Praise for Susan Ouellette's Way

T0006293

"Every once in a decade you read a book like *The Wayward Spy*, which is thrilling, addictive, and sends you reading more thrillers, but you'll go back to this stunning book by Susan Ouellette and reread this tour de force." —***The Strand Magazine**, a Top 12 Book of the Year*

"[A] gripping debut and series launch . . ." —***Publishers Weekly***

"She has walked the halls of the House Intelligence Committee and the CIA and knows those institutions as very few novelists do."
—**Dr. Mark M. Lowenthal**, Former CIA Assistant Director for Analysis

"*The Wayward Assassin* is one of the best books I've read this year. The action is gripping, the plot full of twists and turns [that] draws you into a roller coaster ride. A must read that should be on every thriller fan's bookshelf. Ouellette has hit this one out of the park."
—***The Strand Magazine***

"Ouellette, herself a former intelligence analyst for the CIA, imbues the exciting action with authenticity. Readers will want to see more of the wily Maggie . . ." —***Publishers Weekly***

"VERDICT: An enjoyable spy thriller from an authentic source."
—***Library Journal***

"I couldn't turn the pages fast enough . . . I hope to see much more of Susan and Maggie." —**Tim Suddeth**, Killer Nashville

THE
WAYWARD
TARGET

•THE WAYWARD SERIES•

THE
WAYWARD
TARGET

Susan Ouellette

CamCat
Books

CamCat Publishing, LLC
Fort Collins, Colorado 80524
camcatpublishing.com

Hardcover ISBN 9780744308723
Paperback ISBN 9780744308747
Large-Print Paperback ISBN 9780744308754
eBook ISBN 9780744308761
Audiobook ISBN 9780744308778

Library of Congress Control Number: 2022949458

Cover design/book design by Maryann Appel
Map illustration by Peter Hermes Furian

5 3 1 2 4

For

Andrew, Shawn, and Bryan.

The best boys

a mom could ask for.

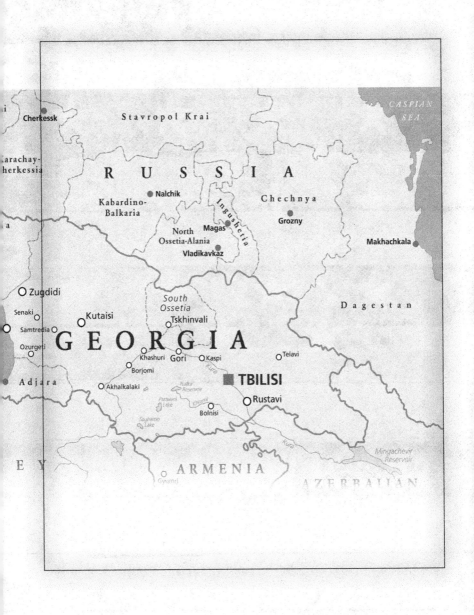

CASPIAN
SEA

Cherkessk

Stavropol Krai

Karachay-
Cherkessia

R U S S I A

Nalchik

Kabardino-
Balkaria

Chechnya

Ingushetia

North   Magas
Ossetia-Alania   Grozny

Vladikavkaz

Makhachkala

Zugdidi

Senaki   Kutaisi   South
Ossetia   Dagestan

Samtredia   Tskhinvali

Ozurgeti   G E O R G I A

Khashuri Gori Kaspi   Telavi

Borjomi   Kura

Akhalkalaki   Tkibuli
Reservoir   ■ TBILISI

Paravani
Lake   Khrami   Rustavi

Sauhaimo
Lake   Bolnisi

Kura

Mingachevir
Reservoir

E Y   A R M E N I A

Gyumri   A Z E R B A I J A N

Adjara

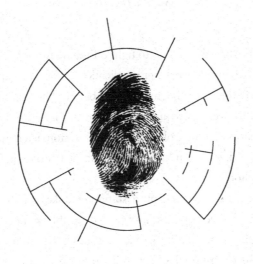

CHAPTER ONE

Tyson's Fitness and Health Club
McLean, Virginia, Sunday, June 12, 2005

Maggie Jenkins increased the pace on the treadmill, her auburn ponytail swaying like a pendulum with every step. She'd boosted her workout regimen over the past several months and the results showed—firm, muscular legs, a trim waist, and well-defined arms. Last fall, Roger had convinced her to join him at the gym. *It'll be good for you*, he'd promised. *Get you out of the house, get your mind off everything.*

Everything. It was his catch-all word for what she'd been through. The terrorist attacks. Zara. All the bloodshed.

An image of hundreds of terrified children flashed in her mind. *No!* She upped the treadmill speed. The faster she ran—the more her body ached—the easier it was to fight off the memories. The gym had become her therapy, sweat her medication. After several months of intensive exercise, she'd begun to sleep better. The nightmares came less often. But every now and then, like last night, the images crept into her dreams and she woke in a cold sweat, stomach churning, pulse pounding. She knew what had triggered it: the hearing on Capitol Hill about the school siege.

Nearby, a man hopped off a stationary bike, grabbed a remote control from the weight rack, and jacked up the volume on the television hanging on the wall. Maggie shot him a look in the mirror, but he didn't notice, absorbed as he was in the breaking news blaring from the TV.

She snatched her headphones and MP3 player from the treadmill console. Volume cranked, the lyrics from "Refugee" filled her ears. The man stood, staring up at the TV. Maggie squinted to read the graphic scrolling across the bottom of the screen.

TERRORIST ISSUES THREAT.

Now what? Another bin Laden missive from some cave in Afghanistan? She didn't want to think about work on her day off. The latest violence and mayhem, whether domestic or international, could wait. In a few weeks, she'd be headed to the beach for a getaway with Roger. After the gym, she planned to go shopping. A new bathing suit, sandals, and a sundress or two were in order. Thoughts of the trip were interrupted by movement on her left. Several more people had abandoned their workouts and gathered in front of the TV. She tugged out an earphone and caught the anchor mid-sentence.

"—*videoed in what British authorities say was his former residence in London.*"

The screen filled with the image of an upholstered chair standing before a vivid abstract painting hung on an otherwise blank white wall. The view darkened for a moment as someone in a blue shirt passed in front of the chair. The person turned and sat, his face level with the camera.

Maggie's fingers punched frantically at the treadmill's off button. She stumbled as it came to a sudden stop, sending her flying forward, her face missing the console by millimeters.

"You okay?" a male voice asked.

She regained her footing, her breath heavy, the weight on her chest suddenly unbearable. "Yeah," she said without looking at him.

"Our brave and glorious martyrs have their reward in paradise. Those responsible for their deaths will be hunted down and executed."

Behind the gaggle of people watching Imran Bukayev speak, Maggie's knees went weak. *Those responsible?* He meant her. She squeezed her eyes shut for a moment before turning her attention back to Bukayev. This video was filmed inside his house, the one she'd broken into in London last year. She'd recognize that garish painting anywhere. And his olive skin and shock of graying black hair were unmistakable.

"Our work is not done. Your children are not safe. No enemy of Allah is safe. Our valiant soldiers are in place and ready to strike again at my command."

Maggie tried to make sense of it. Bukayev wasn't in London anymore. He must've filmed this video after the school attack but before he'd fled. Now, nearly nine months later, the Brits had no idea where he was. Neither did she, despite her spending the better part of every day at Langley trying to track him down.

"I dare him to try something again," one man said, his voice full of bravado.

Sweat coursed down Maggie's face. She steadied herself with one hand on the treadmill rail. The news anchor was speaking, but she couldn't hear him, not with the ringing in her ears. *Roger!* She had to call Roger. *Deep breath. Calm down.* Her lungs felt full, her heart about to burst.

"Is this yours?" A woman's voice cut through the noise in her head.

Maggie blinked. A petite blonde with a bright smile extended her hand, Maggie's headphones and MP3 player resting on her palm.

"Yeah, thanks." Maggie studied the woman for a moment. Something about her seemed familiar.

"You sure?"

Maggie nodded, snatched her phone and water bottle from the treadmill console, and hurried for the locker room. Inside, she slumped onto a wooden bench set across from a row of lockers. After taking a swig of water and counting backward from twenty, she flipped open the phone.

"Roger? Did you see the news? It's Bukayev. I think he's coming for me."

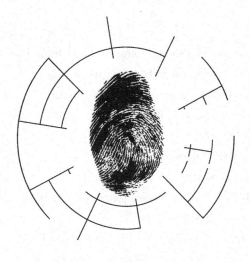

CHAPTER TWO

Makhachkala, Dagestan, Russia

The stooped elderly man dressed entirely in black steadied himself on a cane as two burly men helped him from the sedan. He moved slowly, eyes downcast, his escorts continuously scanning the area around the Grand Mosque of Makhachkala. When they reached the soaring white building, one of the men rapped on an ornately carved wooden door on the far left.

The door swung open, revealing a young man in a flowing white thobe who gestured for them to enter. Inside the dim hallway, the elderly man straightened and shook off his entourage.

The young man stared at the visitor, no doubt assessing his bald head. It wasn't bare with age. Up close, anyone would notice that he'd shaved it clean. And his smooth olive skin and bright brown eyes made him look younger than his forty-two years.

"*As-salam Alaikum,*" the visitor said in greeting.

"*Wa 'alaikum-as-salam,*" the young man replied.

"I'm here to see the office manager."

The young man nodded but didn't move.

"He's expecting me."

The tone of the visitor's voice jolted the young man into action.

"Of course, please follow me."

Twenty feet up the hall, they turned into a hushed, windowless room. The young man gave a slight bow and exited, closing the door behind him. The visitor surveyed his surroundings. Large, dark gray acoustic panels covered the walls, ceiling, and even the floor. The room's only light glowed from four tall lamps, one standing in each corner, and a tabletop lamp set in the center of a round wooden table.

After five minutes, a short man with wire-rimmed glasses entered the room with a security guard. "*As-salam Alaikum.*"

"*Wa 'alaikum-as-salam,*" the visitor replied.

The office manager nodded to the guard, who proceeded to give the visitor a thorough, if not downright intrusive, pat down.

How dare they treat me like a threat. The visitor bit down hard on his tongue. He couldn't afford to assert himself, at least not yet.

"Please, have a seat." The office manager gestured to a wooden chair with a cracked faux-leather seat cushion.

The visitor sat, his hands folded on the table before him.

"Welcome to Dagestan, Imran."

"Thank you, Amar. It's a pleasure to meet you in person."

"Likewise. Although I wouldn't have recognized you. In your video, you had a lot of hair."

"Precisely why I don't anymore." After Zara's name leaked last September, Imran Bukayev had made a video threatening the United

States. He'd been preparing to upload it to the internet when a source in London warned him that law enforcement was investigating his connection to Zara and the school attacks in Russia and America. There'd been no time to waste, so he'd emailed the video to a trusted confidante, shaved his head, grabbed his go bag, and fled.

"We welcome you to the Grand Mosque at great risk."

Imran nodded. "I understand." Now that the video had finally aired, there was no doubt that the world's intelligence services would intensify their efforts to find him. Here in Dagestan, and no doubt throughout the country, Russian security services monitored the comings and goings of the mosque's visitors and employees. As the main mosque in all of Dagestan, it was, perhaps, the least obvious place for him to take refuge. Why would he, Imran Bukayev, one of the world's most wanted terrorist financiers, go anywhere near such a well-known mosque? Which was precisely why he'd chosen it. Sometimes hiding in plain sight was the best way to remain unnoticed. "I came here because it's not safe for me to go home yet." In truth, he had been home—in Chechnya—moving from hideout to hideout for months. But now he needed to be in a place where he could think and plan, not live in constant fear of discovery.

"I understand. Our goal is to protect you and the mosque. As such, there are some rules you must follow while you're here."

Imran pasted on a smile but bristled inside. Who was this mid-level mosque official to dictate the rules? Clearly, the man didn't know how many powerful connections he had. It was these connections that Imran needed to rekindle to get his life back.

He wasn't made for living on the run. He wasn't a warrior. He was a master planner, an orchestrator of warriors. Someone who did his best work when there were no distractions. That meant comfortable surroundings and access to whatever he needed, whenever he needed it.

"First, all communications must pass through us. We've taken your phone from your belongings and will provide you with a new one when the time is right."

Imran had taken to using burner phones since he left London, but kept his old phone, always powered off, because it contained contact information for his many connections. Eyes narrowed, he said, "Make sure nothing happens to it. I'll need it back."

Amar continued without comment. "You will not be able to leave the mosque unless and until it becomes necessary. If there's an emergency, we have an escape route. In the meantime, we have a small apartment set up in our basement for special visitors like you. We will provide you with whatever food and clothing you need."

"How kind," he said without any enthusiasm.

"You may not attend prayer services. We will provide a prayer rug for your room."

Imran's eyes widened. "No prayer services?"

"We are certain that Russian police send informants to our services. It's not safe for you to mix with the general population. Which reminds me, all conversations of a potentially sensitive nature should be held in this room. It's soundproof and swept for surveillance devices regularly."

Imran supposed that a little paranoia was better than a disregard for security. "I'd like my things so I can shower and get settled."

Amar nodded and stepped outside the room. A moment later he was back with the dusty rucksack containing Imran's clothes and toiletries. "This way."

Imran followed Amar down the hall to a door on the right, waiting behind him as he inserted a key into the lock. They descended a set of concrete stairs into a dimly lit basement. A massive furnace filled one half of the otherwise empty, unfinished space. At the far end of the room was a hallway crowded with stacked chairs, rolled prayer rugs, and several boxes of office supplies. Halfway down the hall, Amar nudged open a door on the left, revealing Imran's living quarters.

He followed Amar inside and frowned. A sagging cot and a mismatched nightstand and chest of drawers took up half the room, which was no bigger than a ten-by-ten cell.

Amar pushed aside a purple curtain that hung incongruously on the concrete block wall. On the other side was his bathroom. A dingy commode, a small metal sink, and overhead, a showerhead that would soak the entire bathroom when used. A drain, discolored a putrid green, sat in the center of the floor.

"Over here is a buzzer to the mosque's intercom system. We'll deliver meals three times a day, but if you want a snack or need to speak with me in the secure conference room, simply push the button and I'll be with you as soon as possible."

"Am I your guest or your prisoner?" These accommodations, if they could even be called that, were an outrage. An insult. Bukayev didn't expect to be housed in quarters as swanky as his beloved London row home, but he also didn't expect to be confined to what resembled a cell in a Russian prison camp.

"You have full range of the entire basement, but I must ask that you stay out of sight unless I say it is safe to come upstairs." Amar paused. When Bukayev didn't respond, he added, "I'll have a meal sent down soon."

Bukayev watched him cross the basement and ascend the stairs. He ran his hand across his head, an old habit he hadn't dropped despite the absence of hair. He sank onto the cot, which groaned in protest. Yes, he was safe. But he was stuck, in the basement of a mosque, of all places. Unable to do what he needed to do to get back into the good graces of his benefactors. After the American school operation, which they considered a failure, he needed to convince them his word was still worth the money they'd sent him. Their cash had been used to execute an attack on the children of Washington's elites, but it had all gone horribly wrong. Zara was to blame. She'd had other plans, a personal vendetta, that she'd kept from him. Bukayev had tried to explain that to the benefactors, but all he'd received was scorn for allowing a woman to lead the operation. There was still a chance for redemption, to please the money men and get his old life back. That's why he was here, in Dagestan—so he could execute his plan to kill the people who had murdered Zara. After that, he would launch his next and most ambitious plot to date.

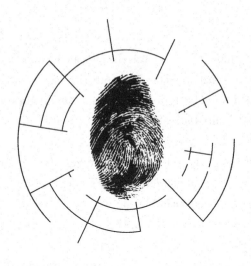

CHAPTER THREE

Dirksen Senate Office Building, Washington, DC
Monday, June 13, 2005

Maggie Jenkins slipped into a seat at the back of the Senate Intelligence Committee hearing room.

"I like the disguise," Roger Patterson whispered from the chair to her right.

Maggie patted her auburn hair which she'd hurriedly twirled into a French twist at the nape of her neck after seeing the large media presence in the hearing room. The reading glasses she sported weren't necessary but helped to alter her appearance a bit. *Just in case.* Wherever Imran Bukayev was hiding, he might find a way to watch the hearing. And although she didn't think he got a good look at her in London last year, she didn't want to take the chance that he'd recognize her.

She wouldn't mind if her face was the last one he ever saw, but before her fantasies of vengeance could play out, she had to find Bukayev, the terrorist mastermind behind the Beslan and Dominion school attacks. Find him and finally, for real and for good, put the past behind her.

Roger eyed her. "You're a sexy secret agent."

She smiled and gave his arm a squeeze. After seeing Bukayev's video for himself, he hadn't left Maggie's side. Even though Bukayev couldn't possibly know that Maggie was the one who'd stopped the Dominion school attack last year, she appreciated Roger's protective show of support.

Maggie forced Bukayev's threats from her mind and focused on the two men at the witness table in front of them. Warner Thompson, the CIA's deputy director of operations sat to the left of the star witness—FBI Director Richard Miller.

Beyond them was an elongated, curved wooden dais where seventeen United States senators sat, all eyes on the witness table. Behind the senators was a gaggle of staffers who occupied an elongated, cushioned bench that ran the length of a soaring twenty-foot wood-paneled wall. To their left stood a large American flag hanging limply on a brass flagpole.

The chairman of the Senate Intelligence Committee gaveled the hearing into order.

Maggie flipped open a brown leather portfolio and scribbled a note. "Do you think Warner will have to testify? What if someone asks about me? He can't lie under oath."

Roger snatched her pen. "He'll say it's classified. Can't discuss in public."

Maggie nodded as the FBI director read from the executive summary of the report on the "Investigation into the Dominion Elementary School Siege." She'd already read it from cover to cover. Twice. There was no mention of her name anywhere.

"In the aftermath of the school siege of September tenth, 2004, the FBI, the CIA, Homeland Security, and state and local law enforcement agencies have implemented unprecedented levels of cooperation." He continued, outlining the report's findings and fielding questions from several senators. Warner, for his part, sat unmoving beside the FBI director. He had no plans to speak but the president had wanted the nation's law enforcement and intelligence agencies to present a united front to the country. It was supposed to be the CIA director at the table with Director Miller, but Warner had offered to fill in after the CIA chief had fallen ill suddenly.

"Mr. Chairman, if I may." It was the senator from California, a brash, well-coifed woman with a penchant for the camera. "I can only imagine the shock and terror those children endured when their school was attacked. If we can't keep innocent children safe in our nation's public schools, then the FBI must come clean and explain why they weren't able to stop this atrocity."

"Senator Canton," the FBI director began, "we have learned many lessons from that day. On the positive side, it is a credit to the FBI and local law enforcement that no students were killed inside the school."

The voices in the room faded as memories flashed through Maggie's mind. AK-47s trained on children. Teachers crying. Zara sneering and determined to exact her brand of twisted revenge. She shook her head and blinked rapidly, forcing herself to focus on the hearing.

The senator smoothed her blonde highlighted hair and leaned forward, hands folded behind the nameplate that sat on the dais in front of her. "About that 'success'"—the senator made air quotes—"why don't we know the name of the federal agent who killed the terrorists inside the school? The public deserves to know."

Director Miller, a lanky, middle-aged man with close-cropped salt-and-pepper hair, lifted a document. "And the public will know. This," he explained, "is the truth about what happened last September at Dominion Elementary School. We are releasing our report to the public at the conclusion of the hearing. The only secrets we must maintain involve intelligence sources and methods." He took a sip of water from a tall glass set before him on the witness table and glanced at Warner. "And in this case, the identity of the undercover federal agent must also remain a secret—for personal safety reasons."

The senator smirked at the FBI director. "Perhaps we can arrange for a personal meeting with the agent so I can thank this person for his . . . or her . . . heroics."

Maggie's breath caught in her throat. Roger placed a hand on her knee and gave a gentle squeeze. She slipped her hand over his.

"Perhaps," Director Miller offered noncommittally.

"I'll hold you to that," Senator Canton snapped.

Maggie watched the senator scan the room, a smile plastered across her face for the media. Her gaze met Maggie's and seemed to linger a moment longer than necessary.

Maggie removed her hand from Roger's and acted as if she was taking notes in her portfolio.

"Did you see that?" she scribbled.

"What?" Roger wrote back.

"Tell you later." Maggie shut the portfolio and crossed and uncrossed her legs, her body quivering with the urge to flee the room.

Twenty minutes later, the chairman gaveled the hearing to a close. The FBI director approached the dais and shook hands with the senators who hadn't already made a dash for the reporters lined up in the back of the hearing room. Warner, looking stately as ever in a tailored steel-gray suit that matched the color of his hair, approached Maggie and Roger.

"That went as well as can be expected."

Maggie tugged Warner to the far edge of the hearing room.

Roger followed.

"I swear that Senator Canton gave me a look."

Warner frowned. "What kind of look?"

She pulled off her glasses. They were giving her a headache. "I don't know. She stared at me, like she knew something."

Roger glanced over his shoulder. "Everyone thinks an FBI agent was inside the school. Not a CIA analyst."

"But," Maggie protested, "all the children saw me. The teachers. Police. The FBI agents outside the school. At some point, my name will come out."

Warner glanced around the hearing room. "Look, we're doing everything we can to protect your identity. The Bukayev video is alarming, but he doesn't know who you are. Besides, he's a bit preoccupied running from us, the Russians, and the Brits."

Roger's forehead crinkled in concern the way it always did when the Chechen terrorist's name surfaced.

"I know. I'm just . . . I guess it's . . . reading the report and listening to the details. It's so clinical, so detached from what it was really like inside that school." Maggie shook her head. "Never mind. I'm overreacting."

"You're not, Maggie." Warner placed a hand on her arm. "No report could possibly capture what you experienced that day. Believe me, I understand."

Of course he did. His children had been inside that school.

Warner checked his watch. "Need a ride back to the office?"

"The office?" Roger said. "I was hoping we could play hooky. Grab some lunch at the Dubliner. Get drunk and sing Irish pub songs. You in, Maggie?"

Warner cleared his throat. "You may work for the Counterterrorism Center, Roger, but I'm still your ultimate boss. Get back to work and find Bukayev."

Imran Bukayev. Zara's lover and terrorist financier.

The administration was determined to bring him to justice for his role in the school siege. Now that he was gunning for her, Maggie wanted nothing more than to be the one who smoked him out of whatever hellhole he was hiding in.

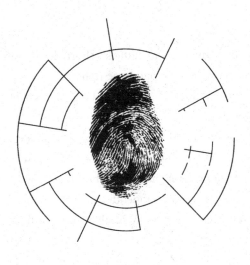

CHAPTER FOUR

Makhachkala, Dagestan, Russia

Bukayev stomped up the stairs behind Amar. Despite his prison-cell surroundings, he'd slept well, relatively secure in the fact that he didn't have to be on alert all night for a sudden Russian raid. "I need access to a computer."

Amar stopped on the top step and scanned the hallway before hurrying them along to the conference room where they'd first met the previous evening. Inside the room, a laptop sat on the table. "The FBI report is already pulled up. As are several related news stories."

Bukayev's name was all over the report. The FBI called him the "mastermind" behind the school attack in the American capital. The fact that it had been Zara's idea would remain buried with her. If he was going to be blamed for the attack's shortfalls, he sure as hell was going to take credit for what had gone right.

"They claim a single federal agent killed Zara and her entire team?" He snorted. "Who was this agent? Rambo?"

Amar looked confused. The man probably had never traveled outside of Dagestan, he reminded himself. As omnipresent as American pop culture was, it probably hadn't reached Amar's world.

He clicked to the report's appendix and took in the photo of Zara. *Damn*. Was she ever gorgeous. A sudden pressure filled his chest. It wasn't that he missed her as one might miss a beloved wife. But he certainly missed the idea of Zara. Dangerous. Unpredictable. A pleasure like no other.

He shook off a memory of her lying naked on his bed, beckoning him with her wide green eyes.

"I need to find out the name of this federal agent."

Again, Amar appeared disinterested. Perhaps this was not his battle. Perhaps he was here only to watch over his guest, a prison guard minding his prisoner.

Then it hit him. "A fatwa," he exclaimed.

Amar tilted his head. "For what?"

"For killing my men."

"But you already put out a video calling for this person's death. Isn't that enough?"

"A fatwa carries more weight. It will smoke out this agent. You know Americans. If you threaten them, they puff out their chests and say, 'Go ahead, make my day.'"

Again, a blank stare from Amar.

Bukayev continued, undeterred. "This person or the agency he works for won't let a threat go unanswered. They'll say something. Do something. Reveal themselves. And once I know who the target is, I will act."

Amar picked at a jagged fingernail. "You're going to go to America to kill this person?"

Bukayev couldn't decide if Amar thought he was an idiot or if Amar was the idiot. "Of course not." *You fool.* "I have resources at my disposal." That wasn't entirely true. Yes, he had a small cell of operatives in the US, but his al-Qaeda financiers had cut off funding and the money he'd been laundering through the Washington-based Central Asian Studies Institute had dried up as well. Last he'd heard, the director of the institute had fled to Chechnya in the aftermath of the school attack.

Had the director been caught, Bukayev's role in the siege might've been discovered before he had time to get out of London. For that, he was grateful.

Bukayev tapped his fingers on the tabletop. He ran an internet search on his name. People speculated that he was hiding in Afghanistan. The Americans and the British might actually believe that, which was good. But it wasn't them he was worried about. It was the Russians. Now that the Brits had revoked his political asylum, he was fair game for the SVR, Russia's foreign intelligence service, or even worse, the GRU, Russian military intelligence. In recent years, the GRU had stepped up its assassination game, especially overseas. Moscow had been hunting him for nearly five years because of his role in planning and financing several high-profile terrorist attacks inside Russia. Fortunately for him, the Russians had refused to share their intelligence with the British, who naively believed his claims of political persecution and had granted him asylum.

After the revelations about his role in the Russian and American school attacks last year, he wouldn't be surprised if British intelligence had shared every bit of information they had on him with the Russians. And the Russians were smart. They wouldn't limit their search to Afghanistan.

"I need to issue a fatwa as soon as possible, Amar. It will alert my assets in America to prepare for another attack."

"I'm afraid you can't issue a fatwa from the Grand Mosque. We are not jihadists." Amar smirked.

Bukayev pounded his fist on the table, causing the laptop to jump. "Don't be so obtuse, Amar. Surely, you can have Abu Idris issue a fatwa."

Amar paled. "We don't have the best relationship with him. We can't always trust the Chechens."

"I'm Chechen." His lips curled into a smile. "And you seem to trust me. Besides, I thought we were all in this together. Against the West, against the Russian imperialists. Should we allow minor differences among us lead to the slaughter of Muslims all over the Caucasus?"

"Of course not. But even you must know Abu Idris is no friend of Dagestan."

True, Abu Idris, otherwise known as Shamil Basayev, had led a Chechen invasion of Dagestan several years prior that resulted in a Russian crackdown on Dagestani Muslims. Basayev's intentions had been pure—to help liberate the oppressed people of Dagestan from their Russian overlords. His actions, however, had led to great suffering for Dagestanis.

"There will be a fatwa, Amar. But don't worry, I'll make sure there's no connection to this mosque," Bukayev promised, his tone soothing. "I need my phone, just for a minute."

Amar bit the corner of his lip, then stood and left the room. In his absence, Bukayev resumed searching for information on the federal agent who killed Zara but came up empty. He peeked out into the hall. With no sign of Amar, he rushed back to the laptop and logged into his webmail account. Though it was risky, he had to act now, while the world's attention was on him. He'd be cryptic but get his message across.

Hello, my dear friend. I trust you've seen the news about me. It's urgent that we issue a fatwa on the matter. On video, for all the world to see. I'm unable to do this from my current location, and besides that, it will have more weight coming from you. I plan to visit again soon. Currently, staying nearby with friends. Kindly attend to this matter immediately.

Bukayev hit send just as the door handle turned. He closed the browser and affected a bored expression. Now that he'd emailed Shamil Basayev, there was no need to text his contact, but he would anyway, so as not to raise Amar's suspicions.

Amar slid Bukayev's phone across the table. "Keep cellular and Wi-Fi off."

"I need to send a text."

Amar's eyes widened. "You can't text Shamil Basayev from here. Especially not on your personal phone."

"Fine, then give me a burner phone and I'll text one of his associates."

Amar grumbled as he yanked open a file cabinet drawer and extracted a black flip phone.

"Thanks," Imran muttered as he powered up his phone and jotted down the number he needed before shutting it off. He took the burner phone and typed in a message to one of Basayev's henchmen, directing him to alert his boss to an important email. He turned off the burner phone and folded his hands together on the table. "There. That's all I needed."

Amar stood.

"I'd like to eat breakfast in here, if I may." Even this windowless office was less dank and depressing than his basement cell.

"Very well," his host replied as he pocketed both phones.

Bukayev contemplated his next move. There was nothing he could do until Shamil Basayev issued a fatwa against the agent who'd slain

Allah's loyal servants in the American school. Perhaps the odds of finding this agent were longer than he cared to admit, but he had to start somewhere if he hoped to secure a big enough victory to get his life back on track.

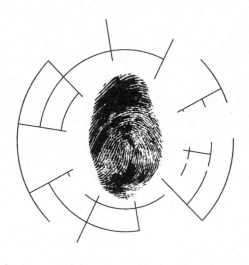

CHAPTER FIVE

CIA Headquarters, Langley, Virginia

Maggie clicked on the television in a conference room located on the fourth floor of the Agency's original headquarters building. She scrolled through the channels until she came to a panel of pundits seated around an oval glass table, a massive image of the US Capitol aglow on the studio wall behind them.

"After months of delays, the FBI released a much-anticipated report on the September tenth siege at a suburban Washington, DC-area elementary school. Critics say the report didn't go far enough toward explaining how terrorists were able to take over a school so close to the nation's capital."

The news anchor, whose chiseled features were capped by perfect-ly styled jet-black hair, nodded to the woman on his right.

"It seems to me, Bob, that the American people, and parents in particular, should know more about what happened that day. Especial-ly now that Imran Bukayev, the man who claims to be the mastermind behind the attack, says he can and will launch additional attacks on American soil."

The dark-haired woman leveled her gaze at the camera.

"Frankly, I find it laughable that the FBI is trying to conceal the identity of the federal agent who was inside the school that day. This is Washington, DC. It's only a matter of time before the name is leaked."

Maggie lowered herself onto a black stackable chair and tugged at a loose cuticle on her thumb. Another panelist, a gaunt young man with wire-rimmed glasses chimed in next.

"I give it a week, tops, before this undercover agent shows up on all the talk shows. Two weeks until he signs a book deal."

"Or she," added the woman.

Maggie cursed under her breath and nearly jumped out of the chair when Roger materialized behind her.

"You signed a book deal?"

She twisted in the chair. "They're right, you know. My name will leak."

Roger dropped into the chair next to her. "Not if I have any say in the matter."

She gave him a sidelong glance. "You don't." Unfortunately. Roger was fiercely protective of her, but she didn't want to feed his obsession with keeping her safe. After all, she'd managed to survive life-threaten-ing situations without him, although if she were being honest, Roger made a very appealing knight in shining armor. Still, she worried that he'd go too far at some point. "Do you think Bukayev has another network in the US already?"

"If he does, we'll find it. It's my top priority."

"Yours and mine both." Maggie clicked off the television and stood. "I want to check the intel traffic, see if there's any chatter about the hearing." Without waiting for a response from Roger, she wove a path through a maze of identical cubicles until she reached one set in the far corner near a window overlooking a parking lot. There, she fired up her desktop computer and released her hair from the French twist while she waited for the password screen to appear. Auburn curls tumbled to her shoulders.

Roger appeared beside her again. "I doubt Bukayev's cave in Tora Bora has Wi-Fi or cable. He probably doesn't even know that the hearing took place today."

"We don't know that he's in Afghanistan, Roger. Besides, the fact that he released the video the day before the FBI report came out can't be a coincidence. He has to be somewhere with access to a computer and the internet."

"Anyone could've posted the video for him."

"True, but who?" She logged into her account and clicked through dozens of new messages, looking for intelligence that mentioned terrorism. The Agency called these reports "traffic," presumably shorthand for "cable traffic," a broad category of documents that included intelligence reports procured and produced by the CIA and other government agencies. "Most of this information is irrelevant," she commented without taking her eyes off the screen. "I'll have to set up a search." She typed in a few keywords. "Only a few overseas media reports so far." She typed again. "And my name yields zero results."

"I'm starving. Let's go get lunch in the cafeteria."

Maggie continued to scroll through her messages.

Roger knocked on the small safe that stood on the floor next to her desk. "Hello? Anyone home?"

"What, Roger?" Her tone was more impatient than she'd intended. "Sorry, what did you say?"

"Lunch. You. Me. Cafeteria."

"Sure. One second." She powered off the computer and grabbed her purse from inside the desk drawer.

"No need for that. My treat."

She stood. "I'll get lunch. You buy me dinner."

Roger's eyes lit up. "I'd love to, my love."

Maggie smiled. Sappy but charming.

That was Roger.

As they turned to leave, the phone on Maggie's desk trilled.

"Ignore it. They'll call back."

She hesitated a moment before picking up the receiver. "Maggie speaking."

"Is Roger there?"

"He is." *Warner*, she mouthed.

Roger rolled his eyes and leaned toward the receiver. "We're grabbing some lunch. I'll pop by after."

"Put him on, Maggie. It's urgent."

She covered the mouthpiece. "He says it's urgent."

Roger exhaled dramatically. "Fine." He slid behind her and took the receiver. "Roger Patterson reporting for duty."

Maggie suppressed a laugh. How Warner had put up with Roger's antics all these years was a mystery. They'd had a professional falling out shortly before the September 11 attacks, but that was long forgotten now.

"You sure?" Roger's expression grew serious, his mouth set in a straight line, his brow furrowed. "I'll be right up." He hung up and turned to Maggie. "Rain check on lunch?"

"What was that about?"

"I'm afraid it's compartmented. Operational stuff."

Maggie understood. Roger couldn't tell her everything he knew. And vice versa. But she pressed. "Anything to do with Bukayev?"

His gaze flitted upward for a moment. "I gotta go."

"Roger?" she called after him as he broke into a trot toward the elevators. Dammit. If there was one thing she couldn't stand, it was people keeping information from her for her own supposed good. Both Warner and Roger should have learned that lesson by now. They needed to tell her everything they had on Bukayev, if that's what this was about, no matter how sensitive the intelligence.

She ignored her growling stomach and fired her computer back up. *Imran Bukayev, where are you?*

CHAPTER SIX

Maggie rolled over and slapped at her alarm clock. She'd stayed up way too late waiting for Roger. First, he'd called to cancel their dinner date with a promise to bring take-out. Then, he'd called at 9:30 to say he was still at work. Close to midnight and several glasses of wine later, she'd ignored his third call and crawled into bed, a headache already forming.

She tottered downstairs and shoved a coffee pod into the coffeemaker. Irritation nipped at her. What was so urgent that Roger had to stay at work so late into the night? If it was related to Bukayev and he was keeping it from her—

Maggie turned on the television as her mug filled with a final hiss of steam. Footage borrowed from Russian television showed unrest in Uzbekistan. She was supposed to pay attention to these sorts of developments, but all she could think about was Imran Bukayev. She sipped at her coffee, then dumped in an extra spoonful of sugar to take the edge off her mood and the thrumming in her head.

"In response to yesterday's senate hearing on the September 2004 school attack in Great Falls, Virginia, a leader of the Chechen independence movement in Russia has issued a legal opinion, known as a fatwa, calling for the death of the unidentified federal agent responsible for taking down the terrorists inside the school."

With a shaky hand, Maggie lowered her mug to the kitchen counter. Last year, Yuri Markov, a former KGB officer, had tried to convince her that the Chechens were going to issue a fatwa targeting her for her involvement in the deaths of several Chechen rebels. The fatwa never materialized. It had been a ruse, concocted by the Russian to extract information from her. But this was different. If the news report was accurate, and the fatwa was real—

She dashed to the living room to get her laptop.

A British newspaper article popped up first. "Shamil Basayev," she breathed. The leader of the Chechen separatists. Someone Imran Bukayev probably had worked with to execute the Beslan school attack and possibly even the Dominion Elementary siege. Had he issued the fatwa at the request of Bukayev? Certainly, the Agency must be watching Shamil Basayev.

She tugged on a knot in her curls and called Warner.

"I just saw the news," Warner said upon answering. "It's pathetic. That guy's no scholar."

Maggie noted Warner's avoidance of any specifics. You never knew who might be listening in on the CIA spymaster's line. "Technically, you're right, but he did it anyway." Under Islamic law, only qualified legal scholars—muftis—can issue a fatwa. Shamil Basayev was a warlord, not an Islamic scholar. "He's surrounded by people who won't give a damn about his qualifications."

"He is. But there's no evidence that his reach extends beyond his little corner of the world."

"I don't think we should assume anything." There'd been no evidence that Bukayev and Zara could carry out an attack on US soil. Yet they did. "Do we have eyes and ears on him?" By him, she meant Shamil Basayev. It shouldn't be difficult. They knew he was somewhere in Chechnya.

"Not sure. I'm looking into it."

Maggie frowned. Warner didn't know if they were eavesdropping on Shamil Basayev? "Maybe he'll help lead us to our other friend." *Bukayev.*

"That would be fantastic."

"Did you know this was coming?" Unlike her, Warner had access to every piece of intelligence that made its way into the CIA's hands. If he knew the fatwa was forthcoming and didn't tell her—

"What? No," he protested a little too quickly.

"My friend worked awfully late last night. You sure you didn't know?"

"There are some things I can't—"

She cut him off. "Save your breath. I have to get ready for work."

CIA Headquarters, Langley, Virginia

"Close the door, Roger." Warner sat at his desk, shoulders slumped in fatigue.

"Did you confirm it?" Roger stood across from Warner, his body jumpy, fueled by too much caffeine.

"NSA just got back to me. They've confirmed that the email to Shamil Basayev originated in Dagestan. We can't determine the exact location." Warner frowned. "Problem with the IP something or other. But the point is, we've been watching Basayev's comms for months and this is the first hit we've had that might be from Imran Bukayev."

"Might be? It has to be from Bukayev. Who else would ask Shamil to issue a fatwa against Maggie?"

"Technically, it's not directed at her."

Roger grunted. "Let's not play semantic games, Warner. If Bukayev finds out that Maggie was the one inside that school—"

"I know, I know." Warner sighed. "It's just, I think we should be careful with how we phrase things. Maggie's on edge, understandably, and I don't want to push her into panic mode. As it is, she already thinks we're keeping information from her."

"Aren't we?"

"Yes, but it's for her—"

"—own good," Roger added.

Warner and Roger had come to a sort of unspoken agreement that they would protect Maggie from harm at any cost. Sometimes, this meant keeping unverified information from her so that she didn't overreact, or worse, try to take matters into her own hands. "We've got to reassure her that we're on top of this fatwa matter. The question is, what do we do next?"

Roger leaned his hands on the edge of Warner's desk. "We kill the sonofabitch."

"No, I mean what do we do about Maggie? Do we tell her that Bukayev might be in Dagestan?"

Roger pushed away from the desk and ran a hand through his tousled black hair. "If we tell her—"

"She's liable to run off to Dagestan," Warner offered. "But if we don't—"

"She'll never speak to either of us again."

The men shook their heads in unison.

Roger paced a path in front of Warner. "She'll figure out that something's up. The woman's a living, breathing polygraph machine. We have to tell her."

Warner sipped from a mug of cold coffee and made a face. "I suppose so. Let me do it. Unlike you, I have some professional authority over her."

Roger smirked. "Like that's ever stopped her."

As Maggie pulled the Jeep into the CIA's south parking lot, her phone rang for the third time. Roger. Again.

"Are you okay?"

"Of course I'm okay, Roger. Why? Is there something I should be worried about?" Sarcasm dripped from every word.

He was silent for a moment. "I'm sorry about last night. I wanted to leave work, but I couldn't get away."

Did he really think she was upset about dinner? "Oh, really? What was so urgent?"

"I can't—"

"Of course you can't."

"I don't make up the rules, Maggie."

"But you're willing to break them when it suits you."

"What's that supposed to mean?" Now he sounded irritated.

Roger had a history of sidestepping the rules. If he had information on Bukayev that he wasn't supposed to share, he could break the rules, if he really wanted to. "Nothing." She pulled the key from the ignition and checked her lipstick in the rearview mirror. It seemed obvious he'd continue stonewalling her.

"Warner wants to talk to you."

"About what?"

"Hell if I know."

Her pulse picked up. She grabbed her purse, slammed the car door, and ran across the parking lot. Maybe Warner would bring her into the loop.

She found Roger on the seventh floor, waiting for her outside of Warner's office suite. "I got you coffee."

"Thanks." She took a sip. As always, it was fixed exactly how she liked it. "I should go in."

He nodded. "Maybe you've been promoted."

She studied Roger for any sign that he knew more than he was letting on. His blue eyes held her gaze without a flicker of nerves or deception. But that didn't surprise her. After all, he was a CIA operative. Half-truths were par for the course.

In his perfectly tailored Armani suit, Warner looked more like a Wall Street executive than a government employee. "Have a seat." He gestured to the tufted leather chairs across from his desk.

Maggie swallowed, her mouth suddenly dry. Something was wrong. "Did you find him?"

"Who?"

"Bukayev."

Warner rubbed his hands over his eyes and across his cheeks. "Not yet. What I'm about to tell you can't leave this room."

She shifted in her seat.

Warner cleared his throat. "I just got word that the director's health issues were far more serious than we knew."

Were? "What's wrong with him?"

"He had a massive stroke over the weekend. He passed away late last night."

"That's awful. So young." Maggie had met the CIA director in a meeting last year when she'd convinced the Agency that Zara was plotting to attack American schools. And after the attack, the director had presented her with an Intelligence Commendation Medal in a private ceremony inside his office. Warner and Roger were the only other invitees. To this day, the medal remained in a plain cardboard box, locked away in the safe tucked under her desk.

"The deputy director has been named acting director effective immediately."

Maggie nodded, still not sure what this had to do with her.

"The president isn't a fan of the deputy director. He intends to nominate me as the new CIA director."

A smile spread across her face. "Oh, Warner, that's fantastic." She jumped up and ran around the desk to hug him.

He reached up and patted her on the shoulder. "Thanks. I think."

Maggie pulled away. "What's the matter?"

"You know there are things in my past that would derail my nomination if they became public knowledge."

She frowned. "No one knows. Not even Roger." The only other people, besides herself, who might possibly know anything about Warner's brief indiscretion with a Russian agent—a male Russian agent—were all dead. Congressman Carvelli, Yuri Markov. And Ed, the honeytrap agent himself.

He rocked back in his plush leather office chair. "That issue aside, I hardly see the girls as it is. Being CIA director will be even more demanding on my time."

True, his professional obligations curtailed the time he spent with his twin daughters, a situation made worse by the fact that they lived with his bitter ex-wife. "You can always delegate responsibilities to your deputies. And make sure to schedule time with Emma and Abigail."

"I never had any ambition to be the director."

Maggie leaned against the side of his desk. "If you don't accept, who will the president nominate instead?"

"Rumor is that it will be Congressman Blevins."

She laughed. "You're kidding." She didn't know the congressman personally, but her old friends on the House Intelligence Committee said he was a pompous jerk. "Do you really want that guy to run the CIA?"

"No. Which is the only reason I'm contemplating taking the job." He locked eyes with Maggie. "I'd like you to be my chief of staff."

Maggie blinked. "Me? But I don't know anything about running an office. Never mind the CIA. I'm just an analyst."

Warner stood and faced her. "But I trust you. Completely."

"Even after all my shenanigans the past two years?" Warner had been entirely too forgiving of her unauthorized exploits that involved chasing terrorists around the world.

He laughed. "I figure I can keep a closer eye on you if you're sitting in the office next to mine."

This would be a huge promotion. But she hadn't ever imagined herself in a management role. She loved the mystery intrinsic to her job as an analyst. She loved piecing together disparate pieces of seemingly insignificant information to discern an adversary's intentions. "But what about Bukayev? Tracking him has been my sole focus for months."

"We're not going to give that up, especially now that he's threatened to hit us again. Finding him, and bin Laden of course, will remain the Counterterrorism Center's top priority."

"But I won't be involved?"

"Not directly."

As a senior member of the CIA director's staff, she'd have access to all the intelligence she wanted, but she wouldn't have the time to focus on Bukayev. "Can I think about it?"

"Only if the answer is yes." He turned his head, taking in the intelligence awards that lined the bookcase behind his desk. "You know, speaking of enemies, I have a lot of them in this building. And elsewhere in Washington. I need someone whose instincts I trust. Someone who has my back and isn't afraid to tell it like it is. You're that person, Maggie."

"If I say yes, can I get a code name?"

"I was thinking 'Secret Agent Now-What-The-Hell-Has-She-Done.'"

Maggie laughed. "When will the White House announce your nomination?"

"This morning, after the deputy director reveals the news about the director's passing over the in-house video channel. The president is pressing the Senate Intelligence Committee to begin hearings on Thursday."

"That's in two days," she yelped. She scanned through a mental list of the senators on the Senate Intelligence Committee. There were a couple of concern. "I'll do an assessment of the key senators, both allies and foes."

Warner grinned broadly. "That's why I'm hiring you as my chief of staff."

"I haven't accepted," she protested.

"Yet." He sank into his chair. "Now get out, I have calls to make."

"Yes, sir." Maggie saluted and slipped into the reception area outside his office before turning back. "Can I tell Rog—"

Warner held up a hand. He was already on his call.

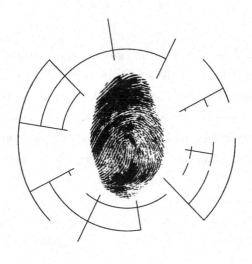

CHAPTER SEVEN

The Grand Mosque, Makhachkala
Dagestan, Russia, Thursday, June 16, 2005

Bukayev took a final swig of coffee, now lukewarm, and carried the mug and breakfast plate up the basement stairs. He might be safe from the Russians hiding out in the mosque, but couldn't remain here without a reliable means of communicating with his people in Chechnya. He'd also had no contact with his Arab benefactors and no news yet on progress with finding the person who'd killed Zara.

Certain kinds of men wait passively for help to arrive. Or for the perfect timing before acting. *Not me*, he thought. All his achievements were a result of taking action, often at great personal risk. Today, he would act.

He placed the plate, mug, and utensils on the top step and leaned his ear against the door. Silence. He tested the doorknob, knowing it was futile. The door was locked, and the keyhole was on the other side.

Bukayev lumbered back down the stairs to his room. He shoved his belongings into his rucksack then pressed the intercom button every few seconds until, finally, an exasperated voice floated through the speaker.

"What is it?" Amar said.

"I'm leaving. There's business I must attend to."

"You can't just walk out in broad daylight. Someone might recognize you."

"Unlock the door, Amar, or I'll really make a racket." Instead of waiting for a reply, he grabbed his bag and headed for the stairs.

Upstairs in the windowless room, he laid out his demands. "I need my phone back. And several new burner phones. And the laptop."

Amar frowned.

"Now," he barked, causing the younger man to flinch.

Amar disappeared into the hall, returning several minutes later with the requested items. Bukayev powered up the laptop and navigated to his email account, where he found a message from Shamil's man. His new point of contact in Dagestan was someone Bukayev already knew, although they'd never met in person. He turned on one of the burner phones and dialed the number Shamil's man had sent in the email.

"I need a taxi in thirty minutes," Bukayev said, following the script.

The man on the other end told him where to wait and hung up.

Bukayev smiled as he tossed the phones in his bag.

"I understand that you must go," Amar said, hands clutched together in front of his chest. "But the police regularly patrol the area outside the mosque."

"I'm leaving."

"Of course. But for your own protection, I must insist you wear a disguise."

For my protection or yours? Bukayev didn't want to admit it out loud, but Amar was probably right. He'd come so far. Why take an unnecessary risk now? "What kind of disguise?"

Relief spread across Amar's face. "Wait here."

A few minutes later he returned with a roll of black cloth under his arm.

"What is this, Amar?"

He shook out the garment. "An abaya."

Bukayev shook his head. "I'm not dressing like a woman."

"It's the perfect disguise, Imran. The police don't harass our women, especially those who dress modestly."

He thought for a moment. It would work, and as soon as he was a block or two away, he would shed the costume. Snatching the garment, he slipped the abaya over his head.

"Don't forget the hijab."

He grabbed the smaller pile of fabric from the table and pulled the hijab over his head. It already felt hot and a bit claustrophobic. Bukayev cursed under his breath. He'd never felt so ridiculous.

Bukayev tugged off the abaya and hijab, balled up the fabric, and tossed it in a nearby trash can. A man strolling along the beach stopped and stared at him in astonishment. He swore at him in Russian and the man resumed his walk at a quickened pace. Bukayev sat on a splintery wooden bench and stared out at the vast Caspian Sea. Off to the right, children splashed and shrieked as they played in the water while their mother watched from her spot on the sand. He checked his watch. His contact was supposed to be here by now.

As relieved as he was to be out of the mosque, he wasn't looking forward to living on the run again. Always wearing the same clothes. Having no access to fine foods. Or his nightly drink. Alcohol was *haram* in Islam, but he'd never been all that observant, though his supporters didn't know that.

In any event, he missed London, where he could do whatever he wanted, whenever he wanted. Now, he lived at the mercy of those who hid and fed him.

Just then, a slight, olive-skinned man with jet-black hair approached. Dressed in khaki shorts, a striped polo shirt, and sandals, he might be mistaken for a tourist at a much nicer beach resort, perhaps one in Abu Dhabi. Makhachkala didn't have many tourists these days, not with all the violence between the local Islamists and Russian security forces.

"Nice day for a boat ride," the man said in Russian.

Bukayev stood. "It would be nice to catch some fish."

The younger man nodded after Bukayev's recitation of the prearranged code phrase.

"You must be the young man from the institute?"

The man blinked rapidly and nodded.

Why so nervous? "I never got to thank you for all the work you did for us last year, Daud."

A thin film of sweat formed along the man's upper lip. "It was an honor, sir. I only wish I was still in the States."

Bukayev raised an eyebrow.

"To . . . to help, from there, with the funds," he stammered. "So I could continue to help further the cause."

He patted Daud's arm. "You are helping. Allah's reward will be great."

"*Inshallah*," Daud replied.

"Let's go, shall we? I don't want to be out in public too long."

Daud led him to a silver Toyota Camry parked along the boulevard that ran parallel to the beach. He started the car, adjusted the air-conditioning, and turned the radio up. "The emir wants to see you."

"Rasul?"

"Yes."

Another lifetime ago, Bukayev had been Rasul Makasharipov's mentor. Or perhaps babysitter was a more apt description. After being kicked out of his home in Dagestan, Rasul had moved to Chechnya and quickly ingrained himself with the leadership of the Chechen rebel movement. At his heart, he was a rash, wannabe jihadist. Passion drove him—hatred for Russia, love of his native Dagestan, and a burning desire to unify Muslims into an Islamic state that spanned the Caucasus. It wasn't that Bukayev didn't share those same passions, at least some of them, it was that Rasul acted without thinking. As such, he'd counseled the young radical on the need to step back, consider alternative scenarios, and seek guidance from more experienced men. Despite these efforts to guide the younger man, Rasul had ended up imprisoned in Dagestan. Fortunately for him, he was released in a general amnesty a year later. In the intervening four years, he'd founded his own group, Shariat Jamaat, an organization known for assassinating Russian police officers, government officials, and journalists.

"How many times have the Russians claimed they killed him?" Bukayev said, laughing. At the beginning of the year, police had raided a Jamaat safe house, killing several militants, including Rasul. Or so they'd claimed. Rasul resurfaced four days later, alive and well. Rasul Makasharipov was a man gifted with nine lives. At least. But eventually his luck would run out. Bukayev hoped that wouldn't happen until he no longer needed his help.

"At least twice," Daud replied, glancing over at Bukayev. "How long do you plan to stay in Dagestan?"

Bukayev shot him a look. "That's not your concern."

Daud blanched. "Of course not. I apologize. It's just such an honor to meet you after all this time."

Bukayev frowned. In his capacity as the head of the Central Asian Studies Institute in Washington, this young Chechen had done a fine job funneling money for the Beslan school attack, but perhaps he knew too much. Daud certainly knew more about his financial network than the American or Russian governments did.

Even if he was entirely trustworthy, he didn't seem the type who could withstand an interrogation. If the Russians ever got their filthy paws on this young man, odds were, he would spill everything. "Are we almost there?"

The young man nodded as he turned down a narrow side street about ten minutes outside the city center. Around them, four- and five-story Soviet-era apartments rose to the sky. Each identically constructed in drab concrete, each showing the neglect of time. How Bukayev hated Soviet blight. Even with care and attention, this architectural motif would remain depressing and uninspired.

Thirty yards up, Daud pulled to the side of the street, typed a message into his phone, and waited, his eyes focused on a third-floor window across the street. "Okay," he said as he turned off the ignition.

The men exited the car, crossed the quiet street, and entered the building. Bukayev found himself slightly breathless by the time they reached the third-floor landing.

A burly, bearded man with dark, suspicious eyes let them into the apartment without a word.

Bukayev wrinkled his nose at the kitchen sink piled high with dirty dishes. He'd call the apartment's décor retro Soviet chic, but there was nothing at all chic about the ratty, sagging green sofa or the mismatched chairs set around a scarred wooden table.

The bearded man knocked on a door at the far side of the apartment. A moment later, a powerfully built man with short but unkempt curly hair and a full beard laced with a hint of red emerged.

"*As-salam Alaikum*," Bukayev said, a wide smile breaking across his face.

"*Wa 'alaikum-as-salam*," the man replied, pulling Bukayev into a bear hug.

Bukayev gasped for breath as Rasul Makasharipov, a man ten years his junior and in far better shape, lifted him from the floor.

"Look at you, Imran. You haven't changed at all. How long has it been?"

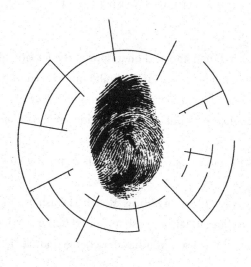

CHAPTER EIGHT

Dirksen Senate Office Building, Washington, DC

M aggie settled into the first row of chairs behind the witness table, just to Warner's right. If he needed to consult
with her about anything, all he had to do was glance over
his shoulder and she'd jump. Capitol Hill police officers guarded the
hearing room—two inside the room, two outside the entrance and another half dozen scattered around at the elevator and stairways on the
building's third floor.

An hour before the hearing started, the Capitol Hill police bomb
squad had swept the room using both electronic detection devices and
two massive Belgian Malinois dogs. Such security measures weren't
normally afforded to Senate Intelligence Committee hearings, but

given the elevated threat level and the presence of the soon-to-be CIA director, security pulled out all the stops.

As they awaited the start of the hearing, press photographers, who were positioned between the senators' dais and the witness table, jostled for the best camera angle. Warner ignored them and pretended to study his notes. He needed no more preparation, Maggie knew. They'd worked late into the night the past two days. Thanks to her extensive research, he knew where each senator stood on the country's most pressing national security issues. And he could recite the president's policies and concerns in his sleep. As for the Agency side of things, Warner had spent his entire career at Langley. No question they threw at him would leave him fumbling for a coherent answer. For Maggie, it felt like the end of a marathon but also the beginning of a new one. As she yawned and stretched her stiff neck, it occurred to her that she might not catch up on sleep for weeks. Maybe months.

Warner rose as the senators filed in. Up at the dais, he pressed the flesh with members from both sides of the aisle. From the tight smile pasted on his face, Maggie knew that the political side of the job would be Warner's least favorite part. He couldn't abide the Washington culture, where flattery got you everywhere, as long as an exchange of money or influence was included.

Intelligence Committee staffers filtered in through a door at the back of the hearing room and took up positions behind the senators' chairs. With a few notable exceptions, most of the senators on this committee relied entirely on unelected staffers to explain the issues at hand to them and to write their statements and witness questions. Maggie should know—she'd been a committee staffer, only on the House side of the Hill.

Her phone buzzed. A text from Roger.

Good luck. Just pulled into the parking lot after grabbing lunch. Call my desk number if anything comes up. Probably can't watch the hearing.

Why wouldn't he be able to watch the hearing from headquarters? What was taking up all his time?

Okay, she texted back. She spun in her chair. The Agency's director of Public Affairs, general counsel, and director of Congressional Affairs were all supposed to be here by now. When she faced front again, she noticed Senator Canton approaching Warner. He offered his hand. Hers remained folded together in front of her. Not only did this woman have a distaste for all things CIA, but she also seemed to have a personal animus toward Warner. Maggie had warned him that Senator Canton was the one to watch out for today. But no matter how nasty she got, the senator wouldn't be able to derail his nomination. Nevertheless, Maggie was certain that she'd do everything she could to smear Warner's reputation.

As Warner moved on to the next lawmaker, Senator Canton locked eyes with Maggie. She glanced over her shoulder to see if perhaps the woman was looking at someone else. There was no one behind her. Maggie raised her phone to her ear as if receiving an urgent call. As she turned away and let her hair cascade down to hide the side of her face, the senator finally turned her attention elsewhere. Maggie carried on the charade of a phone call until she noticed who had captured Canton's attention.

She clapped her phone shut and watched as the senator and a petite blonde woman in a tight-fitting red dress spoke in the corner of the hearing room. The younger woman looked familiar, but Maggie didn't know why. Maybe she'd seen her around Capitol Hill back when she'd worked for the House Intelligence Committee.

Just then, the committee chairman made his way to the center of the dais. He tapped the gavel on the sound block. Senators drifted to their seats and Warner headed for the witness table. Maggie noticed a waif of a brunette enter the hearing room from the side door. It was Wendy Carlson, the former administrative assistant for the House

Intelligence Committee. Wendy and Congressman Richard Carvelli had an affair two years ago.

At the time of his death, Wendy was pregnant with his child—a scandalous story, but not nearly as scandalous as the congressman's dealings with the Russian mafia.

Maggie ducked, afraid Wendy would spot her. It had been at least a year since they'd spoken. That had been Maggie's decision, one she'd made because she couldn't bear the weight of the lies that hung between them.

"Everything okay, Maggie?" It was Warner, who'd yet to take his seat.

She unclenched her fists and nodded. "Yeah, why?"

"You look a little stressed." He patted her arm. "Everything will be fine."

"Of course." She offered a bright smile and scanned the room. Wendy was gone. "You've got this."

The rest of the CIA entourage arrived and settled into the seats to Maggie's left. After exchanging perfunctory greetings with them, she turned her attention to the front of the hearing room. Photographers knelt in front of Warner's table, waiting for him to sit so they could snap shots until they got the exact image they needed for whatever spin their news organization wanted to put on today's hearing.

A confident Warner Thompson. An evasive Warner Thompson. An arrogant Warner Thompson.

Then it occurred to her. She was right in the photographers' line of fire. A quick scan of the room revealed only two television cameras. One trained on the row of senators up front, the other on Warner. She tapped him on the shoulder. "I'm going to move a few seats over. Feeling a bit camera shy." The only time her face had been plastered across television and newspapers had been in the aftermath of Congressman Carvelli's death a year and a half ago. The official story had obfuscated her role in his demise, but still, Maggie didn't want a curious reporter or TV viewer to recognize her and dredge up questions about what had really happened in the congressman's brownstone.

Warner pointed to the Agency's Public Affairs director. "I'll slip her a note if I need any information from you."

"Sounds like a plan." She took a seat several rows back on the far left of the hearing room. To her right, she watched as the woman in the red dress handed Senator Canton a note before taking a seat with the rest of the media contingent. *A reporter?*

At last, the chairman gaveled the hearing into order. Most of the senators' questions were political statements posing as questions, some praising the CIA, others questioning its efficacy, what with Osama bin Laden still on the run almost four years after the September 11 attacks. As for Warner, he handled compliments and criticism with equal aplomb. If he was at all nervous or irritated, it didn't show.

As the second most junior member of the intelligence oversight committee, Senator Canton's turn came more than an hour and a half into the hearing. Warner easily deflected questions about Agency involvement in alleged torture and gender inequality in the Directorate of Operations. Seemingly placated, or at least stripped of further angles of attack, Canton settled back into her leather chair, arms crossed. She glanced over at the press pool and then leaned toward the microphone set in front of her on the dais.

"Mr. Thompson, there is a matter of serious concern that no one has raised. Yet."

Warner folded his hands on the table and waited.

"According to my sources, your very close associate, Maggie Jenkins, was inside the Dominion School last September during the siege. Is this true?"

Maggie gripped the seat of her chair, her face suddenly hot. *How does she know?*

Warner leaned forward to speak directly into the microphone. "I'm not familiar with your sources."

"May I remind you that you're under oath, Mr. Thompson."

He stared back at the senator, his face expressionless.

"It's a yes-or-no question. Was Maggie Jenkins, an intelligence analyst, inside the school, shooting people who were seeking to redress their grievances against—"

"By people, you mean the terrorists, correct, Senator Canton?"

Murmurs and a few laughs filtered through the hearing room.

"You ran an illegal CIA operation on US soil, inside an elementary school."

"I've spent my entire adult life in the employ of the Central Intelligence Agency, senator." His tone was like steel. "I'm well aware that the CIA may not operate on US soil."

"Hundreds of children could've died that day, Mr. Thompson."

Warner's jaw twitched. "Hundreds of children would have died had agents of the US government not moved in when they did."

"It was an illegal CIA operation."

"With all due respect, it was no such thing."

The senator's voice grew more insistent. "Not only do I oppose your nomination, I intend to request a Department of Justice investigation into the matter. And into your role that day."

"I would welcome such an investigation."

Maggie blinked rapidly, trying to keep the room in focus. *Who told Senator Canton?*

"Perhaps you'd like to explain to the committee why you also were in the school if there was no CIA involvement?"

A murmur arose in the hearing room. Several senators exchanged confused looks.

How did she know that? There was no mention in the FBI's report about Warner slipping into the school. He wasn't there on official business. He was there to help Maggie and to get his daughters, who were students there, out of the building. Warner threw Maggie a look over his left shoulder. It was a mistake.

"Mr. Thompson," Senator Canton said, her tone laced with venom, "if you have something to say to Ms. Jenkins," she pointed a perfectly manicured finger directly at Maggie, "please state so on the record."

Every camera turned Maggie's way in unison. Beyond the reporters, she watched as Senator Canton passed a note to a staffer, who then scurried over to the chairman, handed it to him, and scrambled back to her seat. Maggie craned her neck to watch the chairman open the note. He frowned and focused in on Warner. Then Maggie. *Not a good sign.*

"The Committee will take a brief recess." He banged the gavel.

Warner stood, turned his back on the cameras, and motioned Maggie over to the rear corner of the room. "How the hell did she know about us?"

Maggie felt eyes and camera lenses on her, so she did her best to keep her expression neutral. "I don't know." Her throat was dry, her voice hoarse. "But, thanks to her, now Bukayev knows my name."

Warner's eyes flashed with anger. "There will be hell to pay for this, Maggie."

The Agency's general counsel approached. "Mr. Thompson, the chairman would like to see you."

"Give me a minute."

"We should go now."

Warner crossed his arms.

"Please. Sir."

"Fine," Warner snapped as he turned and headed toward the front of the hearing room.

Maggie lowered herself into a chair.

The general counsel nodded at her. "You too."

"Why?"

"Let's go," he said brusquely.

She knew she hadn't done anything wrong, but with all eyes on her and cameras clicking and whirring, it felt like a perp walk.

From her seat in the press section, Anna stared across the hearing room at Senator Canton, trying to catch her attention. Finding a source who confirmed that Maggie Jenkins was the federal agent inside the school during the terrorist attack was quite an intelligence coup. But sharing that information with the senator might've been a huge mistake.

Anna had known about the Russian teacher for months, but hadn't considered contacting her until after Imran Bukayev's video aired on Sunday. She'd been at the gym, observing the CIA woman, Maggie Jenkins, when news of the video threat broke. Jenkins's visceral reaction could only mean one thing: she knew something important about the school siege. That realization had prompted Anna to pay a visit to the teacher.

It had been surprisingly easy for Anna to track her down. Her father, a former KGB bigwig and reputed Russian mafia boss, was the only civilian killed at the school that day. If it had been her family member gunned down, Anna would've made herself scarce until Imran Bukayev was apprehended. But Svetlana Markova's name and address were right there in the white pages.

Anna had presented herself as a consular officer from the Russian embassy stopping by to check on Svetlana and her young daughter. They were doing okay, Svetlana had said, but were looking forward to an upcoming visit home to Russia. *Fantastic*, Anna had enthused before probing into what had happened inside the school. Svetlana couldn't remember the name of the woman who killed the terrorists. *Megan or Maddie or something like that?* Anna described Maggie Jenkins. *Yes. Yes, curly red hair, that's her.*

What Svetlana revealed next had been a surprise. A second federal agent had been wounded during the siege. Shot, in fact. Svetlana thought his name was Walter Thomas or Thompson, or something like that. It didn't take long for Anna to figure out that the man was Warner Thompson—the CIA's spy chief.

Anna had wanted Maggie and Warner's names to remain secret until she could leverage the information for something. Maybe for *kompromat* on the new CIA director. That's what Moscow wanted her to do. But now that it was all public, perhaps she could use it for her own purposes. She'd never stopped thinking about Imran Bukayev. At last, she might finally have the opportunity to exact her own form of revenge.

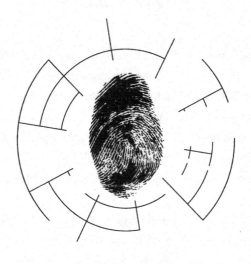

CHAPTER NINE

Maggie circled around the witness desk and followed Warner to the left of the hearing room and out a door in the far corner.

A Capitol Hill police officer waved them into a small window-less room furnished only with two brown leather couches and a coffee table. The chairman and vice chairman of the Senate Intelligence Committee fell silent when Maggie, Warner, and the Agency's general counsel entered.

"Warner," began the chairman, "why didn't the FBI report reference you being inside that school?"

"Because it wasn't relevant to the material facts involving the terrorist siege." He folded his arms. "I made my way inside before the SWAT team, but I wasn't acting in an official capacity."

The committee's vice chairman snatched Senator Canton's note from the chairman's hand. He read for a moment then looked up at Warner. "You got injured inside the school?"

"I got shot." Warner offered with a tight smile. "It was just a flesh wound."

Maggie bit her lip to avoid laughing at their running joke, the one they'd used to lighten their dark moods in the months following the school siege. Not surprisingly, the vice chairman didn't pick up on the Monty Python reference. He looked like a man who spent more time buttering up donors than watching classic comedy films. Or any comedy films, for that matter.

"Who shot you?" the vice chairman asked.

Maggie and Warner exchanged a quick glance.

"That's not really relevant," Warner said, jumping in before Maggie could speak.

"I'm afraid I have to disagree," the vice chairman huffed. "A CIA official getting shot inside a school where terrorists are holding hundreds of hostages sounds entirely relevant to me."

"It was personal," Maggie chimed in.

Warner's eyebrows shot up. The senators stared at her, slack-jawed.

"What I mean—"

"Look," Warner interrupted, "Maggie is under intense stress after what Senator Canton just did. In case you haven't been paying attention, there is a fatwa directed at the agent involved. And thanks to Senator Canton's indiscretion, it is now public knowledge who that agent is." His cheeks grew red as his anger rose. "Canton was either criminally oblivious or knew full well that outing Maggie's name would put her life at risk. And the worst part is, she did it to score political points."

Maggie put a hand on Warner's arm to try to calm him. "If I may explain things for myself?"

Warner frowned.

Maggie ignored him. "What I was trying to say is that Warner entered the school for personal reasons. He wasn't there as a CIA officer."

The chairman spoke next. "Don't your children attend that school?"

Warner nodded. "I didn't want that information to be made public. My girls' safety is the main reason I wasn't included in the FBI's report. But thanks to Senator Canton, my children may now be in jeopardy."

The chairman tsked in disapproval. "I'll speak to the senator about her outburst."

Outburst? Maggie opened her mouth to object. Warner shot her a look.

"So one of the terrorists shot you?" the chairman asked.

Maggie raised a hand. "Actually, it was me."

Both senators stared at her in disbelief. Finally, the vice chairman spoke. "Did she actually shoot you, Warner?"

"Technically, yes," he said, his face betraying no emotion.

"Thank goodness I'm a terrible shot," Maggie let slip. Strike two with the jokes. These men weren't in any mood for humor. Frankly neither was she, but it was her tried-and-true coping mechanism. If she didn't break the tension, it might just break her.

"If I recall, Ms. Jenkins," the chairman intoned, "the FBI report says you killed three of the terrorists."

She cleared her throat. "Four, actually."

The senators exchanged glances. "So you're not a terrible shot, then?" the chairman asked, his downturned mouth betraying annoyance.

"The situation was fluid. I had Zara held at gunpoint. I saw the flash of someone in the hall as she shouted one of the terrorist's names. I thought I was about to be ambushed, so I fired."

"Like I said, it was a minor wound," Warner offered. "The FBI director himself decided to leave the specifics of this friendly fire incident out of the final report. Both because it's irrelevant to the outcome of the siege and because of security concerns for my children. And if it's of any interest to you, the girls didn't even know I'd been shot. I bandaged up my arm before they saw me."

The vice chairman ran a hand through his thinning gray hair. "But you see our problem now, Warner. Senator Canton isn't going to let this go. As far as she's concerned, you're a liar. Next, she'll be accusing you of violating the statute against CIA operations on US soil."

"She already has," Maggie said.

The chairman shot her a look as he smoothed his yellow paisley tie. "This is going to get ugly in the press. Really ugly."

"It doesn't need to." Warner closed his eyes and exhaled. "Look, I can address this incident in front of the entire committee, but only if we do it in closed session. No press. No staff. Just the senators."

The two senior senators considered his suggestion. "Ms. Jenkins," the chairman said, "are you prepared to go on the record?"

She glanced at the general counsel, who gave a nod. "I'd be glad to. I have nothing to hide."

Warner gave her a grateful smile.

"All right. Give us fifteen minutes to gather the members and get rid of the media."

The vice chairman poked his head outside the room and summoned a Capitol Hill police officer. "Please ensure that Mr. Thompson and Ms. Jenkins don't speak to each other."

"Excuse me?" Maggie said.

"Maggie," Warner said, his tone a warning.

"I don't want you refreshing each other's memories about that day," the vice chairman said.

"You can't stop us from talking. This is still America——"

"Fine, then, Ms. Jenkins," the vice chairman said. "You can come with me and testify first."

She looked to the Agency lawyer for support. He simply shrugged.

"You'll do fine, Maggie," Warner called as she left the room with the senators.

Back in the hearing room, Maggie saw the last of the committee staffers filing out of the room through a door behind the dais. Security herded the media through the rear door. There was no sign of the blonde reporter who'd spoken with Senator Canton. Maggie sat at the witness table in the same chair Warner had occupied just minutes before.

As the senators returned to their seats, they looked at her in surprise. All except for Senator Canton, who appeared mildly amused. *Or maybe plastic surgery has frozen her face that way*, Maggie mused.

Once the room was secure, Maggie swore to tell the truth, the whole truth, and nothing but the truth.

The chairman explained that Senator Canton was correct. Warner Thompson had entered Dominion Elementary school during the siege. And that not only had he been in the school, but he'd also been shot. By Maggie Jenkins, the woman sitting at the witness table.

Every muscle in Maggie's body felt taut. If she thought she could get away with it, she'd flee the room. Her hand trembled as she lifted a glass of water to her lips. If only Roger were here, sitting where she could see him so she could pretend he was the only one in the room with her.

"Ms. Jenkins," began the senator from Texas, "I have to say it is an incredible honor to meet you in person. The entire country owes you a debt of gratitude."

Several of the senators applauded.

"Mr. Chairman," objected the vice chairman. "Committee decorum?"

The chairman turned to senators on his right. "If the senators would refrain from personal commentary, please."

The Texas senator gave Maggie a thumbs-up and a huge grin. She smiled back, grateful. If things got ugly, she'd turn to him for support.

With each senator's turn to question or comment, Maggie's confidence rose. All, so far, seemed sympathetic.

Then came Senator Canton. After the chairman gave her the floor, she busied herself, jotting down notes—or doodles, for all Maggie knew—on the legal pad set before her.

Maggie folded her hands in her lap, then placed them on the table, hoping it would make her look more relaxed than she felt.

"Ms. Jenkins." The senator finally lifted her head and tucked a stray wisp of hair behind an ear. "I understand the school shooting wasn't the first time you were involved in such an incident."

Maggie's stomach lurched. She couldn't possibly know about her being on-site at the terrorist attack in Beslan, Russia. That information had been compartmented and locked away. Or was she referring to something else? She leaned forward to the microphone set on the table. "I'm afraid I don't know what you mean." Her voice came over the speakers far too loudly.

"Oh, I think you do."

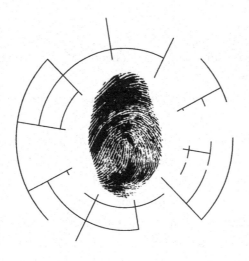

CHAPTER TEN

Maggie moved her hands to her lap so that Senator Canton wouldn't see her fists balled up tightly. She stared back at the woman, whose skin was preternaturally smooth for someone her age.

Senator Canton tilted her head to the side ever so slightly as if looking for a better angle of attack. "Two years ago, you shot Congressman Carvelli. He died, did he not?"

Maggie flushed and turned to her left.

The general counsel hurried over and squatted next to her. "What does this have to do with Mr. Thompson's nomination?" she whispered.

The lawyer stood and raised a hand. "Mr. Chairman, may I address the committee?"

"Yes. Please." The chairman shot an exasperated look at Senator Canton.

He sat at the table to Maggie's right. "Ms. Jenkins agreed to testify about a specific event that occurred during the school siege last year. If the committee would like to bring the witness back at a future date to discuss other matters, we'd be happy to arrange it."

"Mr. Chairman," Senator Canton said, "Warner Thompson was also at Congressman Carvelli's the night he died. As I understand it, Mr. Thompson was shot in the leg. I think we have the right to know if Ms. Jenkins shot him that time too?"

Murmurs arose among the senators. "I remember seeing your faces on television," one said, waggling a finger in Maggie's general direction. "Couple of years ago, if I recall."

"Mr. Chairman?" Maggie said.

He nodded, his mouth pinched in uncertainty.

She cleared her throat. This was not a part of her past that she'd expected to have to relive today. "In November 2003, Congressman Carvelli shot both Warner Thompson and me inside his Capitol Hill home." Several of the committee members stared at her in astonishment. They were either new to the Senate or hadn't been privy to the classified briefings that occurred in the aftermath of Steve's murder and Carvelli's death.

The details fed to the media had pinned Carvelli's death on a Russian spy who was trying to blackmail the congressman. It was all nonsense, all made up to keep the country from knowing how close it had come to a devastating terrorist attack caused by the treacherous actions of a congressman. "If you'd like to know more, there is a classified report that explains everything." She wasn't going to spoon-feed this crowd any more details. If they were really interested, they could contact the Agency and arrange a briefing. She doubted any of them would. Most of them were all talk, no action.

"It's not often that a sitting member of Congress is shot dead in his own home. And what are the odds of you being present the two times Warner Thompson has been shot?" Senator Canton leaned back in her chair. "If he is confirmed, which isn't all that certain given everything we've learned today about his involvement in a domestic terrorist attack—"

The chairman banged his gavel. "Senator Canton, this may be a closed hearing, but everything you say is on the record. If you want to accuse Warner Thompson of any illegalities, stop with the insinuation, and come out and say it."

Maggie let herself breathe.

"All I'm saying, Mr. Chairman, is that without more details about what happened inside Dominion Elementary School and Richard Carvelli's house, I will be voting no on his nomination."

As if she'd vote to confirm Warner under any circumstances. Maggie leaned toward the microphone. "Senator Canton, your confusion surprises me."

The senator frowned. .

Maggie grabbed the leather portfolio from inside her valise, opened to the dossier she'd compiled, and acted as if she were reading from it. "According to my records, you were present at all the classified briefings on both the Carvelli matter and the school siege. You already know the answers to all your questions. Unless you've forgotten them?"

The senator from Texas snickered.

Senator Canton's face flushed. "There is no mention of Warner being in the elementary school or the fact that you shot him."

"Both are issues that he will address once I am dismissed from the room."

The senator's mouth opened wide as if she were about to protest or sling another accusation.

Maggie cut her off at the pass. "Before I go, I'd like to know why you just told the entire country that I was the one inside the school the day of the siege. That I was the one who took out four terrorists whose goal it was to slaughter as many children as possible." Her entire body buzzed with adrenaline. "No doubt you are aware of the fatwa that Shamil Basayev just issued. Your actions have placed a bull's-eye squarely on me. So let me ask you, who gave you my name and what do you have to gain from leaking it?"

"Mr. Chairman, I move to strike these accusations from the record." The senator glared at Maggie.

"This is a closed hearing, Senator Canton. Ms. Jenkins's statement stays right here inside this room. And it would be highly unusual for the committee to strike anything from a witness's statement."

"A witness does not get to ask me questions," she objected.

The chairman ignored her. "Ms. Jenkins, unless there's anything else you'd like to add, you're free to go."

"Thank you, Mr. Chairman." She scanned the dais. "The only thing I would like to add is that Warner Thompson will make an exceptional CIA director. He knows the Agency better than anyone else in the building, and perhaps most importantly, he understands our security and intelligence strengths and weaknesses. This country needs him leading the CIA. He is a patriot and a hero, and I am proud to call him my friend."

Senator Canton snorted.

Maggie hadn't planned to say another word, but the smirk on the senator's face was like an accelerant to her temper. "If Imran Bukayev kills me or Warner Thompson, let the record show who is responsible for leaking our names."

"Mr. Chairman," Senator Canton objected again.

"Thank you for your time, Ms. Jenkins. You may go." The chairman turned to the clerk. "Please bring in Mr. Thompson."

Maggie stood and pasted on a smile that belied her jumping nerves and shaking legs. Not sure she could withstand another withering glare from Senator Canton, she hiked the valise over her shoulder, and marched out the door without a glance back.

· ★ ★ ★ ·

Maggie slumped onto a bench that stood along the far wall opposite the hearing-room entrance.

"Miss?" A young Capitol Hill police officer approached. "Are you okay?"

She inhaled deeply, held her breath, then exhaled audibly, hoping the breathing exercise would calm her wildly beating heart. What had she done? Did she just blow Warner's chance at confirmation by being so flippant and turning the tables on Senator Canton?

"Miss? Can I get you anything? Water?"

Maggie pushed away the hair that had fallen over her face. "I'm okay. It's just . . . some of those senators . . ."

The officer gave a knowing nod.

"Did you happen to see where all the reporters went?"

The officer pointed to her left. "Once the hearing went into closed session, we relocated them to the ground floor."

Maggie stood, feeling slightly steadier on her feet. "If anyone comes out of the hearing looking for me, could you tell them I'll be right back?"

The officer nodded.

"Thanks." Maggie headed down the hall, the clicking of her heels echoing off the white marble floor. She passed the brass elevator doors in favor of the staircase sign she spotted ahead. Three floors down, she pushed open the stairwell door and peered down the hall. Sure enough, there was a gaggle of reporters milling about in the lobby, cordoned off like a herd of cattle by red velvet ropes hanging from a dozen gold-plated stanchions. It was hard to pick out individuals from this distance, so she squared her shoulders and marched toward the lobby.

As she got closer, Maggie noticed the blonde woman standing away from the other reporters, typing something into her phone.

What am I doing? She hadn't thought this far ahead and had no idea what she was going to say to her. No, it would be better to keep her distance until she talked to Warner. *Warner!* She glanced at her watch. It had only been five minutes, but there was no telling how long he'd be jousting with the senator from California. As his soon-to-be chief of staff, she should be outside the hearing room when he was done.

Just as she turned, someone called her name. Maggie looked back. The blonde reporter.

"Hey!" She waved her hand in the air and ducked under the velvet rope. "Can I speak with you a moment?" A broad grin spread across her face, revealing bright white, perfectly straight teeth. The smile didn't reach her cold blue eyes. She handed Maggie a white business card. "Anna Orlova, *Russia Today.*"

Maggie didn't look at it. "How do you know Senator Canton?"

"I know many American politicians." She cocked her head. "I was hoping we could chat."

"I don't talk to the media." Maggie turned and headed for the stairs.

"Maybe I can help you. With finding Bukayev," the woman called. Maggie faltered, as if someone had kicked her in the gut. She squeezed her eyes shut, ordered herself to breathe, and picked up the pace.

Inside the stairwell, she fell against the cool cinder-block wall. What the hell was going on? Why was a US senator friendly with a

Russian reporter? And what did this reporter know about Bukayev? Her phone rang, slowing the merry-go-round of panicked thoughts.

"Hello?" she said, whispering without realizing she was.

"What's going on over there? I saw that the hearing went into closed session."

"It's bad, Roger. I'll fill you in when we get back." She disconnected the call and ascended the stairs.

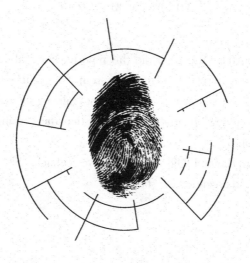

CHAPTER ELEVEN

CIA Headquarters, Langley, Virginia

Maggie splashed cold water on her face and gripped the edge of the sink. The pale green eyes and lightly freckled skin reflected in the mirror looked the same as they had this morning. But suddenly, because of a single sentence uttered by a government official, everything was different. Maggie was a target. Bukayev's target.

Last year, she hadn't known she was in Zara's sights until it was almost too late. But now, the reality of the situation—the fact that any given moment could be her last—seemed to squeeze every cell inside her. Her entire body ached. Thoughts flew from every direction, jumbled and incoherent. *What now?*

The sound of the restroom door whooshing open startled her. She blotted her wet face with a paper towel.

"Maggie?"

"Roger?"

"Can I come in?"

"I guess." She tossed the paper towel in the general direction of the trash can. It fell to the floor, landing silently on the ceramic tile below.

A woman exited a toilet stall behind Maggie and shot Roger an angry look as he entered the ladies' room.

He rushed to Maggie and grabbed her hands. "I couldn't find you anywhere, I—"

"I'm fine," she protested. "Bukayev can't get to me inside CIA Headquarters."

"This is a serious situation, Maggie."

She tugged her hands free and grabbed her purse. "You think I don't know that?"

"Warner wants to talk to us."

"Now?"

Another woman entered the restroom and emitted a yelp at the sight of Roger.

"Sorry," Maggie said to the woman as she brushed past her. "We were just leaving."

Warner took one look at Maggie and knew she wasn't okay. Her pale skin looked nearly transparent, and her lips were drawn in a tight line. She hadn't said much on the ride back from the Hill, which was okay with him. He'd needed the time to absorb what Senator Canton had done to Maggie. And to him. But more importantly, to Maggie.

"Please, have a seat. Priscilla made us a fresh pot of coffee."

She lowered herself into a chair, eyes locked on Warner.

Roger scrambled for the carafe, poured, and handed Maggie a white mug emblazoned with the blue CIA logo.

Maggie accepted it without a word, her fingers wrapping tightly around the smooth, warm ceramic.

"I've directed security to set up physical and video surveillance at your house. There will be security guards there twenty-four seven, and personnel on-site to monitor the feed from the video cameras. Someone will always be with you in the house and—"

"In my house?" She placed the mug on a side table. "Are they in my house already?"

"Yes."

She popped up from the chair. "You didn't even bother to ask me if it was okay to break into my house?"

"In all fairness, you were hiding in the bathroom," Roger said.

Her head whipped in his direction. "I wasn't hiding."

Warner raised his palms. "Maggie, I told you that if there was any hint of trouble, anything at all, I would pull out all the stops to keep you safe."

She sank into the chair, closed her eyes, and massaged her temples. "My house is my sanctuary, Warner. It's the only place I can . . . think. The only place I can be alone."

Warner noted the expression that flashed across Roger's face. Even if the comment wasn't directed at him, it looked like it stung. Maggie took no notice. "This is temporary. Until we neutralize the threat."

"I'm going to find Bukayev, Maggie, if it's the last thing I ever do," Roger said, sounding like the Boy Scout he wasn't.

Maggie rolled her eyes. "Bin Laden's been on the run for nearly four years. How's that manhunt going?"

Clearly, this approach wasn't working. She was at her worst when she felt vulnerable and at her best when she was on a mission. Right now, there was no plan, nothing for her to focus on other than the realization that Bukayev wanted her dead. "We need to head out of town for a couple of days," Warner said.

Her gaze shifted between them in suspicion. "Who's we?"

"The three of us," Roger said, his voice brimming with forced cheerfulness.

Maggie looked from Roger to Warner and back again. "You can't go anywhere, Warner. You just got nominated . . . and I have to work. There's Bukayev, and I am, or soon will be, your chief of staff, and—"

"The Intelligence Committee isn't voting on my nomination until next week. In fact, the Senate is out of session until Tuesday. So we're in a holding pattern."

"But Bukayev," she objected.

Warner nodded at Roger. He'd offered to take the flack for the news about Dagestan, but Roger insisted that he be the one to tell her.

"We have a lead on him."

Her eyes widened as she sat up straight. "Where is he?"

"Dagestan."

"Right under the Russians' noses," she breathed. "Wait, how did you find out?" Her gaze moved to Warner. "And when?"

Warner took the "how" question. It was the easier of the two. "A few months ago, we tasked the NSA with watching Shamil Basayev's communications."

"You said you didn't know if we had eyes and ears on him," she said, her tone accusatory.

"We were on an open line, Maggie."

She pulled her hair up to the top of her head and held it there a moment before letting it fall back into place. "What else have you lied about?"

Warner ignored her question. "As you know, Shamil Basayev and Imran Bukayev have a history together. Our signals intelligence picked up an email to Basayev that originated in Dagestan. Based on the verbiage in the email, we think it was from Imran Bukayev."

"I want to read it."

The folder Roger pulled from the top of Warner's desk was emblazoned with TS-SCI/SI/TK. Top Secret, Sensitive Compartment Information, Special Intelligence, Talent Keyhole.

"Talent Keyhole," Maggie commented. "That satellite intelligence-collection platform we discussed the other day?"

Warner nodded.

She read through the intercept. "It could be him." She glanced back at the document. "Wait a minute. This is dated two days ago. You knew about this on Tuesday and didn't tell me?"

Uh-oh. Warner jumped in to save Roger's hide. "I was going to tell you Tuesday, but then the director died and everything spun out of control."

"It's been two days, Warner. What if Bukayev's already moved to another location?" She waved the folder in the air. "What if he disappears again?"

"We're monitoring the email account and we'll—"

"This is inexcusable, Warner."

His eyes grew wide. "Careful, Maggie."

If any other CIA employee said such a thing to him, they'd never get away with it, and she knew it. "Sorry, it's just that—"

"Maggie," Roger said, his voice pleading. "I'm in contact with a source I've been cultivating in Dagestan. And I've been monitoring all the intelligence."

"That's supposed to be my job," she shot back.

"I needed you to get me ready for the confirmation hearing," Warner interjected. "While you were busy with that, Roger began working on a plan to capture and exfiltrate Bukayev from Dagestan."

"Capture?" Her voice cracked. "I want him dead."

Warner closed his eyes for a moment. So did he. "The president wants him brought here for trial. To bring justice against the person who attacked our most innocent citizens."

"If we kill him—"

"We can't, Maggie." Warner pulled the folder from her hand.

She leaned her head back and studied the ceiling. "So what am I supposed to do? Sit in my house with a bunch of armed strangers and hope we find Bukayev before he finds me?"

"That's where our little beach getaway comes in. We'll go to my house in Hatteras a few weeks earlier than we planned."

She shook her head, not understanding Roger's plan.

"The media is all over your neighborhood already, Maggie," Roger said. "It's best to keep out of the spotlight until the story dies down. And, if you're not home, security can work around the clock to get your house wired and secured."

"But the beach?" she groaned. "How are we supposed to get updates on Bukayev at the beach?"

Warner jumped in. "Security is bringing a secure mobile phone. We'll be in constant touch with the Ops Center. And there's a boat captain on the island who may be able to help us."

Maggie squinted at him. "A boat captain?"

"He has close ties to Dagestan. He can help," Warner explained.

"I still don't understand."

"He's former Agency. We need to talk to him."

"Why can't he come up here instead of us trekking all the way to the Outer Banks?" Maggie asked.

"Let's just say it'll be easier if we go to him," Warner said. "Long story."

Her shoulders slumped. "Do I have a choice?"

"Not really," Roger said. "Unless you'd rather stay in a hotel somewhere."

She threw up her arms in surrender.

"Then it's settled." Warner clasped his hands together. "I suggest you let Rich bring you home so you can pack."

"Rich?"

"One of the security officers who will accompany us to the beach."

She sighed. "Probably a good idea."

"You'll like him. He's one of our best," Warner said, trying to sound cheerful. "Roger will pick you up in the morning and Rich will follow."

She ran a hand through her hair. "When I woke up this morning, I had no idea that today would be the day I lost control over my life." Blowing air through her lips, she added, "No more secrets. I need to know everything you know, when you know it. That's the only way this will work."

Warner didn't ask her to elaborate. He'd learned the hard way that if Maggie Jenkins decided to go rogue, there was no way to stop her.

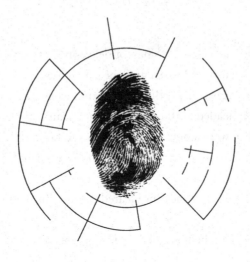

CHAPTER TWELVE

Makhachkala, Dagestan, Russia

The last time Bukayev had seen Rasul, nearly six years ago, he'd tried to talk the hot-tempered young man out of launching a military operation from Chechnya against Dagestan. Rasul had ignored the advice and proceeded to lead a failed operation that led to his imprisonment for a year. Despite that detour, the time since his release had been kind to him as he acquired more power and scored multiple successful attacks against Russian targets throughout Dagestan.

"Look at you, Rasul. You've become everything you always dreamed, and more."

"*Alhamdulillah*." Rasul smiled, then waved at the man who'd led Bukayev and Daud into the apartment. "Tea."

The man made quick business of delivering hot tea from the kitchen. Bukayev examined his teacup to be sure it was clean.

"*Shukran*," Rasul grunted as he waved the man away.

The man headed for the door, grabbing Daud on the way out.

Once they were alone, Rasul got down to business with Bukayev. "What brings you to Dagestan, my friend? I thought you'd be with your people in Chechnya."

"I was there for a time. But I feared that the Russians were closing in."

"So, you need shelter until the Russians are convinced you've vanished again."

"Yes." Bukayev sipped his tea. "I also need resources to help carry out Shamil Basayev's fatwa against the American who killed our fearless warriors inside the American school."

Rasul's light blue eyes, a nod to Slavic blood coursing through his veins, fixed on him over the rim of his steaming cup. "Shouldn't you be asking Shamil for those resources? It's his fatwa."

A wave of exhaustion swept over Bukayev. What he wanted to say, or rather shout, was that he was tired of begging for help. He wanted his life back. He wanted the freedom to roam the streets, surround himself with beautiful things, have others jump at his every command. But he knew how that would come across to Rasul, a man who respected action, not complaints. "He is working on it, but I'm losing patience. I want to deploy foot soldiers to America. Perhaps they can smoke out the target."

Rasul tugged at his beard. "My men, the ones I trust most, do not speak English."

Bukayev clenched a fist under the table. He didn't want Rasul's men. Sure, they were loyal and focused, but they were nothing more than uneducated barbarians. What he craved was the assistance of someone who could think strategically, who could help him plan and execute the next attack. It was times like this that he desperately missed Zara and her cold, calculating, and brilliant mind.

"You're welcome to stay with me and my men while you wait for Shamil to respond. As long as you don't mind being constantly on the move." He looked around the apartment. "I'll be sorry to leave this place. It's one of the nicer hideouts I've had in recent months."

Bukayev frowned, unsure if the younger man was joking. When no laugh or smile materialized, it became obvious he wasn't. Clearly, his time living life on the run, bouncing from hellhole to hellhole, wasn't over. Maybe he should've stayed at the mosque.

"We can stay with my cousin, Abdel, to begin with. He's planning the next attack here in Dagestan. Perhaps you can help."

Bukayev forced a dishonest smile. "It would be an honor, Rasul."

When they arrived at Abdel's apartment, Bukayev's mood lifted considerably at the news that greeted him on the television. "*Alhamdulillah*," he shouted. He now had a name and a face for the person who'd killed Zara. *Maggie Jenkins*. He turned the name over in his head. Who was this woman?

"I need a computer, Rasul. And an internet connection." The sooner he learned everything he could about her, the sooner he could launch an attack. Where did she live? What were her vulnerabilities? Did she travel alone? Leave her house or her car unlocked?

"There's no way to connect to the internet here, Imran." He waved at the television in the corner of the room. "At least you know who killed your team in America. This is great news, no?"

Bukayev paced around the dingy basement apartment as he ran a hand across the spikes of hair growing atop his head. The assets he had in the US weren't part of a unified cell, but that could be remedied with funding and logistical help. Unfortunately, the only place he could get that was from his al-Qaeda benefactors. "Of course it's good news, but I need the internet. Today. There must be another safe house?"

"But we just got here, Imran. And you said you'd help me plan my next series of attacks." Rasul narrowed his pale blue eyes at his former mentor. "We had a deal. I protect you and you help me."

"And I will. I'll be back. My word is good and you know it." In truth, Bukayev had no intention of returning to Rasul's rundown hideaways unless absolutely necessary. "I have to get a message to Shamil as quickly as possible."

Rasul frowned. "I can't guarantee your safety if you're not with me."

"I understand." Realistically, he would be safer away from Rasul, the most wanted man in Dagestan. He glanced at the television as the news anchor repeated the same story they'd heard a half dozen times already. A photo of the woman sitting on a jetty, the sea behind her, filled half the screen. Bukayev approached the television, flipped open his phone and snapped a picture of her.

He squinted at the phone screen. It wasn't the clearest photo, but it would suffice for now.

"Maybe you could kidnap her and bring her to me." Rasul's tongue flicked across his lips.

"You'd like that, wouldn't you?" Bukayev smiled to hide his disgust. Yes, the woman was attractive, but that was entirely beside the point.

"If you're so desperate for the internet, perhaps I should take you back to the mosque?"

"No. There are too many people coming and going there." And he didn't want to return to his basement prison, waiting hours on end for the privilege of coming upstairs to scan the internet on a borrowed computer. "Where's Daud? Perhaps he knows somewhere I can go."

Rasul tugged at his beard. A telltale sign of uncertainty.

"Daud can act as the go-between for us," Bukayev continued. "He can deliver messages from me to you, which will keep our electronic footprint untraceable."

"Very well," Rasul said. "I'll call him."

Two hours later, Bukayev met Daud outside of the basement apartment. They ducked into his car before speaking.

"Have you seen the news?" Bukayev asked.

"What news?"

"About the American woman."

Daud reached for the radio. "I haven't had the chance to listen to the news."

"They identified the woman who killed Zara Barayeva and the others at the American school."

Daud's eyes widened.

"Her name is Maggie Jenkins."

"Who is she?"

Bukayev flipped open his phone and showed the photo to the younger man.

Daud's fingers slipped from the radio power button. Something between a gasp and a cough escaped from his mouth.

"Are you okay, Daud?"

He covered his mouth with one hand and coughed. "I'm fine. Really. Just a scratchy throat."

Bukayev studied him for a moment before continuing. "Now that I have a specific target, I need to talk to Shamil Basayev."

"But isn't he in Chechnya?" Daud's voice cracked on the final syllable.

"Yes, but I'm not going to Chechnya, Daud. I need to go somewhere where I can think. And plan. And access the internet so I can contact him."

Daud started the engine and pulled away from the curb. "There are a few people I can ask."

"Where are you staying?"

Daud paled. "With my cousin."

He studied the young man's profile, watching the way the corner of his eye twitched. "Why aren't you back in Chechnya?"

"Like you, I'm worried that the Russians may be looking for me. I don't know if they know about my role in the transactions that financed the attacks."

"Makes sense." Bukayev looked out the window as they began to leave the heart of the city. "If the Russians haven't found you at your cousin's house, it sounds like the perfect spot for me." He watched as Daud caught his breath. "Is there something wrong?"

"No, of course not. It's just that my cousin's house is very small. The neighbors are nosy. Probably not a good place to hide."

"Let me be the judge of that."

Daud blinked rapidly, then spoke in a tone that sounded almost triumphant. "And there's no internet."

"Then find me a café or somewhere I can go online for a while. After that, I'll go to your cousin's for the night."

The younger man nodded, his eyes fixed on the road. "Maybe it would be better if I took you to another safe house. One with internet."

Bukayev studied Daud. "Tell me, why do I make you so nervous?

Daud glanced at him. "You don't. I mean, I have so much respect for you, Imran. It's an honor to work with you in person. I don't want to do the wrong thing," he rambled. "Or put you in danger. Or anyone else. And I—"

He placed a hand on Daud's right arm. "It's all right. Everyone thinks I'm in Chechnya or perhaps even Afghanistan. And I promise you, your help now will not be forgotten."

Daud smiled, but it seemed forced. "No reward needed. The honor alone is enough."

Daud's reward would be to keep his life. He might be good with financial transactions, but he clearly lacked the calm needed for operations. If he slipped up even once, Bukayev would end him.

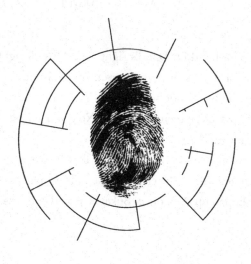

CHAPTER THIRTEEN

The Outskirts of Makhachkala, Dagestan, Russia

As soon as the young Chechen dropped him at the internet café, Bukayev hailed a taxi. Daud had seemed skittish at the prospect of bringing him to his cousin's. Was it simply a protective instinct, or was more going on? Either way, he intended to find out. At Bukayev's direction, the taxi driver followed Daud's car at a good distance. Ten miles west of Makhachkala, the younger man's silver car turned onto a dusty road dotted with a few small houses. Bukayev imagined them as once belonging to relatively prosperous communist party members. Now, the neighborhood looked like a place where poor peasants went to live out the remainder of their miserable existences.

He paid the driver and walked up to a dilapidated farmhouse on the left. He leaned in, his ear against the front door. When he heard nothing inside, he tried the doorknob. It gave way, leading him into a small living room anchored by a threadbare sofa and a wooden rocking chair. A dark-haired beauty wearing blue jeans, a jade green blouse, and a matching headscarf yelped in surprise.

"Daud!" she shouted.

From a room to Bukayev's left, Daud emerged. "What's wrong—" His mouth dropped open. "Imran."

Bukayev's gaze flowed from the woman's high cheekbones to the curves of her chest and hips. "You must be—"

"Karina," Daud said, his voice not quite steady. "This is my cousin Karina. Karina, this is Imran."

Karina stared at him, her eyes wide.

Bukayev felt a sudden yearning. There had been a few village girls here and there since he'd left London. But while they sufficed for his purposes, none of them had been beauties. Beauty had been absent from his life since the day that Zara died. Karina had the most desirable of qualities—she had absolutely no idea how gorgeous she was.

Daud interrupted his trance. "How did you . . . I thought you would be at the internet café for a while."

Bukayev shrugged. "You can take me back to the café in a bit. After I get settled here."

Daud splayed his hands in front of him. "It's a small house. No place to stay."

Bukayev peered into the room on the left. It was nothing more than an oversized closet containing a cot, a wobbly nightstand, and a wire rack for hanging clothes. He dropped his rucksack on the bed and meandered from the living room into the kitchen, at the rear of the house, where he found Daud and Karina whispering in sharp tones. They stepped aside as he rifled through the cupboards hanging on the wall.

"Ah, I knew I could count on you, my dear," he said to Karina as he extracted a bottle of vodka from where it was stashed behind a large piece of crockery. He snatched a small glass from the drying rack next to the sink and poured himself a generous shot. The vodka burned like hell going down, but filled him with that old familiar warmth he'd missed so much since leaving London. Vodka wasn't his drink of choice. Unless it was Ketel One—top shelf, but most importantly, not Russian. But given that he hadn't had a drink in more than six months, and that this was his only choice, it would more than suffice.

"Imran, I'm going to find you a place with internet."

"There's no need. I can stay here for the night." Bukayev's gaze wandered up the length of Karina's lithe body as he poured another shot.

Bukayev watched something pass between their eyes. It wasn't desire or a secret. It looked more like fear. He grinned. It had been a long time since someone feared him.

Karina averted her gaze and set about wiping down already dried dishes in the rack next to the sink.

"Of course, you're welcome to stay here tonight. In the meantime, I'll work on a better arrangement for tomorrow." Daud patted his pants pockets. "I left my phone in the car. I'll go make a few calls, see what I can arrange."

Bukayev winked at Karina. "I'll keep your cousin company."

Daud started to speak, then stopped himself.

"I must finish weeding the vegetable garden," Karina said a little too brightly. "Please make yourself comfortable. I won't be gone long." She offered a slight bow and slipped out the back door, which stood between an old white refrigerator and a mustard yellow stove.

Daud fixed his eyes on the back door.

"I thought you were going to get your phone," Bukayev said.

Daud nodded vigorously and headed for the front door.

Bukayev poured a third shot and considered the situation. He needed to get online to check his messages, but maybe a few hours off would do him good. A few hours of delight with Karina and some drink. His body pulsed with excitement for the first time since he'd left London. He'd have to send Daud on an errand so he could get to know Karina better.

The third shot went down even easier than the first two. He closed his eyes and felt his entire body relax. Time to dispatch Daud. Hurrying to the front window, he looked out. *Where'd he go?* Back in the kitchen, he pushed aside a faded yellow floral curtain covering a small window over the sink. Out in the garden, Daud and Karina were engaged in what looked like a heated exchange. He let himself out the front door as quietly as possible, crept around the side of the house, and paused when he arrived at the back corner.

Daud's tone was urgent. "I can't get a signal, but I must tell him. Warn them."

Bukayev frowned. *Warn who? About what?*

"Please don't leave me alone with him."

"I have to make the call, Karina. Maybe you can cook him dinner. Distract him that way. I won't be gone long."

Distract him? Daud was up to something, and one way or another Bukayev would find out what it was.

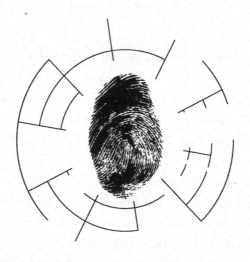

CHAPTER FOURTEEN

Bukayev slipped back inside through the front door and made a beeline for the kitchen. He rummaged around in the drawers until he found the perfect knife. In the bedroom, he took another swig of vodka, tucked the bottle inside his rucksack, and walked outside to wait for Daud.

Two minutes later, the young Chechen hurried around the side of the house, stopping short in his tracks at the sight of Bukayev leaning against his car.

"That looked like an intense conversation."

Daud flushed. "I was just telling Karina what to do if the police showed up here asking about you."

Bukayev pushed himself away from the car and approached Daud, so close he could smell the sweat coming off him. *Ah, the scent of fear.* "Why haven't you made your phone calls yet?"

"There's no signal. I'll have to drive closer to the city to get one."

"I'll save you the trouble. Hand me your car keys and I'll take care of it."

Daud's fingers wrapped reflexively around the key ring in his right hand. "There's no need. I'll be back before you know it."

Bukayev extended his arm, palm up. "The keys, Daud."

Daud made a move to get past Bukayev, but he wasn't quick enough. With his left hand, Bukayev grabbed his arm and with his right hand, he snatched the knife from where he'd laid it on the car's hood. "I will hurt you, Daud. I don't want to, but I'll do what's necessary." He ran the tip of the knife under the trembling man's jawline. "The keys."

The keys landed in Bukayev's hand with a clack. He released his grip on Daud. "Don't do anything stupid while I'm gone. Remember, I know where Karina lives. And you and I both know what I want to do to her."

With that, he picked up his rucksack and sauntered around the front of the car to the driver's side. Without a glance backward, he slid into the seat and started the engine. "What a shit box," he muttered. The last car he'd driven was in London. His beloved Audi convertible.

He hadn't been in Makhachkala long enough to know his way around. At first, he found himself heading away from the city center on roads that grew narrower by the minute until they eventually became dirt paths barely wide enough for Daud's car. Eventually, he turned around and headed back toward Karina's house, continuing past it for fifteen minutes until he saw signs for the Grand Mosque. He navigated down a side street and parked next to a restaurant situated on the ground floor of a building newly refurbished with a cladding of beige shell rock. The sign outside the restaurant identified it as an establishment for fine Georgian dining. His mouth watered at the thought of *khinkali*, which were simply the best dumplings he'd ever tasted. But first, he had phone calls to make.

He dialed the number he was supposed to use to get a message to Shamil Basayev.

"It's Bobby," he said, using his code name, a nod to London's police force, which he'd managed to evade several times during his exfiltration from England. "We must discuss our business plan sooner rather than later. Today, in fact."

He stuffed the phone in his pocket and turned to find the white cotton *taqiyah* he'd seen in the backseat earlier. Shoving aside a blanket, empty water bottles, and several food wrappers, he snatched up the cap and placed it on his head. It wasn't much of a disguise, but it was better than nothing.

Inside the restaurant, he settled into a corner table and had himself a feast of *khinkali* and Georgian cheese bread. On his second glass of *Saperavi*, his phone buzzed. He took a final swig of the red wine and answered. It was Shamil Basayev's contact.

Having a detailed conversation in code was nearly impossible because he had only a few code words with which to work. It was a risk to speak openly, but he had little choice. "My contact has no internet at his current location. I can't come to you, so you need to find me a place where I can work on the project." He listened, memorized the address, and hung up. After paying the bill, Bukayev emerged onto the street and spotted an intoxicated man talking to himself as he swayed along the side of the road.

He approached. The man didn't appear to be Russian, but most people in the republic's thirty-odd ethnic groups spoke at least some Russian. "Pardon me, sir. Could you tell me where Ulitsa Mirzayeva is located?"

The man laughed, his foul breath turning Bukayev's full stomach. He pulled a five-ruble note from his pocket and waved it in front of the drunk. The man swiped at the money but missed.

"Ulitsa Mirzayeva," Bukayev repeated.

The man offered directions that seemed straightforward enough, although Bukayev wondered if the man even knew what day of the week it was. On the positive side, based on his slurred speech and unstable gate, the drunk wouldn't be able to describe Bukayev or remember giving directions if anyone asked. Bukayev handed over the money and ducked back into Daud's car.

Ten minutes later, he turned onto Ulitsa Mirzayeva and parked in front of a five-story building with an off-white concrete façade. The buildings on the street, carbon copies of one another, had seen better days, but not for at least three or four decades. A stray dog trotted up the street past the car, sniffing at assorted bits of rubbish strewn along the pavement. Ahead, two young boys ran, shooting their finger guns at each other. Bukayev watched as one of them collapsed dramatically onto a sparse patch of grass while his friend cheered in victory. Bukayev thanked Allah for not burdening him with children. Such odd and annoying creatures. He sent a text to the designated number and waited. Not a minute later, a dark-haired teenage boy poked his head out of the building's main doorway and waved in Bukayev's direction.

He tossed the skull cap into the backseat, grabbed the rucksack, and entered the building behind the boy. If this location didn't work, he'd have no choice but to slip back into Chechnya and go straight to Shamil Basayev.

Upstairs in the apartment, the boy showed Bukayev into a small sitting room with a laptop set on a coffee table in front of a couch with gawdy floral upholstery. A phone line trailed from the wall to a side portal on the computer.

The boy stood silent, watching Bukayev as he sat. The computer screen lit up after a minute. Bukayev clicked on the service-provider icon, unleashing the familiar squealing squawk as the laptop connected to the internet. He looked up at the boy. "You may go."

The kid hesitated as if expecting something. *Money?* Bukayev waved him away. *Young people today have no principles*, he thought. It's all about money. "Pathetic," he muttered.

Navigating to the browser, he logged into one of his many email accounts. This one he shared with Shamil's assistant. The intricacies of electronic eavesdropping weren't something Bukayev understood, but it seemed like a good idea to avoid communicating directly with Shamil unless absolutely necessary, like when he'd been hiding out at the mosque.

I trust that he's seen the news about the target. I'm going to move against her soon, but need help with funding.

Next, he opened the email account he shared with Omar, his contact in London. There was one draft message waiting for him.

I'm still trying to find her address.

Bukayev groaned. How could he plan the hit on Maggie Jenkins if he didn't even know where she lived? Maybe Omar was too stupid to figure it out. *Maggie Jenkins*, he typed into the search bar. A *Moscow Times* article was the first hit.

According to a Washington Post *story due to be published tomorrow, Ms. Jenkins is a CIA employee. An FBI report released earlier in the week identified the US government official inside the elementary school near Washington, DC, as a federal law enforcement agent, not a CIA officer. Ms. Jenkins briefly made headlines in 2003 in connection with the shooting death of a US congressman from New York.*

Bukayev scratched at the stubble on his cheek. Who, exactly, was this woman? Did she have a child who attended that school? Or was she some highly trained CIA operative who might pose a threat to him? He returned to the search results. A BBC article contained a photo of a man and a woman inside a silver Audi. The caption read, *Maggie Jenkins and an unidentified man near her home in Virginia.*

Bukayev brought the laptop closer to his face. The man in the photo was looking directly at the camera. It couldn't be, could it? "What the hell is going on?" He placed the computer back on the table and reached for the rucksack. Without looking inside, he closed his hand around the vodka bottle. He took a large gulp. It burned all the way down his throat. He studied the photo again. If only Zara were here to confirm it. Was this really the man who'd broken into his London row home?

He felt dizzy, suddenly exhausted by the day's events, the vodka and wine, and the late hour. He added to Omar's draft email.

Keep on trying. I need her address NOW.

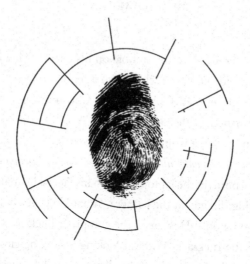

CHAPTER FIFTEEN

Makhachkala, Dagestan Republic, Russia
Friday, June 17, 2005

Bukayev slept fitfully on the sofa, having forgone the lumpy bed in the tiny bedroom off the kitchen. At one point, around two thirty in the morning, he woke covered in sweat, his head pounding. He'd been dreaming of the man in the photo, the one who looked so much like the man he'd captured skulking about his London home in the middle of the night last September. Inexplicably, the unidentified man, who'd he'd beaten unconscious, had managed to free himself from the ropes binding his hands and feet together and escape through the back courtyard. Had Zara snuck out of his bed that night and freed him? He sat up and rubbed at his temples. No, that couldn't be. The man in the newspaper had been photographed days ago with the woman who'd killed Zara, which meant that he probably was CIA too. There was no way in hell that Zara would've helped a CIA officer escape his house.

He groaned and lay back down, bracing himself for the hangover that was infiltrating his head. Stumbling into the bathroom, he relieved himself, then checked the medicine cabinet, which was tucked behind a small mirror with rusted metal trim. An unlabeled bottle of pills and a used toothbrush were the only items inside. He sniffed the pills before putting them back in place.

He tried to fall back to sleep, but his mind wouldn't stop racing. Shamil seemed to be dragging his feet. Issuing a revised fatwa naming Maggie Jenkins as their target would be simple. All that required was a brief, fiery speech. The real question was whether Shamil would put his money where his mouth was and fund the attack. Bukayev cracked his knuckles one at a time. He needed a backup plan. *Omar?* The Jordanian expat didn't have money, but he lived in London and had access to people who did.

It was just past midnight in England. He flipped open his phone. Calling Omar was risky. If his phone was tapped, British intelligence would jump into overdrive to trace every overseas call he received. Then what if they tipped off Moscow? Bukayev pictured heavily armed Russian police crashing through the apartment door.

After considering all his options, he knew he had to take a chance on Omar. He scrolled though his contacts, stopping at *O* and hit send.

"Hello?" a gruff voice said.

"My friend. Do you recall the nightclub China White?" He heard a sharp intake of breath on the other end. Several years back, he'd treated Omar to a night of western decadence at a trendy club. The next day, the portly Jordanian thoroughly condemned the debauchery in which he partook, but he hadn't complained at the club when a scantily clad blonde led him off to a private room. "Are you there?"

"Yes. I'm just shocked to hear your voice."

"I don't want to stay on the phone too long."

"I understand," Omar replied.

"I need your help placing an order for a new carpet. Remember the one I purchased for my house?"

"Not specifically."

"Go to the shop in the morning and ask the owner if he remembers the red carpet."

"Okay." Omar sounded uncertain.

"And check your email." Bukayev hung up and rubbed at his tense, aching neck. The upscale oriental and Persian rug restoration shop in London was one of the places he'd used to communicate with his al-Qaeda benefactors in Riyadh. The owner, a man named Khalil, sent messages on his behalf to terrorist financiers in Saudi Arabia. Perhaps Khalil would be able to secure him the funding he needed to pull off the assassination of Maggie Jenkins. Without it, he wouldn't be able to pay his asset to carry out the hit. And he wanted to strike soon, while the world's attention was on her.

Bukayev paced the worn, brown carpeting inside the claustrophobic apartment, stopping occasionally to glance out the window to the street below. Cars rolled by here and there, all on their way toward the main road. Other than an old woman walking her dog, he saw no other pedestrians. Daud's car remained parked against the curb. He studied the apartment building across the street. There was no obvious movement or activity behind any of the windows within his line of sight.

Once it was ten o'clock in the morning London time, his pulse picked up. Omar was supposed to call from a burner phone at 10:05.

Finally, one minute late, his phone rang.

"Good morning, my friend."

"It's a fine morning here. In fact, I decided to stop into that carpet shop you like."

Bukayev felt the tightness in his chest ease. Omar was following the script he'd left for him in the draft email folder. "Perhaps I should speak with the shop owner myself."

"Of course. Here he is," Omar said.

"Good morning." The accent was British, familiar.

"Khalil, how lovely to speak with you. You remember that red carpet I had my eye on?"

"Yes, of course. I wasn't sure if you had changed your mind."

Yes, I'm fine, Khalil. Still alive. "I wouldn't change my mind about such an important purchase."

"Very well, then, how would you like to proceed?"

"I'm thinking of buying a home in Jeddah. Do you ship there?" Jeddah was the base of operations for his primary benefactor. Bukayev knew him only as the "sheikh." Unfortunately, he didn't know how to contact him directly. That was Khalil's job.

"Yes." The clicking of a keyboard traveled over the line.

"Wonderful. Before I go to Jeddah, I must stop in Washington to attend to a very important business matter."

More typing and then a protracted pause. "I'm afraid there's a problem with our inventory. I'll call you back."

"What kind of problem?" Bukayev struggled to keep desperation out of his voice. The line went dead. "Khalil?"

He slapped the phone shut and let out a roar of frustration. While they were on the phone, Khalil must've messaged the benefactor. Surely the sheikh knew about the fatwa against Maggie Jenkins and understood the reference to Washington. He ought to jump at the chance to help Bukayev kill the American woman. After all, she'd killed their foot soldiers. Humiliated them, in fact. So why the abrupt end to the call? Bukayev had proven his ability to carry out a major attack. Beslan had been a huge success. That should count for something. Maybe if the sheikh understood that killing Maggie Jenkins was just the first of many such attacks, he'd be willing to help. If only the sheikh knew what was to come, the funding would start to flow.

He called Omar back. "What the hell happened with Khalil?"

"Wait a minute." Omar grunted over the phone. A bell jangled in the background. "Okay, I just left the shop."

"What did Khalil say?"

"He said he'll let me know if the carpet comes back in stock."

If? "Bloody hell!"

"This isn't about a carpet, is it?"

Bukayev squeezed the phone. The more people who knew about his plans, the more danger he'd be in. But between Shamil Basayev's tortoise-like pace in replying to his requests for funding and Khalil's abrupt hang-up, perhaps he had no choice. He'd have to bring Omar into the fold.

"Buy another phone. Send me the number through our usual channel. I'll call you back."

"Now?"

"Yes, now."

"It's just that I've got to get back to the mosque for *zuhur*."

Bukayev glanced at his Rolex and did the math. "That's not for three hours."

"Right. Of course. I'll go buy a phone at the corner shop."

Bukayev hung up without another word. It should take Omar a half hour to buy a phone, return home, and send his message. That gave him enough time to run to the grocer's market up the street. His stomach grumbled as he put the laptop and the rest of his belongings in the rucksack. After so many months on the run, he'd learned to plan for the unexpected. If someone recognized him, he'd have to go to ground. It was best to take his things with him everywhere he went.

Twenty minutes later, he was back at the apartment with a bag of food—potato chips, apricots, grapes, and a loaf of fresh baked bread. He'd been pleased to find a tea service at the market and had prepared a steaming hot cup for himself. It wasn't quite English breakfast tea, but it would suffice. He peered out the window onto the street below and breathed a sigh of relief. A man he'd noticed inside the store had trailed behind him the entire way back to the apartment. But now, he was nowhere in sight.

Bukayev retrieved the laptop from the rucksack, powered it on, and tore open the bag of chips.

Omar had left his new cell number in the draft email folder as instructed. Bukayev placed the call from one of his burner phones.

"Where are you, Omar?"

"Home."

"Go outside and start walking."

"Why?"

"Just do it." For all the help he'd provided over the years, Omar still had no sense of operational security. If British authorities knew of their connection, they may have bugged Omar's house.

"Okay, I'm outside now."

"Good. Now listen. I have operatives in the United States. I need you to contact the one in Washington, DC." He'd prefer to do this himself, but what if the CIA or the FBI knew this operative was tied to him? It was better to burn Omar than to put himself on the Americans' radar.

"Is this about the fatwa?"

"Yes, Omar."

There was silence on the other end before he replied. "What do I say?"

Bukayev popped a grape into his mouth. "It's simple. He needs to take out the woman."

"Will he need money?"

"Yes, but that won't be a problem." It would, actually, but he didn't want Omar to know that yet. The British had frozen his bank accounts and what remained in his Swiss account was rapidly dwindling. That's precisely why he needed Shamil or the sheikh to finance the operation. "Tell him ten thousand dollars for a clean hit. I'll throw in an extra thousand if he finds the target's address before you do."

"A thousand?"

"Yes. Listen, I've got to run. Be careful. You never know who's listening."

Bukayev sipped on his tea, which was now room temperature, and checked the email account he shared with Shamil's assistant. Finally, a reply.

We don't have an answer from the bank. Check back next week.

"Next week?" he sputtered. The message was clear. The "bank," Shamil's word for his own al-Qaeda money man, wasn't interested in funding the fatwa. Maybe Shamil hadn't even bothered to request the money, or worse, maybe he'd received funding but kept it for himself.

Just wait, he thought. When images of Maggie Jenkins's bloodied, lifeless corpse appeared on TVs around the world, everyone who'd doubted him would come crawling back. Bukayev liked to think himself a magnanimous man, but he would remember everyone who'd refused to help him.

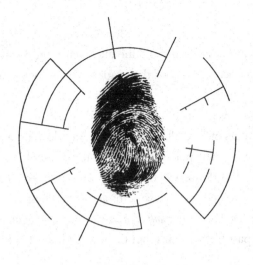

CHAPTER SIXTEEN

Vienna, Virginia

R oger took his driver's license back from the police officer and slid it into his wallet as he turned onto Maggie's street. When he'd driven by the previous evening, several media vans had been parked near the police barricade. He'd called to see if she wanted company, but she'd demurred. Clearly, she was furious that they'd kept her in the dark about Bukayev being in Dagestan. If she could just learn to trust him—and Warner for that matter—there'd be a lot less tension between them.

He pulled into her driveway and braced himself for an icy welcome. All his plans for a romantic getaway to the beach in a few weeks had been swamped by unexpected developments. Warner's nomination as CIA director and the intelligence on Bukayev's where-abouts hadn't been on any of their radars. Roger jogged up the brick staircase.

The door swung open before he could knock.

"Mr. Patterson?" A tall, burly African American man in tan cargo pants and a navy blue polo shirt stood on the threshold.

"In the flesh. Please, call me Roger." He extended a hand.

The man folded his massive arms across his chest.

This guy could snap me in half if he wanted to. "Is Maggie ready?" He tried to see past his blue shirt, but the man's broad shoulders blocked the view.

"She's grabbing her bag. I'll be following behind you. I have Maggie's cell number. If I call it, you pull over. Instantly."

Roger popped an eyebrow. "Are we driving to the beach or through downtown Baghdad?" He'd planned to stop for lunch at one of his favorite seafood restaurants, but not if Mr. Beefy Security Guy was going to join them. "If we lose you in traffic, you can just meet us in Hatteras."

"Or Maggie can ride with me."

The hell she will. "No, I'm good, uh, sorry, didn't catch your name?"

"Rich."

"Nice to meet you, Rich. One question—am I allowed to speed?" He smirked. "I'm kind of a rebel that way."

Rich stared at him, clearly not amused.

He tried again. "You're a big guy. You play football in high school? Maybe a little college ball?"

Again, Rich didn't reply.

"Played a bit myself." Roger rotated his right shoulder. "Until the old arm gave out, right about freshman year. Of high school. Still aches sometimes, usually when it's going to rain. On the bright side, I'm pretty much a human barometer."

Another steely stare.

Roger gave up trying to engage the man. Mercifully and at last, Maggie's voice floated up from behind her security guard.

"I'm ready, Rich. Is he here yet?"

Roger stood on his tiptoes and waved over the man's shoulder. "Over here. Just hanging out, chatting with Rich."

Rich stepped aside, revealing Maggie in black gym shorts, a pink V-neck T-shirt, and white flip-flops. While he took in the sight of her, Rich snatched Maggie's small suitcase.

"Thanks, Rich," Maggie said, her voice all sunshine and light. "You're late," she said to Roger, her tone now flat.

Actually, he was on time. She was the one holding them up, but he knew better than to say that. "I grabbed coffee and bagels on the way over." He flicked his head toward Rich. "I would've grabbed breakfast for three, but I didn't realize we'd be so . . . chummy."

"We can stop and get you something," Maggie offered to Rich.

He held up a hand. "I'm all set. Thanks anyway."

Roger had had just about enough of this fellow and it had only been five minutes. He descended the stairs and opened the silver Audi's passenger door. "Your carriage awaits, m'lady."

Maggie followed and slid into the seat without a word. Rich heaved himself up into a massive black SUV with tinted windows. The vehicle wouldn't draw attention in DC where such cars were used to shuttle VIPs from one federal building to another, but it would stick out on the island.

"A little obvious, isn't it?"

"He's nice, Roger."

"I mean the tank he's driving."

Maggie shrugged. "Had I known three days ago that Bukayev was in Dagestan, maybe I could've found him by now. Then there'd be no need for any of this." She waved her hand around in front of her face.

Here we go. Roger swallowed a comeback, instead, picking up his disposable coffee cup and taking a cautious sip of the still piping hot liquid. "You talk to Warner?" He offered a curt nod to the police officers at the end of the street.

"An hour ago. He left at five a.m. with his security detail."

"Since when does he travel with security inside the US?"

"Since he was nominated to be CIA director." Maggie stared out the window. "What is she doing here?"

Roger glanced in the rearview mirror. The only thing he saw was Rich's car. "What are you talking about?"

She craned her neck to look behind the car. "A reporter who tried to talk to me at the hearing the other day."

"Damned media," Roger muttered.

"I swear I've seen her somewhere before."

"Seen who?" Roger asked as he concentrated more on merging into early rush-hour traffic than on what Maggie said.

"Never mind."

"Maggie?"

"Mmm?" she replied as she sipped her coffee.

"Are we okay?"

She looked sidelong at him. "I guess." Suppressing a yawn, she added. "I'm going to close my eyes for a bit. Didn't sleep well last night."

Pea Island National Wildlife Refuge
Hatteras Island, NC

"Roger, you've got to stop the car!"

"What's the matter?" He edged the Audi to the side of Highway 12. "Don't tell me you get car sick."

Maggie jumped from the car and ran across the two-lane road to a massive sand dune that shimmered in the midday sun. She scrambled up the dune, sliding back a foot for every two feet she ascended.

"What are you doing?" Roger called through the driver's-side window. Behind him, the SUV pulled to a stop.

She paused her climb and hollered back. "The ocean! You said it's another hour to the house. I can't wait that long." Atop the dune, she stretched her arms wide above her head. "Roger, come on!"

By the time he got up the dune, his T-shirt was damp with sweat. "You grew up on Cape Cod. I assume you've seen the ocean before?"

She swept her hand around in front of them. "But look at this, Roger. It's like we're the only two people in the world. No houses. No people." She grabbed his forearm. "Let's go check the water."

"Check it for what? If you're looking for sharks, I can assure you there's no need to check. They're out there."

"Come on, you big chicken." She tugged him down the dune. They half slid, half ran down to the empty beach. "Race you to the water!"

Maggie beat him to the water's edge, where she kicked off her flip-flops and waded into the warm sea. The rumble of surf, fed by a continual loop of tumbling waves, filled her ears. She squatted to take a closer look at the shells careening off her feet. Gray and blue whelks; pink, white, and blue scallops shells. "Look at this one, Roger." She held up an orange-and-white shell. "It looks like a tiny little helmet. And it's plaid. Have you ever seen anything like this?"

He knelt beside her. "It's a Scotch bonnet. That's a great find." He tucked her windblown hair behind her ear. "Just like you."

Maggie leaned in and kissed him. As irritated as she'd been with Roger over the Bukayev issue, she felt a surge of happiness. It was an unfamiliar sensation, one she hadn't felt since before Steve died. A lump formed in her throat. There was no need to feel guilty. It wasn't like she and Roger were *that* serious. "Thanks for bringing me here. It's so much better than hiding out in a hotel for a few days."

Roger stood and pulled her up with him. "I wish we were here under less stressful circumstances. I really want you to feel like this could be your home away from home."

Roger's new beach house had once belonged to his old girlfriend, Jane Manning, a woman who was married to a CIA coworker. Their affair ended abruptly on September 11, 2001, when Jane boarded Flight 93 to meet Roger in San Francisco for a secret getaway. Jane's husband, Carl, never learned about the affair and never would. He'd died last year of an apparent heart attack.

"It would be nice to sit on the beach, read, and drink wine." And not think for one second about Imran Bukayev.

"I think you'll love the house. It needs some work. As far as I know, Carl only came down here once or twice after Jane . . ." He cleared his throat. "Do you think it's weird that I bought the house?"

Maggie didn't know what to say. She brushed sand off Roger's arm instead.

"When Carl died, his estate put the house on the market . . ." He squinted up at the sun high overhead. "Jane loved it down here and I wanted to . . . preserve it, I guess you'd say. I didn't want a developer coming in and replacing it with beach condos."

"I get it. I probably would've done the same thing."

"Just so you know, a few of Jane's things are still in the house. I don't think Carl could bring himself to clean the place out. Maybe he intended to at some point, but then—anyway, I want to make this house my own. Put up some fresh paint. Get some new furniture, that kind of thing."

Maggie dug her toes deeper into the wet sand and caught sight of a shrimping boat bobbing along the water. "Does Warner know this was Carl's house?"

Roger picked up a smooth, flat stone and skipped it over the water. "No. He never knew about Jane. I'd prefer to keep it that way."

"Okay." Maggie didn't know what she felt. A mixture of sadness and envy? Maybe it was just sorrow over the loved ones they'd both lost. Whatever it was, the magic of the moment had vanished. Her pale arms were already turning pink and a trickle of sweat ran down her back. "We should get on the road." She spotted Rich at the top of the dune. "And we don't want to get on Rich's bad side."

"It's probably too late for me on that count," Roger said with a smirk.

The hot sand burned on the way back up the dune as they trekked together in silence. Rich, arms folded across his broad chest, glanced at his watch before leveling a cool stare at Roger.

"Beautiful, isn't it?" Maggie offered.

Rich grunted and led the way down the mountain of sand.

Back in the car, Roger spoke, eyes on the road. "Where's Rich staying?"

"The security detail wants us all in one place, so they don't have to divide and conquer."

He frowned. "So it won't be just the two of us at my house?"

"Nope. You, Warner, and I will be housemates. The security team grabbed a room at a nearby motel. They'll cover us in rotating eight-hour shifts." She saw Roger's face fall. "Security will stay outside the house. Maybe we can get Warner drunk, put him to bed early, and, you know, hang out."

Roger's face brightened. He reached over and squeezed her hand. "I love it when you talk devious to me."

Maggie laughed and her eyes widened as they entered Rodanthe, the first village on the island. To the left was the ocean, its waves breaking just a few dozen feet away. To the right, not far off, was the Pamlico Sound. "How often does this road wash out?"

"Pretty much every hurricane and tropical storm. Locals don't seem to worry about the road going out, even when they're cut off from the mainland for months at time."

"I wouldn't mind being stranded on an island."

"With me?" Roger winked, his eyes a sparkling blue.

Maggie relaxed into the leather seat. "Maybe."

Roger applied the brakes to let a family cross the road. The father carried two chairs and a beach ball while the mother tried to herd three young children weighed down with pails and assorted beach toys.

Would that ever be her? A wife? A mother? She glanced at Roger. *Maybe.*

CHAPTER SEVENTEEN

Hatteras Village, North Carolina

Forty-five minutes later, they pulled into a driveway hidden behind the local Methodist church. Before them stood a little white cottage sitting on five-foot-tall stilts. Rich pulled in behind Roger's car, the rumble of his SUV reminding Maggie of her new reality. Not twenty feet away, to the left of the house, was a creek. A smattering of elevated houses stood on the opposite bank. "Where's that go?" she asked, pointing to the calm, dark water.

"It leads out into the Pamlico Sound. There are kayaks stored under the house if we want to go explore." Roger grabbed Maggie's suitcase and hefted it up the steep front steps. A heavy, somewhat weather-beaten front door creaked open into a living room anchored by a pale green couch and love seat. Seascape paintings hung on two walls. In the rear left corner, a spiral staircase led to an upper level.

"The bunk room's up there." Roger winked. "Would be a good place for kids to sleep."

Maggie avoided eye contact with him. Had he spent time here with Jane on one of their secret getaways? A part of her hoped she'd never find out. She peered into the kitchen. It was perfectly appointed for a beach cottage, with wooden cabinets painted a nautical blue. "It's lovely, Roger. Adorable, homey."

"There are two bedrooms and a bathroom over there on the right side of the house. And through that door," he gestured past the spiral staircase, "is the master bedroom."

She made a show of checking her watch, suddenly uncomfortable. What if this weekend together proved them incompatible? What if they were too flawed, too scarred, too alike to ever have a normal life together? "I wonder where Warner is."

A sudden thudding up the front steps was followed by a knock on the door. "Speak of the devil," Roger said.

Maggie felt the tension release from her shoulders. She'd only been here a few minutes but already felt like an intruder, as if she were a stranger imposing on Roger and Jane. She slipped in front of Roger to greet Warner. "Mr. Director, welcome to Hatteras Village."

"Haven't been down this way in a while. Far too long, actually." He flashed a bright smile and pulled off his aviator sunglasses before leaning in to give Maggie a hug. "It's gorgeous, isn't it? Maybe we should open a satellite office in the village."

Even though this wasn't exactly a carefree beach weekend, Warner looked relaxed. *Good*, she thought. Because the director's job would be anything but relaxing.

"Don't just stand there, Maggie. Let the man in. How about a beer, Warner?"

"Why the hell not?" he replied.

"Maggie, a drink?"

"Maybe in a bit. After I put some of my things away." She rolled her suitcase across the carpeted floor and between the two couches. Gazing up the spiral staircase, she caught sight of broad wood paneling that climbed the walls and extended across the ceiling. Just beyond the stairs was the master bedroom. She closed the door behind her and took in the room. On the dresser to her immediate left stood a lavender-scented candle. Over to her right, the closet stood ajar. Maggie didn't want to look, but she couldn't stop herself. She exhaled in relief when she saw that it was empty. At one time, it must've been filled with Jane's brightly colored sundresses, perfect for the beach; strappy sandals; and maybe a pair of tennis shoes. Maggie peered down the length of the closet, catching sight of a shoebox tucked in the far corner. She knelt on the floor and opened the box. Inside were several framed photos of Carl Manning and, Maggie presumed, his late wife, Jane. Dark hair fell to the woman's shoulders, framing a face with soft features and high cheekbones. She was beautiful. Maggie stared another moment. Had Carl packed up the photos after Jane died on 9/11? Or had Roger done so after Carl died last fall?

Maggie replaced the box, closed the closet door, and dashed over to the dresser. The drawers were empty, except for a stray earring she found in the back of the second drawer from the bottom. A sterling silver starfish dangled from the earring hook. Had Jane held on to this earring in case she found its missing mate? Or had someone—Carl or Roger—overlooked it when they cleaned out her belongings?

She peered into the mirror hanging on the back of the door and dangled the earring in front of her earlobe. Did Roger buy these for her? She pictured them at an island gift shop, laughing, touching. *Stop it.* She tossed the starfish back into the drawer and sank onto the bed. Jane's bed. A bed that Carl had shared with his wife and Roger may have shared with her as well. "I don't think I can do this," she whispered. Not with everything going on. The fatwa. The on-again off-again tension with Roger. All the baggage they both carried.

"Maggie!" Roger bellowed from the living room. "We're going to the dock to find Warner's friend. You joining us?"

She took another look around the bedroom, Jane's bedroom, and decided she'd rather be anywhere but there. "Yep, I'll be right out." She pushed aside the curtain and caught sight of Rich talking with two other well-built men out in front of the house. They must be part of Warner's security detail. She sighed, ran her fingers through her hair, and dotted on some lip gloss. "Good enough," she muttered at herself in the mirror.

She found Roger and Warner sitting in the screened-in porch at the back of the house, finishing their beers. A breeze kicked up off the creek. Several seagulls made an impressive landing on the lapping water.

"Nice spot, isn't it, Maggie?" Warner stood from a wicker chair.

She eyed his outfit. Blue shorts and a yellow polo shirt. "Might want to work on that tan, Warner."

"You should talk," he shot back, teasing.

"I'll be lucky if I don't get sun poisoning."

Roger slid next to her, draping an arm over her shoulder. "I'll make sure you don't. Happy to reapply sunscreen all over you every twenty minutes."

"Get a room, you two," Warner said.

Maggie blushed. Obviously, Warner knew about their nascent relationship. But it wasn't clear if he approved. Her late fiancé, Steve, had been Warner's protégé, a rising star among CIA operations officers. And even though she and Roger had been dating unofficially since after the holidays, she had a feeling Warner was still trying to adjust to them being a couple. Of course, Maggie didn't need his approval, but he was the closest thing to a father figure she had, and if she were being honest, she wanted his blessing. If their relationship got to that point.

"Let's get going," Roger said, giving Maggie's shoulder a squeeze. "Head over to the dock to meet Warner's friend and then check out the beach. Might be some decent surfing later."

Warner slid his sunglasses from the top of his head to his face. "I hope you're prepared to meet a true CIA legend."

Roger slid his hand into Maggie's. "I thought we were all legends, Warner."

Maggie laughed. "In your own mind, Roger."

CHAPTER EIGHTEEN

Maggie and Roger followed Warner along the dock at Hatteras Harbor Marina. The security detail trailed behind, their eyes hidden by mirrored aviator sunglasses. Most of the boat slips stood empty. Tourists willing to fork over a couple of grand for a day's worth of deep-sea fishing were still out on the open ocean, hours away from shore. An enormous brown pelican waddled along the dock ahead of them before taking a brief flight to the top of a nearby wooden mooring post.

"This way." Warner gestured toward the rear of the marina's store, a large clapboard building painted baby blue. Docked in a slip tucked away behind the store was a gleaming white fifty-eight-foot fishing boat with *Sea Creature* emblazoned on the stern. Warner hopped across the gap between the edge of the pier and the boat's port side. "Permission to come aboard, sir?"

Roger exchanged a look with Maggie.

The cabin door swung inward. "Sonafabitch! If it isn't the most important man in America." A well-built man with a salt-and-pepper beard, heavy on the salt, emerged onto the boat deck. "Permission granted, sailor." A shock of white hair curled out from under a red baseball cap.

Warner embraced the man, clapping him on the back. "Nice boat, Creature."

"She's been mine for years now. Glad you could finally grace us with your presence."

Maggie detected a southern drawl in the man's voice.

"You know how it is in DC."

The man laughed. "Of course I do. Why do you think I haven't stepped foot there for a decade?"

Roger slipped his hand into Maggie's and tugged her closer to the boat.

"Come on board," the man said. "It's hot as the devil out here. Cocktails await in the cabin."

Maggie and Roger leaped onto the deck, which rocked slightly at the disturbance.

"The name is Creature," the captain said. "Right this way."

"Creature?" Maggie whispered to Roger.

The captain looked back over his shoulder. "Yes, ma'am. It's a nickname I picked up in the jungles of Nicaragua early in my career. I was young, dumb, and reckless. Whatever creature the locals put on my plate, I'd eat, no questions asked. I still can't believe I didn't die." He laughed, a low rumble rising from his chest. "The name 'Creature' stuck ever since."

He led them into an air-conditioned cabin with brown carpeting and white walls that rose to an arched ceiling with wooden beams spanning the length. Warner snagged a comfortable-looking leather captain's chair while Roger and Maggie sank onto a sectional couch positioned under two large windows. Gleaming dark-wood cabinet doors lined the rear wall, which was bisected by a steep staircase leading belowdecks.

Creature rummaged around in a minifridge in the small kitchenette adjacent to the staircase. "It's five o'clock somewhere," he chuckled, handing each of them a bottled light beer. He sat in the chair next to Warner's. "You must be Roger, and you," he added with a broad grin, "the one and only Maggie Jenkins."

She shifted, the leather beneath her bare legs emitting a squawk, as she leveled questioning eyes at Warner.

"As I mentioned yesterday," Warner said, "Creature is one of us."

"That's right. Former Agency," the boat captain said. "Or maybe not so former. As they say, you can leave the Agency, but the Agency never leaves you."

Maggie felt herself relax. "And you worked with Warner?"

"Worked with?" Warner laughed. "This man taught me everything I know. Got me out of more than one scrape back in the day." The two men shared a knowing look.

"I can honestly say I never thought you'd make it this far. CIA director? Damn. I feel like I should kiss your ring, or something."

The former colleagues erupted in laughter.

"Where were you stationed?" Roger asked.

"Here, there, and everywhere. At my prime, I was running money and guns to the Afghan rebels back when the mujahideen were the good guys fighting the evil commies." He shook his head. "Some of those rebels remained great allies, even after September eleventh. Others . . ." His voice trailed off.

Roger gulped the rest of his beer, probably, Maggie assumed, because he didn't want to talk about 9/11. That meant thinking about Jane.

Warner fetched second beers for everyone. "Part of the reason I wanted us to come all the way down here is that Creature spent time in the Caucasus after the Afghan war."

Creature studied his beer bottle.

"He knows Dagestan," Warner added. "And people in Dagestan."

Maggie leaned forward. "But you're retired. Why would you still have sources there?"

The boat captain suddenly looked tired.

Warner jumped in, changing the subject. "Roger has an asset in Dagestan."

"You already told me that, Warner," Maggie said, exasperated.

Roger glanced at Warner as if asking for permission to go on. Warner nodded.

"You know him," Roger said.

"I know him?" She frowned. "I don't know any Dagestanis." This discussion was getting more convoluted by the minute. She flicked a hand in the air. "Can someone just tell me what the hell is going on?"

"It's Daud," Roger said.

Daud? "From last year? The guy at the Central Asian Studies Institute?"

"Yup, my old asset is now my most valuable operative."

It took her a moment to remember his face. He was young. A bundle of nerves. In hindsight, she couldn't blame him for being so skittish. He'd been an unwilling pawn in a much larger game that involved funneling money through the Institute to Imran Bukayev's terrorist network. And although Daud hadn't been privy to Bukayev's and Zara's plan to attack an American school, he'd inadvertently revealed enough information that it allowed her to put together the pieces of the puzzle and thwart the attack. In any event, she hadn't given much thought to Daud since his disappearance last fall. She assumed he'd returned to Chechnya.

"Why is he in Dagestan?"

"He's afraid to go to Chechnya. He thinks the Russians know that he has ties to Bukayev."

Bukayev had financed and organized the school siege in Beslan, Russia. Hundreds of innocents had been slaughtered over the three-day siege. Memories of bloody children, of the little girl who'd died right in front of her flashed through her mind. Maggie took a sip of beer to help clear the lump forming in her throat. "Do you know Daud, Creature?"

He shook his head.

"Then what—"

Warner glanced out the port-side window. Maggie's eyes followed. Three sets of legs clad in identical khaki pants were visible on the dock. The security team.

"A couple of months ago," Warner began, "I asked Roger to have Daud meet with one of Creature's contacts in Dagestan."

"Why?" She looked at Roger, who shrugged.

"Warner never gave me a why, did you, Warner?"

Warner's face was unreadable.

Roger continued. "I did as I was asked and told Daud that this person was reliable and could provide him a place to lie low if circumstances warranted."

"That's where I come in," Creature said, his tone serious, a marked departure from his initial affability. "I needed eyes on my contact. Her mother was recently killed when a suicide bomber attacked the police station where she worked. This young lady knows the men who were behind the attack. I'm worried they'll come for her next." His blue eyes clouded over. "I had to be sure she's okay."

"Wait," Roger said, his words directed at Warner. "You had me use Daud to . . . what . . . check on someone who has nothing to do with Bukayev?"

Maggie felt the anger emanating from Roger's body. She placed a hand on his leg. "I still don't understand. Who is this contact and why do we care?"

"Her name is Karina." Creature locked eyes with Maggie. "She's my daughter."

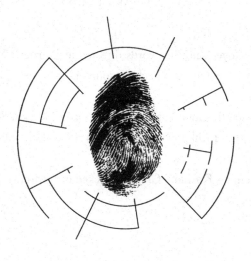

CHAPTER NINETEEN

"Your daughter?" Roger asked, turning to Warner. "You didn't tell me I was doing a personal favor for"—he waved a hand in Creature's direction—"him."

The boat captain's eyebrows drew together, forming a wiry, gray line.

"All this time, Daud could've been focused on looking for Bukayev instead of hanging out with his daughter."

"If Daud needs a place to hide, he can go to Karina's," Warner offered.

Roger was not reassured. "How do we know if Daud can trust this woman? I mean, Creature just said she knows a bunch of terrorists."

Creature leveled a steely gaze at Roger. "Her mother was killed by Islamic militants. Karina hates them with every fiber of her being."

"If she hates them so much, why is she living there?" he shot back. "Why don't you get her out?"

"Roger—" Warner snapped.

"How long has she been in Dagestan?" Maggie interrupted, hoping to settle the situation.

"Her whole life," Creature said. "And for your information, Roger, I tried to get her and her mother out years ago. Thanks to the jackasses in Langley, Vera is dead and Karina is stuck there." He sank against the back of his chair, his body slumped as if weighed down with sorrow.

The cabin filled with silence. Eventually, Creature spoke. "I ran Operation Cyclone on the ground in and around Afghanistan in the mid-1980s."

"Operation Cyclone?" she asked.

"Code name for the CIA's program to arm, train, and finance the Afghan mujahideen against the Soviet invaders. Anyway, I spent some time recruiting foot soldiers for the CIA from places like Chechnya and Dagestan. These were the guys who would run the guns and money into Afghanistan for us."

Roger leaned forward, elbows on his thighs, suddenly intrigued. "You were in the Soviet Union under diplomatic cover?"

"Nah," he scoffed. "Nonofficial cover. It's a miracle I didn't get discovered sooner than I did. Then again, the KGB and the GRU were consumed with the Afghan war and all the internal unrest under Gorbachev."

"Because of glasnost and perestroika," Maggie commented.

"That's right. Old Gorbachev thought he could reform communism." He snickered. "Anyway, the domestic situation and the war were more than enough for Soviet intelligence to handle. With a lot of

American money at my disposal, I was able to move about the Caucasus fairly easily."

"What was your cover?" Roger was now fully engrossed in the story.

"Professor of anthropology with a focus on the peoples of the Caucasus region of the Soviet Union, if you can believe it." Creature laughed. "One of the universities we partnered with from time to time agreed to put me on staff as an adjunct professor. Fortunately, I never had to teach a single class. Anyway, I met Vera in Dagestan." He stared up at the cabin ceiling. "She was Russian. A dark-haired beauty. Exquisite. One thing led to another and, well, when I returned to Dagestan after a six-month absence, I learned she was pregnant with Karina."

Silence filled the cabin again as all eyes fixed on Creature, who appeared to be lost in a memory. He cleared his throat and continued.

"When Karina was a year old, I finally got busted. Local police arrested me and brought in the KGB. They threw me in a rat-infested cell for a few days, but the Agency managed to pull some strings and get me out." He looked at Warner. "Didn't we trade one of the mujahideen leaders for me?"

"Yeah, but he wasn't all that important to the war effort. The Soviets thought he was, but that's only because we're such good bullshitters."

"You've got that right. Of course, I was grateful to be rescued, but then it all went south. After everything I did for the CIA, after literally putting my life on the line for years, the bastards in Langley refused to help me exfiltrate Vera and Karina. Langley was none too pleased when they realized I had fathered a child with a Soviet woman, especially one who was of no value as an intelligence asset. Vera had no connections to Soviet military or intelligence sources. She was just an ordinary citizen. Therefore, she was useless to them."

Maggie didn't know the Agency's rules for CIA officers in the field. Were they encouraged to sleep with assets if it would result in obtaining valuable information? Or was such behavior prohibited? She'd never asked Steve, because she hadn't wanted to know. And she hadn't asked Roger, for the same reason.

"The Soviets and then the Russians blacklisted me. The Putin government will never grant me a visa to enter Russia." He ran a hand along the side of his beard and locked eyes with Warner. "The only person who has ever lifted a finger to help is this man right here."

Warner's smile was tinged with sadness.

"He delivered letters and money to Vera during the remainder of the Soviet years. And every few years, Warner helped them travel to places where I could visit. Georgia and Armenia, mostly. I'll always be grateful for that, Warner." He sighed. "But even with letters and visits every year or two, I'm basically a stranger to my own daughter."

"Couldn't the US government help get them out of Russia after the Soviet Union collapsed?" Maggie asked.

Creature clenched his fists. "The State Department wouldn't issue them immigrant visas. I don't know how many times they rejected my applications. I can't prove it, but I'm certain that the CIA has blacklisted me too."

"Why would they do that?" Roger asked, sounding skeptical.

"Maybe because I testified to Congress about how the Agency knowingly let money and sophisticated weaponry fall into the hands of the most radical Islamists in Afghanistan. We had our allies, guys who weren't terribly radical, who just wanted to get the Soviet Union out. And then there were the crazy jihadists." He shook his head. "Our efforts to track the money and weapons was pathetic. So pathetic that they never knew what happened to the rest of the slush fund they'd given me to recruit gun runners, bribe Soviet officials, and so on."

Warner cleared his throat. "We probably don't want to know too much about that slush fund. Some of us still have to pass polygraph exams."

"Right. Well then, enough about me." Creature stood and pulled four more beer bottles from the fridge. "Aside from Karina, I still have contacts in Dagestan who might be easily incentivized by some greenbacks to report on Bukayev's whereabouts."

Roger popped off the sofa to grab the beers from Creature. "Now there's an idea. If any of your sources get any information on Bukayev, they can report it directly to Daud."

"And when this Bukayev business is all over, my Agency friends—" he pointed a finger at each of them, one by one—"will help get Karina on a flight to Jamaica."

"Jamaica?" Maggie asked.

"No visa required for Russian citizens." He patted the cabin wall with his empty hand. "I'll be docked there waiting for my daughter."

"And you'll bring her here?" Roger guessed.

"Precisely. I have friends who can provide her with a new identity." He winked at Warner. "And finally, she'll be safe."

Maggie stole a furtive look at Warner. Smuggling Creature's daughter into the US and providing her with false documentation would put his career at risk.

"If it means we get Bukayev, I'm all in," said Roger.

Creature raised his beer. "I think this is the beginning of a beautiful friendship."

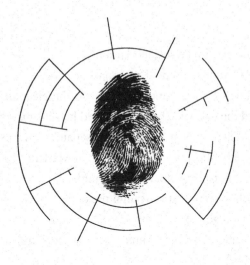

CHAPTER TWENTY

Dupont Circle, Washington, DC

Anna Orlova opened her apartment door and ushered in Senator Canton. "Anyone follow you?"

"No."

"You sure?"

"Of course I'm sure, Anna." The senator from California smiled, revealing exceptionally white and perfectly straight teeth. "I disguised myself so no one would recognize me." She removed oversized Gucci sunglasses and pulled out the clip holding her platinum blonde hair in a French twist. "Besides, if anyone noticed me, I could always say I was visiting a friend in the building." She sighed. "Aren't you going to offer me some wine?"

"Marlene, this isn't a social occasion."

Senator Canton pouted. "Don't make me beg."

Anna rolled her eyes and strode down the gleaming hardwood floors toward the galley kitchen. She busied herself uncorking a bottle of a Napa Valley sauvignon blanc, the senator's favorite, while she considered the best approach. Blowing up at Marlene would be counterproductive, but the woman had to understand that secrets were meant to remain secret. At least until the optimal moment to unleash them. "Here you go," she said sweetly, handing the senator a full glass.

Canton's fingers brushed Anna's as she accepted the drink. "Aren't you having any?"

Anna shook her head. "I'm working."

The senator eyed her over the glass. "All work and no play?"

"Marlene, I wouldn't have asked you to come over if it wasn't urgent. I tried calling a half dozen times yesterday."

"I had constituent business to deal with after the hearing." She sighed as she lowered the glass to the granite countertop where it landed with a clink. "Then dinner with the husband. I simply couldn't get away."

Anna leaned against the counter and folded her arms across her chest. "Why did you leak Maggie Jenkins's name yesterday? I asked you to keep it quiet."

The senator frowned. "I know, but the opportunity was too great to let pass by. Warner Thompson will end up as CIA director, but he's going in as damaged goods. And I won't stop going after him. At least not until I know the real reason he was at Richard Carvelli's house the night he was murdered."

Last year, when Anna stumbled on an article about Senator Canton's refusal to accept the official story surrounding Richard Carvelli's death, she'd sensed an opportunity. She'd approached the senator as a Russian journalist seeking the truth about what happened that night on Capitol Hill. Had a Russian intelligence officer really killed an American congressman, or was that a story concocted to hide CIA involvement in his death?

In the eight months that she'd known the senator, it was clear to Anna that the woman was obsessed with the death of Carvelli. She and the congressman had been tight. Anna suspected they'd had an affair, although Marlene was older—a lot older—than the congressman's usual type. Based on gossip column articles from the early 2000s, Carvelli's appetite had been for young women—interns, recent college graduates. Whether the two had had an affair mattered little. Senator Canton was convinced that Warner Thompson and an intelligence analyst named Maggie Jenkins were responsible for her friend's murder.

Anna wasn't so sure until one night, when Marlene, who'd consumed an entire bottle of wine herself, offered information so potentially explosive that Anna had to bite her tongue to keep from screaming in excitement.

Richard told me, Anna, that Warner Thompson has very dark secrets. Secrets so dark that he has no business working for the CIA.

That was the moment when Anna's objective changed. Yes, Moscow was thrilled that she was recruiting a prominent United States senator to spy for Russia. That, alone, would send her career into orbit. But now she had even more valuable information—the future CIA director had deep secrets that rendered him vulnerable to recruitment.

It was almost too good to be true. Recruiting a CIA director would make her a legend. It wasn't going to be easy, she knew. For one, it was nearly impossible to get access to such a senior government official. That's where Maggie Jenkins came in. She would provide the pathway to Warner Thompson. And maybe to Imran Bukayev.

But first, she had to rein in the senator. "Look, Marlene, I understand your loyalty to Richard. But it would've been better to keep this information secret so we could use it later."

The senator poured herself more wine. "There's no time like the present."

Anna pressed her lips together. For someone with such great political instincts—if you believed the Beltway pundits—Marlene could be terribly dense. "We could've waited until Thompson became CIA director and then given him an ultimatum. Either he come clean about his role in the death of Richard Carvelli or we reveal everything to the media. That both he and Maggie Jenkins were present at the scene of the congressman's murder. And that both were inside the school that the terrorists attacked."

The senator's expression soured.

"Don't you see, Marlene? We might've been able to take out Warner Thompson even without knowing the deep, dark secrets he supposedly harbors."

"Perhaps you're right." She emptied her glass. "We can still dig for the dirt on him, can't we?"

Anna had to repress a smile at the use of the word "we." That the senator saw them as a team was a very good sign. Eventually, Marlene Canton would realize that there was no team. That, in fact, she'd been co-opted into working for Russian intelligence. And if she didn't want her privileged lifestyle to end in infamy, she'd do Anna's bidding. She poured herself some wine. "Of course we can keep digging for dirt, Marlene. In fact, I'll never stop, because I believe in you and everything you stand for." She raised her glass. "To us."

"To us," a smiling and slightly drunk senator replied with gusto.

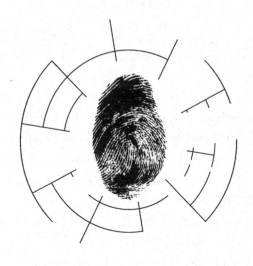

CHAPTER TWENTY-ONE

Hatteras Village, North Carolina

After returning from a couple of hours at the beach, Maggie and Roger found Warner napping in a chair on the back porch, the sound of his light snoring interrupted only by the splash of jumping mullets in the creek.

"Dad," Roger shook Warner's shoulder. "Dad, wake up. We're home."

Maggie laughed at the idea of Warner and Roger being related. Talk about a dysfunctional family.

Warner grumbled and pulled his sunglasses down his nose. "For crying out loud, Roger. I'm on vacation."

"Some vacation," Roger said. "A Soviet love child, gun running, people smuggling."

Warner threw an empty beer can in Roger's direction.

"Assault and battery," Roger called as he disappeared into the house.

Maggie sat next to Warner. "Can I ask you something?"

"Can't stop you," Warner mumbled, his voice still thick from sleep.

"Why did you risk so much to help Creature? I mean, I'm not sure that I'd do that sort of thing even for you."

He grunted and pushed himself up in the chair. "Creature wasn't just my mentor, Maggie. He saved my life."

She pulled a bottled water from the cooler in the corner of the porch and handed it to him. "What happened?"

He opened it and downed half the bottle. "I was a young case officer in East Berlin on my first tour. I had an asset, a senior Stasi officer." He stared out at the creek. "We were at a safe house, having a couple of drinks, talking. He wanted out, to defect. We wanted him to stay in place, of course. He was an incredibly valuable source—" His face contorted in pain.

Maggie waited.

"His wife had just had a baby. A little boy. He was so proud." He took a moment to collect his thoughts. "And the next thing I knew, the Stasi kicked down the door. They were all over me and my asset. Guns. Shouting." He closed his eyes.

Maggie put her hand on his. "Where does Creature fit in?"

"He was chief of station in West Berlin. He knew I was going to meet this asset. Turns out he had a bad feeling, so he sent backup. Two of our guys tailed me to the safe house, and when they saw the Stasi, they followed them into the flat and . . . it was a bloodbath. One of our guys was shot in the face. Three of the Stasi officers were shot dead. The fourth fled with my asset. I never found out what happened to him."

"I'm so sorry, Warner."

"If it hadn't been for Creature's gut instinct, I might not be sitting here today."

"So, you owe him."

"I do. If the Agency knew everything I've done to help Karina, and Vera when she was alive, I'd be screwed. But helping him was always the right thing to do."

"That's incredible, Warner, to have someone who will always have your back."

He squeezed her hand. "I know."

At that moment, Roger burst into the screened-in porch. He stopped short. "Am I interrupting something?"

"Nope," Maggie and Warner said in unison.

"Then let's talk." Roger plopped himself down on a third chair. "I called the office just now. Daud's supposed to check his AOL Instant Messenger account daily. Before we left this morning, I posted a message written in French asking how his mother is. That's the signal that I need to speak to him immediately. He hasn't responded."

"Do you think he's in trouble?" Warner asked.

"I don't know. He's a bright kid, but he's not exactly trained in spy tradecraft."

"We need experienced people on the ground," Maggie declared.

"I can't just move people from Moscow Station," Warner said.

"Yes, you can. You're the director of the CIA."

"Maggie, the president has signed a covert action finding permitting the Agency to apprehend and exfiltrate Bukayev from wherever we find him. But until we know exactly where he is, we can't risk sending in a team and alerting him to our presence. Never mind that the Russians will get suspicious rather quickly."

"We could have the Russians take him out," Maggie opined.

Warner frowned. "The president wants Bukayev alive so he can show the American people that justice will be done."

"Justice," Roger snorted. "I'm going inside to fix a drink."

"But Warner," Maggie continued, "the Russians could—"

He raised a hand. "I told you that Roger's been working on a plan. In fact, the president has authorized the Agency to send a Special Operations Group team to capture Bukayev, but we can't deploy them until we know where, exactly, he is."

"By the time we get a team like that in place, Bukayev will have vanished again," she protested.

Warner's cell phone, which sat before him on a brown wicker coffee table, chirped. He looked at the incoming number and frowned. "Creature," he said as he lifted the phone to his ear. He listened for a moment. "You sure it wasn't a random hang-up?"

"What?" Maggie mouthed.

Warner held up a hand. "Can't you call back now? Five thirty? Okay, we'll be there." He hung up and looked at his watch.

"What was that about?"

"Creature thinks Karina's in trouble. They have a prearranged signal that someone just used. If there's something wrong, she's supposed to call his cell phone and hang up after he says hello three times."

Roger emerged from the house and handed Warner a beer and Maggie a glass of pinot grigio. "What'd I miss?"

Warner explained the situation.

"Is Creature going to call her back?" Roger asked.

"Yes, but he wants to do it from his satellite phone. Out at sea."

"A satellite phone? Why?" Maggie asked. "Does he really think the Russians, or the Americans for that matter, will be listening for a call from North Carolina to Dagestan?"

"Creature is extraordinarily cautious when it comes to protecting Karina. He figures that making a satphone call from somewhere out in the Gulf Stream will make it more difficult for the NSA or the Russians to figure out what's going on."

"Assuming they're even listening," Maggie added.

"Which they're not, Warner," Roger said, his eyes flashing. "This is ridiculous. What are we supposed to do in the meantime? Stare out at the horizon, waiting for his boat to return to shore?"

"Not exactly," Warner said. "We're going with him."

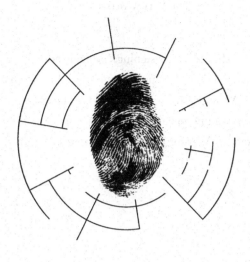

CHAPTER TWENTY-TWO

The late-afternoon heat beat down on them as they congregated on the boat deck. Maggie sat on a cushioned bench seat, her feet propped up on a cooler containing sandwiches, beer, wine, and water. Roger spun around in the fighting chair, watching as Warner tried to calm the security detail. They were insistent that one of them accompany the trio on the boat.

"We're just going on a little sunset cruise, gentleman," Warner said.

Roger stopped spinning. "I checked the forecast," he called out. "Chance of terrorists killing us out on the water is currently zero. The chance of dying in a shark attack is considerably higher."

"Sir," Rich began insistently.

"Rich, I know you're just doing your job, but I am technically the highest-ranking person among us."

"Says who?" Roger said as he popped the cap off a beer. He winked at Maggie. "Whoops, did I say that out loud?"

She laughed. "Try not to irritate the boss, Roger."

He hopped off the chair, slid onto the bench next to her, and kissed her cheek. "We all know you're really the boss."

She threw her head back and laughed again. He loved her smile. And everything else about her. He leaned in for another kiss.

"All right you two, save it for later." Warner hopped onto the boat, leaving Rich and the other two security guards standing on the dock, looking irritated.

"Bet they rent a speedboat and chase after us." Roger shouted up to the flybridge, "Creature, how fast can this baby go?"

Creature muttered something that was drowned out by a sudden rumble as *Sea Creature*'s twin 700-horsepower diesel engines roared to life.

"Guess we'll find out," Roger said as he took Maggie's hand in his.

They took a winding path through the Pamlico Sound to navigate a narrow and constantly shifting channel leading to the open ocean. Out the port side, they watched as the boat passed the island's southern end. Marsh grass and cedar trees framed the narrow strip of sandy beach, which was reachable only by foot or kayak.

After twenty-five minutes, the engines throttled up as they entered Hatteras Inlet, their path to the Atlantic Ocean. Off in the distance on the starboard side was Ocracoke Island, a spit of land that had been connected to Hatteras Island until a violent storm in the mid-1800s. As they passed the tip of Hatteras, the boat began to rock.

"Oh geez," said Roger. "Is it going to be like this the whole time?"

Maggie craned her neck to look him in the eye. "You get seasick?"

"I don't know." He braced his free hand against the side of the bench. "I've never done this before."

"Focus on the horizon," she said.

"Hey Creature, how long until we get there?" His voice was lost in the engines and the wind. "Wherever *there* is," he muttered. Hatteras was still visible off in the distance, but it was growing smaller by the minute.

Maggie leaned her head on Roger's shoulder. "You okay?"

He nodded, the sudden movement of his head making his stomach lurch. He moaned.

She righted herself. "If you're going to be sick, do it over the side of the boat, not all over me."

"Won't that attract the sharks?" he croaked.

Maggie squeezed his hand. "You're awfully cute when you're miserable, Roger Patterson."

He wanted to kiss her again but thought it better not to move his head. "Are we there yet?"

"Soon," Maggie promised.

Twenty minutes later, with nothing but the endless ocean around them in every direction, the engines eased and the boat slowed.

When Creature climbed down from the flybridge, Roger straightened and pasted on a smile.

"Heh," Creature needled. "Looking a little green around the gills there, Roger."

"Can you please hurry up and make the call so I can get back on solid land?"

"Let me grab the phone." Creature ducked into the cabin, returning a moment later with a black valise and Warner at his side.

The boat rocked side-to-side as it idled in three-foot swells.

Roger groaned again.

Maggie leaned in and whispered in his ear, sending a chill through him. "You'll be fine as soon as you can see land."

"Promise?" He closed his eyes, and quickly realizing his mistake, ran for the side of the boat, where he emptied his stomach.

Maggie rushed to his side and placed a hand on his back. "You okay?"

"No." *Way to show the lady a great time.* "Could you get me a water?"

She dashed to the cooler and back.

"Thanks." His smile came across as a grimace. As soon as he saw Creature holding a satellite phone, he forced the misery aside so he wouldn't miss a single detail. The satphone was a large contraption, reminiscent of the first mobile phone he'd purchased over a decade ago.

They all watched in expectant silence as Creature dialed and raised the phone to his ear. "It's just after one in the morning," he said, "so she should be home." After an excruciatingly long moment, his face brightened. *"Eto ya." It's me.*

They spoke rapidly. Roger lost half of what Creature said to the wind, which had shifted and now rocked the boat not only from side to side but also from bow to stern. It felt like he was trapped inside a giant washing machine.

Creature lowered the phone and motioned for them to follow him into the cabin. Roger held onto the door frame for dear life. Maggie looked ashen, but he was sure it was from worry, not the seas.

"Karina's okay. Daud's with her. But Bukayev followed Daud to Karina's house and stole Daud's car."

"Sonofa—" Warner cursed. "What's her address? Just in case—"

Creature scribbled something down on a notepad and tore off the top sheet.

Maggie took the paper from him and tucked it in her purse.

"Some asset you have there, Roger," Creature spat. "Putting my daughter in danger like this."

"I told you, he's not a trained intelligence officer. His only assignment is to report on Bukayev. His whereabouts, his contacts." He leveled an intense gaze at Creature. "How do you suppose Bukayev found Daud? Maybe a certain young lady has a relationship with him."

Creature tossed the phone on his captain's chair. "If you're insinuating that Karina is mixed up with terrorists—"

"Sometimes a girl's gotta do what a girl's gotta do."

"Roger!" Maggie interjected.

"Everyone calm down," Warner shouted. "Daud's not incompetent and Karina's an innocent bystander in this whole mess." He glanced from Creature to Roger. "Our primary goal is to capture Bukayev so he can't get to Maggie. Our secondary goal is to keep Karina safe."

"The priority of these goals depends on your perspective," Creature grumbled.

Roger looked like he was about to jump at Creature, so Maggie intervened. "It does indeed, and from where I stand, neither of the goals is within easy reach."

"Look," Warner said, a sudden weariness lining his face, "we've got to get back to headquarters to try to connect with Daud and set a trap for Bukayev. Without Creature's help, we probably wouldn't have this information. So everyone put your egos away and focus on the mission. Got it?"

"Fair enough," Creature grumbled.

Roger gave a weak salute. "Aye, aye, captain." He turned and headed back to the fighting chair out on the deck.

Maggie appeared at his side. "What's with you and Creature?"

"Hell if I know. He rubs me the wrong way with his legendary-spy macho thing."

Maggie spun the chair until she was behind it. She wrapped her arms around Roger's shoulders and leaned in. "I kind of like him," she whispered. "He reminds me of someone I know." She kissed his neck.

He responded with a quiet moan.

"Are you going to be sick again?" she asked, her tone tinged with panic.

"No." He spun to face her. "That was all you."

Her face flushed. With her curls blowing in the air in all directions and her seafoam green sundress clinging in all the right places, she was a vision. "Maggie Jenkins, I think I'm—"

"We're heading back to the marina," Creature said as he stomped past them on his way to the metal ladder that led to the flybridge. "The winds have picked up, so expect a rocky ride."

"Fabulous," Roger muttered.

Despite the growing swells, he was able to keep down what remained in his stomach. And by the time they caught sight of the island, the sun had begun to set, painting the summer sky with streaks of red.

"I'm starving," Maggie declared, as she surveyed the cold cuts and bread they'd thrown into the cooler in haste before heading to the marina.

Roger's stomach felt better the closer they got to land. "Let's ditch the old men and have a romantic sunset dinner. Just the two of us." He wrapped his arms around Maggie's waist.

"But Warner said we have to get back to Langley as soon as possible."

"What's one night," he murmured, his face buried in her hair.

"Roger," Warner hollered from inside the cabin. "Have you checked your phone?"

He groaned. "Can we just have a moment?"

Maggie sighed. "Apparently not."

He pulled the phone from his pocket. Of course he hadn't checked it. There was no signal out in the middle of the ocean. "Hang on." He flipped open the phone. "Crap. Three missed calls."

Maggie followed him into the cabin.

Warner waved his phone in front of his face. "I just talked to head-quarters. They've been trying to reach you, Roger. Daud's called in several times from a landline."

"Let me guess, from Karina's house?"

"Probably." Warner lowered his voice. "Let's keep this between us until we know more. Creature might go off the deep end if he thinks Karina's in danger."

Maggie and Roger nodded in agreement.

Roger glanced up at the flybridge. "Any details? Did he leave a message?"

"They couldn't say, not over an open line. They just said that your friend had called in several times hoping to speak with you." Warner frowned. "As soon as we get back to the house, we've got to pack up and hit the road."

By the time they reached the house, the sky had transformed into a rich paint palette, from the darkest, deepest purple high above to a rich rose red that faded into the palest pink at the horizon's edge.

"At least we got a spectacular sunset on our day away," Maggie said as they paused on the back porch to watch the sun sink behind the houses along the Pamlico Sound. Roger was disappointed with the sudden changes of plans. As was she, but how could she possibly stay here knowing that Bukayev was within their reach?

"We're coming back here in a few weeks, Maggie. Just the two of us. No phones, no laptops, no clothes."

She laughed. "Two out of three ain't bad."

"Which two?" Roger smiled, his dimples deepening, his crystal-blue eyes bright. She could get used to looking at that face every morning.

Back inside, she gathered her things from the bathroom and headed for the bedroom. Through the open door, she caught sight of Roger, his back to her, holding something in his hands. She crept closer. It was a framed photo of Jane. After staring at it for a moment, he knelt and tucked it into his duffel bag.

CHAPTER TWENTY-THREE

Vienna, Virginia, Saturday, June 18, 2005

Roger turned onto the road adjacent to Maggie's street. Up ahead, the police blockade remained at the entrance to her neighborhood. On the left, a single news truck sat parked on the shoulder. Maggie stirred in the front passenger seat. Between the time they'd left the beach and when she'd fallen asleep, somewhere near Williamsburg, she'd hardly said a word to him. Her silence was a bit unusual, but she didn't seem angry. More troubled. Or upset.

He handed his license to the officer and pointed to the passenger seat. "This is Maggie. The security detail is right behind us."

Maggie opened an eye. "What's going on?" Her voice was thick with sleep.

"We're back. They're just checking IDs."

"What time is it?" She shielded her eyes from the officer's flash-light.

"Almost two in the morning." Roger suppressed a yawn. For the past hour, he'd driven with the window open to keep from nodding off at the wheel. The coffee he'd picked up at a rest area had barely made a dent in his fatigue. "Thanks, Officer." Ahead, he pulled into the driveway and parked next to Maggie's Jeep. Rich's black SUV pulled up along the curb.

Roger popped the trunk and jumped out of the car. He grabbed Maggie's suitcase and his duffel bag and met her on the passenger side. Newly installed motion-sensor lights lit up the driveway with a harsh glow.

Maggie squinted against the glare, reached for her suitcase, and turned for the stairs. "Thanks, Roger."

Thanks? He'd just driven thirteen hours round trip, suffered through seasickness, and eaten crappy drive-thru takeout, and he didn't even get a kiss for his efforts? Rich, the burly security man brushed by him and grabbed the suitcase from Maggie before she was halfway up the stairs.

"Good night," he mumbled as he dragged himself back to the car. It was probably all the stress, he told himself. They'd had a nice time, nonetheless. They'd even had a few moments, moments that gave him confidence that he wasn't the only one falling in love.

Five hours later, Maggie woke, her mind already churning before she even threw back the covers. As if worrying about Bukayev wasn't enough, she couldn't stop thinking about Roger staring at Jane's pho-tograph. He was entitled to his grief and memories, of course. After all, her engagement photo still hung on the wall in the living room. And there were photo albums full of her adventures with Steve on the bookshelf in the den. So why did Jane's picture bother her so much?

She checked her cell phone. No missed calls. In the bathroom, she slid into workout clothes, threw her hair up in a ponytail, and tossed clean clothes into her gym bag. She stomped down the stairs to the kitchen, where she half expected, half hoped she'd find Roger waiting for her with coffee and a bagel.

She let out a little yelp when a man in khakis and a blue shirt appeared at the top of the basement stairs. *The overnight security guy?*

"My apologies, Ms. Jenkins. I was just getting coffee for the surveillance team." He gestured toward the basement.

She offered a weak smile in reply. This was going to take getting used to. All these strangers in the house, day and night. After prepping a travel mug full of coffee, she grabbed a banana and her car keys and hurried to the front door. Outside, she rushed down the steps, stopping short at the walkway when she discovered Rich's black SUV blocking her driveway.

The heavily tinted driver's window descended with a quiet hum. "Good morning, Maggie."

"Hey. Late night last night, huh?"

"I caught a few hours of sleep." He pointed at the gym bag. "Where you going?"

"The gym. Then the office."

"Why don't you hop in? I'll drive you."

Maggie slumped. "No offense, but I'd like to drive myself."

"No offense taken." He lowered mirrored sunglasses over his eyes. "I'll follow."

Ten minutes later, she pulled the Jeep into the fitness club's parking lot with the black SUV trailing closely behind. As she grabbed her bag from the backseat, Rich jogged over.

"Listen, Rich. I'm here almost every day. Everyone knows me. It's not necessary for you to come inside—"

"I'm just going to look around. Then I'll hang out near the entrance to see who's coming and going."

Maggie sighed and slung the bag over her shoulder. "You don't want to work out? I could get you a guest pass."

"Already hit the gym this morning." He flexed his rather impressive bicep.

"Clearly." Maggie laughed. "I should warn you that they won't let you into the women's locker room no matter who you say you work for."

"If you're in there too long, I'll bust in anyway."

"You'll be doing so at your own peril." Inside, she told the front-desk attendant: "This is my friend, Rich. He's going to hang here while I work out."

The teenager wrinkled his forehead. He'd seen Maggie and Roger come to the gym together many times. "You can wait for me here, hon." She winked at Rich, who exchanged a confused look with the attendant.

Ten minutes into her run on the treadmill, heart pumping, sweat dripping, she slipped into what she called the zone. Her worries weren't exactly melting away, but it was easier to forget them with every pounding footstep. She cranked up Tom Petty's greatest hits on the fancy new MP3 player Roger had bought her and picked up the pace. Once she hit the three-mile mark, Maggie slowed the treadmill to a light jog and eventually to a walk.

Through the glass partition separating the cardio and weight rooms, she watched a woman with a blonde ponytail place a pair of dumbbells on a rack and trot in the direction of the yoga studio. She brought the treadmill to a complete stop. Although she hadn't seen the woman's face, there was something familiar about her.

Maggie quickly wiped down the treadmill, grabbed her belongings, and hurried through the weight room for the yoga studio. Through the glass door, she scanned a class full of women twisting themselves into painful-looking poses. There were a few blondes among them, but not the woman she was looking for.

She retraced her steps and found Rich in the lobby.

"You see a woman with a blonde ponytail?"

Rich glanced up from the morning paper. "Several. Why?"

"I thought I saw someone I know. Not a big deal," she shrugged. "I'm going to shower. That's allowed, right?"

He looked at his watch, then switched to another chair so he could monitor the hall leading to the women's locker room. "Five minutes."

"Ten," Maggie declared over her shoulder as she walked away. Inside the locker room, she stripped out of her sweaty clothes and hopped in the first shower stall. The falling water drowned out all other sounds. She turned off the water and listened. Zara had been brazen. No doubt she would've followed Maggie to the gym and killed her in the shower. The question was, did Bukayev have other assets like Zara? People who could blend into American society and engage in stealth attacks? It would be foolish to think he didn't.

She quickly dried herself and stepped into the adjacent changing stall. Nearby, she heard a toilet flush, followed by a rush of water from the sink area. She balled up her sweaty clothes, stuffed them in her gym bag, and pulled open the curtain. The woman at the sink smiled at Maggie in the mirror as she tugged off the elastic band securing her ponytail.

Maggie's breath caught in her throat.

The woman shook her head, splaying blonde hair around a heart-shaped face accentuated by bright blue eyes. "Hello, Maggie. Fancy meeting you here." Her tone was artificially cheery.

Anna Orlova. "What the hell are you doing here?"

CHAPTER TWENTY-FOUR

Tyson's Fitness and Health Club, McLean, Virginia

E ven as every instinct told her to walk away, maybe even run, Maggie didn't move. She felt paralyzed by an odd mixture of fear and curiosity. Anna Orlova, a Russian reporter who was friendly with Senator Canton and claimed to know how to find Imran Bukayev, went to the same gym as her? A coincidence? *There are no coincidences*, she reminded herself.

What did Anna want from her? Had Bukayev sent her? She edged away and glanced from the glowing exit sign to her watch. Rich had given her ten minutes. Eight down, two to go. "Why are you following me, Anna?"

Her bow-shaped lips curved into a smile. "Who says I'm following you? I live in the area. I like to exercise." She lifted her hands as if surprised. "And here we are, at the same gym."

"I saw you outside my house yesterday morning at the crack of dawn."

Her eyes grew wide in mock surprise. "I'm a reporter. I go where the stories are."

Maggie scoffed. "A reporter?"

"You doubt me?"

Back in the Soviet days, every Russian reporter ultimately worked for the KGB. And even in the fourteen years since the collapse of the USSR, the CIA remained highly suspicious of state-owned Russian media outlets. Was every reporter a tool of Russian intelligence? Probably not. But many were. Perhaps Anna really was a journalist. Or perhaps, journalism provided her with the perfect cover.

"You're awfully young for such a prestigious assignment, Anna. You must have connections. Is your father some kind of VIP, friends with Putin, or"—she pretended to contemplate that thought for a moment—"no offense. I'm sure you're great at your job."

"I am, actually. And you know what my favorite part of being a reporter is?" She paused, but not long enough for Maggie to answer. "Digging up people's deepest, darkest secrets."

Maggie stared straight into the smaller woman's cold, blue eyes. "Is that some sort of warning?"

"Why? Do you have dark secrets?"

Maggie hefted her gym bag over her shoulder. "Stay away from me, Anna."

As she turned to leave, heart pounding, Anna grabbed her arm. "Wait. Please. We got off on the wrong foot. I just want to chat. We have mutual interests."

Maggie shook her off. "No, we don't. I don't even know you."

"I'd love to buy you dinner. Or a drink. I'll tell you everything I know about Imran Bukayev."

Every counterintelligence warning the CIA had pounded into her went off like sirens in her head. "Not interested."

"I'd like to interview you."

Maggie headed for the exit.

"About Zara Barayeva."

She stopped, her back to Anna.

"She was a most wanted terrorist in Russia. You hunted her down and killed her."

Maggie's gut clenched.

"The Russian people want to hear your story. You should see the newspapers in Moscow today. There are so many articles about you."

Maggie looked back over her shoulder. "You can write your story without me."

With that, she pushed open the locker-room door and hurried to find Rich. Perspiration dampened her fresh shirt.

"Ready?" Rich stood from his chair.

"Yes."

"Headquarters?"

"Yup."

Anna Orlova had been watching her for a while. Of that she was certain. The question was, why?

Out in the parking lot, Maggie turned to Rich. "Do you mind waiting a few minutes while I make a quick call?"

"Sure." He sauntered over to the SUV, which was parked to the immediate left of the Jeep.

Maggie pulled out her phone. No messages from Roger or Warner. If there was news, one of them would've called. She pretended to dial and lifted the phone to her ear. Certain that Rich was watching her from behind his car's dark, tinted windows, she carried on an imaginary conversation. Which car was Anna's? After several minutes, she ran out of things to say to her pretend friend, and tossed the phone onto the seat. If Anna was going to stalk her, eventually she'd figure out which car she drove. Just as Maggie turned the key in the ignition, the Russian exited the gym. She pulled down the visor and pretended to check her makeup in the mirror. Once Anna passed by, she flipped the visor back into place, gave a little wave in Rich's direction, and put the car into drive.

Several rows away, Anna let herself into a blue BMW. If Rich weren't here, maybe she'd follow the BMW and try to figure out who Anna Orlova really was.

· ★ ★ ★ ·
Vienna, Virginia

The man slowed to a jog as he approached the neighborhood. The heavy, humid summer air left him sweating profusely. He pulled his Washington Nationals baseball cap low over his forehead and pushed mirrored sunglasses further up his nose. Taking a swig from a water bottle, he checked his watch. Between the street map and the new on-line map website he'd consulted, he'd learned that the woman's street was a dead end. Far from ideal for a casual jog meant to attract no attention. Even less ideal for the task at hand.

At the intersection, he decided to proceed as planned and dashed across the street, reducing his pace so he could read the house numbers emblazoned on the mailboxes. Up ahead, a black SUV blocked one of the driveways. That seemed odd. He slowed to a walk, hands on hips as if he were winded. The vehicle also blocked the mailbox so he continued to the next townhouse, whose street number was higher than the one he was looking for. The house with the blocked driveway had to be the one. When he reached the dead end, he squatted down to tie a running shoe that didn't need tying and glanced up at the house in question. It would be too risky to attempt to execute the plan with neighboring townhouses right on top of one another. Maybe another location would work better. There were lots of possibilities.

Using the damp sleeve of his Hard Rock Café T-shirt, he wiped at the sweat trickling down the side of his face. This wasn't going to be an easy job, especially given the time constraints. As he jogged back up the street, he let his eyes wander to the townhouse. He'd have to investigate what was behind this neighborhood to make sure he wasn't missing another line of attack or means of escape.

A muscular, dark-skinned man stepped out of the SUV that blocked the driveway. "Excuse me."

He startled. He hadn't noticed anyone inside the vehicle, not with the tinted windows.

"You don't live in this neighborhood," the man said as he approached.

The man jogged in place. "I'm out for a run."

"You have any identification on you?"

He sized up the man looming over him. Pound for pound, he couldn't beat this guy. He was a third-degree black belt, but if the man had similar training, he'd be at a physical disadvantage. "Is there a problem?" He regretted his tone as soon as the words escaped his mouth. Keeping a low profile was paramount. *Shut up*, he told himself as he bounced on his toes.

The man stepped closer. "What are you doing here?"

He wanted to push back, put this jackass in his place. But what was that expression? Never bring a knife to a gun fight? In this case, he was the knife and this guy was the gun. "Like I said, I'm out for a run." He stepped toward the middle of the street. "Have a nice day." With that, he sprinted for the main road without a glance back.

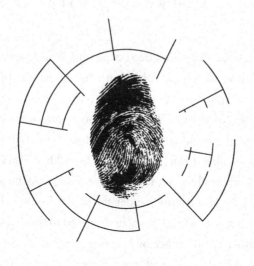

CHAPTER TWENTY-FIVE

CIA Headquarters, Langley, Virginia

R oger headed for the seventh floor after showering in the basement locker room. Once he'd dropped off Maggie in the wee hours of the morning, he'd decided to drive straight to headquarters to try to contact Daud. Eventually, he'd given up and crashed on a lumpy couch in the fourth-floor conference room.

Up in the ops center, few staff were present, not surprising for a Saturday morning. He poured himself a cup of coffee and approached the ops center manager, Bill. Or was it Bob? Maybe Billy Bob? Yeah, he'd go with that one. Blinking rapidly, he tried to focus. He was punch-drunk tired. Four hours of sleep was enough in his wild youth. Now? Not so much.

"Roger Patterson. You have some documents for me?"

"I do, indeed." Billy Bob flipped through a stack of papers. "Ah, here it is, right here. RF-YOUNGGUN."

Every time Roger heard Daud's code name, he wanted to laugh. RF was the country designation—in this case, the Russian Federation. But YOUNGGUN? That was the last name he would've assigned to the timid and mild-mannered Chechen, but, he supposed, that was the point. If the code name ever leaked, the Russians would never suspect that it referred to Daud.

"When I got here a few hours ago, no one could find these files." Roger's tone was accusatory.

"It's highly compartmented information."

"Which I'm cleared for." Roger rubbed at his unshaven chin. "Someone could've left the overnight staff a note so they could find it."

Billy Bob pursed his lips as if to say, *Are you finished complaining?*

"What did YOUNGGUN say? Why'd he call the emergency number? Did he even try contacting me through our online channel?"

Billy Bob held up a hand and muttered to himself as he read through a document. "Ah . . . hmmm . . . my friend Roger . . . emergency."

Roger balled his free hand into a fist to keep from snatching the papers right out of the guy's hands. "May I see the notes?"

The man looked at him over his glasses then resumed reading.

"How did the ops center know that I am the Roger that YOUNG-GUN wanted to talk to?"

Billy Bob tilted his head, looking at Roger as if he were a complete idiot. "We had no idea who you are. We simply followed protocol. All emergency calls go to the director. Since we don't really have one at the moment, we called the next best thing."

"Warner," Roger said. "And he told you that I'm YOUNGGUN's case officer."

"He did." Billy Bob extended two sheets of paper to Roger. One was filled with handwritten notes someone took when Daud called in. The other contained the official report compiled from the notes.

Roger took the papers and turned without a word.

"We're going to need those back," Billy Bob called after him.

Roger pushed through double swinging doors and made a bee-line for Warner's office. Inside, moving boxes were stacked at random around the room, creating a maze of sorts. Warner was nowhere to be found in the mess.

He continued to the director's suite, where he discovered Warner staring out a large window. The office itself was empty, save for a massive mahogany desk, a well-cushioned chair, and two leather club seats standing opposite the desk. All of the late director's belonging were gone and the man wasn't even buried yet. "Measuring for curtains?" Roger said.

Startled, Warner whirled around. "Don't you knock?"

"You're already moving in and you haven't even been confirmed yet? What if something goes sideways with the Senate and your nomination tanks?"

"I talked to the Senate Intel chairman last night on the way home. They have the votes."

"Fingers crossed," Roger said with no sincerity.

"Is there a problem?"

"Nope." Roger slurped the remainder of his coffee, eyes locked on his boss.

"Did something happen with you and Maggie?"

Had Warner bugged his car or something? "What makes you think that?"

"A—your foul mood this morning. B—Maggie seemed rather out of sorts when we left last night."

Maggie didn't hide her moods well. Roger loved that about her.

She didn't always explain why she was in a mood, but she couldn't fake being happy if she wasn't. "A—she wasn't happy about having to leave the beach. B—she doesn't like strangers living in her house. And, C—there's a fatwa with her name on it. But Maggie and me? We're fine. Couldn't be better."

Warner widened his eyes. "Okay then."

Roger placed the empty coffee cup on the desk and read through the ops center documents. Daud had called in three times in a space of two hours asking to speak to his friend Roger. The Chechen had said it was an emergency, that another friend of theirs was in town. "I'm sure that friend is Bukayev."

"Agreed," Warner said, "Karina's conversation with Creature confirmed that."

"I bet when Daud couldn't get in touch with me, Karina put out the SOS to her father." Roger rubbed at his temples. He needed more coffee. "I don't understand why he didn't leave me a message online, the way we usually do. Why risk a phone call from Dagestan?"

"I checked with Creature. Karina doesn't have internet."

"Dammit. And let me guess, she also doesn't have a car."

"She does but it died recently."

"So now Daud is stuck in the middle of nowhere because Bukayev stole his car."

"Yup. And Karina's house is ten miles outside of Makhachkala."

"Easy for you to say," muttered Roger.

Warner laughed.

Despite his best efforts not to, Roger burst out laughing too. "I'd like to buy a vowel."

"Or sell off some consonants," Warner said.

They roared, choking, gasping for breath until Maggie appeared, standing in the doorway, arms folded, irritation written across her face. "Am I interrupting something?"

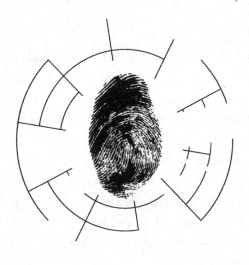

CHAPTER TWENTY-SIX

"Oh, hey, Maggie, I was just going to call you." Roger cleared his throat. "Warner and I were just laughing about the name of Dagestan's capital—" Her steely glare stopped him short. "You okay?"

"I'm great." She marched over to the desk and grabbed the ops center documents before Roger or Warner could react. After a quick scan, she said, "I assume the friend Daud references is Bukayev?"

"It must be," Warner said, "especially since Karina told Creature that Bukayev had been to her house."

"And Daud wouldn't have called the emergency number if he didn't consider his situation a true emergency," Roger added.

She tossed the papers back onto the desk. "Have you tried to contact him?"

"Not yet."

She frowned. "What are you waiting for?"

"He doesn't have internet access at Karina's, so we can't communicate via our usual protocol."

"Which is?"

"An online chat room."

"Then call Karina's house, Roger."

"Maggie," Warner said, "that's risky. For all we know, the Russians are listening."

"The Russians aren't trying to kill me," she snapped. "Bukayev is."

"I have a responsibility to Daud, Maggie," Roger said.

Her face grew hot. "Excuse me?"

Roger blanched. "I mean, he's my agent, but obviously, your safety is the priority. The top priority." He looked to Warner for help but got nothing. "What I'm trying to say, and I'm not saying it very well, is that if Daud gets blown, we're screwed. He's our only asset in Dagestan. If we lose him, we lose our only link to Bukayev."

He had a point, but his fumbling attempt to clarify only made it more obvious that his priority was protecting his asset. Not her. Between his apparently unresolved grief over Jane and his so-called responsibility to Daud, Maggie had no idea where she fit in. What was it with CIA operations officers, anyway? They ate, drank, and breathed the spy life. They were adrenaline junkies who thought themselves invincible. Steve and Roger—she stopped herself, horrified that she was lumping them together. She had to get her thoughts back on track, focused on the mission at hand.

"I need some coffee. You boys get back to whatever it is you're doing." With that, she turned and rushed down the hall for the staircase, hoping Roger wouldn't follow her. And hoping he would.

He didn't.

Down on the fourth floor, she fired up her computer and typed *Anna Orlova reporter* into the search engine. A photo of a smiling young woman with blonde hair popped up in the first hit. A reporter for *Russia Today*. Digging a little deeper, she discovered that *Russia Today* was a new offshoot of RIA Novosti, one of Russia's three state-owned television news agencies. Orlova had authored several stories about Moscow's perspective on US government policies. There were even a few video clips of her reporting from outside the US Capitol and the White House.

She should tell Warner about Anna. Probably Roger too. Maggie squirmed in the chair. *No, not yet.* They needed to focus on Bukayev, not a nosy Russian reporter. Or whatever she was. Then again, Anna had referenced Bukayev. That was a bit unnerving. She pulled a business card from her wallet. Wrong one. Creature had slipped her his card after they returned to the marina from their little excursion. *In case you need anything. Anything at all.* She tucked it back in the wallet and fished around until she found Anna Orlova's. In addition to her name, title, and employer, it included a phone number and an email address. Would there be any harm in calling to ask what she knew about Imran Bukayev? If she was a reporter, probably not. If she was a Russian intelligence officer, most definitely yes. Maggie couldn't put herself in a position of owing Anna anything. That was dangerous ground. *But what if she knows something that leads us to Bukayev?*

She mindlessly flipped the card from front to back and over again in her hands.

"Maggie."

She leaped out of her chair. "Rich! You startled me."

"My apologies." He scanned the empty office. "Something's come up."

She stiffened.

"After following you here, I went back to the house to check on things and make sure the surveillance crew has everything it needs."

Her throat felt suddenly dry. "Did they catch something on camera?"

"Sort of. There was a guy jogging past your house."

Maggie exhaled. "That's probably just my neighbor, Dave."

"Describe him."

"About sixty, I guess. But in good shape for his age. Thinning black hair. I'm pretty sure he colors it."

Rich shook his head. "Not him."

"Then who was it?"

"That's what I'm trying to figure out. I'd like you to go back home and view the surveillance video and the photos I took."

Maggie struggled to keep her voice even. "Meet you in the parking lot in fifteen?"

"I'll follow you home."

She flashed him a bright smile as if all was well. "Thanks, Rich."

"Of course." He backed out of the cubicle.

She sank into her chair. A jogger on her dead-end street wasn't necessarily anything to be alarmed about, was it? It was the weekend. A nice morning. People like to exercise on days like today, right? Rich was just being extremely cautious. That was his job. Maggie inhaled, held her breath for as long as she could, and exhaled slowly in an effort to calm her racing thoughts.

She stared at the calendar on the wall, trying to piece together a time line of events. One thing was certain—Anna had been watching her at the gym well before Senator Canton leaked her name on Thursday. And based on the way the senator and Anna interacted in the Senate hearing room, it was obvious that they hadn't just met. Clearly, the two women knew each other well, or at least reasonably so. But why would a US senator be so chummy with a Russian reporter?

Maggie realized she'd crushed Anna's business card in her hand while she was talking with Rich. She smoothed it out as best she could and laid it on the desk. Why had Anna been following her? And how did Senator Canton fit into this? Her fingers tapped a slow rhythm on the desk. An explanation dancing on the edge of her mind, just out of reach.

She picked up the phone to call Roger. He'd help her sort through all the jumbled thoughts. Then she remembered that he wasn't at his desk. He was three floors up, having a grand time with Warner. Back to the computer. A quick search on Senator Canton brought up article after article. Canton was on her second marriage, with a college-aged daughter from her first marriage and two kids in their early teens from the current husband. There were photos of her on the Senate floor, at White House functions, and at political fundraisers.

Maggie's index finger hovered over the mouse. She clicked to enlarge a photograph and gasped. There was Senator Canton chatting with Congressman Richard Carvelli. The late Congressman Carvelli. The one Maggie had shot two years ago. Despite the shock of seeing the congressman's face, an image she'd studiously avoided since his death, it didn't surprise her to see a photo of him with the senator. *Birds of a feather,* as her mother would say.

Maggie closed the tab and started a new search, this one about herself. There were too many hits, so she narrowed the results by adding Senator Canton's name to the search terms. "That's better," she muttered as she opened an article written by one of the more reputable national-security correspondents. The article's last sentence grabbed her attention:

"Repeated inquiries to Senator Canton's office regarding where she learned Maggie Jenkins's identity have gone unanswered."

There were any number of people who could've leaked her name to the senator. Or to Anna, who then passed it along to the senator.

A slideshow of faces flipped through her mind. No obvious suspects jumped out. Certainly not Warner or Roger. And it was unlikely that any of the law-enforcement personnel who'd been at the school would've released such information. If Yuri, the former KGB man and Russian mafia boss, were still alive, he'd be her prime suspect. But he'd been killed that day, right in front of his distraught daughter and granddaughter. Maggie's hand froze. Svetlana Markova. Yuri's daughter. She'd moved to the US from Russia several years ago and was a teacher at Dominion Elementary. She'd been in the gymnasium and had witnessed the entire siege.

Maggie did a quick internet search for Svetlana's address. There was only one S. Markova in northern Virginia. She scribbled down the address on a sticky note and stuck it in her purse. Her hands were shaking. Did she really want to see Svetlana again? Every time she got too close to that day—the sights, the sounds, the people—it sent her right back to the nightmares, the bouts of insomnia.

She stood on the stage of the elementary school's gymnasium, hands cuffed behind her back, an AK-47 trained on her. Zara summoned Svetlana Markova and her young daughter to the stage. "I know your father," Maggie said, trying to reassure Svetlana that she wasn't alone in this horror show.

Zara had repeatedly said Maggie's name that day. Svetlana must have heard it. What if Anna Orlova had approached Svetlana, a grieving young mother living far from home, offering her the chance to tell the story of her father's death and the terror she and her daughter had endured that day? What if Svetlana had said, "Yes, I remember the woman who saved us. Her name is Maggie."

Maggie exhaled. Even if that was true, why would Anna leak her name to Senator Canton? What was in it for her? She picked up Anna's business card, grabbed her bag, and headed for the elevator.

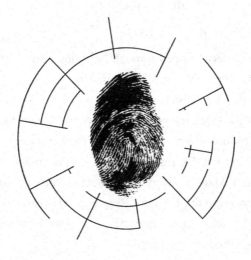

CHAPTER TWENTY-SEVEN

Maggie called Anna before leaving the CIA parking lot. When Anna didn't answer, she hung up, threw the car into gear, and sped toward the onramp to the George Washington Parkway with Rich in close pursuit. When she exited the outer loop of the Capital Beltway onto Georgetown Pike, her phone rang.

"This isn't the way to your house, Maggie."

"I'm popping by to see a friend, Rich."

"You're supposed to notify me of any changes in your plans."

"I just did. It was a last-minute decision." She turned right and slowed, scanning the street signs for Svetlana's road. The area was quite familiar to her. Sometimes late at night, when she couldn't sleep, she'd drive through this neighborhood on the way to Dominion Elementary, where she'd park for a while. Something about seeing the school quiet and at rest helped calm her. "Her street's right here. I'll just be a minute."

She hung up before he could lecture her about protocol and turned into a driveway with a newer model minivan and a child's pink bicycle leaning against the garage. When she rang the doorbell, a petite girl with platinum blonde curls answered. Maggie's breath caught.

"Mama," the little girl screamed as one of the terrorists dragged her up onto the gymnasium stage alongside her mother.

"Mama!" the girl yelled, eyeing Maggie.

A tall, thin woman with blonde hair a shade darker than her daughter's appeared in the doorway. Her expression morphed from cautiously friendly to shock. "Go and play, baby, Mama will be right in."

As her daughter skipped back into the house, Svetlana stepped onto the front stoop. "You're the woman from the school."

"Yes. I'm sorry to bother you, it's just that, well, I've been thinking about you and your daughter and . . . I wanted to see if you're okay."

Svetlana's enormous blue eyes filled with tears. "It is very hard sometimes. Especially for Elena. But we finished out the school year because I want to teach my daughter that we can't run away from what happened."

Maggie pressed her lips together. "I'm so sorry about your father, Ms. Markova."

She swiped at her cheeks. "Thank you. We're leaving for Russia tonight to visit family and scatter his ashes at his old dacha. A part of me wants to stay in Moscow, but bad things happen there too. So . . ." Her voice trailed off.

"Has anyone come to talk to you about what happened in the school? From the government or the media?"

"Oh, yes. The media was very bad at first. I didn't leave my house for weeks. My teacher friends brought food over and walked my dog. It was a terrible time."

Maggie offered a sympathetic smile. "A woman named Anna Orlova contacted me, wanting to talk about that day. I don't know anything about her, so when she mentioned that she spoke to you, I thought I'd stop by to see if you could verify that she is who she says she is."

"Yes. Anna came by last weekend. Sunday, I think? She's from the Russian consulate in Washington. A lovely woman. She offered to help in whatever way she could."

The consulate? "You told her everything that happened?"

"Yes."

"She must've asked about me." Maggie struggled to keep her expression neutral.

"Oh, yes," Svetlana said. "She wanted to know everything about you. And I told her about the man who was wounded. His children are students there, but they're older than my daughter, so I don't know them. Anyway, I think he was a CIA official. Or maybe FBI. No, I think it was CIA." She paused, as if trying to remember the details. "The principal told me. I could always ask her."

Maggie shook her head. "No need. Did you tell Anna about the man too?"

"Yes. I mentioned it when she asked if anyone got hurt. Anna said she needed all the details because the lead terrorist was Russian. Well, she was Chechen, but a Russian citizen."

Zara. "Makes sense." Actually, it didn't make sense that the Russian consulate would wait nine months to check on Svetlana and her daughter. That must not have occurred to her. "And this Anna, she's a blonde woman? Young, very pretty. About this tall?" Maggie raised her hand to the level of her nose.

"That's right. She's very kind." Svetlana smiled. "It was nice to talk to someone who really understands."

"What do you mean?"

"Unfortunately, we have a lot in common because of what happened to our families."

"Your families?"

"Well, of course, they killed my father and Anna's—"

"Mama!" Elena ran to the front door. "There's smoke in the kitchen!"

Svetlana's hands flew to her face. "I forgot about the cookies. I'm so sorry. It was nice to see you." She shut the door, leaving Maggie on the stoop.

· ★ ★ ★ ·
Vienna, Virginia

Maggie sipped from a large glass of Chardonnay. If what Rich was about to show her wasn't enough to start her drinking at three in the afternoon, her encounter with Svetlana Markova was.

"All right, here's the image of the man I saw loitering around outside." Rich turned the laptop toward where Maggie sat at the kitchen island. "Unfortunately, between the tinted windshield, the distance from the subject to me, and the man's hat and sunglasses, I couldn't get a great shot of his face."

Maggie shook her head. "I don't think I've seen him around here before. Then again, I don't normally keep an eye on who's passing by the house."

"I was going to snap another photo, but he took off running before I could." Rich grimaced. "This is the video from the cameras mounted on the house." He clicked on another window. "The guy never looked directly at the camera, so all we can get from this is a profile shot."

She shook her head. "Still don't recognize him. Maybe the composite sketch will help."

Rich had provided the photograph, video, and a description of the man to a CIA sketch artist. "I hope."

Maggie swirled the wine in her glass. "Anything else about him? Was he looking at my house?"

"Couldn't see his eyes, but I got the impression he was checking out the numbers on the mailboxes. See here?" He pointed to the screen. "The way his head's angled a bit to the left like he's looking directly at your neighbor's mailbox?"

Maggie felt a familiar and unwelcome fear pushing against her lungs. *You're not alone*, she reminded herself. There were the cameras. Rich was there during the day. A rotating group of security personnel at night. But their presence didn't diminish the nagging feeling that she was missing something. She topped off her wine and glanced at the digital clock on the stove. Roger was supposed to be here by now. "Your shift's almost over, Rich. How about a beer?"

"I'm not supposed to socialize with my protectees." He looked at the glass in her hand. "As much as I could use a drink after today."

"How about when this is all over?" How long had she been waiting for things to be over? For a return to normal? She didn't even know what normal meant anymore.

"Deal."

The doorbell chimed.

Rich raised a hand, indicating that Maggie should stay put. His other hand moved to the 9mm pistol holstered on his hip.

Maggie lowered her glass to the countertop and hopped off the stool. She peered down the hall that led from the kitchen, through the living room to the front door. Rich's linebacker build blocked her view. When he began to turn her way, she scrambled back to her seat.

"Honey, I'm home."

Roger.

"You started the party without me?" Roger sauntered into the kitchen and kissed her on the cheek.

"Mark's already outside for the next shift," Rich said from where he stood behind Roger. "I'll see you bright and early tomorrow."

"Have a good night, Rich," she called.

He nodded, and with that, he let himself out the front door.

"I went looking for you, but you'd already left the office." Roger drew his lips into a pout. "I thought you might leave a note or something."

If Roger was fishing for an apology or explanation for her whereabouts, he was getting neither.

If anyone was guilty of vanishing without an explanation over the past week, it was him. She shrugged. "I got my things done and came home."

He glanced at the wine bottle and then at her. "What were you working on?"

"Nothing earth-shattering." She spun around and headed for the back deck.

Roger followed, joining her outside in the warm, humid afternoon air. "Did I do something wrong?"

She put her glass on the railing beside her. "How would I know? You don't tell me anything."

"That's why I've been looking for you. I have an update."

Maggie froze. "What is it?"

Roger glanced over the railing at the small fenced yard below. He leaned in close, his breath warm on her neck.

Maggie shivered despite the heat and her irritation with him.

"We called the house."

"The one where—"

"Where our two friends are. Yes."

"And?" Maggie pulled her head away so she could look him in the eye. He was a trained CIA operative. Lying was second nature to him, but still, she wanted to watch his eyes, judge for herself.

"And I talked to him. They're both okay. Our third friend hasn't returned, so without a car, they're pretty much stuck there." Roger's eyes held steady, his dark lashes standing in stark contrast to crystal blue irises.

"Can't they call someone for a ride?"

"My friend doesn't know what our third friend has told their mutual friends about him."

Maggie squinted at Roger. This conversation was getting complicated. "Hang on." She hurried into the kitchen and pulled a small dry-erase board off the side of the refrigerator. Before heading outside, she grabbed a napkin and wiped off the grocery list she'd made. Wine and eggs. She could remember that. Back on the porch, she took the marker and wrote a question. *Daud can't trust his associates in Dagestan because he doesn't know what Bukayev told them about him and Karina?*

"Exactly," Roger said.

Maggie wiped the words off the board. "So what's he going to do?"

Roger took the board from her. *He's afraid to leave Karina in case the evil bastard comes back to her house.* He handed her the board.

But they can't just sit there and do nothing. EB may never come back.

"EB?"

"Evil bastard."

He laughed. She loved the small crinkles that formed at the corners of his eyes. She blinked to break the spell, then wiped the board clean. *What's their plan? We need eyes on EB ASAP.*

"Agreed." He took the board. *I told him to leave Karina locked in the house.* He swiped away his words. "You need a bigger whiteboard." He resumed writing. *Told him to find a ride back to Rasul's safe house.*

"Who?"

Rasul's another EB. Daud's been handling logistics for him.

Maggie's mouth dropped open. She took the board. *Rasul Makasharipov?*

"The one and only." *Bukayev taught Rasul everything he knows,* he scribbled back.

She knew all about Rasul Makasharipov and his ties to Bukayev. Makasharipov was a violent, paranoid, ruthless terrorist. Daud, on the other hand, was a quiet, diminutive man who had no business mingling with such a deranged person. She had a sudden new respect for the young Chechen she'd met last year while investigating Zara's terrorist plot.

"It can't be safe," she said, studying Roger's face, which remained impassive. He seemed completely unfazed by the fact that he'd sent Daud into a viper's nest.

"It's not, but it's part of the game."

She opened her mouth, but her words faltered. *Game?* People's lives were at stake.

"I need more wine."

"I'll get it." Roger returned with the bottle and a glass for himself.

"This isn't a game, Roger."

He met her eyes as he poured. "What's not a game?"

"You just said that putting our young friend in danger is part of the game."

"It's just a figure of speech. He knows what he's gotten himself into."

Was that how all operations officers thought? Had Steve been this calculating? This cold? Some days she wondered if she'd romanticized her late fiancé, turned him into a superhero. The perfect man. Was that why she focused so much on Roger's flaws? To keep the narrative about a perfect Steve alive?

Roger tucked a loose strand of hair behind her ear, a gesture too intimate for her to appreciate in her agitated state. "What were you working on today?"

Her skin felt hot under his touch. Roger was far from perfect, but he had a way of melting her resolve.

She wanted to lean in and kiss him and tell him everything she'd been keeping from him. Instead, she cleared her throat. It wasn't time to bring him in on her suspicions about Anna Orlova yet. Not until she had a better grasp of the situation. "Rich saw some guy jogging past the house today."

"Was it your neighbor? The old guy who always checks you out?"

She flushed. "He doesn't check me out."

"He most certainly does."

"And he's not that old. But no, it wasn't him." She waved him back into the kitchen. He trailed along behind her as she descended the stairs to the basement.

Roger whistled as he took in the equipment filling the house's lower level. "It's like command central in here."

"Everything okay, Ms. Jenkins?" asked one of the two women sitting before several large screens that showed the video feeds from the front and rear of the townhouse.

A second technician, a mousy young woman with large headphones over her ears, didn't so much as glance up at them.

"What's she doing?" Maggie asked the first tech.

"Listening for radio frequency interference that could indicate someone nearby is trying to eavesdrop."

Sounds terribly boring, Maggie mused. "I'd like to show Roger the photos and video of the jogger."

The woman opened a file on one screen.

Roger leaned in to get a better look. "Have you sent these images to headquarters?"

"Yes. We're running them through criminal databases, both local and federal, and our counterterrorism database." The tech clicked
back to the live camera feed. All appeared quiet outside the house.

"You sure you've never seen that guy before?" Roger asked Maggie.

"Never."

Roger's phone chirped. "Yup," he said as he jogged up the stairs.

Maggie followed on his heels.

"I'm leaving now." He hung up. "I gotta go."

"What is it?"

"That was the boss. Our boy called in. He's on the move."

Maggie grabbed her purse off the counter. "I'm going with you."
Just then, her phone rang. A 202 number. *Anna Orlova?*

"Aren't you going to get that?"

She shook her head. "It's just my mom. I'll call her back later."

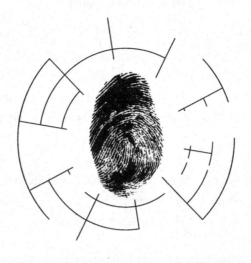

CHAPTER TWENTY-EIGHT

Mostafa cracked open another energy drink. It had been hours since his encounter with the security man outside the target's house. He should've stuck around and watched what, if anything, would happen next. But the encounter had been unnerving. Omar had portrayed this operation as a straightforward hit. The presence of security belied that narrative. Instead of remaining in the area, he'd gone home, changed his clothes, and headed over to the storage facility. To his dismay, the rental unit was empty except for a note from the supplier stating that he needed money to procure the supplies. After that, Mostafa had hurried home and dropped a message in the draft folder to alert his contact to this complication.

For the past hour, he'd been sitting in his car in a guest parking spot at a town house development one street over from the target's neighborhood. Through a row of silver maple trees planted an even eight feet apart, he was able to monitor activity outside her town house. He yawned. Surveillance work was tedious. When he entered the States over the southern border with a group of Central American migrants, he'd been full of optimism, grateful that his training in the mountains of Afghanistan would finally be put to good use. Unfortunately, reality turned out to be quite different from what he'd imagined it would be. For the past two years, he'd mostly done surveillance on government VIPs and written reports on security around federal buildings and national landmarks. His day job was with a landscaping company. The cash pay was decent, but barely enough to get by on in the wealthy suburbs of northern Virginia. A friend at the mosque had suggested he apply for government benefits, but he didn't want to elevate his profile and establish an official paper trail, even using his falsified documentation.

It had been a depressing couple of years, but today, Mostafa felt a glimmer of hope. If he succeeded in this mission, great things awaited him. Surely, he'd be well compensated for his efforts. He looked forward to moving to Florida. He'd never seen the ocean and tried to imagine the feel of waves and the smell of the salty air. And the girls in their bikinis. Beautiful, forbidden Western women.

He shook himself out of his reverie. He needed to focus and plan every step of the operation with meticulous detail. Sniping out the target was the most reasonable option, but his instructions were clear. It had to be a bomb.

A half hour earlier, he'd watched the black SUV with the tinted windows leave the target's neighborhood only minutes after an identical car had pulled up to the house. There was still no sign of Maggie Jenkins, the woman who'd killed several of the jihadists inside a local elementary school last year. The media said she was a CIA intelligence analyst, but he had his doubts. Given the outcome of the school siege, she must have some operational training. No doubt she was going to be a tough target to hit.

He was fiddling with the radio dial, trying to find music that didn't grind on his nerves, when movement outside the target's house caught his attention. Two figures emerged at the top of the steps. He felt around for the binoculars under the seat without taking his eyes off the activity across the street.

"Ah!" he cried in triumph. That had to be Maggie Jenkins. From this distance, what gave her away were the auburn curls that bounced with every step she took. With her was a dark-haired man in jeans and a red T-shirt. Just then, a second man, dressed like the security guard he'd encountered earlier, emerged from the SUV. Who was the guy in blue jeans? A boyfriend? Colleague? Relative? It didn't really matter. If he interfered with the operation in any way, he'd end up as collateral damage.

Mostafa watched as the target and the first man disappeared into a silver sedan. The security man hopped back into the SUV and pulled out behind the first vehicle. A moment of indecision hit. Should he follow the target or take advantage of no security to get a better look at the house? He opted for the latter, waiting five minutes to make sure they were truly gone. There was no telling how long they'd be away, so he left his car and began what he hoped looked like a leisurely stroll toward the target's town house.

The mailbox, he thought, as he neared. That might be the easiest way. He could walk or drive to the house and leave an explosive device inside a package. He veered over to the driveway, glanced up at the empty house, and opened the mailbox to get a feel for the dimensions. It looked big enough for a compact device. He could always buy a cheap mailbox at a home-renovation store to help size the bomb. He extracted a white envelope and saw that it was addressed to Maggie Jenkins. *Perfect.* Of course, there was no way to ensure that Maggie was the only one who opened her mail, but even if her security guard examined her packages before she opened them, most likely she'd be close enough to take the brunt of the explosion.

He closed the mailbox and studied the house to ensure that he wasn't missing another potential angle of attack. The steep front staircase appeared to be solidly built of concrete and brick with no storage space underneath in which to hide an explosive. Where was her car? She must have one of her own. Unfortunately, the garage door had no windows, so he trotted to the left of the driveway and jiggled the handle on a side door. If he wanted to see inside the garage, he'd have to break the lock, rig her car, and get out again without setting off an alarm or alerting the target that something was amiss.

Nope, he thought. Placing a bomb in her vehicle, assuming it was in the garage, was beyond the realm of practical. He walked to the edge of the driveway, his back to the target's house. From here, he could see his car parked in the development across the road, but it blended in well with the vehicles around it. It was a good spot from which to conduct surveillance. Over the next day or two, he'd watch for patterns and anomalies in the target's routine and use that information to plan and execute the attack.

With a final glance at the town house, he retraced his steps toward his car. Just as he crossed the road into the development where he'd parked, the black SUV came careening down the street at a speed well over the residential limit. Mostafa lowered his head and hurried to the car. He slid into the driver's seat and raised the binoculars to his face. The burly security guard was with yet another man in khakis and a blue shirt. How large was this security detail?

Mostafa watched as they peered into the hedges at the front of the house and checked the tiny side yards on either side of the structure.

When a woman emerged from the front door and pointed at the mail-box, Mostafa froze. Someone had been inside the house the entire time he was outside?

One of the men leaned into the SUV and came out with some-thing in his hands. Mostafa adjusted the focus on the binoculars. It looked like the man was putting on gloves. *My fingerprints!* How could he have been so careless? He watched as the man with the gloves opened the mailbox and peered inside. It looked like he was removing the envelopes and depositing them into a plastic bag. The woman on the porch then waved her arm and pointed to the road dividing the two neighborhoods. The security guard took off at a full sprint in his direction, but stopped suddenly and raised a phone to his ear. When the man turned around and shouted something to one of the others, Mostafa grabbed his bag and keys and slid out of the car, staying low to the ground.

About thirty yards away, to the left of the last row of town houses, stood a large rectangular wooden structure. Mostafa straightened and hurried toward it, resisting the urge to look back. As he got closer, he spotted a Recyclables Only sign posted on the front wall. He circled around and discovered that the structure had only three sides and was designed to conceal two blue dumpsters, one labeled Paper Goods, the other Plastics. The back was wide open, providing access to the dump-sters for residents and trash trucks.

Mostafa glanced across the street and spotted the black SUV pull-ing out of the woman's driveway. He slipped between the dumpster on the right and the wooden wall beside it and waited, listening for any approaching vehicles or men.

After an excruciating five minutes, he peered around the wall. Two people remained outside the target's town house, but the black SUV was gone. He heaved a sigh of relief and waited, concealed, for several more minutes.

Rather than draw attention to himself by driving away, he opted to leave his car hiding in plain sight. He skirted along the side of the row of town houses and calculated the way to the nearby convenience store. It should take less than ten minutes on foot. From there, he'd call a cab. He'd screwed up today. But the mistakes hadn't been fatal. He'd be back.

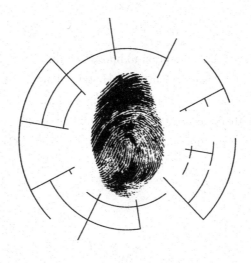

CHAPTER TWENTY-NINE

Makhachkala, Dagestan, Russia

Bukayev arrived at the café ten minutes after leaving the safe house. It was risky to go out in public like this, but he was feeling a bit claustrophobic. And he was starving. Plus, the café had internet access, so he could work and enjoy a good meal for once. He settled at a table in the corner, Turkish coffee in hand. Between the sorry excuse for a couch that he'd crashed on and the anxiety and excitement over finally having a plan to kill the Jenkins woman, he hadn't slept well. He sipped the rich, hot liquid. The strongest caffeine jolt possible would be key to getting him through the morning.

He logged into the email account he shared with Omar and frowned.

There is security outside her house. He says we might have to consider the second option.

No, his mind was made up. There was no other way. He replied.

Proceed with the plan. Get creative.

Shooting Jenkins, the second option, was a much less spectacular statement than a car bomb would be. Spectacular was what he needed.

While waiting for his food, he navigated to a British news site. He snickered at an article about the American president's upcoming speech in which he'd attempt to defend his Iraq policy. As if there was any defense for his imperialistic warmongering. What else? Ah, Wimbledon was well underway. He'd grown quite fond of tennis, and Wimbledon in particular, during his time in London. He'd even taken a few lessons and wasn't half bad for a man who'd never held a tennis racket until his late thirties. Playing tennis would enhance his social life in Jeddah. As would golf. He'd have to look into lessons.

Bukayev finished his coffee and navigated back to the email folder, surprised to find a reply already.

He says it will be almost impossible to put things in place because of the surrounding environment.

Annoyed that anyone would dare question his plan, Bukayev pounded his response: *I want Option 1, whether it involves the subject's vehicle or another one. Figure it out.*

If circumstances were such that the asset couldn't install an explosive device on Jenkins's car, then he needed to park a car bomb nearby and be sure it detonated at the right time. A car bomb in suburban Washington might be a bit of overkill, but the message would be loud and clear. You kill our people, we kill yours. As he closed the laptop, the cafe's door jangled. In walked two police officers, one laughing at something the other said. He couldn't hear them, not with the rush of air pulsing through his ears. He had to get out. Lowering his head, he shuffled from the café, hoping he'd look like a much older man than he was. Outside, and out of the view of the officers, he straightened and broke out in a cold sweat in the warm morning sunshine.

Back at the apartment, there was another draft email from Omar.

The supplier is demanding payment before he delivers supplies.

Bukayev unleashed a string of curses.

How much?

Fifteen minutes later, he had his answer.

$20K.

Twenty thousand dollars? That greedy little bastard would be eliminated as soon as this operation was over. There were ways to get the necessary supplies without money changing hands until later, but there was no time for haggling. It would be best to strike while the iron was hot. He wanted Maggie Jenkins dead before the fatwa story faded from the headlines.

I have the routing number. The money will be there soon. $10K now. The rest after it's done.

He shut the laptop. He knew what he had to do next.

Bukayev found Rasul at the safe house, packing up his few belongings. It was time to move again.

Bukayev despised not being able to settle. Not that any of the places he'd been had been worth settling into. "Why not stay here another few days? There's no sign that the Russians know where you are, Rasul."

"That's because I move so frequently." He checked the chamber on his 9mm Makarov before tucking it into the back of his cargo pants. "You're welcome to join me."

Bukayev gave a tight-lipped smile. "I've hired someone to carry out the fatwa."

Rasul brightened. "So, you're really going through with it?"

"I am."

"When will this happen, Imran?"

"Within the week."

Rasul surveyed the living room, presumably checking for stray belongings he needed to pack. "Congratulations, my friend."

"Thank you. I'm optimistic. But there's a slight logistical problem I must resolve first."

Rasul turned his gaze to his mentor.

"I have to pay my supplier, but I can't access my bank accounts without raising suspicion."

Rasul sighed. "I'm not made of money, Imran. You know that. All my financing comes from outside sources."

"I understand. My situation is similar."

"Then why not ask your network to send money?"

Because they've given up on me, he wanted to shout. Instead, he offered a shrug. "Too many eyes and ears are on them right now."

Rasul didn't appear convinced.

"Fortunately, the intelligence agencies have no idea that we're working together again."

"Are we working together?" Rasul looked surprised.

Bukayev waved his hand around. "We're here, aren't we?"

Rasul chewed on his bottom lip. "How much money do you need?"

"Forty thousand." Double what he needed.

Rasul paled under his beard. "Forty?"

"I'm afraid so. Consider it a loan. Once I get to my new base in the Middle East, I'll have full access to all my accounts."

"And you'll repay us then?"

"Of course," Bukayev said with a smile. But only if he was provided with the resources he needed to live in comfort. He fully expected the royal treatment from his al-Qaeda benefactors to resume once Maggie Jenkins's death made international news.

"Okay. Where do we send the funds?"

"I'll give you the routing number as soon as we can connect to the internet." It was a struggle to keep the excitement from his voice. "You will be rewarded greatly, Rasul."

"Indeed. In the meantime, perhaps you can do me a favor."

Bukayev stiffened. "Perhaps."

"How about you drive me to the next safe house location?"

He relaxed. "I'd be happy to."

"In your stolen car?" Rasul winked.

"It's borrowed."

"Daud would like it back."

If only he had more resources at hand, he'd make Daud disappear. But there was no way to do that without Rasul figuring out that he was responsible.

"Does Daud know where you're staying next?"

"Yes. He arranges all my accommodations."

Bukayev wanted to laugh. Accommodations? As if any of the places Rasul stayed were luxurious getaways. "As long as there's internet access, he can have his car back."

Rasul zipped up his bag and heaved it over his shoulder. "Very well, then. I'll let him know that we are picking him up and that his car will be returned once we're settled into the new place."

As Bukayev pulled up to Karina's house, he saw Daud standing outside, his face twisted in a scowl.

"Perhaps you should let him drive," Rasul suggested. "He knows where we're going, and it's his car."

Bukayev swallowed the irritation he felt bubbling up and stepped out of the idling vehicle. He shot the young Chechen a look through narrowed eyes. A look he hoped would instill fear.

Daud ignored Bukayev as he greeted Rasul with a hearty hello.

Bukayev shoved aside empty food wrappers and sank into the backseat directly behind Daud. He focused on the route, determined to get a better understanding of where they were going in case he needed to make a quick exit. It soon became clear that they were headed back into the city.

That upped the odds of him having internet access but made him feel more exposed and vulnerable. The law-enforcement presence seemed to be more widespread than it had been just two days ago. He spotted police cars at every major intersection leading into the city and sank lower in the seat. "Why all the police?"

Rasul rifled through his duffel. He pulled a cap over his head and slid sunglasses over his eyes. "There have been many attacks against law enforcement in Dagestan this year. Perhaps they heard that more are imminent." He laughed.

Bukayev tensed. "Are you planning something?" If Rasul was going to launch attacks, the manhunt for him would become more intense, putting everyone around him at greater risk.

"Maybe."

Bukayev fought the urge to flatten himself against the length of the backseat, to hide like a scared child. The Russians didn't even know he was in Dagestan. Rasul, on the other hand, was widely believed to be in the republic. He and his Shariat Jamaat organization had engaged in a widespread campaign of violence against local police and Russian security forces, leaving dozens dead the previous year and even more dead only halfway into this year.

"Rasul, you must tell me if you're planning an attack. We shouldn't be together if you are. Imagine the propaganda win for the Russians if they caught the two of us at once."

Rasul craned his neck to look Bukayev in the eye. "They'll never catch me. Unless Allah wills it."

Or unless you screw up. That's when he noticed that Daud, although acting unfazed by the police presence, was gripping the steering wheel so tightly that the skin on his knuckles had faded from tan to bone white.

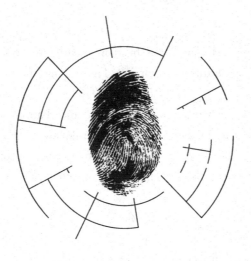

CHAPTER THIRTY

CIA Headquarters, Langley, Virginia

Maggie stared at the computer screen, unable to make sense of the words before her. A message on her work voice mail had left her rattled. There'd been another incident at the house. The so-called jogger had returned to the neighborhood, this time acting even more suspiciously.

"Hey." Roger touched her shoulder.

She yelped. "Don't sneak up on me, Roger."

"I'm a spy. I get paid to sneak." He disappeared for a moment into the adjacent cubicle and returned with a chair, which he placed right next to hers.

"Any update from Daud?" She was desperate for good news.

"Nothing." He shook his head in frustration. "I should be in Dagestan. 'Cause this isn't working. The waiting, the sporadic communication."

Maggie slouched against the back of the chair. "I agree. If we wait to get a team in place, Bukayev might slip away." She swiveled to face Roger. "You know," she began, trying to make it sound like the idea had just occurred to her. "There are other ways we can get to Bukayev."

Roger leaned toward her. "Like?"

She edged forward in the chair, mirroring his body language. "We're not the only ones looking for him."

"You mean the Russians?"

"They want him dead just as much as we do, if not more, Roger."

"Unfortunately, it would take both luck and competence for the Russians to find him." His shoulders sagged. "And we don't have the luxury of waiting for someone else to do our dirty work. Not that I would mind seeing the Russians take Bukayev out in a hail of bullets."

"What if I told you that I know someone." She lowered her voice. "A Russian."

Roger crinkled his nose. "What are you talking about?"

Maggie laced her fingers together. "Anna Orlova."

"Who?"

"Anna Orlova," she said, her tone more insistent. "She's a Russian reporter. But I think she might be SVR."

Roger stiffened. "A spy? How do you know a Russian—"

"I don't know her per se," Maggie explained. "I saw her last week at Warner's confirmation hearing. She seems to know Senator Canton personally."

"Politicians love friendly media," Roger offered.

"Yes, but cozying up to a Russian reporter? There has to be a reason for it. The senator isn't stupid."

Roger tilted his head. "Never underestimate the stupidity of elected officials."

"Believe me, I don't."

Roger rubbed his eyes and stifled a yawn. "I still don't get it, Maggie. How do you know this reporter is a Russian spy?"

"At the confirmation hearing, I saw this Orlova woman and the senator huddled together, chatting about something. Then the next thing I knew, Senator Canton lobbed the grenade about Warner and me being inside the school."

He paused to think for a moment. "That information wasn't in the FBI's report about the siege, was it?"

"Our names weren't, which means someone told the senator." She recalled the smile on Anna Orlova's flawless face as the commotion grew inside the hearing room. "My money's on Orlova."

Roger looked skeptical. "Why's she your prime suspect?"

"Because of the way they were interacting. Because of the fact that the senator blurted out my name moments after talking to the Russian." *Because my instincts are almost always right.* "After I finished testifying, Orlova had the nerve to ask if I'd sit down for an interview for Russian television. She fed me some line about how the Russian people would want to know more about me since I'm the one who killed Zara." Last fall, Russia had conducted a massive manhunt for the female jihadist who'd participated in a school attack in Beslan, Russia. But Zara had slipped through the dragnet, made her way to London to meet up with Bukayev, and then traveled to the US to lead another attack, this time on Dominion Elementary school.

Roger scratched at the stubble on his chin. "Let me backtrack for a second. You think that Anna Orlova gave your name to Senator Canton. How could a Russian journalist possibly know that you and Warner were inside the school?"

"Svetlana Markova."

"Markova." He squinted at her. "Yuri Markov's daughter?"

"Yes. She's a teacher at the school. I talked to her earlier today. Turns out a woman named Anna, who claimed to be from the Russian consulate, showed up unannounced at Svetlana's house last week."

Roger's mouth fell open. "What did she want?"

"According to Svetlana, Anna wanted to check on her, to make sure she was doing well in the aftermath of the attack. They chatted about that day, and guess who Anna asked about?"

"You?"

"Yes. She asked Svetlana what she knew about the woman who had killed the terrorists. Svetlana couldn't remember my name, but she described me. And she told Anna about a CIA official being wounded in the siege."

"Warner?" he asked.

"Yeah. Apparently, the school principal let Warner's name slip."

"Damn." Roger frowned. "It's kind of a miracle that your name didn't leak before now."

"I know. The FBI talked to all the teachers and explained the need for silence. And not only that—they encouraged them to refer to me as Megan in their interactions with students. That way, if any of the kids talked about the attack, no one would figure out that 'Megan' was really me."

"Clever."

"Yeah, but not clever enough to keep Anna Orlova from figuring it out."

"Let's say you're right, that Anna got your name from Svetlana. Why leak it to the senator? Why not just approach you directly to ask if you'd talk to the Russian media about Zara and the school siege?"

That's when it hit her. "Maybe because she doesn't really want to talk to me about Zara. Maybe leaking my name is only part one of her plan."

"Then what's part two?"

"Warner's nomination."

"Meaning?" Roger prompted

"Meaning Anna Orlova told Senator Canton to leak the information about me shooting Warner."

"But why?"

"Russia is desperate for some wins in its own war on terror. They've got the Chechens to deal with. The Dagestanis. Multiple other domestic hot spots. And with their record of human rights abuses, they don't want us watching their every move. What better way to make sure our intelligence isn't paying attention to whatever Putin is doing than to sow trouble for a new CIA director who just happens to be very hawkish on Russia?"

Roger ran a hand across his chin. "So, Anna Orlova leaks this information to try to wound Warner before he has a chance to settle into office."

"Exactly. If the CIA director is damaged goods, his influence at 1600 Pennsylvania Avenue will be diminished. Other intelligence agencies will jostle for primacy. Warner won't have the authority he needs or the ear of the president. Every time he speaks publicly or testifies before Congress, there will be doubts about him."

"I can hear it now. Warner Thompson, the CIA director, who still hasn't explained why he was involved in an illegal domestic operation inside an elementary school. And not only that—his own chief of staff shot him."

Maggie cringed. That's precisely what the media and Warner's political opponents would say. "Do me a favor and don't remind me that I shot my boss."

"Duly noted." He winked but immediately grew serious. "Why would a US senator do the bidding of a Russian journalist? I mean, Canton hates the CIA, but is that enough of a reason?"

Maggie looked up at the acoustic ceiling tiles. "I don't know. Maybe Orlova has something on the senator, some leverage over her."

"Maybe." He closed his eyes for a moment. "I still don't understand what any of this has to do with getting Bukayev."

Maggie stood and peered out beyond the cubicle wall to make sure no coworkers had shown up on a late Sunday afternoon to get a jump on the next day's work. "Orlova says she knows where Bukayev is."

Roger looked up at her. "Why on earth would you trust what she says? If this woman knows where Bukayev is, why hasn't she informed Moscow? He's Russia's most wanted terrorist, after all."

Maggie hadn't considered that. "I have no idea."

Roger leaned forward, elbows on knees. "Let's say that this woman is, in fact, a spy. Think of it from her perspective. Your name is leaked. Now you're vulnerable. Quite literally in danger. She knows you work in some sort of intelligence capacity, so she throws Bukayev's name out there to see if you'll take the bait."

"You think she's trying to recruit me?"

"Dunno." He leaned back in the chair, clasped his hands behind his head, and closed his eyes again.

"Anna goes to our gym."

His eyelids flew open.

"Works out at the same time as me."

"Did you see her there before Warner's nomination?"

"Now that I think back, yes. She was always off to the side, on the periphery of what I was doing. A couple machines away. In the next room. I didn't pick up on it because—"

"Because why would you? You had no reason to think anyone would be watching."

"And she *has* been watching." She grabbed her purse.

"What are you doing?"

"Getting my phone. I need to talk to Anna Orlova." She hurried out of the cubicle.

"That's a horrible idea," he called. "Don't do it, Maggie."

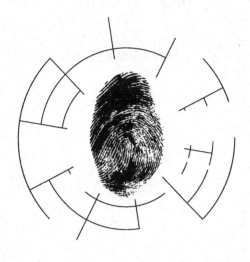

CHAPTER THIRTY-ONE

Makhachkala, Dagestan, Russia

Inside a first-floor apartment, Bukayev lowered himself onto an overstuffed chair. Of all the safe houses he'd been to in the past week, this one was by far the cleanest and most modern. It was nowhere near his standards, of course, but he could stay here comfortably for a few days if necessary.

Daud rustled about in the kitchen preparing a pot of tea while Rasul showered. *Praise Allah for that*, Bukayev thought.

"Tea is ready," Daud offered from the adjacent kitchen.

What he really needed was a stiff drink, not tea, but he thought better of polishing off the vodka bottle that was stashed in his rucksack, at least in front of Rasul. Bukayev pulled a chair away from the table and eyed the young Chechen as he arranged and rearranged the sugar bowl and teacups on the table.

"There's an internet dial-up connection in the living room," Daud said without making eye contact.

"Hmph," Bukayev replied as he selected a cup and waited for Daud to pour.

"I'm sorry about the car, Imran. I overreacted. I know your business is very important."

Bukayev smiled to himself. He was the one who'd taken the car and yet here Daud was apologizing. "I no longer need it."

Daud poured the tea. "Well, if you do, it's all yours."

Bukayev sniffed. Daud was weak. Even if he was as loyal as Rasul insisted, weakness was a liability. He sipped at the tea and kept his eyes fixed on the Chechen.

Daud shifted.

Rasul emerged, shirtless, hair and beard dripping wet. "Ah, much better. I'm refreshed and ready to fight the enemy another day." He flexed a considerable bicep and kissed it.

Bukayev rolled his eyes. "Hurry up before your tea gets cold."

Rasul snatched a black T-shirt from his duffel bag, sniffed it, shrugged, and pulled it over his head before sitting down at the table. "Is everything good here?" He waved a hand between Bukayev and Daud.

"Everything is good," Bukayev answered. "For now." He had no intention of letting Daud fully relax. Better to keep that flicker of fear in him. It might just keep him in line.

Daud blinked and studied the steam rising from his cup.

"What's next, Rasul? Your entire plan can't consist of simply moving from safe house to safe house."

Rasul tilted his head from one shoulder to the other, eliciting a crack from his neck. "You were onto something on the ride over,

Imran. Security is elevated because of threats against the police. Naturally, when the threat level goes up, the police deploy more officers and the Russians send in more FSB." He smiled broadly. "As a result, casualties are likely to be even higher. You'd think they'd understand what not to do by now."

Bukayev gripped his teacup a little tighter. He had nothing against Rasul's little war of attrition against the Russians and their Dagestani collaborators, but it seemed petty, almost pointless. His tactics betrayed a stunning lack of strategic planning. Of course, this came as no surprise to Bukayev. He'd struggled mightily several years ago to help Rasul see the bigger picture. It would be more effective if he sent men to fight the Russians in Chechnya rather than engaging in haphazard attacks in Dagestan that didn't move the needle toward independence for Muslims living in the Caucasus. At least in Chechnya, his people were engaged in actual urban warfare, not just sporadic attacks against police and Russian federal security officers. Chechen freedom fighters had humiliated the Russians on the international stage and proven them to be brutish thugs who would do anything to repress an already oppressed people.

"Keep me apprised, Rasul. If we need to scatter and go into hiding, I'd like as much warning as possible. I cannot be captured or killed until I've carried out the fatwa." Bukayev glanced sidelong at Daud, who flinched and blinked rapidly at the mention of it. "What do you think the reaction will be to the American woman's death?"

Daud busied himself pouring more tea. Bukayev noted a tremor in his pouring hand.

"Here?" Rasul said. "If the Russians don't suppress the news, there will be joy. Any time one of our enemies is slain, we celebrate."

"What do you think, Daud? You lived in America for many years. How will the Americans react to one of their heroes cut down in the prime of her life?"

"Umm," he stammered. "I think that . . . that the Americans will be scared."

"Scared?"

"Yes." He nodded vigorously. "If someone like that woman isn't safe, then no one will feel safe."

"Hmmm. Perhaps you're right." He tapped a finger on his upper lip. "It would be helpful to have a firsthand report from the States, don't you think, Rasul?"

Rasul looked confused.

"Maybe we should have someone on the ground when the fatwa is carried out. Someone like our friend Daud."

Daud paled. "It wouldn't be safe for me to go back, Imran. I don't know what the Americans know about me. And you. My role in—"

"Beslan? Dominion Elementary?"

Daud nodded, his eyes wide.

Bukayev had no plans to send Daud anywhere. Not with the nagging feeling that something was terribly off about him. "I have other resources available, but if it becomes necessary, of course you'll go."

Rasul frowned. "Daud is the one who keeps me safe on the run. I need him."

Bukayev finished the last of his tea and stood without another word. He returned to the living room, where he unpacked the laptop and connected it to the modem. Several minutes later, he opened his draft email folder and read a new message from Omar.

Any update on the payment?

He returned to the kitchen. "Rasul, about the matter we discussed earlier, the transaction?"

Rasul swirled the tea in his cup and exhaled dramatically. "You're so uptight about everything, Imran. I said I'd do it, didn't I?" He ran a meaty hand across his lips. "I'll make the necessary call this evening."

Bukayev dug his fingernails into his palms. He wanted to throttle Rasul. Instead, he returned to the laptop and replied to the message.

Payment coming this evening.

He closed the browser window and opened a Word document containing his personal bank information. He considered asking Daud about the risk associated with such a large transfer of money. After all, Daud had handled the flow of funds for the Beslan and American school attacks. Risky or not, time was running short. The asset needed to be paid so the fatwa could be executed.

"Rasul," he called from the living room. "It really can't wait. My asset is ready to strike the target, but he can't move without the money." Bukayev heard Rasul ask Daud to take a walk outside. Then he stomped into the living room and plopped himself on the sofa, cell phone in hand, a scowl on his face.

"Is there a problem, Rasul?"

"You seem to forget that we're equals now, Imran. I no longer jump when you snap your fingers."

Rasul was like an ungrateful child. He'd be nowhere without Bukayev's mentorship. Anger bubbled up inside him, but he knew he had to remain calm if he hoped to get the money transferred. "I apologize, Rasul. It's just that this operation against Maggie Jenkins is very time sensitive. I can't let her get away. Not after everything she's done."

Rasul chewed on his lower lip, then dialed a number and spoke in rapid Avaric, a local Dagestani language, and one of more than forty spoken in the republic. He paused and looked at Bukayev. "The routing number?" he asked in Russian.

Bukayev hesitated a moment when he thought he heard a noise near the apartment door. *Must be hearing things.* He turned to the computer screen and rattled off the number.

Rasul repeated it back to the person on the other end and disconnected the call.

Bukayev smiled. "Thank you, my friend. Your funds will be returned as soon as I can access my accounts safely. And your reward will be great in paradise."

"*Inshallah.*" With that, Rasul picked up the remote sitting on the table in front of him, turned on the television, and propped his feet on the coffee table.

Bukayev checked his bank account. This was the only one of his accounts that the British hadn't frozen. It was buried deep enough under layers of front companies that it had escaped their notice. He was down to his last $50,000. He'd send $20,000 to the asset now and keep the rest for himself. By the time Rasul realized he hadn't been reimbursed, Bukayev would be out of reach, living in luxury in Jeddah. *Inshallah.*

He filled out the online form to make a wire transfer to the asset's account, which appeared to belong to a small import-export business in New York City. A shiver went through him as he hit the send button. *This one's for you, Zara.*

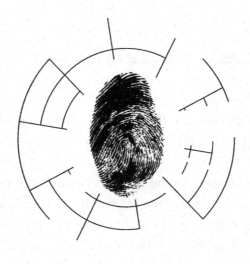

CHAPTER THIRTY-TWO

Capitol Hill, Washington, DC, Sunday, June 19, 2005

Maggie fiddled with the zipper on her purse. She was nervous and felt more than a little bit guilty. Other than leaving Wendy a voice mail last summer congratulating her on the birth of her baby boy, she'd avoided contact with her friend and former Capitol Hill colleague. Wendy had moved from the House Intelligence Committee to the Senate Intelligence Committee early last year, shortly after Maggie left the Hill to join the CIA. Both of them had sought a fresh start and a change of scenery after the death of Congressman Carvelli, albeit for wildly different reasons. Maggie left because Steve's murder and Carvelli's death hung over her like a dense, choking fog.

Wendy left because she was the bereaved, pregnant mistress of a dead congressman.

"Thanks for driving me, Mike."

"Yup." Mike, the second shift security officer, had the personality of a doorknob.

Only a few hours ago, Maggie had realized that it was Wendy's birthday. She'd called to wish her a happy birthday, but that wasn't the only reason she'd contacted her. She wanted to ask Wendy about Senator Canton. She'd offered to take Wendy out to dinner, but she'd declined, saying it was too difficult to get a babysitter with so little notice. That's when Wendy suggested that they order takeout and eat at her place. Her place, a posh Capitol Hill brownstone, had belonged to Congressman Richard Carvelli.

Mike pulled up at ten minutes past seven. Maggie sat staring out the passenger window, fists clenched in her lap. The last time she'd been to this house, she'd been shot, and Warner had nearly bled out from his wounds. The terror of thinking Warner was going to die had faded, but now, outside the scene of the crime, the memory enveloped her like a dark mist.

"You going in?" Mike asked.

She exhaled loudly. "Yeah. I just need a moment." She sat in silence for a bit longer before finally working up the courage to march up the front steps.

Wendy threw open the door. A baby boy sat, squirming, on her hip.

"Hi!" Maggie said as enthusiastically as she could. Her eyes immediately went to the child. He had the dark features of the late congressman, but the shape of his eyes and his mouth were all Wendy. "Hi there," she said to the baby in a singsong voice.

"Maggie, it's so great to see you. Come on in."

She took in the spacious living room, her heart pounding wildly in her chest. Over there, against the wall, was where she'd slumped to the floor after the bullet had entered her shoulder. And beyond the couch was the dining area, where she'd stood and pumped multiple bullets into the traitorous congressman.

"Are you okay?" Wendy placed her free hand on Maggie's shoulder. "You look awfully pale."

"Yeah," Maggie replied trying to steady her voice. "It's just that the last time I was here, it was . . . terrible." Her eyes locked into Wendy's cornflower-blue eyes. There was nothing but sympathy there, no suspicion, no anger. Clearly, she didn't know. The official, unclassified report about Richard Carvelli's death concluded that he'd been killed by a Russian spy who was trying to extort him.

Wendy didn't have the clearances necessary to review the classified report. And even if she did, the truth about Richard Carvelli, the father of her baby, was so tightly held that she'd probably never learn that he had sold his country's secrets and ordered the death of Maggie's fiancé.

"I know it was awful for you." Wendy surveyed the living room behind her.

Maggie noted that Wendy hadn't changed much of the decor. The baby gate at the foot of the stairs and jumble of toys spilling out of a toy box were incongruous amid Carvelli's high-end furniture.

"But I feel at peace here. Like Richard is with us, or something." She kissed the squirming baby on his head. "I know you, of all people, would understand."

Yeah, Maggie thought. *Except Steve wasn't killed in our house. And he wasn't a traitor to his country.* She forced a smile. This was going to be a long night.

"Here." Wendy extended the baby toward Maggie. "Hold him so I can order the food."

"Only if you let me treat you for your birthday."

"Works for me."

Maggie took the baby under his arms and shifted him to her hip. "Wow, he's heavy."

"Already eating me out of house and home and he won't turn one for another ten days," Wendy called over her shoulder as she disappeared into the kitchen.

The baby reached for Maggie's head, grabbed a fistful of curls, and yanked.

She gasped and pried chubby little fingers off her hair. The baby looked up at her, his face in a pout. She bounced him, hoping it would keep him happy, or at least prevent him from wailing for his mother.

Steve had wanted a big family.

Maggie hadn't been so sure.

Children seemed like so much work. It occurred to her that she didn't know if Roger wanted kids or if he'd been joking about turning the beach house loft into a kids' room. Not that she was ready to discuss such matters with him.

Wendy reappeared with a takeout menu in hand. "They have these platters with tacos and enchiladas and fajitas—"

"Sounds great," Maggie said as she moved her hair away from the baby's searching fingers.

"No pulling Auntie Maggie's hair, Richie," Wendy admonished before vanishing back down the hall.

"Auntie Maggie?" she muttered. "I don't think so." She lowered herself onto the couch and let the baby stand on the floor next to her legs, his hands on the seat cushion for support. "Don't turn out like your daddy," she advised, her voice barely above a whisper. Wendy was sweet, if too trusting a soul.

If there was any consolation in this child's father being dead, it was that Wendy would make a far better parent than he ever would have.

Wendy returned with two glasses of wine. "All set."

"Thanks," Maggie said, grateful that her babysitting stint was short lived. Once Wendy had settled on the opposite end of the couch, she began with a few softball questions. "So, you really like it here?"

"I do. Obviously, I wish Richard was alive, but we're doing our best, aren't we, baby?" She ruffled the boy's dark curls. "It's such a blessing to have this house."

Blessing? Maggie had read every sordid detail about Wendy's lawsuit against Congressman Carvelli's estate in the *Washington Post*. All his money was supposed to go to his mother. But then a woman surfaced, claiming that he had fathered her child. And then a second woman. Because Carvelli had no siblings, the estate lawyer was forced to petition for a DNA sample from the congressman's dementia-riddled mother. It turned out that Carvelli wasn't the father of the children in question, although no one had any reason to doubt that he'd bedded both women, and then some. That's when Wendy surfaced, and the world learned about the existence of little Richie. The *Post*'s gossip column had a field day. If the media stories were accurate, Wendy ended up with half of Carvelli's estate, including his swanky Capitol Hill brownstone. The rest went to care for his ailing mother.

"How do you like working for the Senate Intel Committee?"

Wendy sipped her wine and handed Richie a bright blue rattle that she'd plucked from the floor. "It's fine. But it would be more fun if you were there. So many stuffy people compared to the House side of the Hill."

Maggie dodged the rattle as it escaped Richie's hand and came flying her way. "What are the senators like? Are they approachable or do they act all high and mighty?"

"Some are down to earth. Others are, you know." She stuck her nose in the air. "The chairman is nice. A bit intense, but at least he's not a jerk." She jumped up. "Let me grab some more wine. I want to hear all about you."

Maggie sagged against the back of the couch. She wasn't here to talk about herself. But she also didn't want to seem too eager to dig for dirt on Senator Canton.

Wendy returned and topped off both their glasses. "So . . . tell me what's going on in your life."

"I'm seeing someone."

"Ooh," Wendy squealed. "Is it serious?"

"We're exclusively dating, but we're not talking marriage or anything."

"Is he hot?"

"Mm-hmm."

They burst out laughing, and for a moment it felt like they were back on Capitol Hill, trading stories over coffee before everyone else got to the office.

Before everything went horribly wrong.

Maggie steered the conversation back to the Senate. "I think Warner will be confirmed as CIA director early this week."

"Good news for you, I assume. Being so close to the boss?"

Maggie leaned forward and lowered her voice. "Between us, because it's not official yet, I'm going to be his chief of staff."

Wendy's jaw dropped. "That's fantastic."

"Honestly, I'm a little nervous. But excited. I may need your advice from time to time."

"Advice? You're the superstar, Maggie, not me."

"Oh, please," she said as she poured the rest of the wine into Wendy's glass. "You have the inside track on the Senate Intelligence Committee. Maybe you could help me out."

"How?" Wendy asked.

"You could provide some insight into what makes certain senators tick. How we can convince them to fund a program. Things like that. It would be a great help to Warner."

Wendy smiled, clearly flattered. "Sure."

"Like that Senator Canton. What does she have against Warner, anyway?"

"Oh," Wendy waved a hand in dismissal. "She's not that bad. Loves the camera though. And to make headlines. You know what I mean?"

"I know the type." Maggie put down her glass and played a couple rounds of peekaboo with Richie, much to his delight.

"Some of them are prickly old bastards. If they're not talking down to me like I'm some silly airhead, they're hitting on me."

Maggie rolled her eyes. "You should tell them where to stick it."

"I try to ignore them."

"You have any allies? Any other women you can confide in?"

She shrugged. "Not really. There are a couple of recent college grads, but they're wrapped up in their social lives. The other women are older. I'm the only young mother."

Maggie swirled the wine in her glass.

"Maybe one of the older women has had to deal with boorish senators too."

Wendy chewed on her lip.

"How many female senators are on the committee?" She already knew the answer.

"Three," Wendy said as she swiped at drool running down the baby's chin.

"Senator Canton's pretty outspoken on women's issues, isn't she?"

Wendy thought for a moment. "You know, you're right. She is."

Maggie squinted. "Come to think of it, she seemed very friendly with another staffer about your age."

Wendy took a large gulp of wine and placed Richie on her lap. "Really, who?"

"I don't know who she is. I saw them at Warner's confirmation hearing. A very attractive blonde woman. Young. Tiny little thing."

"Ohhh, her. She's not a staffer." Wendy pressed her lips together. "I shouldn't."

Maggie kicked up her best girls-night-out vibe. "Shouldn't what?" She drew a line across her lips with her forefinger and thumb pinched together. "Whatever it is, I won't tell a soul."

"I need more wine first."

Maggie jumped up and hurried to the kitchen for a fresh bottle, which she used to refill Wendy's empty glass.

Wendy lowered the baby to the floor, tucked a leg under her, and took a substantial swig. "This goes nowhere, right?"

"You know me. I'm the world's best secret keeper." In a conversation full of deception, this, at least, was true.

"Okay, well . . . about a month ago, I was working late to get ready for a hearing. I thought everyone had gone home, but when I went to leave, I heard voices in the conference room. I couldn't make them out, but I could tell there were at least two people."

Maggie nodded, encouraging her to continue.

"There are two doors into the conference room. The one off the main hall was shut. I figured maybe there was an emergency meeting or something. Not my business. So, I went all the way around to the other side of the hall to the kitchenette to make sure the coffeemaker was off."

Maggie leaned forward.

"Well, the other door into the conference room is off the kitchenette. And it wasn't shut tight. I heard someone gasp and I probably shouldn't have, but I peeked."

"What did you see?"

"Swear you won't tell anyone?"

"I swear."

"Senator Canton and that woman were going at it."

"You mean—"

"Yup. Making out, fumbling at blouse buttons." Wendy dropped her head into her hand. "I mean, it's fine. It's . . . whatever they want to do in private." She giggled nervously. "I just had no idea that Senator Canton—"

"She's married."

"I know," Wendy added, "with kids. There was a big spread about her and her picture-perfect family in the *Post*'s Lifestyle section a couple of months ago. Who would've guessed?"

No one, except, it seemed, Anna Orlova.

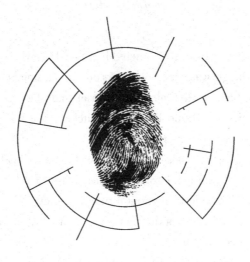

CHAPTER THIRTY-THREE

Vienna, Virginia, Monday, June 20, 2005

Maggie rolled over and groaned. She wouldn't feel this awful if she and Wendy had stopped drinking after dinner. Instead, they'd polished off another bottle and a half of wine. She had a fuzzy memory of being in the SUV with Mike, the security man of few words, singing every song on the radio. She powered up her phone. Four missed calls and one voice mail from Roger.

"I came by late to see you. The security goon wouldn't let me in because I'm not on the list. What list? Put me on it so I can get in. And call me. I miss you."

The night guard must've tightened up security after the mailbox incident. Although she missed hanging out with Roger, she was relieved that security hadn't let him into the house last night. His lingering sorrow over losing Jane still bothered her. She'd been dead for almost four years. Maggie was nearly two years out from losing Steve, yet Roger seemed to be no further along in his grief than she was.

Downstairs, she found Rich at the kitchen table. "Morning," he said, peering over the newspaper.

"Morning," she croaked as she brewed a cup of coffee. "I hope Mike's not upset with me. I got a little drunk last night."

"Mmmm," he offered without further comment.

"I don't usually . . . not during the week anyway."

Rich flipped the page.

"I think I'll hit the gym before work, if that's okay." Maybe a good sweat would clear some of the alcohol from her system.

He folded the newspaper. "Let me know when you're ready."

"Is everything okay, Rich?"

"We'll talk in the car."

"I was going to take the Jeep."

"No can do. Now that there've been two incidents outside your house, we'll be driving you everywhere."

"Great," she muttered as she grabbed her coffee and headed upstairs, feeling like a grounded teenager who'd lost her driving privileges.

"It's for your safety," he called.

Of course it was, but she was already tired of all the constraints on her life. She couldn't wait to get Rich and the others out of her house and out of her business.

· ★ ★ ★ ·

Tyson's Fitness and Health Club, McLean, Virginia

They drove in silence on the way to the gym. After he pulled into his usual spot, Rich threw the car into park and turned to Maggie. "I heard your boyfriend was a bit unhinged last night."

She braced herself. "What happened?"

"Roger showed up looking for you while you were at your friend's house. He demanded to know the latest on the mailbox suspect and why we haven't caught the guy yet."

Maggie's already queasy stomach flipped. "He can be a little . . . intense when it comes to protecting me."

"That's only half the story. He came back later and was even more . . . let's just say, confrontational. If he pulls something like that again, we'll have to take it to the director."

"What, exactly, did he do?"

"He shoved his way past the night crew, demanding to see the surveillance footage. Demanding to see you. A fistfight almost broke out."

Maggie blanched. She hadn't heard a thing. All that wine had knocked her out cold. She wanted to explain to Rich. How Roger had lost a girlfriend to terrorists. How he thought Maggie was going to die inside that school last year. But Rich was not her confessor, and he wouldn't care what motivated Roger. He had one job—to keep her safe—and anyone who disrupted that was a liability. "I'll talk to him." Warner would understand Roger's state of mind, but he wouldn't tolerate his behavior.

And they needed him on the case, especially with them so close to nabbing Bukayev.

Maggie had been so absorbed with the news of Roger's temper tantrum that she'd forgotten to scan the parking lot for Anna's BMW. Inside the gym, she checked all the workout rooms. And there she was, on the ab machine in the weight room. *Let her chase me*, she thought. The more she acted like she was avoiding Anna, the more Anna would pursue her. Or so she hoped.

After a three-mile treadmill run and a 3,000-meter row, the fog began to lift. She waved to Rich on her way to the locker room and slipped into the last shower stall on the left. Five minutes later, Maggie wrapped a towel around her head and stared into the mirror. Roger wouldn't be happy if he knew what she was doing.

"You shouldn't talk to Anna Orlova at all, not even about the weather," he'd said the previous day. *"No offense, but you're not trained in how to handle a Russian intelligence officer."*

Maggie thought back to when she first joined the Agency. Intelligence analysts had the same basic orientation training as operations officers, although people like Roger received much more intensive surveillance and countersurveillance training. Still, she'd been taught the basics.

Be alert for unusual encounters with strangers. Avoid falling into obvious patterns, like leaving home at the same time and taking the same route to work every day. Report close and continuing contact with foreign nationals, no matter how benign the encounters may seem.

Her incoming class of Agency recruits had been warned to avoid specific bars and restaurants that were known hangouts for Russian intelligence officers. So where did the new hires gather for their first happy hour? At one of the denoted watering holes. Maggie was on high alert the entire time, trying to pick out the foreign spies in the bar's dim lighting. The result? A solid hangover resulting from too many white Russians and vodka shots.

She shook her head at the memory and considered the current situation. After the initial rush she'd felt working in the top secret world, her attention to the basics had slipped. She left the house at the same time every day. Went to the gym nearly every morning at the same time. And failed to report her encounters with Anna Orlova up the proper chain of command. She would, though. After she talked to her about Imran Bukayev.

She pulled off the towel, sending damp curls tumbling down to her shoulders. *Come on, Anna.* What the hell was she doing out there?

Training for a triathlon? It wouldn't be long before Rich checked in on her.

"Good morning," Maggie said to a woman who gave a small wave as she passed on her way out of the locker room. She smoothed some foundation over her face and moved on to mascara. Still no Anna. This was the second time in as many days that she would've noticed Rich sitting in the lobby. Had his presence spooked her? If Anna was keeping her distance because of Rich, Maggie would have to find another way to connect. Calling her was the obvious choice, but Maggie wanted to be able to read her expression, her body language. If Anna was a spy, she would excel at lying.

Still, talking to her in person would give Maggie the chance to establish a baseline for her demeanor.

Maggie glanced at her watch. She grabbed her phone from her purse and sent Rich a text message.

Spilled my hair spray. Cleaning up the mess. Out in a few.

She didn't even use hair spray, but Rich didn't know that. Five more minutes, that was all she'd give Anna. Maggie tossed her sweaty workout clothes into her gym bag and returned the makeup to her purse. *Now what?*

When she heard the whoosh of the locker room door opening, she muttered to herself and rifled through her bag, acting as if she'd misplaced something important.

In her peripheral vision, she caught sight of Anna stepping into a shower stall. Either the Russian was playing coy, or she had no interest in chatting today.

Maggie rolled her eyes. *Forget it.* As much as she wanted to talk to Anna, she'd play hard to get, act as if she had no interest in her at all. She tossed her purse over one shoulder and her gym bag over the other and headed for the exit. As she passed the showers, a hand reached out and yanked her into the adjacent changing stall.

"What the hell? Let go of me." Maggie wrenched herself free.

Anna was fully dressed in her workout clothes—black spandex shorts and a crop top—but behind her, the shower rained down. She raised a finger to her lips.

"Have you thought about what I said?"

Her voice was so quiet that Maggie had to lean in to hear. "I have no idea what you're talking about."

"We have mutual interests."

Maggie raised a hand. "You and I have no mutual interests."

Anna made a face. "That's not true, Maggie. I have information about Bukayev that you might find useful."

"Bullshit, Anna. You're the one who leaked my name to the senator. You intentionally put a bull's-eye on my back."

"Why would I do that?"

"I have my theories, and none of them involve Bukayev. In fact, I don't think you know anything about him."

"I know that he intends to kill you." She flashed on a smile. "And I know where he is."

"If you knew that, Anna, why wouldn't you tell your government? You'd be a national hero."

Anna remained mute. All the fire seemed to drain from her eyes.

"That's what I thought. You don't know anything." Maggie smirked and exited the changing stall.

"Maggie, wait." Anna followed. "Bukayev is a dangerous and ruthless man."

Maggie understood that better than Anna ever could. "Either you back off, or I'll leak your secrets to the media."

Anna scowled, her delicate features pinched in anger. "I have no secrets."

"Ah, but you do. And so does Senator Canton."

The Russian's pale skin turned even whiter.

"I can just see the headlines now. SENATOR CANTON'S LESBIAN AFFAIR WITH A RUSSIAN SPY. Her career will be over, and you'll lose your access to the classified information she's sharing with you."

Just then, an older woman entered the locker room and busied herself at a nearby locker.

Anna leaned in, her voice a muted hiss. "If you say anything to the press about me, Warner Thompson's career is over."

Maggie staggered down the hall toward the gym lobby. *What did Anna know about Warner?* All this time, she'd believed that his secret had died with Richard Carvelli. The congressman had set Warner up, putting him in a compromising position with a Russian operative. A young man. There were photos, but Maggie had destroyed them. And Carvelli was dead, as was the young Russian. The only two people alive who knew about the incident were Maggie and Warner. She steadied herself against the wall and took several deep breaths.

That's when it hit her like a sledgehammer to the gut. Maybe she was right. Maybe Anna really was gunning for Warner. What if Russian intelligence knew about the CIA director's deep, dark secret?

"Maggie?" Rich's deep voice sliced through her racing thoughts. "Are you okay?" He looked over her shoulder.

She forced a smile. "I think I should've slept off this hangover instead of trying to sweat through it. I'm probably a bit dehydrated."

Rich's expression hardened. "Let's get you to the car."

Anna stood in the shower and let the steaming-hot water pelt her body. She had to get herself under control. What was she thinking, threatening the director of the CIA when she had no actual *kompromat* on him? She'd been trained to keep emotion segregated from work but had resorted to threatening a potential recruitment target.

Ever since the Bukayev video aired on Sunday, she'd been on edge. Every time she saw his face on the news, it brought her back to September. She'd been in Moscow finishing up her training when the news broke from Beslan. Katya, her baby sister, had been so excited for the first day of school. Mama and Papa had accompanied her, as was customary on Knowledge Day. The three had entered the school and never come out.

Mostafa slipped into the front seat with the egg-and-cheese croissant and coffee he'd purchased from the fast-food joint at the far end of the parking lot. A few minutes later, he watched as the muscular security guard emerged from the gym with the target. Assuming that Jenkins went to the gym every morning and her security guard waited inside with her, he would have plenty of time to set his plan in motion.

Relief rushed through him. After yesterday's scare with the mailbox and his realization that Jenkins's house wasn't, in fact, empty during the day, he'd suffered a sleepless night. The question of how to get to the target was now answered. He bit into the warm breakfast sandwich and relaxed into the seat. Finally, for once, everything seemed to be working in his favor. When he got back home, he'd give his supplier the go-ahead to deliver the supplies to the storage facility. Between the ammonium nitrate, the fuel, and the detonator, he'd be out two thousand dollars, but walking away with eighteen grand for a couple of days' worth of work wasn't a bad deal.

He scanned the tall lampposts scattered around the parking lot. Were there cameras up there? He didn't see any, but he had to assume that the gym and the adjacent businesses had cameras monitoring their storefronts. He'd be sure to keep his face turned away from the building. Mostafa pictured himself pulling up alongside the SUV, parking the stolen vehicle, and sauntering off to his own car, which would be parked a distance away but within the detonator's range. As soon as the target stepped between the SUV and the stolen car, *boom*. He'd drive off, heading due south to sunny Florida.

He finished off the coffee and crumpled the sandwich wrapper. Just as he was about to exit the car to dispose of the trash, he realized that the SUV was still in the parking lot. He couldn't let the security guard see him, not after their encounter yesterday. So he waited and watched as an attractive blonde woman in tight spandex hurried across the lot. He'd avoided Western women the entire time he'd been in the US. Their sinful attire and complete absence of morals disgusted him. And yet, Mostafa stared, unable to look away.

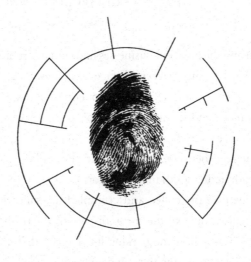

CHAPTER THIRTY-FOUR

CIA Headquarters, Langley, Virginia

"Oh, there you are, Maggie." Priscilla, Warner's long-time administrative assistant, closed the drawer on the file cabinet next to her desk. "Warner's been looking for you. The full Senate is voting on his nomination today at ten."

"Yes," she said, pretending she knew. As his chief of staff, she should've known before Warner. The encounter with Anna had thrown her completely off her game. "I was just coming to find him."

"What do you think will happen?"

After the initial media hysteria over the revelation of Warner being inside the elementary school last year, there'd been no further leaks of classified information. Perhaps Senator Canton had decided her

seat on the intelligence committee was more valuable to her than de-
railing Warner's directorship. Or perhaps she was holding her fire for
another day. Anna's words echoed in her mind. *Warner Thompson's career
is over.* "I think he'll be confirmed. Easily."

Priscilla smiled broadly, revealing deep lines around her eyes and
mouth. She was close to retirement but as loyal as the day was long.

"You're staying on, right, Priscilla? As the CIA director's right-
hand woman?"

She bounced in the seat before composing herself. "I never imagined, but yes, I will stay as long as Warner wants me to."

"Great." Maggie meant it. Having another trusted ally so close to
Warner was reassuring. Every new director had enemies, both within
the intelligence community and in the political world. Warner would
be no exception. In fact, based on Anna's threat alone, he was at exceptional risk. If Anna knew about Warner's one-time indiscretion,
she would try to co-opt him, force him to hand over classified information in exchange for keeping his secrets secret. If he succumbed to
the Russian's demands, it would be the greatest spy scandal in history.
Would he? she wondered for a moment.

She found Warner in his office, tossing a few final items into moving boxes. "Hey, boss!" She forced herself to sound cheerier than she
felt.

"Ah, there you are."

"I just got in from the gym." She eyed a plate of muffins on his
desk, her stomach rumbling.

"Have one. Please. They're Priscilla's finest."

Priscilla was an excellent baker. Maggie bit into a blueberry muf-
fin. "As CIA director, can you order her to stop baking? It's not in the
national interest for us to gorge ourselves every day."

He laughed and clasped his hands together. "Can you believe this
is happening?"

"Steve would be so proud, Warner."

He reached down to a box on the floor, extracting from it a framed photograph of himself awarding Steve a citation for outstanding operational work. "I miss this guy."

They would've been married a little over a year now. "Me too." Her voice was barely more than a whisper.

Warner cleared his throat and placed the frame back in the box. "Just under two hours until the Senate vote. I should probably record the speech now."

Maggie had arranged for Warner to record his first address as director for broadcast over the CIA's internal television channel. "I'll call the studio to see if they're ready for you." She pointed at the phone on his desk. "May I?"

"It's all yours."

Maggie made the arrangements. "They'll be ready in a half hour." She gave him the once-over. "Nice tie. Bright blue will look good on-screen. And it brings out your eyes."

"Thank you, Ms. Chief of Staff, for telling me what to wear."

"Get used to it, Warner. I'm running your life from here on out."

He laughed.

She couldn't.

Warner sobered. "I heard about the man showing up outside your house again. We've doubled security so that one officer will always be with you, and one will always be in the house."

"Thanks."

"You okay?"

Dread welled inside her, turning her stomach and pressing down on her lungs. She closed the office door and turned back to him. "Do you think anyone knows about what happened with you and Carvelli?"

The creases on his forehead deepened. "Which part?"

There was no use dancing around the issue. "The photos of you and the Russian." The young man who went by the name of Ed.

"I don't think so. Carvelli's dead. Ed's dead. And even if Yuri knew, he's dead too." He swallowed. "Why do you ask? Did you hear something?"

The look on his face made her want to cry. She couldn't tell him about Anna, not today, not on his most triumphant day at the CIA. "I haven't heard anything. It just bothers me that Senator Canton brought up Carvelli's death and the fact that we were both inside his house when he died. It's like she trying to . . . I don't know."

Warner exhaled, the tension in his face softening as he did. "I have political enemies everywhere. If the senator knew the sordid details, she would've used them to derail my nomination, don't you think?"

Maggie nodded even though she didn't necessarily agree. "You're probably right. I'm going to keep an eye on her, though. Track every word she says about you and the Agency."

He rubbed a hand across his face. "As you know, Maggie, I have my share of secrets. But I've tried to live a life of integrity. If Senator Canton or anyone else comes for me with knives out, I'll leave this agency knowing I've done my job well."

She blinked rapidly. "That you have." She had her answer. If Russian intelligence tried to co-opt him, Warner would not compromise his integrity. Her job, or at least one of them, was to make sure they got nowhere near him.

Warner stood at the far end of the conference room on the seventh floor, a smile on his face, a bottle of champagne in his right hand.

"Speech!" Roger said.

Several senior Agency executives laughed, while others continued side conversations.

Maggie's eyes met Warner's. He raised the bottle. She left Roger's side and joined her boss at the back of the room. "If I could have everyone's attention." The buzz in the room continued unabated. She grabbed a champagne flute and a fork from the food table on her right, and tapped stainless steel against glass. The resultant *ting* caught the attention of the VIPs in attendance—the Agency's deputy directors for intelligence, operations, science and technology, and administration, and their most senior staff.

"As the new director's chief of staff, I would like to thank you for joining us as we celebrate. Warner, champagne?"

Warner loosened the wire cage and tore off the foil. A few twists of the bottle later, and the cork flew off.

"Incoming!" yelled Roger, which elicited more laughs and a few eye rolls.

Priscilla hurried over with a tray of flutes as Roger got to work opening several more bottles.

Once everyone had a glass in hand, Maggie raised hers. "To Warner Thompson, the most loyal and capable man I know. The Agency and the country are lucky to have you."

A chorus of "cheers" spread throughout the large room.

"Thank you, Maggie. And Priscilla. I'd be lost without both of you." He bowed, eliciting applause, then faced the guests. "I'd like to thank you all for your support, professionalism, and dedication to our mission. As you know, these are dangerous and difficult times, but I'm confident that we can lead the way in securing our country and ensuring stability around the world."

"Here, here," one of the men shouted.

Maggie watched the faces of the attendees—mostly men—to ascertain who looked genuinely pleased with Warner's ascendance and who didn't. A couple of these senior officers already were on her radar based on their reputations alone. This was part of her job now—to keep drama and intrigue at bay, whether it came from within or without the Agency.

Warner checked his watch. "Enough with the ceremony. Let's eat," he proclaimed.

After ensuring that Priscilla and Warner were well situated with food and drink, Maggie scanned the room for Roger. *Now where is he?*

Maggie found Roger in a conference room on the fourth floor, pages full of notes spread out before him. From her vantage point in the hall, she watched him shuffling the papers, scribbling notes. If only she could explain her suspicions that Anna knew about Warner's secret. But she couldn't. Because she'd sworn that she would tell no one about his tryst with Ed, the young Russian agent.

If she broke that promise, Warner would never forgive her. And she'd never forgive herself.

He looked up from the table. "Hey, what are you doing out there?" He waved her in.

"Looking for you." She gestured to the papers. "What's all this?"

"Daud called."

She hurried over to the table and slid into the chair next to him.

"He gave me the address of Bukayev's current location."

Maggie clutched his arm. "Oh, Roger, this is fantastic."

"It is." He shuffled through the papers. "Here it is."

Maggie scanned his notes. The street name was ridiculously long. She repeated it in her head five times. "Is our team on the move yet?"

"They're on their way to Tbilisi."

"They're not even in Georgia?" She slumped back in the chair.

"Nope, which means they're still a few days out. And Daud says that Rasul moves frequently, sometimes daily. That means Bukayev will move with him."

"So, by the time the good guys get there, the bad guy will be gone."

"Probably. But there's good news."

Maggie looked at him expectantly.

"Daud's in charge of securing safe houses. He's going to call me later with the list of places Rasul might go next."

She got up to shut the conference-room door and returned to her seat.

"I don't know what you're up to, but I think I like it." He winked at her. "You lock the door?" He leaned in and nuzzled her neck.

"Roger, we have to talk."

"The words every man dreads." He grinned but quickly sobered when he saw her expression.

"Bukayev could be dead within twenty-four hours if we act."

"How?"

"What if we gave the safe house address to Anna Orlova?"

Roger searched her face. "We don't even know for sure that she's Russian intelligence."

"If it walks like a duck—"

"But we don't know for certain."

"I'd bet my life on it," she retorted. "Even if I'm wrong, even if she's a journalist, she would get this information to the right people in the Russian government."

Roger stood, leaned his palms against the table, and spoke in a staccato tone. "We. Can't. Give. Classified. Information. To. The. Russians."

"No one would have to know."

"Other than the SVR. And the guy who gives me my next polygraph." He pushed away from the table and threw up his hands.

"Would I like to tell the Russians? Absolutely. Can we? Absolutely not. Not in a million years."

"If you knew it would eliminate the threat to me, you wouldn't do it?"

He pointed a finger at her. "That's not a fair question and you know it."

Roger was right. She couldn't demand that he put himself on the line for her. Not like this, anyway. If they gave Anna classified information and that fact ever surfaced, not only would their careers be over, but they might also end up in federal prison. Besides that, even if the Russians killed Bukayev, the fatwa might not die with him. "I'm sorry. I'm just, I don't know, feeling a bit desperate. And frustrated that everything takes so damned long to do."

Roger squatted beside the chair and took her hands in his. "I know. And I'm going to do everything I can to get our paramilitary guys in place as quickly as possible." He looked up into her eyes. "And when this is over, we are going on a long tropical vacation. We'll drink frozen beverages with tiny umbrellas in them and we'll sleep on the beach and go sailing."

"You don't know how to sail."

"I'll learn."

Maggie smiled. "Okay." She wanted to believe that day would come. But the way things stood, it felt very far away.

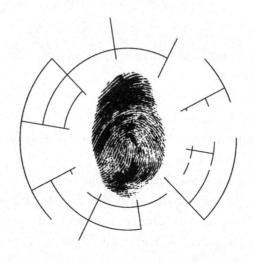

CHAPTER THIRTY-FIVE

Tyson's Fitness and Health Club
McLean, Virginia, Tuesday, June 21, 2005

Mostafa shifted in the front seat of the stolen Honda Civic, a common enough car that it wouldn't stand out, even in swanky McLean. The interior smelled like weed. Empty food wrappers were strewn across the backseat. He sniffed. Maybe not entirely empty. As long as the owner, a student at nearby George Mason University, didn't need the car before 7:00 a.m., he wouldn't report it missing until it was too late. It had almost been too easy. Not only had the car been left unlocked, but the owner had also left the keys under the driver's seat. Under the yellow glow of a nearby parking-lot light, Mostafa exited the car and walked a loop around its perimeter. His source had left five hundred pounds' worth of ammonium nitrate fuel oil at the storage facility. He'd opted to use just slightly less than half of it. Even so, with an extra couple hundred pounds stowed in the trunk, the rear of the car hung lower than normal. But, he decided, unless Jenkins or her security guard were actively scanning the area for a suspicious car, they were unlikely to notice anything amiss.

Mostafa wiped his sweaty palms on his T-shirt. He'd made several IEDs when he was at the training camp in Afghanistan. He'd been a star student, in fact. But this was his first unsupervised project. And he'd never made a vehicle-borne device. Still, he trusted the training. A quick glance at his watch sent him jogging away from the parking lot to the gas station on the corner. He'd call for a cab from there so he could retrieve his car from the university parking lot before campus security towed it. There would be almost no traffic at this time of day, but he wanted to be back at the fitness club no later than 6:00 a.m. so he could move the stolen vehicle into place at the optimal time.

Maggie rode with Rich in silence. Roger had called her multiple times last night. Clearly, her idea about feeding Anna information on Buka-yev's whereabouts had alarmed him. He'd wanted to spend the night, but Maggie suspected it was more to keep an eye on her than to keep her company. She'd demurred. It would be weird, she'd told him, for him to stay over when there were three CIA security professionals roaming around the house. His last call had come in just after nine. He hadn't heard from back from Daud with the list of safe house addresses yet, probably, he speculated, because the Chechen couldn't slip away to make a call.

Was Bukayev on the move? Did Daud have more information on the fatwa? The questions had swirled through her mind in a relentless loop, keeping her awake until late into the night.

They pulled into the shopping plaza at 6:15. Rich jumped out of the SUV and surveyed the lot before giving her the okay sign.

She didn't usually go to the gym this early, but she had a lot to do now that Warner was officially the CIA director. And she wanted to work with Roger to plot out every possible scenario for capturing Bukayev.

After watching Jenkins and her security guard enter the fitness club ten minutes earlier, Mostafa had moved his personal car to the far side of the fast-food restaurant. Even though he'd been up all night, he was wide awake and brimming with energy. Another coffee would be nice, but he was already so amped up that he feared more caffeine would make his hands shake when dialing the number. He forced himself to walk as casually as possible into the restaurant. After a quick stop in the restroom, he ordered a breakfast sandwich with juice and parked himself at table that afforded him a view of the fitness-club entrance.

He scarfed down the sandwich, grabbed the juice bottle, checked his watch, and left the restaurant. The stolen vehicle was parked halfway between the restaurant and the black SUV. Even though he'd driven it here from the storage unit without incident, and even though he knew that the bomb wouldn't detonate without him making the phone call, he broke out in a cold sweat the moment he slid into the driver's seat.

He held his breath as he started the Civic, exhaling only when no noise or flash of light materialized. The distance from the restaurant to the SUV was about four hundred yards, far enough to prevent a bomb this size from doing major structural damage to the restaurant, although the windows might shatter from the concussive blast.

As he approached the SUV, he smiled. The driver's side faced the gym entrance. He parked the Civic in the adjacent space, next to the passenger side—the side that the target would be on. Not only would she be in the direct line of fire, the black behemoth of a vehicle would conceal the Civic from view until it was too late.

Mostafa took a final look around the inside of the vehicle. If the ammonium nitrate fuel-oil bomb hidden in the trunk failed to detonate, he would set off the smaller IED, the one filled with nails. That device, hidden inside a backpack in the backseat, was attached to a different cell phone. Given the proximity of the Civic to the SUV, even the smaller bomb would most certainly kill the woman.

Mostafa exited the car and headed back to the restaurant, where he resumed waiting and watching.

Maggie was rinsing conditioner from her hair when she heard a woman scream. She fumbled with the shower nozzle as she reached for the towel hanging in the adjacent changing stall. She wrapped the towel around her torso and threw open the curtain.

"Get out of here, you pervert!" an older woman yelled as she ducked into a toilet stall and bolted the door.

"Roger, what the hell are you doing in here?"

Roger whirled around, his face pale, tired. He grabbed her bare arms. "I just got off the phone with Daud. It's supposed to happen in the next twenty-four hours."

Water dripped from her hair to her shoulders, sending a shiver through her. "What's supposed to happen?"

He lowered his voice. "The attack." His eyes darted around the locker room. "On you."

Panic rose inside her. "Where? How? What did he say?"

"He doesn't know the—" He cut himself off and smiled apologetically at a woman who stopped short when she caught sight of him. Once she passed, he whispered, "I tried calling you, but you didn't answer. So I called Rich. He said everything was fine." He swallowed. "But I had to see for myself, so I drove here right away."

Maggie's eyes darted from one end of the locker room to the other. "We should get out of here. Just give me a minute, I'll get dressed." She spun around, entered the changing stall, and swiped the curtain shut. She leaned against the metal wall and exhaled. *The attack would happen in the next twenty-four hours?*

As she pulled on her blouse, a plan began to come together in her head. Rich could bring a few days' worth of her clothes to headquarters. She could order meals from the executive dining room. And when Warner went home at night, she could sleep on the couch in his office.

"Ready?" Roger said, his voice strained.

She nodded.

Rich was waiting for them right outside the locker room.

"I think it would be best if I stay overnight at work for the next few days," she said to both of them. "I'll need some clothes and a few other things."

Roger's hand shot up. "I'll do it! I'll go to your house now."

"Okay. Thanks. Call me when you get there, and I'll tell you what to bring."

She turned to Rich. "That okay with you?"

"Yeah. I'll let the rest of the crew know." He jerked his head in Roger's general direction. "So they're prepared for him this time."

Roger ignored the jab.

Rich led the way through the lobby. When he opened the door to the parking lot, he paused, scanning.

Maggie peered around him. There was no sign of Anna's blue BMW. On any other day, that would have been cause for relief.

Not today. Not when the clock was ticking.

"Once we start walking, you stay close to me, Maggie. We'll get in the car and head straight to headquarters. When Roger was in the locker room with you, I called ahead. The guys at the gate will be ready for us. We won't have to stop at the light or for an ID check."

Twelve years prior, a terrorist had shot at cars waiting at a traffic light to turn into CIA Headquarters. Two Agency employees were killed in the attack. "Okay, good." She blinked. "But what if—" Her voice trembled. "What if we're ambushed on the way?"

Roger took her hand.

"Security is sending more officers this way as we speak," Rich said. "They'll surround my car, keep us well protected."

This was good. Rich had a plan. She squeezed Roger's hand. "Maybe you shouldn't go to the house. The jogger or someone else might be there, waiting—"

"More security is on the way there too. And the county police are setting up the roadblock again." Rich nodded at Roger. "He'll be fine."

"Perfect. Thanks, Rich," Roger said. As they stepped outside, he leaned in for a soft kiss. "It's going to be okay, Maggie."

"Anna, three o'clock," she said, her tone urgent.

He pulled away from her and looked to his right.

"No, my three o'clock."

Roger caught sight of the Russian. "She's obnoxiously persistent. I'm going to have a word with her."

Maggie grabbed his arm. "Don't waste your time. Besides, the security detail will be waiting for you at my house."

"Right." He gave her another quick kiss and jogged off to his car.

She turned to Rich, who waited patiently, his alert eyes watching Roger before fixing on the petite blonde across the parking lot.

"Let's move out, Maggie. The sooner we get to headquarters, the better."

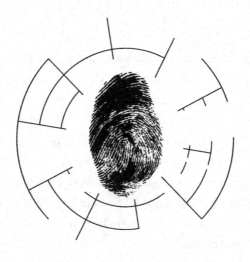

CHAPTER THIRTY-SIX

Mostafa jumped from the chair, knocking it backward with a loud clatter. An older gentleman who was nursing a coffee while he flipped through the newspaper frowned at him. Mostafa silently berated himself for the spectacle. The last thing he wanted was for people at the scene to remember him. He righted the chair, disposed of his trash, and made a beeline from the restaurant to his car. He peered through the windshield with binoculars, watching as Jenkins, the guard, and another man emerged from the fitness-club entrance. Then he powered on the cell phone with a trembling finger and waited. Once Jenkins and the bodyguard began to move across the parking lot, Mostafa started the car. As soon as he hit the *send* button, he'd spin it around in the opposite direction and merge into traffic on the main road.

His heart pounded. His entire body dripped with sweat. "*Allahu Akbar,*" he whispered as he entered the phone number.

As she and Rich hurried across the parking lot, Maggie watched Roger's car turn left into traffic. Rounding the rear of the SUV, Maggie muttered, "That's obnoxious." She pointed at the small white car parked immediately next to Rich's vehicle. "With all these open spaces, they park right here?"

Rich stopped. His eyes landed on the trunk. "Maggie, run!" He lunged, grabbed her wrist, and pulled her toward him.

She stumbled but his powerful arms caught her and propelled her forward. Adrenaline coursed through her as she tried to look back to see what was going on.

"Go, go, go!" he shouted.

She ran hard until a sudden force threw her forward toward the pavement. Heat and darkness combined with an unearthly roar, stopping time. Car alarms sounded, but they were strangely muted, as if alerting from miles away. A tremendous weight pressed down on her as she blinked her eyes open. She couldn't move. There were more sirens. Closer. Louder. Police? Fire truck? She struggled against the weight and the darkness.

"Maggie!"

She couldn't speak.

"Maggie!"

There it was again. Someone calling her. But it sounded like a voice inside her head.

"Maggie! Oh, dear God. Maggie!"

She struggled against the darkness, her eyelids heavy.

"Don't move!"

Roger?

The voice grew closer. "I'm right here, Maggie."

Her eyes fluttered open. A man's shoe, a pantleg were in her line of sight. Then the leg shifted and a face appeared. "Roger?" It was barely a whisper, but he heard.

"Oh, thank God. Can you feel your arms? Legs? What hurts?"

"Heavy. My back."

Roger's face crumpled. "There was an explosion, Maggie." He brushed his fingers across her cheekbone. "Rich shielded you. He's on your back. That's the weight. We can't move him until the paramedics—"

"What happened?" she croaked.

Wailing sirens grew louder.

"Over here!" Roger shouted.

She tried to lift her head, but couldn't. A cacophony of strange voices erupted around her. Someone shined a light in her eyes. Checked the pulse on her neck. Black boots passed quickly in every direction. The ringing in her ears and all the voices made it impossible to figure out what was going on. "Roger?"

No one replied. She had no sense of time. It could've been two minutes, or twenty, until suddenly there was no weight on her back. She tried to roll to her side. Multiple hands grabbed her—one on each arm and leg.

A man she didn't know knelt next to her and lowered his face to the pavement.

It wasn't until that moment that she even understood she was lying on the pavement. Her mind flashed back. They'd been outside the gym. Roger had just left. It was her and Rich. And Anna Orlova. And then they'd run. "Anna? Roger, where's Anna?"

Roger straightened. "That's right. She was here." He scanned the parking lot. "She's over there getting checked out."

"Is she—"

"I'll be right back."

"Roger, no. Don't leave me." It was too late. From the corner of her eye, she saw Roger sprinting away across the parking lot.

Hands ran over her entire body. Male and female voices converged in an urgent hum above and around her.

"Maggie?" The man wore a white short-sleeve button-down shirt with a shiny badge on the chest pocket. "We've checked your limbs and your back. I don't think anything is broken, but we're concerned about your head. You're probably concussed."

She squeezed her eyes shut.

"I'm going to touch your limbs. Give me a thumbs-up if you feel anything."

It seemed like forever before she felt something brushing her left leg. Then her right. And finally, her upper arms.

"Blood's not hers. Feeling in all extremities. Bring the backboard over!" He knelt again and met her eyes. "Does anything hurt?"

"My head. Ears. Ringing."

A wave of nausea hit her when they rolled her onto the board. The next thing she knew, she was on a stretcher and Roger was brushing hair from her face and grasping her hand. His eyes brimmed with tears.

"I'm okay."

He kissed her softly.

"Rich? Where's Rich?"

"They're working on him."

When Maggie turned to look, her stomach lurched. She closed her eyes, and the world went dark.

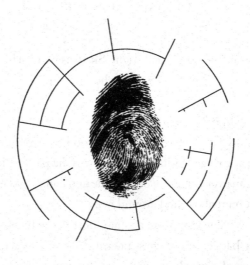

CHAPTER THIRTY-SEVEN

Interstate 95, Richmond, Virginia

Mostafa decided to drive five miles per hour over the speed limit so as not to draw attention to himself on I-95 south. But when all manner of cars and trucks flew by him on the left, and those in the right lane began to ride his bumper, he accelerated and set the cruise control. He gripped the steering wheel and tried to focus on the road. Once he passed through Richmond, his body stopped shaking. Now, every limb ached from post-adrenaline fatigue. He'd fled the scene immediately after hitting the phone's *send* button. The outgoing call went straight to the phone attached to the bomb's circuitry. The explosion had been violent, rocking his car even from four hundred yards away. Shrapnel from the stolen Honda had flown in every direction and a great, dark plume of smoke had formed around the wreckage. Jenkins had to be dead. Even if she'd tried to run, she wouldn't have been able to get far enough away. And if the force of the concussive blast hadn't turned her organs into mush, shrapnel would've taken a limb or cut a major artery.

He wished he could see the body, to be 100-percent sure, but that was too risky. "She's dead," Mostafa announced to himself as he searched the radio for a Washington news channel. "She has to be."

· ★ ★ ★ ·

INOVA Fairfax Hospital, Falls Church, Virginia

Roger stood in the doorway to Maggie's hospital room, conferring with the FBI agent and the county police officer who stood in the hall, keeping watch over her and everyone who entered the room.

Her entire body hurt, but other than a few cuts on her extremities that required a stitch here and there, she was largely intact. The ER doctor had diagnosed her with a mild concussion—a damned miracle, he'd declared—but nevertheless insisted that she be admitted overnight for observation. The morning's events were coming into clearer relief now that she'd ingested an anti-nausea medication, some water, and a few saltines. Something about the car parked next to the SUV had caught Rich's attention. She remembered him staring at the back of it. Maggie closed her eyes to try to see what he'd seen. Maybe he'd remember when he regained consciousness.

"Hey, baby." Roger was at her side.

"Rich knew something was wrong with that car. I'm sure he'll tell the investigators."

Roger dropped his head.

"What's wrong?" She pushed herself farther up the bed.

"Rich—" He swallowed. "He didn't make it."

Maggie's breath caught. "No. No, Roger, that's not possible."

"He took the brunt of the blast. The worst of it was the shrapnel to his femoral artery. He was extremely unstable and had a heart attack on the way to the hospital."

That's why there'd been so much blood. "He shielded me? He——"

Roger gathered her left hand in his and kissed it. "He did. If he hadn't made you run. If he hadn't covered your body with his——" his voice caught in his throat.

"He saved my life." She closed her eyes as tears streamed down her face. A knock on the door broke their silence.

"Ms. Jenkins?" A woman wearing a navy-blue windbreaker stepped into the room. "The doctors say you're able to speak with us."

She swiped at her cheeks. "Of course." She pushed the button on the bedside remote and raised herself to a sitting position. "Can Roger stay?"

"I'm afraid not, since he's a witness. We can't have your statement influencing his, or vice versa."

"Can we just have a moment?"

The agent nodded and slipped into the hall.

She lowered her voice. "Do I say anything about Anna being at the scene?"

Roger exhaled. "I don't know. I mean, I doubt she was involved. A car bomb is a little over the top, even for the Russians."

"Yeah, poisoning is more their style."

"If you think she's coming after you, I'll be your food taster."

Maggie smiled. "Anna wants information from me. She doesn't want me dead. I think I should keep quiet about her unless the Feds ask me directly." After the death of Richard Carvelli, she'd learned her lesson about offering up unsolicited information to law enforcement. Trying to be as transparent and helpful as possible had landed her in the middle of a months' long FBI investigation.

"Agreed."

"Do you know if Anna got hurt?"

"She was seen at the hospital for a few cuts and bruises but wasn't admitted. Apparently, she dove under her car when the bomb went off. And she was quite a distance away."

Maggie turned in the bed. "How do you know all that?"

"I chatted up the FBI agent who interviewed the witnesses."

Of course he did. His charm and looks didn't always work with men but usually did with the ladies. "Did he . . . or she say whether Anna saw anything or anyone? The bomber? An accomplice?"

"She asked Anna, but Anna claims to have seen nothing." He frowned. "You know what's weird? When I saw Anna in the parking lot, she was nearly hysterical, screaming something about Bukayev."

Maggie sat up straighter in the bed. "What did she say?"

"I couldn't really hear her, and I was worried about you, so I didn't home in on what she was saying. No doubt she was reacting to the bomb. It was massive. I heard it and felt it and I wasn't even in the parking lot."

The sound of the explosion reverberated in Maggie's head. "I should be dead. If it weren't for Rich . . ." She slumped against the pillow. "This is never going to end, Roger."

"I promise it will." He kissed her forehead. "If it's the last thing I do, I will put this to an end."

As Roger exited the room, the FBI agent entered and proceeded to fire off a series of questions about Maggie's movements since the moment she woke up earlier that morning. The more questions she asked, the more Maggie's head ached. "It's the fatwa," she croaked. "Imran Bukayev was behind this."

The agent rifled through a briefcase she'd placed on the floor near the door and handed Maggie a photo printout.

"Recognize him?"

She frowned at the grainy picture pulled from a surveillance camera. "Where was this taken?"

"From a camera outside a nearby restaurant."

Maggie squinted. The man, who appeared to be tanned or olive skinned, wore a baseball cap pulled low over his brow and a George Mason University T-shirt. "Without seeing his face, I can't be sure."

The agent stepped closer. "Sure about what?"

"The man jogging in my neighborhood."

"What man?"

"Rich saw him up close. We got him on surveillance video when he was casing my house."

The agent flipped open a portfolio and scribble furiously. "Rich who? And who was casing your house?"

"Rich is . . . was part of my security detail. He's the one who shielded me from the bomb."

"The one who died?"

Maggie blinked at the agent. Her dark hair was pulled back tightly from her face, enhancing the severity of her angular features. "Yes. The bomb killed Rich." She realized she didn't know anything about his private life. Was he married? Did he have kids? Her throat constricted as she tried to swallow back tears.

"What footage?"

"You haven't talked to my security detail yet?" *Seriously?* More than four years after the most devastating terrorist attack on US soil and the FBI and CIA still couldn't get their collective acts together?

"What footage?" the agent repeated, her lips drawn together in thin line.

"Outside my house. The other day they caught this guy looking in my mailbox, casing my house. They have video." She waved the printout in the air. "Although if this crappy photo is all you've got, I'm not sure you'll be able to figure out if it's the same guy."

The agent's phone buzzed. "Yup . . . Uh-huh . . . Thanks," she said, before hanging up. "We found the car's license plate in the rubble and ran the tags. It belongs to a college student at George Mason University."

Maggie's eyes shifted to the man in the photo wearing a Mason T-shirt.

"Student's name is Brandon Davis. Virginia resident. Blond hair, light skin."

Maggie dropped the photo. "Not the same guy."

"Davis says he didn't realize his car was missing. He claims to be enrolled in a summer class and works at a nearby restaurant. He last drove the car on Sunday when he returned to campus from his bartending job. We're working with university security and local businesses to review camera footage to see if this guy's story holds up."

Maggie understood that they had to run down every lead, but if this college student was involved, he'd be on the run. The FBI could theorize about a wider conspiracy, but her gut told her that the man in the photo stole the car in question. "Someone rigged that car with explosives. Parked it next to Rich's SUV. And tried to—" she couldn't finish the sentence.

"Are you sure you don't recognize the man in the photo?"

Maggie threw up her hands.

"I can't even see his face."

A knock at the door spared her, at least momentarily, from answering more questions.

"Maggie," Warner said as he rushed to the bedside. "I had to brief the president, or I would've been here earlier."

"Excuse me, sir, but I'm not finished speaking with Ms. Jenkins."

Warner ignored her. "Are you okay?"

"Yeah, but Rich didn't make it."

His expression fell. "I heard."

Maggie didn't think she could handle another memorial wall ceremony. She'd have to speak, tell everyone assembled what Rich had done to save her life. And then there was his family. She'd have to face them, bear the weight of them wondering whether she'd done something that led to his death. A sob escaped her mouth. She was so tired. Tired of everyone dying. Tired of the past two years. Tired of always looking over her shoulder.

Warner leaned over the bed rail and smoothed her hair. "I'm so sorry, Maggie. I promised it would be okay. And I failed."

She swiped at a tear. "Just promise me we'll get him, Warner."

He glanced over his shoulder at the FBI agent. "Let's talk about this after you've had some rest."

Roger entered the room. "I just got off the phone with Priscilla. Once you get discharged, you'll have a comfortable place to stay. You'll be safe and there's a doctor on-site at the clinic."

It dawned on her that she might not be going home for a very long time. Not until they got to Bukayev. Her eyelids drooped despite her effort to keep them open, and her mouth felt as dry as sandpaper.

"She needs to rest," Warner said to the agent.

Maggie heard the woman turn and leave the room. "We have to find Bukayev," she mumbled as she forced her eyes open.

Roger lowered the bed rail and sat beside her. "Leave that to us."

"When Bukayev hears that I'm still alive, he's going to come back at me."

Roger interlaced his fingers with hers. "Warner and I talked. We think we should put out a statement saying you didn't survive."

Maggie snatched her hand from his. "What? Absolutely not. I'm not doing that to my family, especially not my mother." It made sense for them to pretend she was dead. Bukayev would relax, maybe even put out a video celebrating her death, or something that would help them pinpoint his whereabouts in case Daud lost the trail.

But the thought of putting her mom through that was too much.

"We can call your mother before we put out the statement," Roger offered. "Explain the situation."

"You don't know her, Roger. There's no way she could pretend to be a bereaved mother."

"What if we say you're gravely wounded, in critical condition with multiple life-threatening injuries?" Warner suggested.

"That might work," Roger said. "We'll say you're under medical care in a secure, undisclosed location."

"Okay." This should keep Bukayev from coming after her, at least for a little while.

"The couch in my new office pulls out to a bed. And there's a shower and a little kitchen." Warner paused, thinking. "We'd have to keep you up in my office suite for a while. We can't risk employees seeing you and telling the media that you've had a miraculous recovery."

"Especially not Anna," Maggie muttered, her voice thick with fatigue and the sedative effect of the medication.

"Anna?" Warner said. "Who the hell is Anna?"

Maggie didn't answer. She was fast asleep.

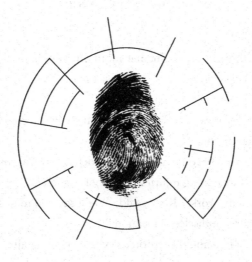

CHAPTER THIRTY-EIGHT

"I can't believe you didn't tell me about this Russian woman, Roger," Warner hissed.

"I planned to after I looked into her background." Roger stepped to the side of the hall as an orderly passed by pushing an empty gurney. "Maggie thinks she's SVR."

Warner closed his eyes and counted to five. "I'm the CIA director, Roger. And no one told me that my chief of staff has been talking to a Russian spy?"

The officer guarding Maggie's room stared at them from up the hall.

Warner gave him a nod and returned his fury to Roger. "What were you thinking, Roger?"

"She only told me her suspicions yesterday. Or maybe it was Monday, I don't remember." He ran a hand through his already disheveled hair. "Look, this Anna woman claims to know something about Bukayev. Maggie wanted time to figure out if there's any truth to it."

Warner's gray eyes widened. "This is unbelievable, Roger."

Roger threw up his hands. "Should I have come to you immediately? In hindsight, yes. But don't forget I've been burning the midnight oil trying to track Daud and Bukayev. Isn't that the priority here?"

"Is there anything else you're not telling me about this woman?"

He shook his head. "That's it." He twisted his hands together. "Although I wouldn't be surprised if Maggie hasn't told me everything."

Warner fought to keep his expression neutral. In the conversation he and Maggie had yesterday, she'd asked if anyone else knew about the naked photos of him and Ed. He leaned against the wall, grateful for its support. Maybe someone did. "What's the Russian's last name?"

"Orlova. Anna Orlova."

· ★ ★ ★ ·

CIA Headquarters, Langley, Virginia

Back at CIA Headquarters, Warner logged into his computer, the only thing that seemed to be in its proper place in his new office. On the built-in bookcase behind him, books stood stacked in disarray. Boxes of unclassified paperwork lay scattered across the floor. He felt terrible leaving Maggie at the hospital, but she needed her rest. And he had work to do. Congressional Affairs wanted him to brief six different committees on the Hill over the course of the next two days. The press office needed him to sign off on multiple press releases. And the FBI director wanted to discuss whether the CIA had withheld information about the suspected bomber.

He'd get to all that, right after he investigated Anna Orlova. First, he checked the internet. According to multiple websites, Orlova was a reporter for *Russia Today*, a new government-owned media organization with a recently opened office in Washington. Maggie was right to be suspicious. A number of Russian news correspondents were undercover intelligence officers. Did Orlova really know anything about Imran Bukayev?

Maybe. Maybe not. Either way, dropping Bukayev's name was a classic agent recruitment technique—dangle a treat so tempting that the target can't resist going after it. He hoped Maggie hadn't made a huge mistake.

He closed the search window and opened the link to the Counterintelligence Center's page. As director, he had access to every piece of information the Agency had on foreign intelligence activity around the world. He typed Anna's name into the search field. No hits. Perhaps she was too new to have a paper trail.

Warner hated the thought of Maggie contending with a persistent and persuasive Russian intelligence officer. As soon as she was fully healed, he'd talk to her about it.

Warner waved Roger into his office but put a finger to his lip and pointed to the phone in his hand.

"Yes, Mr. Chairman, I'm certain that Senator Canton's leak led directly to today's attack." He paused and listened. "I can't advise you how to handle your business, but if it were up to me, the senator would never step foot inside your committee again. Yes, of course I'll brief the committee, but tomorrow might not be feasible. There's a massive

manhunt for the bomber and we're still searching for Imran Bukayev."
He thanked the chairman for calling and dropped the phone into the
receiver. "How's Maggie?"

"Still sleeping, last I heard. I'll head over to the hospital in a bit."

"Any word from Daud?"

"Yes." Roger's expression was grim. "There was quite a celebra-
tion when word of the bombing hit. They all think Maggie is dead.
Daud got a bit overwhelmed and left the safe house."

"He what?" Warner shouted.

"He feels responsible for what happened, for not stopping Bukayev."

"For crying out loud, Roger, Daud has to go back." He pounded
the desk. "We don't have time for a meltdown."

"I told him to get his ass back to the safe house." He exhaled loudly. "Even if he does, he's not trained for this sort of operation, Warner.
I need to go to Dagestan."

"No you don't. The Special Operations Group will be in Georgia
tomorrow."

"But then they have to sneak into Russia separately and meet up
again in Dagestan without getting caught. It's a risky operation, and,
frankly, we don't the luxury of time." He leaned forward, eyes pleading. "Send me."

"To do what?"

Roger stared, his expression cold, hard. "You know what."

Warner held his gaze. "Look, the presidential finding explicitly
states that we're supposed to capture Bukayev. You can't go to Dagestan, guns blazing, and kill the man."

Roger rubbed his hands together. "Then we come up with a story.
We can say you sent me to Dagestan to help my asset. But then there
was some kind of incident and Bukayev died."

"What kind of incident?"

"I don't know. I'll come up with something. If the story doesn't fly, then you can say I went rogue. Fire me. I don't care. The only thing I care about is Maggie's safety."

Warner turned to his bookshelf and rearranged several leather-bound tomes. "Okay," he said quietly.

"Okay, I can go?"

Warner turned.

"Yes, but nothing better happen to you, Roger. I don't know if Maggie can withstand another . . . disaster."

· ★ ★ ★ ·

INOVA Fairfax Hospital, Falls Church, Virginia

Maggie unmuted the television after the medical entourage left her room. Sometime during her lengthy nap, the FBI had put out a nationwide alert for the man seen outside her house earlier in the week. Cable news alternated between the artist's sketch of the jogger Rich had first encountered, stills from the surveillance cameras mounted on her house, and the photo the FBI agent had pulled from the restaurant security camera.

"The FBI is on the hunt for this man, who may be connected to the car-bomb explosion that happened early this morning in a suburban shopping plaza outside of Washington, DC."

The screen filled with an aerial view of the wreckage. Although the frame of the fortified SUV remained largely intact, if a bit warped, the vehicle itself was on its side and not in the same place that Maggie remembered it being parked. Yellow police tape encircled the blackened, twisted, skeletal remains of the car that had served as the bomb. The next bit of footage showed boarded-up storefront windows, including the gym's.

"One man was killed in the explosion and a woman is in critical condition with multiple life-threatening injuries. The FBI has not linked this bomb to a

specific terrorist group or individual and is investigating all possible scenarios, including the involvement of domestic extremists."

"Domestic extremists," she muttered as Roger came in carrying Chinese food and a duffel bag.

He smiled, but the smile didn't reach his eyes. "I hear they're going to spring you first thing tomorrow."

"They are?"

"I was eavesdropping on the nurses' station while security searched the bag." He lowered the duffel bag onto the end of the bed. "I brought you some clothes and stuff from your bathroom. Shampoo and that hair mousse or whatever it is."

"Thanks." She studied him. "Are you okay?"

The lines in his forehead deepened. "Yeah," he said, "just worried about whether you're okay."

"I'm fine." She ran a shaky finger across a butterfly bandage near her eyebrow. "Otherwise, they wouldn't discharge me, right?"

He lowered himself onto a chair several feet from her bed and sat, hunched forward, forearms resting on his thighs. "That's not what I meant, Maggie."

She tried to make eye contact but his gaze was focused on the floor. "I'll be a lot better once Bukayev is captured."

He pushed himself back to his feet. "Our guys are on the move over there. We'll get him."

Something was off. His suddenly bright tone didn't match his facial expression. "Everything's good with your asset?"

"Yup. Just a few more days, Maggie, and I promise you, this will be over." He stared up at the TV. "Can you mute that?"

She clicked the television off. "What's really going on, Roger? You seem . . . sad or—"

He gathered her hands into his and kissed her palms. "I thought I was going to lose you today."

"I know." She leaned toward him and placed a soft kiss on his lips. "I'm glad you were nearby. I don't know what I would have done without you."

· ★ ★ ★ ·
Jacksonville, Florida

Mostafa stepped out of his car and stretched out the kinks that had settled in after driving ten plus hours with only two pit stops. Across the street was the campground he'd seen signs for during the last ten miles of the drive. He watched as a truck pulling a large camper stopped at a guard shack at the property's entrance. The driver presented paperwork to a woman in the shack, and after a brief exchange, she waved him inside. Mostafa considered his options. He wasn't sure how to go about making reservations at the campground, and asking the attendant might draw too much scrutiny. He could park here at the strip mall and sleep in the car for a few hours. But his aching body craved a shower and a bed, not the cramped backseat. A hotel was too risky at this point. Better to lie low and avoid surveillance cameras and crowded hotel lobbies. Just then, a middle-aged couple walked into the campground without stopping at the shack. Was it that easy? Five minutes later, with a backpack slung casually over his shoulder, Mostafa strolled past the guard as if he were a registered guest returning from an evening walk. It worked. The woman barely gave him a glance.

Inside the campground, he acted like a curious tourist, peering inside cabins that dotted the site. All but one appeared occupied. Satisfied that he'd found a place to sleep, he returned to the car to wait for nightfall and to catch the news. Even hundreds of miles away, the bombing was the top story on all the AM radio channels. The fact that police were looking for a man based on surveillance photographs unnerved him. But it didn't seem like they knew his name, and from what he heard on a talk show, the photos were grainy and revealed little of his face. Besides, the police probably thought the bomber would try to flee the country. They wouldn't expect him to drive to Disney World.

Just after 9:00 p.m., Mostafa sauntered into the campground. He tried not to think about snakes as he slapped at mosquitoes and other buzzing insects dive-bombing his head. Laughter and the musky smell of campfires wafted at him from several directions. Off to the right was the empty cabin he'd scouted earlier, but there was no way to get to it without being seen, not with so many people still out and about.

It was after ten o'clock when he'd finally decided that it was safe to emerge from his hiding spot behind a bathhouse. He slipped to the back of the cabin and tried the three rear windows. All locked. Fortunately, a window on the right side gave way. The problem was, he couldn't hoist himself in without making a racket. He needed something to stand on. Five minutes later, he returned with a plastic crate he'd found two campsites down. One by one, he'd removed a toy bulldozer, a tiny backhoe, dozens of matchbox cars, and a frisbee from the crate, laying them on the grass. He returned to the cabin with the crate and a couple of beach towels he'd pinched from a nearby clothesline. Within a minute, he was inside the cabin, fumbling around in the dark. As he felt his way along the wall, he found a couple of cots on the far side of the main room. A sliver of light emanating from one of the lampposts that rimmed the campground leaked into the cabin, revealing a small galley kitchen and a bathroom.

Mostafa tossed the beach towels onto the cot, unlocked the front door, and returned the crate to the campsite. Then he set an alarm on his phone, covered himself with the pilfered towels, and fell dead asleep in seconds.

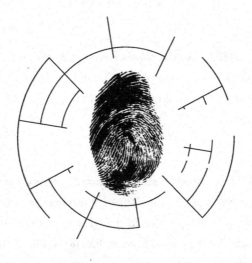

CHAPTER THIRTY-NINE

Makhachkala, Dagestan, Wednesday, June 22, 2005

Imran Bukayev stared at the British news presenter, mouth open, eyes flashing. "Turn that off," he barked.

Daud grabbed the remote and powered off the television. The gravely wounded woman had to be Maggie Jenkins. She was alive! *Alhamdulillah!*

Bukayev slammed the laptop shut, stood, and paced the length of the safe house living room.

"Relax, Imran," Rasul said from the sofa.

"You saw the photographs, Rasul. How could anyone survive that?"

"Whether or not she survives, you've made a statement that no one is safe from Allah's reach."

Bukayev snorted.

Rasul edged forward on the sofa. "You doubt Allah's will?"

Daud watched as the two men stared each other down. For a moment, it seemed like they might have a physical confrontation. Rasul, the younger and stronger man, looked ready to pounce. Bukayev's hands twitched as if he wanted to slap some sense into Rasul. "I want her dead."

Rasul relaxed into the sofa and shrugged. "She'll probably die from her injuries. And if she doesn't, you go after her again."

Bukayev scowled but remained silent.

What do I do? What do I do? Daud's racing thoughts were outpaced only by his galloping heart. He had to tell Roger that Bukayev knew Maggie was alive. Daud edged toward the door.

"Hey! Where do you think you're going?"

"I thought I'd get some food, Imran."

"We have food," Bukayev replied, his tone sharp.

A thin line of sweat formed above Daud's upper lip. "It's been a stressful day. A nice meal from that Georgian restaurant you like would—"

"Why are you always disappearing, Daud?"

"I don't disappear, Imran." His eyes darted to Rasul, who was gnawing on a cuticle. "I run errands for Rasul."

Bukayev marched over and yanked him away from the door. "Let's get one thing straight. When I'm here, I'm in charge. And you're not going anywhere without my approval."

· ★ ★ ★ ·

Jacksonville, Florida

Just before 6:00 a.m., Mostafa stepped outside into the swampy air. If Florida's weather was always this oppressive, he might think twice about relocating here permanently. As his eyes adjusted to the dim pallor cast by the campground lights—tall lampposts made to look like old-fashioned gas lanterns—he made his way to the clothesline to return the beach towels. After securing them with wooden clothes pins, he turned to head for his car.

"Morning."

He startled, looking around. The glow from a lit cigarette caught his attention as a figure emerged from between two tents. A heavyset middle-aged man with a scruffy beard exhaled a puff of smoke as he approached.

"Good morning," Mostafa replied.

"You a late arrival? Didn't see you around here yesterday."

"Yes," Mostafa said. "I'm on my way from Florida to North Carolina."

The man dropped his cigarette and smashed it out with the bottom of his worn leather sandals. His eyes took in all of Mostafa, before settling on his face. "Where were you before you got here?"

These questions were making him nervous. "Disney," he blurted out.

"Disney?"

"Maybe I'll see you around later." Mostafa gave a weak wave and headed off toward the campground entrance. When he looked back over his shoulder, the man was still watching him. Curling his hands into fists, he forced himself to walk casually toward the strip mall. Although the stores were still closed at this hour, he could tell the man, or anyone else who might be watching, that he was simply out for a morning stroll. In front of a shuttered beauty salon, he dropped three quarters into a newspaper vending machine.

After a quick glance at the headlines—TERRORIST ATTACK IN POSH DC SUBURB—he squinted into the hazy dawn light. No one appeared to be following him or loitering outside the campground, but that didn't mean he was in the clear. He hurried over to his car and headed for I-95 south.

· ★ ★ ★ ·

After seeing only one police car over the next ten miles, Mostafa tried to relax. He was hungry, but every time he looked at the *USA Today* lying on the passenger seat, his stomach churned. Had the man in the campground seen the surveillance photos? Was that why he'd been staring at him so intently? Had he recognized him?

No matter, he assured himself. Even if the man called the police, they'd be looking for a suspect who was driving to North Carolina. Still, it might be best to avoid Disney World since he'd mentioned being there recently. Police might swarm the park, searching for people who'd seen someone matching his description. It was smarter to head straight to his ultimate destination—Miami. With his olive skin, a sun hat, and sunglasses, he might pass for Hispanic and blend right in with the locals.

After another half hour, he exited the highway, tossed the newspaper into the backseat, and drove to a doughnut shop. The manhunt for him would rage for a time but Americans were easily distracted. All he needed was a well-timed celebrity scandal or, even better, another terrorist attack, and people would forget to be on the alert for someone who looked like him. And as for Maggie Jenkins, the news reports said she had multiple life-threatening injuries. If she succumbed to her injuries, his contact would wire him a second tranche of ten thousand dollars. If she didn't, he still had a pocket full of money. Time for a little fun in the sun.

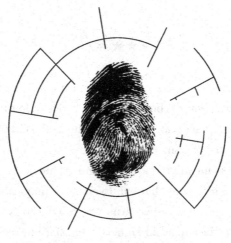

CHAPTER FORTY

CIA Headquarters, Langley, Virginia

J ust before nine in the morning, a black SUV carrying Maggie and two CIA security officers pulled up to the gate outside of CIA Headquarters. As soon as the vehicle was safely inside the compound, a chaser van full of heavily armed FBI agents spun around and returned to the main road.

Maggie clutched her duffel bag and stared out the darkly tinted passenger window. Although they hadn't discussed it last night, Maggie had assumed that Roger would come to the hospital this morning with coffee. But he didn't, and he wasn't returning her calls.

Maybe he was setting up her office, ensuring she'd have everything she needed to make her stay at Hotel Langley, as he'd dubbed it, comfortable. Or maybe he'd been so occupied with the Bukayev operation that he hadn't been able to get away.

As the headquarters building came into sight, the SUV took a sharp left and proceeded a short distance to a ramp leading to the underground executive parking garage. The barrier gate rose as the driver waved to an armed security officer standing outside a guard shack. This was where Warner and the other CIA brass parked.

The driver glanced in the rearview mirror. "Ms. Jenkins, please remain in the vehicle until we're certain there are no unauthorized people in the director's elevator or suite. We'll give you the all-clear signal when we're ready to move."

She considered saluting.

The two men jumped from the vehicle, which idled in front of a pair of gleaming brass elevator doors. One spoke into a corded phone that hung incongruously on the wall beside the elevator call button. After a minute, the other trotted to Maggie's door and pulled it open.

"Ready?"

They ushered her into an elevator cab lined with dark wood panels. The elevator rose with a smooth and swift *whoosh* up to the director's suite on the seventh floor. The security men led her to her new office, which was adjacent to Warner's. A computer sat atop a gleaming wooden desk. Next to the keyboard was a sealed envelope.

"The combination to your safe," one of the men advised.

Maggie glanced around, searching for the standard-issue gunmetal-gray cube with a black combination dial.

"It's here." The man pressed on a wood panel set into the wall. The panel sprang open, revealing the safe. "And over here," he pressed the adjacent panel, "is your shredder and a full supply of burn bags."

"Great. What about meals and—"

"The director's assistant will be along shortly to fill you in on the rest. Is there anything else we can do for you?"

"I don't think so." She was feeling a little lightheaded. "Thanks."

As soon as they left, she sank into her new office chair, a leather-cushioned throne of a seat. She could get used to this.

"Maggie! Oh, my dear girl." Priscilla rushed into the office and threw her arms around her. "I can't believe what happened."

Maggie patted her on the shoulder. "I'm okay, Priscilla. Really."

The wrinkles around Priscilla's eyes deepened. "I understand that we're keeping your presence here a secret."

"That's the plan."

"I've ordered several days' worth of meals from the executive dining hall."

"Won't that raise suspicions?"

Priscilla shook her head. "Not at all. During a crisis, the staff prepares and freezes meals in advance. I'll say the food's for Warner."

"Got it. And I'll be sleeping in his office?"

"Yes. There are fresh sheets and blankets in his wardrobe and plenty of towels and toiletries for you too."

It really was Hotel Langley. "Did Roger set up my office?"

"No, that was our facilities people." She spun around, surveying the space with a critical eye.

"Have you seen him?"

"Roger? Not today, but don't worry, he's one of the few people on the list."

"The list?"

"The list of people who are allowed to see you."

"Oh. Well, I suppose I should get to work."

Priscilla frowned at her. "Don't push yourself too hard, Maggie. Concussions are no laughing matter."

As soon as Priscilla was gone, Maggie dialed Roger's extension, but it went to voice mail. She tried his cell number again. Same thing. *The Ops Center.* That's where she'd find him. As soon as she stood, it hit her. She wasn't allowed to go anywhere but Warner's office.

"Hey, there you are." Warner breezed into the office. His cheerful demeanor struck her as forced. "How are you feeling?"

"I've been better. Where's Roger?"

He clasped his hands in front of him. "He's working on a few things for me. He'll be out of pocket for most of the day, but as soon as he can, he'll call."

"What's he doing?" Whatever it was, he could at least check in on her.

Warner shook his head. "He'll update you."

"I need to know—"

He slid into one of two upholstered red chairs that stood across from her desk.

"The Agency doctor has reviewed your discharge papers. He says you're to rest as much as possible for the next few days. No stress, no—"

"No stress? You've got to be kidding me."

"He's going to check on you every few hours."

Her tone brightened. "Roger is?"

"No, the doctor." Warner looked around the office. "I don't think he'd object to you unpacking some boxes. This place could use some decorating. Maybe you should hang a few pictures."

Her world was imploding, and he wanted to talk interior decorating? "Seriously, Warner, what am I supposed to do all day?"

He patted the arms of his chair. "These recline and swivel, so you can watch TV, close your eyes. Just take it easy."

Her green eyes flashed in anger. "What's going on?"

"Just trying to help you settle in, that's all." Warner tilted his head as if confused. He was rarely confused.

"Are you cutting me out of this investigation?"

"Of course not," he protested as he averted his gaze.

"You're being evasive," she snapped.

He sighed. "We don't have much to work with at the moment. Roger's trying to get more information from Daud."

Maggie blinked a few times. Her thoughts were still fuzzy. "That reminds me, Daud was supposed to give Roger the addresses of their other safe houses. I could do some research—"

"We don't have the addresses. Not yet, anyway."

"That's great. Just fantastic." She powered on her laptop, hoping he'd take the hint that she wanted to get back to work.

Warner stood. "I'll let you know as soon as Roger hears from Daud. I promise."

She ran a hand through her hair and winced when her fingers hit a tender lump.

"Maggie?"

"What?" she said, more sharply than she intended.

He searched her face. "Why didn't you tell me about the woman—"

"What woman?"

"Never mind. It can wait. I'll let you get settled." He disappeared into the hall.

Maggie shut the office door and leaned against it. *What woman? Anna?* Her head pounded and her thoughts were a jumbled mess. Tears of frustration stung her eyes.

Just when she thought she could count on Roger, he'd disappeared without a word. All those times he said she was the most important thing in his life?

Where were the actions to back up his words?

She swiped at a tear and lowered herself into one of the red chairs. When she pushed a button tucked into the right armrest, a footrest emerged, and the chair reclined. She closed her eyes and saw Roger's face. That smile and those dimples. Aqua-blue eyes that danced with mischief. *Dammit, Roger.* Half the time, he was funny, affectionate, and attentive. The other half, he was evasive, withdrew into his work, and vanished when she needed him most. She realized she didn't want only half of Roger. It was all or nothing. At this moment, she leaned heavily toward nothing.

CHAPTER FORTY-ONE

B ack in his office, Warner called his driver. "I want to go to the bombing site."

"Now, sir? Your schedule says—"

"In a half hour. Just you and me."

"I'm afraid that's not possible. The CIA director travels with at least two security officers."

"Well, I'm the director. Just you and me."

There was a long pause. "I'll have the car ready in thirty minutes."

Warner hung up and cracked his knuckles. Roger should be landing in Dagestan shortly. The plan was for him to extract Daud from the safe house and surveil it until he received further instructions. Roger had boarded the Agency airplane under the assumption that he'd be the one to take out Bukayev. But Warner never intended to put him at that kind of risk.

Warner exhaled, picked up the phone, and punched in *67 to block his number. It wasn't a necessary step, he knew, given that his phone was one of the few in the building specially equipped with scrambling technology designed to disguise his location, even when he placed a call to a nonsecure line.

But, he decided, he couldn't be too careful. He steadied his hand and dialed the number that Roger had pulled from Maggie's cell phone while she slept in her hospital bed.

Warner greeted the driver in the underground parking garage with a gruff, "Ready?"

The man appeared rather unhappy about breaking protocol. "Yes, sir."

Ten minutes later, they pulled into the far end of the parking lot.

Warner looked to his left. The windows on the storefronts closest to the blast site were boarded up and a smattering of unidentifiable debris lay scattered on the sidewalk. "Get as close to the police tape as you can," he directed the driver.

The blast site itself was largely cleaned up. The bomb-laden car was gone, no doubt taken to the FBI's crime lab, as was the Agency's SUV. A car-sized crater several feet deep marred the pavement. Chunks of blacktop and charred bits of metal dotted its perimeter. Nearby, a lamppost lay on the ground, twisted by the blast into a giant question mark.

"Good Lord," he said under his breath. Maggie should be dead. Warner forced his eyes from the crater to the strip mall. At the far end stood a used-book store. When he'd phoned earlier, the owner assured him that they were open for business today.

He scanned the mostly empty parking lot. Across the busy main road stood a series of town houses with a direct line of sight to the bookstore. He'd given Anna Orlova just twenty minutes to get here, probably not enough time for her to deploy a surveillance team. He slipped a baseball cap on his head. "Could you drive to that store on the end?"

The driver eyed him in the rearview mirror before spinning the vehicle around and rolling toward the bookstore.

"Just pull up to the curb right here."

The driver seemed to hesitate.

"A retired Agency officer's wife owns that bookstore," Warner said. "I'm going to pop in and say hello. Maybe grab a few books for my kids."

"Sir, we haven't done a security check. I'm afraid I can't let you do that."

Warner threw open the door. "Wait here. I'll only be a few minutes." As he walked in front of the vehicle, he gave the driver a smile and a wave.

A strip of hanging bells affixed to the door alerted a woman behind the checkout counter to his presence

"Good morning," she said as she closed a book and eyed Warner. "Can I help you find anything?"

"No thanks, I'm just browsing." In the corner behind her, a security camera hung from the wall. It could be a fake, placed there to deter thieves, although Warner couldn't imagine that thieves targeted bookstores. He averted his face, just in case it was a real camera, and found his way to the romance section. Most of the paperback covers featured voluptuous women locked in embraces with muscular, bare-chested men.

The bells on the door jangled again. Warner's stomach jumped. This could be the biggest mistake of his life.

"You like romance?"

He glanced to his right. A petite woman with blonde hair smiled up at him. She was the walking definition of a honeytrap—an attractive young Russian that the SVR would deploy to seduce foreign government officials. If the honeytrap is successful, the foreigner is forced to choose between exposing his infidelity or cooperating with Russian intelligence. It was the oldest trick in the book. Warner would never have fallen for it had Ed, an attractive young Russian, not slipped something into his drink that night.

"Romance? No. I prefer spy novels." He glanced around. "We've come into possession of information that might be of great interest to your government."

She blinked at him. "I'm just a journalist, Mr. Thompson. I don't know anything about—"

"Spare me the cover story. I've been directed to share this information with you."

"I don't understand."

Warner reached into the inner pocket of his suit jacket and pulled out a slip of paper. "If you want to capture Imran Bukayev, you've got to act immediately." By capture, he meant kill. But he wasn't going to say that out loud. He placed the note in Anna's hand. "This is his current location, but he's on the move every few days."

Anna's gaze darted around the store as if she feared an ambush. "You're mistaken if you think—"

"I'm not mistaken." He turned and walked to the children's section, where he grabbed a couple of chapter books without glancing at them, paid for them at the counter, and returned to the waiting SUV.

He shook the plastic bag as he slid into the backseat. "My girls have been dying to read these books."

The driver nodded, the lines around his mouth relaxing now that his charge was back in the safety of the vehicle.

Warner spent the rest of the ride in silence as the reality of what he'd done hit him in waves, each stronger than the last. He'd just provided classified information to a suspected Russian intelligence officer. Granted, all he'd shared was the location of a common enemy, but the information itself had originated with a human asset on the ground. If Anna was good at her job, if she was more than just a pretty face, she'd race to get the address to her superiors. The way he'd phrased his pitch—I've been directed to share this information—implied orders from on high. As in the White House. That would grab Moscow's attention.

He put a hand on his aching chest. The stress was getting to him. What was the advice he used to give to trainees? Focus on what you can control and remain alert for what you can't. The only thing he could control was Roger. He'd tell him there was intelligence indicating that the Russians had homed in on Bukayev's location and that he and Daud must move a safe distance away.

An equal mix of dread and anticipation filled him. When the Russians came for him, Bukayev would either blow himself up or die trying to stop them. Either way, his death would mark the end of a long, difficult saga. Finally, Maggie would be free to write the rest of her story. He owed her that much. Steve would have approved. The thought eased his guilty conscience.

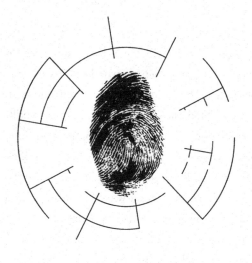

CHAPTER FORTY-TWO

Makhachkala, Dagestan, Russia

R oger found an airport bathroom and locked himself inside a stall. Using his CIA-issued phone, he called a number that ostensibly connected to a corporation in Eastern Europe and left a message. "It's me," he said in accented English. "The flight was smooth." He wondered when Warner would tell Maggie where he really was. If he didn't tell her soon, she'd figure it out. And she'd be furious. He imagined a flush rising on her cheeks, her green eyes flashing. She was a fireball, a woman of great passion and tender vulnerability. The more she revealed of herself, the more he wanted to know her. The sound of the bathroom door opening shook him from his reverie. He couldn't allow himself to think of Maggie now or he'd lose his edge. After leaving Maggie at the hospital the previous night, he'd rushed home to pack, then returned to CIA Headquarters tó retrieve his cover documents and a Russian cell phone. Roger's cover name was Aleksei Mikhailovich Smirnoff. Like the vodka. He wished he could claim credit for choosing the surname, but those honors went to an employee whose job it was to create false identities and legends for Agency personnel. Because of the quick turnaround needed to get Roger on an airplane, his legend was built around the life of a real Belarusian citizen, a risky but necessary shortcut.

The real Aleksei worked as a tax accountant for an international consulting firm. As such, Aleksei frequently traveled to neighboring countries on business, which was the perfect background for Roger. Not the accounting part. He hated math. The travel part. Someone like Aleksei would be a seasoned traveler, a fact that Roger could use to explain to Russian customs officials why he'd been out of the country.

The Office of Technical Services created a passport for him using an expertly crafted Belarusian template. Because of Roger's blue eyes, dark hair, and sharp features that could, in the right light, help him pass as a Slav, the disguise officer decided against altering Roger's appearance.

"It's hard to improve on perfection, isn't it?" Roger had joked, evoking a blank stare from the disguise man.

As far as the Office of Technical Services was concerned, Roger was flying to Turkey on a mission for which they were not cleared. The pilot and first mate on the CIA's Gulfstream G550 knew nothing of Roger's Belarusian cover. Their job was to deliver him to Istanbul in the shortest time possible. On board the aircraft, Roger had searched the wet bar for Smirnoff vodka so he could offer a toast to his new identity. He breathed a sigh of relief when he realized that he'd have to settle for Grey Goose. He'd stopped at two vodka tonics, which were just enough to ease his nerves and more than enough to knock him out for several hours in a reclining leather seat.

After landing in Istanbul, Roger became Aleksei. His passport showed that he had landed in Istanbul from Jordan, where, he explained to the customs officer, he'd helped a client to implement a new accounting system. The officer's eyes glazed over at the word "accounting." He breezed right through to the ticket counter, where he purchased a one-way flight to Dagestan.

The two-and-a-half-hour flight from Istanbul into Russia's southern Caucasus region was scenic, if a bit harrowing. Roger made a mental note to avoid flying on a discount Turkish airline in the future. Inside Makhachkala Uytash International Airport, the customs officer asked him why he wasn't flying directly from Istanbul to Minsk, his home city.

"My brother is a police officer here in Dagestan," he'd said in fluent Russian.

The officer regarded Roger with suspicion.

That's when he deployed his new secret weapon. "I'm an accountant. A tax accountant." The officer grunted something and stamped the passport. If the CIA made every operative an accountant, he mused, they'd never have issues crossing international borders.

After grabbing some caffeine in the form of can of cola, Roger exited the airport just after 6:00 p.m. local time.

The preliminary work Maggie had done mapping out the neighborhood surrounding Bukayev's last known location helped him plan his next move. He'd memorized the information during the last hour of the flight on the Gulfstream, then shredded the document and flushed it down the aircraft's toilet.

He hailed a taxi that took him to a Turkish restaurant several blocks from the safe house and ordered a plate of *borek*, a Turkish appetizer made of phyllo dough, feta cheese, spinach, garlic, and onion. He washed it down with a cup of piping-hot Turkish coffee. As the fog lifted from his travel-weary body, Roger prepared himself for his next move.

At this point, he had no choice but to contact Daud directly. If Daud couldn't speak over the phone, he'd direct him to a small park a block away from the safe house. If Daud didn't answer his phone, Roger would have to approach Bukayev's hideout and try to make visual contact. He dialed Daud's number and willed him to answer.

"*Da?*"

His pulse quickened. "Is this the Central Asian Studies Institute?" he said in English. As the former director of that institute, Daud would know immediately that it was Roger calling.

"*Da*," he repeated.

"I'm here. Meet me at the park one block southeast of the safe house."

The line went dead.

"Shit," Roger said under his breath. He threw several rubles on the table and left.

Bukayev muted the television. "Who was that, Daud?"

"Wrong number," he said, his face growing red.

Bullshit. He rose from the couch and walked toward the kitchen where Daud had taken the call. "No. it wasn't."

Daud, eyes wide, sputtered. "It was just . . . it was Karina. She's worried about me, that's all."

"Give me the phone."

"But if she calls again, I need—"

Bukayev snatched the phone. The last three calls had originated from the same local number. "If I call this number, she'll answer?"

"Of course. But, she said she was going to work in the garden, so if she doesn't answer, that's why."

Bukayev glared at Daud, then pocketed his phone.

Daud lowered his eyes and returned to the kitchen, where he'd been hand-washing two days' worth of dishes when Roger called. He couldn't believe that Roger was here, in Dagestan. How had his call come across the phone as Karina's number? Was Roger with Karina? No, he said he was a couple of blocks away. What if he called back and Bukayev answered? His hands trembled under the hot, sudsy water.

Back in the living room, an argument erupted between Imran and Rasul after Rasul cranked the TV's volume.

"I like this *Big Brother* show," Rasul said.

Daud dried his hands and peered around the corner into the living room.

Imran was on his laptop, typing furiously. He paused and looked up at the television. "It's utter trash."

Rasul, who was seated beside Imran on the sofa, gave the older man's shoulder a playful shove. "It's fun. You need to loosen up, Imran. Not everything has to be so serious."

"Watching drunk Russians jump into bed with somebody new every five minutes isn't fun." Imran slammed the computer shut. "It's depraved."

Rasul scowled. "Lighten up. You're such a prude, Imran."

This was it, his chance to slip away while they were arguing. Daud turned and slipped out the front door.

From the corner of his eye, Bukayev saw movement. He sprang from the couch and found the kitchen empty. "Daud," he shouted over the blaring television. He wasn't in the bathroom or either bedroom. With a glance back at Rasul, whose face twisted in delight at the sight of nubile Russian women splashing around in a hot tub together, Bukayev left the apartment in search of Daud.

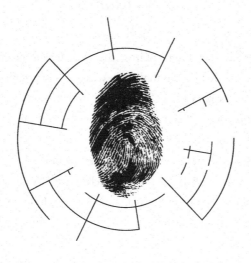

CHAPTER FORTY-THREE

CIA Headquarters, Langley, Virginia

Warner waved off Priscilla as she scolded him for leaving the building without so much as a note. Inside his office, he opened the safe and flipped through a folder until he found the number for Roger's Russian cell phone.

"It's me," Warner said, relief flooding him at the sound of Roger's voice.

"Not a good time," Roger replied. "Daud's meeting me a block from the apartment. I'll call you after."

"You've got to get away from there. Immediately."

"Hell no. I'm a block away from the sonofabitch."

"I just received an intercept from the FSB office in Dagestan." Roger would eventually find out that there was no such intercept. He'd figure out how to explain away that lie when the time came. "They know where the safe house is." That part was true. "They're moving in."

"When?" Roger's voice rose an octave.

Warner glanced at his watch. "I don't know, but soon." And it would be soon, if Anna had acted on the intelligence he'd given her. "Get Daud. Then if you can, get Karina, and get the hell out of Dagestan."

"I didn't come this far to leave the mission unfinished."

Warner scratched at his head. Roger's response didn't surprise him. When you're that close to your target, you don't cut and run. "Listen, the Russians are coming. If you're still there when they arrive, they'll either kill you or capture you."

"I'll be fine," Roger snapped. "I'm not leaving until I know he's dead."

"You don't need to see his body. The Russians will be shouting it from the rooftops when they kill him."

Roger fell silent.

Warner squeezed his eyes shut. "Just get out."

"But—"

"That's an order, Roger."

"This is a mistake." The line went dead.

· ★ ★ ★ ·

Makhachkala, Dagestan, Russia

Outside the apartment building, Samir, one of Rasul's men, stood, lit cigarette in hand, ostensibly keeping an eye out for any possible threats. He was a large man, over six feet tall. And young, rippling with muscle.

"Hey," Bukayev said. "Which way did Daud go?"

Samir dropped the cigarette on the sidewalk and smashed it un-
derfoot. He jerked his head to the left. "Toward the park."

Bukayev hadn't noticed a park nearby. "Come with me." If his
suspicions were correct about Daud, that he was up to no good, it was
better to bring some muscle along for the inevitable confrontation.

Samir shrugged and fell in step behind Bukayev. He slowed as he
saw a rusted iron gate bisecting a row of unkempt hedges. "That the
park?" he asked over his shoulder.

"Yes."

Bukayev proceeded to the gate. From here, the park appeared
small, perhaps no larger than a half acre of land. A gravel path meandered from the entrance, then split in two paths, one arcing to the
right and the other to the left. There was no sign of Daud, but he
wasn't comfortable walking into the park with no cover. The nearest
tree, standing about twenty yards ahead, was too narrow for him to
hide behind. He rushed past the gate and continued until he reached
the next corner.

Before taking a left down the adjacent side street, he motioned
for Samir, who was lighting a fresh cigarette, to catch up to him. Up
ahead on the left was another gate, this one opening to a jumble of
overgrown weeds, tall, uncut grass, and, most important, a high row of
hedges. Bukayev crept toward the hedges and peered over the green-
ery. Across the park, two men stood huddled together. One of them
was Daud. The other had his back to Bukayev.

I knew it! Daud was up to no good. What if the other man was Russian intelligence? Or the local police? Bukayev scrambled to formulate
a plan. He was about to tell Samir to retrieve Daud's car when the two
men turned and walked in his direction. He shrank low and waited for
a count of thirty. Then he peered over the hedge and watched Daud
shake his head. The other man put his hands on Daud's arms and held
them there. Were they lovers? He'd suspected that Daud might be one

of *them*, soft and sensitive as he was. Daud, seemingly placated by the other man's assurances, exited the park along the main road. Bukayev rushed out the side gate and directed Samir to follow Daud. Then he returned to the hedge.

When Daud's friend turned to take a seat on a nearby bench, all the air went out of Bukayev's lungs. *Him!*

· ★ ★ ★ ·
CIA Headquarters, Langley, Virginia

Maggie rubbed at her eyes, momentarily disoriented, then checked her watch. A two-hour nap? *Dammit.* She scrambled from the chair and hurried over to the desk. No messages on her phone.

A dull pain thrummed behind her eyes. The doctor had said she might feel this way for several days. Her breath quickened as she heard Rich's voice echoing inside her head. *Maggie, run. Go, go, go!*

She gulped down some water, fluffed her hair, and marched into Warner's office. She found him sitting at his desk, staring at the phone. "Waiting for a call?"

He startled. "Hey there. How are you feeling?"

"Fine." She sat in one of the leather chairs across from his desk. "Where is he, Warner?"

He glanced to the window and back again. "Dagestan."

"What?" she yelped. "You've got to be kidding me. Did you know he was going?"

"Actually, I sent him." His tone was flat, his face drawn in concern.

"You . . . why?"

"Daud isn't up to the task. I think he's cracking under pressure. Roger persuaded me to send him so he can do the necessary surveillance ahead of the Special Operations Group's arrival."

"When did all this happen?"

"We made the decision yesterday afternoon. He flew out of an airfield in Maryland last night."

The throbbing in her head grew stronger. When he'd brought her dinner and her things, he'd known he was going to Dagestan. And he hadn't said a word. After all this time, he still thought she was too fragile to handle the truth? That she had to be protected from it?

"I decided not to tell you," Warner said, interrupting her thoughts. "Doctor's orders were to keep stress to a minimum. But after everything you've been through, you deserve to know."

She threw up her arms. "I can't believe you sent him to Dagestan. Bukayev will recognize him." Her voice rose. "In case you've forgotten, he captured Roger sneaking around his house last year. He's going to—"

"Everything's going to be okay. I promise."

She stood, shook her head in disbelief. "You can't promise that," she spat before walking out of his office.

· ★ ★ ★ ·
Makhachkala, Dagestan, Russia

Bukayev almost couldn't believe his eyes. It was the man he'd seen in the news photograph, driving Maggie Jenkins to her house. The same man he'd caught in his London brownstone last fall. Bukayev had beaten him unconscious. He and Zara had tied his hands and feet and moved him into the guest room on the lower level. Sometime during the night, the man had managed to free himself and escape. To this day, Bukayev didn't know how he'd gotten away or who he was. But in this moment, one thing became crystal clear. *This man must be CIA.*

Daud was a dead man walking. But he could take care of that matter later. Right now, he had to worry about the CIA man. He must know about the safe house, which could only mean one thing—they were coming for him.

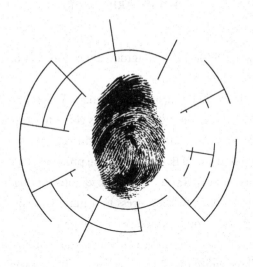

CHAPTER FORTY-FOUR

CIA Headquarters, Langley, Virginia

Warner burst into Maggie's office, his face flushed.

Her stomach dropped. "What's wrong?"

"Police in Florida have detained a man driving a car with Virginia tags. He matches the description of the bomber."

For a moment she forgot how furious she was with him. "The description isn't very detailed, Warner."

"Yeah, I know, but there's more. He told police he'd been vacationing in Florida for weeks, but they found a receipt in his car from the fast-food restaurant near the gym. With yesterday's date on it."

Maggie stood and gripped the edge of the desk. "Are they bringing him back up here?"

"The FBI's Jacksonville field office is transporting him to Quantico now. I'm heading there in a few."

"Why? You can't interrogate a suspect, Warner."

"Not on US soil, no," he noted. "But I can feed the FBI questions."

This was good news, their first break. "Let me go with you."

"Absolutely not."

Based on the steely expression on his face, she knew it was useless to argue. "What about Roger? What if he calls in and you're not here?"

"I'll have a phone with me the entire time. If Roger needs me, the Ops Center will find me." He bounded for the door. "Don't forget the pullout couch in my office if you need to rest. And the fridge is stocked with meals Priscilla ordered for you from the executive dining room." And with that, he vanished.

Maggie kneaded her temples, then picked up the phone.

"Creature? It's me."

"Hey, you," he drawled. "How you feelin'?"

"I'm okay." She wasn't okay and wouldn't be until Bukayev was dead and Roger was home safe. "It could've been a lot worse."

"Well, I suppose, but you gave our mutual friend the scare of a lifetime."

"I know." She paused, considering what to say, knowing he might call Warner immediately after she hung up. Then again, she didn't need anyone's permission to call Creature. "You talk to your person recently?"

"Not since yesterday." The cry of a seagull filled a brief silence. "Why?" His voice spiked with concern.

"My person, the one you met, is over there to keep things on track." She swallowed and cleared her throat. "I haven't heard from him, so I was wondering if you knew anything."

"Doesn't the boss know what's going on?"

Hell if I know. "I can't ask him. He's indisposed at the moment."

"Oh yeah?" Creature asked, obviously curious as to what could be more important than the status of Roger and Daud.

"Yeah. If anything comes of it, you'll hear it on the news."

"Sounds promising."

"I hope so." She took a sip of diet soda. "Will you let me know if your person calls?" Maybe Karina was already with Roger. Maybe they were making their way to safety and didn't have time to call.

"Of course I will. And you'll let me know if you hear from your person?"

Roger wouldn't call her and Warner wasn't telling her much. "Absolutely. Right away."

"You hang in there, darlin', okay?"

"I'll try." She disconnected the call and leaned back in the chair.

There had to be something she could do. *Maybe . . .* No, Warner would have her head if he found out. But it wouldn't hurt to prepare, just in case. She spun around and pressed her hand against the wood-panel door, revealing her safe. Inside were both her personal and US government employee passports.

· ★ ★ ★ ·

Makhachkala, Dagestan, Russia

"Imran, is that you?" Rasul shouted over the noise emanating from the television.

Daud searched the kitchen for his keys. Where were they?

"It's just me, Rasul. Where'd Imran go?" Had he taken the car?

Rasul scratched at his stomach. On the couch with him was one of his security men. Another sat on the floor on the opposite side of a coffee table. On the table was an open backpack ringed by a half dozen handguns.

Daud drew closer to get a better look. He gasped when he saw the contents of the backpack. "Are those grenades?"

Rasul smirked. "No, they're tennis balls."

The men laughed.

"What are you doing with them?"

Rasul shot him a glance. "That information would be classified as none of your damned business."

Daud's legs went weak. He had to get out of here. He dashed into the bedroom where Imran had slept. The place was a mess. Clothes on the floor. Imran's rucksack on the unmade bed. He rifled through the bag—clothes, several cell phones, and a nearly empty vodka bottle.

He whirled around, eyes taking in the rest of the space. *There, on the dresser!* As he crossed the room to grab the key ring, a loud thud followed by the sound of splintering wood filled his ears. Then came shouting. *Politsiya?*

Daud dove into the small closet in the corner of the room and began to pray. Gunfire erupted in a cacophony of booms. More shouting. Then he remembered the hand grenades. Rasul would sooner die than be captured. He peered out the bedroom door. At the end of the hall stood two heavily armed Russian police, clad in black tactical uniforms, helmets, and bulletproof vests. Their semiautomatic rifles and eyes were fixed in the same direction—toward the living room.

"*Bros' eto!*" One shouted. "Drop it!"

Daud stepped into the hall, arms raised. The officer closest to him whirled around and trained his weapon on him.

"Please, help me," he begged, tears streaming down his face.

"Drop it!" the first officer shouted, drawing the attention of the second for the briefest moment.

This was his chance to get out. As he neared the policeman, he saw what had captured their attention. Rasul Makasharipov stood just feet away, arms raised, a grenade in each hand. And a snarl on his face.

"No!" Daud yelled, but it was too late. Rasul released his thumbs from the levers. A bright flash of light filled the hall as an explosive force tore into everyone inside the apartment.

Bukayev noticed a commotion near the apartment building. The CIA man seemed to have noticed it too, as he rushed from the bench to the park's front gate. Bukayev stood from his semi-crouched position and ran for the side gate. He needed to see for himself.

Ahead at the corner, Samir came sprinting his way. "The police. They're everywhere."

Bukayev's eyes widened. It couldn't end like this. He wasn't done yet. "They're coming for me?"

"They're inside the apartment building." He looked around in disbelief. "I heard gunfire."

Sirens wailed in the distance. A muted *boom* hit the air.

Bukayev's hands flew to his head. His computer. His phones. Daud's car keys. Everything was inside the apartment. Panic rose in his throat. "Do you have keys for the other car?"

Samir's face brightened as he pulled a keychain from his pocket. "I'll go get it." With that, he dashed up the street in the opposite direction from the apartment.

Bukayev hurried back to the side gate. The CIA man paced in front of the bench, then sank onto it, his head lowered, face cradled in his hands. A moment later, he looked up and sniffed the air. He must smell what Bukayev did. Smoke.

Roger inhaled deeply. It was definitely a fire.

Maybe Daud had seen the police approaching the apartment building and run off somewhere. That was the best case but least likely scenario. Odds were, Daud had been in the apartment when the police arrived and had died, if not from gunfire, then in what seemed to be a rapidly spreading inferno. Overhead, black tendrils of smoke danced and weaved in the light summer-evening breeze.

I'm so sorry, Daud. He was an accidental and very reluctant spy, a hapless young man who was too good to do evil but too weak to stop it. Roger had lost another agent once, but Daud was different. He was just a kid. *Dammit all.*

He stood and shook out his arms. At least there was good news. No, great news. Imran Bukayev was dead. They'd need confirmation, but just a few minutes ago, Daud had said that Imran was in the apartment. As was Rasul Makasharipov, a thug who'd made a career out of slaughtering Russians.

As much as Roger wanted to stick around to monitor the outcome, the entire neighborhood would soon be crawling with Russian security and intelligence personnel. This was no place for a CIA officer traveling on a Belarusian passport. He didn't dare place a call to Warner, at least not until he figured out a way out of the city.

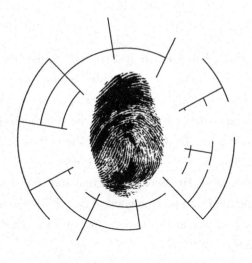

CHAPTER FORTY-FIVE

Makhachkala, Dagestan, Russia

Bukayev's back ached and his legs burned from squatting behind the hedge. He felt nearly paralyzed by indecision. He had to get the hell away from the safe house, but he also needed to know what the CIA knew about him. What secrets had Daud revealed? Were all the safe houses blown? Who told the Russians where they were staying? His survival depended on answering those questions. That's when it occurred to him. If he captured the CIA man, his cachet with al-Qaeda financiers would skyrocket, especially when he released a video of the American's slow and painful death. And if Maggie Jenkins recovered from her injuries, the images from the video would make her wish she hadn't.

A sudden movement on the other side of the hedge jolted him back to the present. Hands on thighs, he pushed himself to a stand to see what was afoot. It was the CIA man, standing just feet away. Bukayev panicked and rushed for the gate.

"Hey, are you okay?" the man asked in Russian.

Bukayev tried to run, but the CIA man was faster. He grabbed Bukayev's shoulder and whirled him around.

Imran stared up into bright blue eyes that narrowed for a moment before widening in surprise. Bukayev took advantage of the man's shock to wrench himself free and escape through the gate.

The man followed, this time shouting in English. "Stop, you motherfu—"

The sound of screeching tires drowned out his voice but didn't slow his speed. He lunged for Bukayev, managing to hook an arm around his neck. From the corner of his eye, Bukayev saw Samir and another man scramble out of a black sedan. A moment later, Samir tackled the CIA man, freeing Bukayev and sending the American tumbling to the sidewalk, where his head met concrete with a sickening thud.

"We need to take him with us," Bukayev shouted as Samir pummeled the spy's face. Blood flowed from the man's nose, chin, lips, and the side of his head. He grabbed Samir's arm. "Enough. I need him alive. Gag him and tie him up."

Samir smiled, admiring his handiwork. He popped the trunk and pulled out a length of rope. Sirens wailed ever louder.

"We don't have time. Put him in the trunk and drive."

· ★ ★ ★ ·

Quantico, Virginia

Warner passed through the security checkpoint inside an innocuous-looking brick building located a distance away from the FBI Academy complex, which itself was situated at Marine Corps Base Quantico. A smartly dressed FBI agent escorted him down a set of stairs into the basement. A sparsely furnished conference room with a glass outer wall sat to the left of the stairs. To the right were three doors evenly spaced along a short corridor. The escort opened the first door. Two middle-aged agents, one man, one woman, sat at a small oval table.

"Director Thompson," said the woman as she stood and extended her hand. "Agent Mullen. This is Agent Barrett."

Warner offered a curt nod. "Thanks for having me. Where's the suspect?"

Mullen pointed at the darkened two-way mirror on the wall. "In the interrogation room."

"Do we have a name?"

Mullen handed him a piece of paper imprinted with a photocopied Virginia driver's license. "Mostafa, huh? This his real identity?"

"We don't know yet. We're running his face and the surveillance footage through our facial-recognition software to see if they match," she said. "He claims to work for a landscaping company and to have fled Afghanistan when the Taliban destroyed his village a few years back. The address on his license and car registration point to a boardinghouse in Falls Church. We've deployed an agent to talk to the landlord."

This had to be the bomber. He was in possession of a receipt from the restaurant near the gym. He lived and worked just outside of DC. *Seems like a slam dunk.* "How does the interrogation work?"

She pointed to her ear. "I'll have an earpiece in so you can comment or ask questions. And you'll be able to watch through the mirror. We'll also have a live video feed streaming on that laptop."

Warner took in the setup. Since he couldn't beat the truth out of the suspect, this would have to do. He pulled out a folding chair and put his phone on the table.

Agent Mullen pursed her lips. "I'm afraid you'll have to leave your phone in the bin near the stairs."

"If it rings, I need to be notified."

"Of course." Agent Mullen left the room with his phone.

Agent Barrett clicked the computer mouse several times until a video feed filled the screen. Next, the large two-way mirror on the wall lit up, allowing Warner to see clearly into the interrogation room. The suspect—Mostafa—sat with cuffed hands folded together on the table. He looked calm. Was that a result of training, or was he innocent? It had to be the former. Even the most innocent foreign Muslim would be shaking at the prospect of an FBI interrogation.

Warner watched on the laptop as Agent Mullen entered the interrogation room and greeted Mostafa, who remained impassive. She read him his Miranda rights, emphasizing that these were the same rights the arresting officer had read to him.

"I don't need a lawyer. I didn't do anything. I have nothing to hide."

Big mistake, buddy, Warner thought.

Mullen began the interrogation with questions about Mostafa's childhood and his eventual journey to the States. Warner checked his watch. Couldn't she just cut to the chase already?

Someone rapped on the door. A young man entered the room.

"I'm sorry to interrupt, Mr. Thompson. Someone's trying to reach you on your phone."

"The session's being recorded," Agent Barrett said. "If you miss anything important, you can watch it when we're done with him."

Warner followed the young man down the corridor and grabbed his phone from a bin on a table near the stairs. Two missed calls from the Ops Center. "Do you have a STU-III here?" Warner didn't want to have to speak in code when he called in. The STU-III, the intelligence community's secure telephone system, would allow him to speak freely.

"Yes, sir. In the conference room."

"Great." He let himself into the empty room and shut the door behind him. Pulling a chair up to the credenza where the secure phone sat, Warner dialed.

"Thompson here." He recited his employee ID and a PIN that he used only when calling into the Ops Center.

"Sir, Moscow Station received word that there was a shootout in Dagestan."

He gripped the receiver. "Do you know where?"

"Based on what they've picked up from Russian comms, they've narrowed the location down to five city blocks in Dagestan's capital."

Off the top of his head, he couldn't recall the street name where the safe house was located. "What roads are in that vicinity?"

The duty officer began to recite streets names, butchering their difficult pronunciations.

Warner stopped him. "What was the last one?"

The duty officer repeated it.

"Yes, that's it." His heart raced. "Have we heard from Roger?"

"No, sir. In fact, we've been trying to call him for the past hour. He's not answering."

Warner rushed back into the observation room. "Did I miss anything?"

Agent Barrett glanced up from the video feed on the laptop. "Nothing of significance yet. Agent Mullen is building rapport with the suspect."

"Rapport?" He moved to the two-way mirror. "That man in there tried to kill my chief of staff yesterday. And he murdered one of our security men."

"Understood, but this is part of the process." Barrett kept his attention on the computer screen.

"I've got an extremely serious situation going on overseas. I don't have time for this getting-to-know you BS."

Barrett squinted up at Warner. "We don't want to elicit a confession that can be thrown out in court because of procedural missteps."

Warner closed his eyes and counted to five. The agent and the suspect were discussing the family he'd left behind in Afghanistan. "As if anyone cares," he muttered. "How long until she asks him about the attack? Where'd he get the bomb? The money? The instructions on what to do and when?"

"With all due respect, sir," Barrett began, "I can't answer that for you because I can't hear what they're saying with you firing questions at me."

Warner bit down on his tongue. It would do him no good to alienate the FBI. He sat in the folding chair next to Barrett. "How do I talk to Agent Mullen?"

His finger hovered over the mouse. "I click here and you can speak to her. The suspect won't be able to hear you."

Warner snatched the mouse and clicked. "Ask him about Bukayev's network in the US. And whether there are follow-on attacks planned. And how we contact Bukayev." He stared at the video feed.

Agent Mullen cleared her throat, then continued with her line of questioning.

"Dammit, Mullen, cut to the chase already."

She raised her eyes and stared up at the camera hanging in the corner of the room. "No," she mouthed.

Warner slammed a fist on the table. "One of my officers is in grave danger and you suits can't demand answers from this evil little piece of shit?"

"Director Thompson—" Barrett protested.

Warner stood with such force that the chair toppled over behind him. "If anything happens to my officers because of this pathetic excuse for an interrogation, the FBI director will hear from me." He pointed a finger at Agent Barrett. "And I will hold you and your partner personally responsible." With that, he stormed from the room. It would be up to him to save Roger himself. If it wasn't already too late.

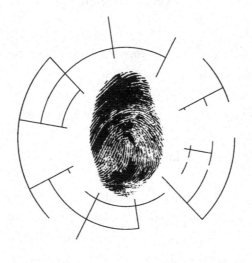

CHAPTER FORTY-SIX

CIA Headquarters, Langley, Virginia

Warner rushed into his office, his heart beating erratically, sweat dotting the chest and armpits on his blue dress shirt. The ride from Quantico had been the longest hour of his life. And still no word from Roger. He logged on to his computer, dropping his head into his hands while it booted up. This couldn't be happening. Not again. He couldn't lose another officer.

Maggie would never survive this. Let alone forgive him.

"Come on, come on," he muttered as he navigated to his inbox. Moscow Station was supposed to send updates as often as events warranted. He wanted every detail, even the most minute or seemingly insignificant ones.

Russian media short on details. Reports claim a major success in the country's war on radical extremism.

He clicked to the next message.

Police in Dagestan say there was police action in the republic's capital, resulting in multiple casualties.

If this message was in Maggie's feed, she'd make the connection to Roger.

And she'd demand answers he didn't want to provide.

Hoping against hope, Warner tried Roger's Russian cell phone. No answer. He hung up and tried to gather himself. Maybe he was in police custody. Not good, but at least not dead. Or he might've left the scene at the first sign of trouble and lost his phone. Except, he would've found a way to call by now. It had been hours since the shootout.

Warner remembered the day he had to tell Maggie that Steve was dead, but he didn't remember how he'd gotten through it. Roger wasn't Maggie's fiancé, but the two of them were good for each other, he could see that. She was still raw from her brush with death last year, but he'd seen the light return in her the closer she got to Roger. And now, just when it seemed that she was turning the corner . . .

Maybe he's not dead. Warner bit down hard on his lower lip. If Roger was dead, it was all his fault. He'd sent him to Dagestan. He'd tipped off the Russians.

The office door flew open. Maggie's pale, tortured expression told him everything he needed to know. "Have you heard from him?" Her voice was barely above a whisper.

He shook his head, unable to speak.

A hand flew to her mouth, absorbing the sob that burst from her.

Warner rushed to her side. "He might be in hiding. He might be okay."

"I turned on the BBC," she said, tears running down her cheeks. "They said at least a half dozen people are dead. There was gunfire, an explosion, a fire. Roger would have called by now. He wouldn't let me think—" Another sob engulfed the rest of her sentence.

He placed a hand on her arm.

She shook it off. "You did this, Warner. You sent him there."

Warner had no words.

She stared over his shoulder at the photograph of Steve on his bookshelf.

"Maggie—"

"What?" Her eyes drilled into him.

"Roger swore he'd never let anything bad happen to you again. He had to go and take care of this himself." It was the last thing he'd said to Warner before leaving for the airfield. "He loves you."

Her lips trembling, she looked away. At the door, she turned to him. "I quit."

· ★ ★ ★ ·

Makhachkala, Dagestan, Russia

It took Roger a few minutes to realize where he was. The metallic taste and smell of blood assaulted his senses. His head throbbed. The last thing he remembered was seeing Imran Bukayev, but he knew that old, doughy, stump of a man couldn't have knocked him out and thrown him in the trunk of a car without help. How was Bukayev alive? He must've left the apartment before . . . before whatever it was that happened. The details were a little fuzzy. He remembered thinking that Daud had been killed. That's right, there'd been gunfire. And maybe an explosion. A fire. Definitely a fire. *Damn.* Poor Daud.

Panic rose in his throat. *Is this how it ends?* An unbidden image of Jane in her final, terrifying moments onboard Flight 93 flashed through his mind. He'd carried around the remorse and guilt for her death for nearly four years. And although he'd never fully recover from her loss, he was ready to lay Jane to rest in the soft recesses of his heart. After returning from the beach trip with Maggie, he'd tucked Jane's photograph away in a box of family pictures for safekeeping. And there it would remain because Maggie was his future. He would fight his way back to her no matter what it took.

The car slowed. Roger struggled to put together a plan. How many men were there? A moment later, a rush of fresh air enveloped him, but he remained still. He'd pretend to be unconscious until he got a better read of the situation.

Nearby, a man barked orders in a language he didn't recognize. Welcome to Dagestan, the land of a million languages. A second man replied.

Then came a third, speaking in Russian. "Russian or English only," the man snapped.

Imran, Roger thought.

Two sets of hands grabbed at his arms and legs. He left his body limp and willed his stomach not to revolt. But every time his head moved, his gut felt like it was going in the opposite direction.

The men grunted and huffed as they carried him a short way. Roger cracked one eye. It was dark out, but there was light coming from nearby, enough to illuminate the grass below. What sounded like a slamming door startled him. A few feet ahead, he could tell he was inside a building. The summer sounds—insects, rustling tree leaves— had fallen silent. And light permeated his closed eyelids. Another safe house?

The men dropped him on a hard surface. A wood floor, maybe? He bit down on his tongue to keep from yelping in pain.

One of the men spoke. "I'm back, Karina."

Karina? It had to be Creature's daughter. Roger knew Bukayev had been to this house at least once before. He needed to get her attention, get her to call for help.

He moaned and tried to roll to his side.

"Secure him," Bukayev ordered.

A foot shoved his shoulder, first rolling him onto his back and then onto his stomach again. "There's rope in the car," one of the other men said.

"Easy," Roger said as the foot pressed into his spine, "I'm an American diplomat, not some sea creature flopping around on a dock." He hoped Karina knew her father's boat was named *Sea Creature*.

"Get me a rag, Karina," Bukayev demanded.

A shuffling of feet ensued, but Roger, whose eyes faced a wall, couldn't see which direction Karina had gone.

When he heard the same soft shuffle, he said, "I used to visit Dagestan all the time during the Soviet war in Afghanistan. I met a beautiful woman named Vera." If these men knew their history and their math, they would realize that Roger would've been a child during the war. They didn't react, but he hoped the message got through to Karina. *I know your father. Your mother's name was Vera.*

"Gag him," Bukayev said.

Before he could react, someone shoved a rag into his mouth. He inhaled deeply through his nose and kicked at the man closest to his feet. His reward was a swift kick to the gut.

Bukayev's goons tied his feet together and bound his hands behind his back. Roger began to gasp and wheeze as if he couldn't breathe. One of the men flipped him onto his back and at last he could see Karina, a beautiful young woman with striking dark eyes and hair. She stared at him and gave an ever so slight nod. At least that's what Roger hoped it was. A sign of understanding.

Bukayev disappeared into a room on the left, returning quickly. "This will do. I'll film the video in there."

Roger's blood ran cold. A video? Like those ones of Western hostages dying in the most brutal ways? Beheadings, mainly. The thought of Maggie watching him die that way tore at his chest. Bukayev's men sat him up and dragged him into a tiny room to the left of the living room. They propped him against a wall next to a metal cot that sat flush against the back wall. A dirty, fraying roller shade covered a window on the front wall. From here, there were only two ways out—the window or the front door. He twisted his hands, trying to loosen the rope around his wrists. But just then, one of the thugs plopped himself down in a wooden chair that the other had fetched and placed in the bedroom doorway.

Out in the living room, Bukayev barked something at Karina, who vanished from Roger's field of vision. She returned shortly with a small pad of paper and a pencil.

"Are you really that stupid, Karina? I need a large piece of paper. Or cardboard. Something that will show up on video."

"I don't know if I have anything like that, Imran. I'll . . . I'll keep looking." Karina locked eyes with Roger as if she was trying to convey something. Was she stalling for time? Trying to distract Bukayev? Or so terrified of him that she didn't know what to do?

"Go search the house for supplies," he ordered his men. They pushed past Karina, eyes locked on her breasts.

Roger gave her a slight nod, then dropped his head to his shoulder as if cradling a telephone. He looked beyond her, then back into her eyes. This time, he gave a bigger nod, so she wouldn't question what she'd seen. Then he slid to his side, kicked his bound legs violently, and used his shoulder to push his body away from the wall. Bukayev ran into the room. Roger thrashed and grunted as he tried to land kicks to Bukayev's legs.

Bukayev shouted for his men to help restrain Roger. Despite their kicks and punches, Roger kept thrashing, trying to give Karina as much time as possible to call Creature.

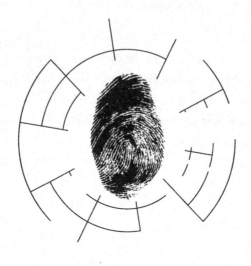

CHAPTER FORTY-SEVEN

CIA Headquarters, Langley, Virginia

Maggie leaned against the door and slid down to the floor, her entire body shaking. This couldn't be happening. Roger, for all his faults, loved her, despite all of hers. And lately, she'd been an overly suspicious, envious shrew to him. She wrapped her arms around her legs, rested her forehead on her knees, and fought back tears. He couldn't be dead. Not Roger. It couldn't be true.

She wiped her eyes with the hem of her shirt and stood, moving about the office robotically, looking from shelf to shelf, drawer to drawer while she debated what to take home with her. Quitting had been a rash decision. But maybe it was time. *Yes*, she decided, it was. There were only a few personal items she didn't want to leave behind, most notable being Steve's photograph. A pain seized her. What had Roger thought about her having a picture of Steve but not of him? Sure, she had photos of Roger, but none were displayed in her office or home.

She tucked a few things into the duffel bag that Roger had brought to the hospital. Her hand felt something smooth and thin. A vacation brochure for a Caribbean resort. A sticky note inside read:

Come sail away with me, my love.
xoxo, Roger

Tears began to well again. She shoved aside clothes that Roger had packed and found a package of her favorite chocolate candies that he'd tucked in the bag. And her cell phone. Someone must've taken it from her at the hospital and put it with her belongings. Having it inside headquarters violated Agency regulations, but it didn't really matter at this point. She'd just quit. What would they do if they found it? Fire her? From the safe, she retrieved her passports. Then she reached for the remote to shut off the television just as breaking news interrupted a broadcast.

"Authorities say that at least one high-profile terrorist was killed in the counterterrorism operation in Dagestan. Also among the dead are two police officers and three other men. Authorities say it may be days before the bodies are positively identified due to a fire that ripped through the first-floor apartment after an explosive detonated. Thus far, the Kremlin has neither confirmed nor denied rumors that Imran Bukayev, the mastermind behind two separate terrorist school attacks, is among the dead."

Maggie muted the television, grabbed a tissue, and blew her nose. The screen filled with a photo of Bukayev. "Come and get me, you bastard," she muttered.

The sound of voices out in the hall grabbed her attention. She hurried to the door and pressed her ear against it, but couldn't make out the words. She cracked it open and heard Priscilla's voice.

"Now? At this hour?"

"The president saw the news on Dagestan and summoned me to his private residence." Warner's voice was flat.

Maggie froze. Once the president found out that Warner had deployed Roger to deal with Bukayev instead of waiting for the Special Operations Group to swoop in, he'd go ballistic. Maybe he'd fire Warner. No. It would be a political disaster if he fired his brand-new CIA director for insubordination. Instead, he'd probably leave a powerless Warner in place and appoint a shadow director to run the Agency.

"I suppose you can't say no to the president, can you?" Priscilla said.

Nope. But if you weave a good enough story, there won't be any consequences. No doubt Warner would concoct a compelling tale justifying his decision to send Roger to Dagestan ahead of the SOG team. And knowing him, he'd probably planned for this exact scenario in case Roger's operation went sideways. Yup, she thought with more than a little bitterness, Warner would remain CIA director. Even if Roger never came home.

"I definitely can't say no to the president," he huffed loudly enough for Maggie to hear. "It's late, Priscilla. Why don't you head home. It's been a long day."

"Should I check on Maggie, first, make sure she has what she needs?"

"She's resting," Warner said, his tone still flat.

Maggie closed the door. A part of her felt terrible about the way she'd stormed out of Warner's office. But she couldn't pretend that everything was okay. Not now and maybe not ever. She checked her watch. In another five minutes, she'd be the only one up here and she'd be able to slip out and go home. For a split second, she thought about calling Rich to come pick her up. But then it hit her all over again. Rich was dead. She closed her eyes, trying to calm her thoughts. A cab. She could have a cab pick her up at the gate.

She shook the computer mouse and searched for local taxi companies. As she reached for the phone, it rang. Her insides seized. Roger?

"Maggie?"

Her heart sank. "Hi, Creature."

"I saw the news."

She dug her nails into her palm to keep from crying.

"I just tried calling your boss but he didn't answer."

Maggie frowned. "He got called to a meeting."

"That's what I figured. As soon as you see him, let him know that I have news."

She gripped the phone.

"My family member called. The guy you're tracking just brought an American man to her house."

She heard the words but didn't comprehend them.

Creature filled the silence. "I think it's him."

"Him?"

"The American. He said something to my person about a sea creature."

"Is it—" she yelped.

"Let's not say names over this line," he warned.

"Right. Sorry." She exhaled to steady herself. "Is he okay? What about the bad guy?"

"I wish I knew more, but she had to hang up."

If Roger was with Bukayev, he was in great danger. But he was still alive. "Thank you, Creature. You have no idea how worried we've been."

"I do, actually." He cleared his throat. "You'll update your boss?"

"Yes." As angry as she was with Warner, of course she'd tell him. Creature sighed. "You going to be at the office all night?"

"I don't know. If you hear from your family member, call me immediately. If I don't answer this number, try my cell." After she gave him her number, she hung up and sank into the desk chair, feeling stunned, elated, and fearful all at once. Roger was so good at what he did. Brilliant, actually, letting Karina know he was on her side by working the phrase "sea creature" into conversation. The thought of Bukayev harming him . . . she pushed away dark images. They'd paralyze her if she let them in.

She double-checked that she had everything she needed, grabbed her bag, and made a final stop in Warner's office. His collection of baseball hats remained packed inside a box on the far side of the room. The CIA director wasn't a sports fan. As such, his hat collection consisted of caps representing intelligence agencies from around the world. Maggie sorted through them, foregoing the KGB hat in favor of the French DGSE agency. Warner would never notice it missing.

She twisted her hair atop her head and secured the hat in place. It wasn't much of a disguise, but she wasn't too concerned. It was late, so few employees would be around. And the guards at the gate wouldn't recognize her since she'd been whisked onto the compound this morning in an SUV with black-tinted windows.

She clattered down seven flights of empty stairs. As she neared the turn for the lobby, she slowed to ensure the people approaching from the opposite direction would exit in front of her. Pulling the bill of the cap lower, she nodded to the guard at the security desk and glanced sidelong at Steve's star on the Memorial Wall. She would do whatever it took to make sure Roger would not be the next star to be added.

Outside, she walked briskly down the granite steps and turned right onto the sidewalk. The gate was only a quarter of a mile ahead. Several cars passed but none slowed. As she approached the guard shack, she caught sight of a yellow cab parked in one of the three spaces where noncleared spouses, friends, and cab drivers could pick up employees who needed a ride.

She waved to the guards without looking in their direction and let herself into the backseat of the cab. "Dulles Airport, please."

Dulles International Airport, Sterling, Virginia

Maggie scarfed down a burger and fries at the bar and grill near her gate and checked her phone for at least the tenth time. She thought for sure Warner would've notice her missing by now, but after what must've been a difficult meeting with the president, he may have decided to avoid her altogether. She couldn't blame him. She'd been brutal in her disdain for him. Even though he'd deserved it, she had to admit that he'd done what he felt necessary to protect her.

A pang of guilt stabbed at her. She should tell Warner about Karina's call to Creature. No doubt he was worried to death about Roger. Even if he had set all this in motion, or at the very least had allowed it to happen, he deserved to know that Roger hadn't died in the Russian raid. She paid for her meal, which now sat in the pit of her stomach like a lead weight, and returned to the gate, where they were just beginning preboarding. She sat in a corner, far away from the rest of the passengers, who were already gathering their belongings so they could be first in line. She called Warner's cell phone. No answer. Same for his office.

Finally, the home phone. She couldn't get on the plane without alerting him to Roger's situation.

She left the same message on all three lines. "I'm sorry to leave without explaining. But I had to go. Call the boat captain. He'll fill you in."

Next, she scrolled through her contacts, found the number she was looking for and dialed. Although it had been a while—they'd last spoken after the school attack last year—she was certain her old friend would be willing to do her one more favor.

"Tamaz?"

There was a pause. "Maggie?" The man's voice was heavy with sleep. And raspy from decades of smoking *papirosi*, those vile, unfiltered Soviet cigarettes.

"I'm sorry to wake you."

"What's wrong?"

"I need your help. I'm flying to Tbilisi tonight."

· ★ ★ ★ ·

CIA Headquarters, Langley, Virginia

Warner hung up the phone with Creature, stunned relief flooding his body. Roger was by no means out of the woods, but at least he was alive. He tried Maggie's cell phone. Voice mail. The security detail answered her home line. No, she hadn't been there all day.

He had a sinking feeling she'd gone after Roger. "Oh, shit," he groaned.

He had officers in the CIA's stations in Georgia, Armenia, and Azerbaijan, all of which were closer to Dagestan than Moscow Station was. Maybe he could send one of them to intercept Maggie. But they would need visas before traveling, and the Russians made the process overly complicated. Did Maggie realize that? How was she planning to get into Russia?

He scrolled through his "eyes only" feed, the one the Special Operations Group used to communicate their progress with him. They were in Tbilisi now and planned to cross the Russian border separately over a period of two days. There had to be a way to expedite their travel so they could rescue Roger, kill Bukayev, and free Maggie if she needed freeing. He paced the length of his office. The entire operation was fraught with peril. If only he had leverage, someone in the Russian government who owed him a favor. He stopped short. Anna Orlova? Even though Bukayev had survived the raid, he'd done her a favor by providing the tip about his location. Still, could he really trust the Russians with Roger's and Maggie's lives? They tended to go in guns blazing, with no regard for the lives of innocent bystanders. And even if they didn't kill Roger and Maggie, they might arrest them for conducting an espionage operation inside Russia.

"Dammit, Maggie," he sputtered. He could always count on her to complicate things.

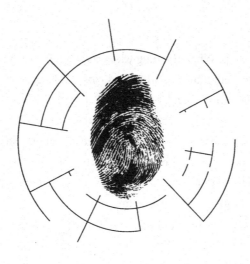

CHAPTER FORTY-EIGHT

Makhachkala, Dagestan, Russia
Thursday, June 23, 2005

Roger woke to sunlight peeking through holes in the window shade. During the night, when he'd realized that the goon guarding him was snoring on the floor nearby, he'd hoisted himself up onto the cot and had a decent nap. If it weren't for his arms being tied behind his back, it might have been an excellent nap.

Now, the chair in the doorway was empty. He could hear the low hum of male voices, but couldn't make out their words. Roger assessed his wounds. His head ached, his lip was swollen, dried blood lined the right side of his jaw, and the ribs that had taken the brunt of the beatings hurt if he breathed too deeply. But he was alive, and help was on the way. He hoped. The previous night, Karina had been tasked with feeding him soup. When the thug who was watching them hollered for a refill for himself, Karina had leaned close to Roger's ear and whispered, "I called my father."

That was the only verbal exchange they'd had, but it had been enough to fuel hope. The other positive development was that Bukayev's phone battery had died, so he was unable to make his hostage film. Apparently, his charger and the rest of his belongings had gone up in smoke inside the safe house fire.

Just as Roger pushed himself to a sitting position on the bed, Bukayev entered the room. "I want to know everything, beginning with your name."

Roger stared back at him. "My identification is in the backpack I was carrying."

"If your name is Aleksei Smirnoff, then I'm the king of England."

"There is no king of England," Roger pointed out, "which you should know since you used to live in London."

Bukayev's furrowed brow betrayed annoyance. "Your name," he repeated more sharply this time.

"Bond. James Bond."

Bukayev's face grew red. "Why were you in my house?" he roared.

Last year, Bukayev had caught Roger snooping around his house in London. Thanks to Maggie, he'd managed to escape. "I was visiting friends, got drunk, and walked into the wrong house. You didn't have to beat me and tie me up over it." He glanced at his bound feet. "I think someone here has a thing for bondage."

Bukayev turned on his heel and stormed from the room. Roger braced himself for the next beating that was sure to come—unless he found a way out or at least a way to fight back. *Never give up or give in,* he told himself, remembering the mantra his first trainer at the Agency had repeated ad nauseum. The man had been a tough-as-nails bully, but his voice in Roger's head was enough to revive his resolve. Roger took a deep breath, stood, and hobbled over to the window. Using his shoulder, he nudged the shade aside and peered through a grimy pane of glass. A small front yard abutted a dusty road. Across the road stood a barren field dotted with a few shrubs. If he were to escape, he'd have to make a run for it as there seemed to be nowhere to hide. He struggled against the rope binding his wrists together without success. That's when he spotted it—a hook on the wall to the left of the window, the kind meant to hold a towel or a light jacket. It hung loosely as if it had borne too much weight over the years. Roger shuffled past the window and clamped his teeth around the hook. He pulled, twisting his head left and right like a puppy battling a chew toy. When the hook popped loose, he stumbled backwards, landing with a thud on the floor. The hook and a two-inch-long screw dangling from the back of it clattered onto the uneven wood planking several feet away. He lunged for the screw, something he could use as both a weapon and a tool to shred the rope binding his wrists. But before he could secure it, one of Bukayev's men ran into the room, dragged him across the floor to the cot, and kicked him in the gut for good measure.

· ★ ★ ★ ·

Tbilisi, Georgia

Maggie fought off the fatigue of her fifteen-hour journey from Dulles Airport to Istanbul and finally to Tbilisi. It was nearly seven in the evening, local time, before she cleared customs. Outside the airport, the air was warm, and the sun was low in the sky. She tugged her ponytail through the back side of the baseball cap and hurried over to the first cab in line.

The taxi sped through the outskirts of Tbilisi, the city where she'd lost her fiancé almost two years ago. When she'd been here ten months earlier, she'd run away from Roger, who Warner had sent to escort her back to the US embassy in Moscow. The third time had to be the charm, she told herself. Less chaos, violence, and death would be a nice change of pace.

Gazing out the window, she took in the Mtkvari River as it wound its way through the capital city. Eventually, the driver slowed as they entered Old Town Tbilisi. Homes seemingly stacked on one another clung to rocky hills, and the rounded central spire of Sameba Cathedral soared toward the darkening sky. Someday, Maggie thought, she'd come to Tbilisi to explore every narrow side street, every ancient cathedral, every restaurant. She'd visit when there was no turmoil, no tragedy, and no danger pressing down on her.

When they reached Tamaz's apartment complex, she paid the driver and headed for the entrance. The building looked older than ever with its drab concrete exterior and small sliding windows aligned in precise horizontal and vertical symmetry. Inside, the elevator groaned as it climbed. The same worn carpet lined the hallway. But when she got to his apartment, everything lit up, from Tamaz's broad smile to the tasteful Georgian artifacts he'd accumulated over a lifetime.

"Maggie!" he exclaimed, kissing her on each cheek "Come in, come in. I have cheese and bread. And wine."

"Tamaz, it's so wonderful to see you again." And it truly was. Two years ago, he'd been a sympathetic shoulder to cry on after Steve's death in Tbilisi. As for Tamaz, he was forever in Maggie's debt for rescuing his brother from the hands of a deranged CIA officer. She and Tamaz had reunited last year when his home served as a temporary respite from her frantic pursuit of Zara.

Tamaz grabbed Maggie's bag and carried it inside with Maggie following behind. The enticing scent of fresh-baked bread wafted toward them. "You didn't cook for me, did you, Tamaz?"

He laughed, a deep, rumbling laugh arising from his chest. "No, that was Mikhail."

"Mikhail?"

"At your service." A man stepped from Tamaz's tiny kitchen into the combined dining and living rooms. Had he been born in America, Mikhail Khmaladze would've been destined for Hollywood or the pages of *Gentlemen's Quarterly*. The six-foot-three Georgian had the physique of an elite soccer player and the face of a leading man. Black, curly hair framed piercing blue eyes and a disarming smile. He was, Maggie thought, a thing of beauty.

"Maggie Jenkins, I'd like to introduce you to my nephew, Mikhail."

Mikhail took Maggie's hand in his. "*Ochen' priyatno*, Maggie. And, please, call me Misha," he said in heavily accented English.

Maggie smiled up at Mikhail, forgetting about Tamaz for a moment. "*Ona krasivaya amerikanka*," Mikhail said to his uncle.

"Yes, she's quite beautiful, and she speaks Russian, Misha," Tamaz said with a smile.

Misha threw his head back and laughed. "So, she is beautiful and smart."

She blushed. "The bread smells wonderful."

"Let's eat." Tamaz pulled out one of four chairs tucked under a round table that was covered by an intricately patterned lace cloth. "Please, have a seat."

Maggie felt the tension drain from her tired body. It amazed her that she felt so at home in a foreign country with a man she'd spent just a few days with over the course of two years. "How are you, Tamaz?"

"A bit bored." He'd retired from the Georgian Ministry of Foreign Affairs after his brother's brush with death.

"You need a hobby. Or maybe a lady friend," Maggie said.

"Both," chimed in Misha as he brought freshly baked bread from the kitchen. He sat across from Maggie and drew a serrated knife across the loaf, releasing steam and an intoxicating aroma.

Maggie bit into the soft, fragrant bread and smiled.

"You like it?" Misha asked.

"It's wonderful."

He smiled that dazzling, disarming smile, forcing her to focus again on Tamaz. "I hate to keep popping in only when there's an emergency."

Tamaz frowned. "What have you gotten yourself into now?"

She glanced at Misha. "It's extremely sensitive."

"Misha is very trustworthy, Maggie. In fact, he's going to help you with whatever it is you need."

"Oh?" she said, her eyes shifting to Misha. "And what is it that you do?"

"I'm a businessman."

"He's a smuggler," Tamaz chimed in. "He knows people."

A smuggler? Tamaz appeared to trust Misha implicitly. If he was willing to vouch for his nephew, she would trust him too. She took a generous sip of wine and let its warmth travel through her before proceeding. "Well, I could use a few people to help rescue a colleague who's being held captive in Dagestan."

Tamaz and his nephew exchanged glances.

"It's Roger. You remember meeting him briefly last year, Tamaz?"

He nodded.

She continued. "We've been hunting Imran Bukayev."

Tamaz's substantial eyebrows shot up.

"Bukayev is holding Roger captive. I need to rescue him."

Tamaz leaned forward, clasping his meaty hands together. "Maggie, this is dangerous."

"I know many people in Dagestan," Misha said. "People who hate the radicals."

"I'm willing to pay them, as soon as I get back to the States." She'd spend whatever she had to free Roger, even if it meant dipping into the trust-fund money she'd inherited after Steve's death. He'd approve.

"I don't like this one bit, Maggie." He shook his head.

"Last year I traveled to Grozny. Alone. In search of one of the world's most wanted terrorists." She flung her arms out. "And here I am. Back for more."

"I like this girl," said Misha.

Tamaz ignored his nephew. "It's an eight-hour drive to Makhach-kala. And I assume you don't have a visa?"

She shook her head. "Not enough time to get one. I was hoping there was a way to smuggle me into Russia. I have cash if we need to bribe the border guards."

"Does Warner know about this?" Tamaz had met Warner once at a Georgian embassy function in DC. And he'd spoken to him over the phone last year when Maggie skipped out of Tbilisi without either of them knowing.

"Not yet, although he'll probably figure it out sooner than later."

"Terrific," Tamaz muttered.

Maggie stood. "While you two make your phone calls, I'd like to shower and freshen up, if that's okay?" What she really wanted was a nap, especially after the long trip, but Roger needed her. The sooner they jumped into action, the better the odds of rescuing him.

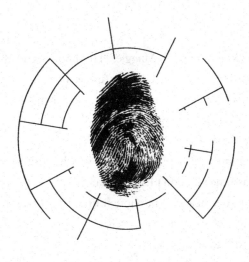

CHAPTER FORTY-NINE

Tbilisi, Georgia, Friday, June 24, 2005

Just after midnight, Misha, Maggie, and Davit, a middle-aged counterterrorist expert who'd worked for Tamaz's brother for years, jumped into Misha's blue Skoda and headed north from Tbilisi toward Vladikavkaz. For the first three hours, Maggie slept soundly in the backseat, secure in the knowledge that she was safe while they were still in Georgia. Fifteen minutes before they reached the Russian border, Misha turned up the radio to wake her. She sat up, groggy and confused. "Are we there?"

"Almost in Russia," he said as he pulled to the side of the road. "You'll have to get in the trunk."

"What?"

"You have an American passport with no visa. So into the trunk you go. With any luck, they won't ask to search it."

Maggie grabbed her duffel bag and followed Misha to the rear of the car. "What if they find me?"

"I have vodka and such to distract them with. It works every time. They've never asked to see inside the trunk so just don't make a sound."

"I'll try." She climbed inside, clutching her bag to her chest. Once Misha slammed it shut, it was so dark she couldn't see her hand in front of her face.

At the border stop, she heard muffled conversation. Then footsteps. The voices grew louder and sounded harsher. A swell of panic rose inside her. If the Russians found her, she'd never get to Roger. At the sound of a key in the trunk lock, she bit down on her tongue and tasted blood. The border patrol was right there, just seconds away from discovering her.

"Ah, yes, for you, my friends, only the finest vodka."

The trunk popped up about eight inches. Maggie shrank inward as far as she could and suppressed a yelp when someone patted her calf.

"I know it's in here somewhere," Misha said. "Ah, here it is."

"*Spasiba*," an unfamiliar voice said.

"To your health, comrades," Misha said as he slammed the trunk shut.

Maggie's entire body went weak. What was Misha thinking, leaving bribes for the border guards—in the form of liquor—in the trunk with her?

After what felt like an interminable wait, the car slowly accelerated. Every bump jarred her body, every curve made her stomach lurch. How long until they let her out?

It was ten, maybe fifteen minutes later when the car finally slowed to a stop and the trunk popped open. Misha shined a flashlight at her.

She recoiled from the light, which blinded her for a moment. The next thing she knew, his hand clasped hers as he pulled her up and out of the trunk.

"You okay?"

"Yeah," she said, breathing in the fresh night air. "I'm fine. But you scared me half to death. What were you thinking?"

He shrugged. "If I open the trunk to get a bottle of nice vodka out, the border guards will think I have nothing to hide in there."

"You could've warned me," she snapped as she climbed into the backseat.

"Well, here's your warning. The same thing might happen on the way back."

"Great," she muttered. "How much longer do we have?"

"About five hours," Misha said.

A sense of unease permeated her. There were so many unknowns. What if her plan put Roger in even graver danger? *No,* she thought, she didn't come all this way to lose him. And if she backed out now, chances were he'd end up dead.

The sun rose as they exited Chechnya and entered western Dagestan. She sat up and drank from a thermos of tea Tamaz had made them. "Are we driving straight to the target's house?"

"First, we go pick up my men," Davit said.

Twenty minutes later, they pulled into an alleyway on the outskirts of the capital city. Misha waited with Maggie while Davit disappeared around the corner to meet his team. Both men, bearded and muscular, squeezed into the backseat with Maggie without a word.

"We'll surveil the place first," Davit explained. "These guys are exceptional at urban warfare. They both fought in Chechnya."

"They're Russians?" The Russians were responsible for the mess that had brought her here. If Anna Orlova hadn't leaked her name to Senator Canton, Imran Bukayev never would've sent a car bomber after her, Rich would still be alive, and Roger never would've been kidnapped.

"Yes, but they're no longer in the military. They're very experienced, and believe me, they'll have no problem killing whoever tries to get in our way."

Mercenaries? *Great*, Maggie thought, not the least bit reassured. "How far is this address?" she asked Davit, who was tracing a route on a paper map.

"Ten minutes, maybe fifteen."

Maggie sat silent, staring out the window as the city gave way to countryside. Off to the distance on the left, the foothills of the Greater Caucasus mountains rose against an azure-blue sky. She chased away dark thoughts, closing her eyes, picturing Roger's smiling face. *I'll be there soon.*

Scattered along the winding road were small farmhouses, some with crumbling stone façades, some with faded wood siding, others a patchwork of both. When they arrived at the end of a dusty road, the men conferred in rapid Russian.

"Hey," she interrupted. "Why doesn't everyone get out except for Misha and me? We'll get a feel for the neighborhood and any possible security issues."

Davit tried to object.

"A car with five strangers in it is going to look a lot more suspicious than a car with two people," Maggie said.

Davit translated for the Russians, who exited the car and followed him to the shade of a large sycamore tree. Maggie slid into the front seat.

"Ready?"

"Ready," said Misha. "And, ah, don't do anything risky, Maggie. My uncle told me stories about you."

Tamaz knew well her penchant for acting without planning. But she only did so when absolutely necessary. "I'll try not to." In truth, she'd do anything to rescue Roger, risky or not.

The car bumped and shuddered down the rutted dirt road. As far as she could see, there were only two houses on the left and one on the right. "Stop the car, Misha."

He threw her a look but did what she requested.

"There aren't any numbers on these houses." She turned around in the seat to check the façade of the house they'd just passed.

Misha followed her gaze. "I bet everyone here knows everyone else. No need for numbers."

Her shoulders drooped. "Then how will we figure out where Roger is?"

Misha shrugged. "We check each house? Or pick one and move in on it? After all, the odds of choosing the right place are one in three."

Maggie frowned. An old man swept the front stoop of the house on the right. She concentrated on the two houses on the other side of the road.

Her breath caught. "You see that?" She pointed to the first house on the left.

"See what?" Misha asked.

"I thought I saw someone outside." There it was again, movement. Just then, a young woman with dark, shoulder-length hair came around the corner of the house and squatted down among the weeds. When she stood, Maggie saw that she had a garden spade in her right hand, and a stone in her left. The woman proceeded to scrape the spade across the rock. Back and forth in a sawing motion. "It looks like she's trying to sharpen it, Misha. Who sharpens a garden shovel unless you're trying to turn it into a weapon? That's got to be the house."

"You think a tiny woman like her is going to stab a terrorist with a shovel?"

Maggie opened the passenger door. "Give me five minutes."

"What are you doing?" Misha hissed.

"I'm going to talk to her. Pick up the others, but make sure they're ducked down in the seats so they can't be seen."

"Maggie—"

"Just go." She shut the door and hurried toward the home's side yard just as the woman disappeared behind the house.

Slowly, and watching the ground in front of her to ensure that she didn't step on anything that might give away her approach, Maggie crept along the side of the house. To her right, perhaps a quarter of a mile away, stood the closest neighbor. What if that was where Roger was being held and someone spotted her? *Stop.* She forced herself to disengage from catastrophizing. *Focus.*

At the rear corner of the house, Maggie squatted and peered into the back yard. The woman sat on a small wooden bench, elbows on knees, face in hands.

"*Privet,*" Maggie said quietly.

The woman startled and whirled around.

Maggie stood and held up a palm, before raising an index finger to her lips.

The woman's dark eyes darted from the house to Maggie and back again. She stood and shuffled away.

"Karina?"

The woman's retreat halted.

"You speak English?"

"*Da.*"

"I know your father. And Roger. The American."

The woman's eyes grew wide.

Maggie pointed to the house. "Is Roger in there?"

"He is."

Every muscle in Maggie's body tensed. "Is he okay?"

"Yes," Karina said, nodding vigorously.

The sound of an approaching car drew Maggie's attention away for a moment. It had to be Misha. She held up a finger to Karina and peered back toward the street.

Sure enough, the car was idling in the exact location where they'd parked a few minutes ago. She waved at Misha, then held up a palm, signaling for him to wait.

Maggie turned her attention back to the woman. "How many men?"

Karina licked her lips. "There are three including Imran, but one left to pick up supplies."

Maggie pointed to the car and urged Karina to follow her. Before the team moved in on the house, she needed to make sure Karina was out of the line of fire.

Karina hesitated for a moment, finally relenting when Maggie assured her that she would be safer in the car while they rescued Roger. She swiped at tears as she hurried alongside Maggie and gave a final glance at her house. She had to know, Maggie thought, that her humble little dwelling would be marred by bullets and blood by the time this was over.

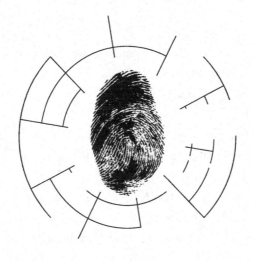

CHAPTER FIFTY

The Outskirts of Makhachkala, Dagestan, Russia

Misha rolled down the window, blue eyes flashing in anger. "Who is this?"

Davit sat in the passenger seat. The two Russians popped up from where they were crouched in the back.

Karina gasped.

"This is Karina. Imran Bukayev and one of his men are holding Roger hostage inside her house."

Davit glanced at Karina. "Why would they let her out of their sight?"

"Because Imran Bukayev stayed here recently, and Karina didn't call the police on him. He must think she's trustworthy." Maggie glanced at the woman. "Look at her. She's terrified. I think it would be better if she stayed in the car."

"With you," Misha said.

"No, I'm going in—"

"Absolutely not. My uncle will kill me if anything happens to you." He turned in the seat and spoke to the men, who checked their Makarov pistols one final time.

Maggie placed a hand on Karina's arm to reassure her.

The men exited the car.

"Stay here," Misha warned before hurrying across the road.

Maggie gestured for Karina to climb into the backseat. Then she popped the trunk and searched through the men's bags, tossing aside bottled waters, spare clothes, and passports until she found a fully loaded Makarov. A quick glance back at the house confirmed that the men had disappeared behind it. As for Karina, she was curled in the fetal position, lying on the backseat.

Maggie dashed across the road, crept along the side of the house, and peered into the backyard. The two Russians stood, weapons raised, on either side of the rear entrance. Misha and Davit crouched behind a three-foot-high stacked stone wall that ran along the length of the yard. She withdrew, not wanting to distract them.

Moments later, shouting erupted, then gunfire. She closed her eyes for a moment and offered up a silent prayer. *Please don't let Roger die!* When she looked around the corner again, the Russians were gone. In their place stood Misha and Davit. They nodded to each other and entered through the kicked-in door that now hung, lopsided, on its hinges. More gunfire. She ran low to the ground and followed the men inside.

All the commotion emanated from the front of the house. The acrid odor of gunpowder filled the air. She side-shuffled along the linoleum floor, hugging the wall as she made her way toward the living room. Peering around the corner, she saw the two Russians sprawled across the floor, one on his back, the other on his side, their blood merging into a gruesome Rorschach pattern staining a threadbare gray rug. The large front window lay shattered. To the right, Misha and Davit aimed their Makarovs at the chest of a man dressed in tactical gear. The militant, in return, trained his weapon first on Misha, then on Davit, and back again.

"Where's Roger?" Davit shouted.

Just shoot him! If they weren't going to take the shot, she would. Maggie steadied herself on one knee and raised the pistol. As her index finger found the trigger, a sudden movement caught her eye. There, behind the militant, a door that had been closed, was now open a fraction. Misha and Davit were so focused on the militant that they hadn't noticed.

Maggie shifted her sights to the door. But before she could fix her aim, someone flung it wide open and fired into the room.

Misha and Davit hit the floor. Maggie turned to the militant and squeezed off two shots. He clutched at his stomach and fell to his knees.

As Misha's eyes found hers, Imran Bukayev emerged through the door, shoving a battered and bloody Roger in front of him.

Maggie clamped her mouth shut to smother a gasp.

His feet bound, Roger stumbled. Bukayev grunted and righted him with a swift tug on the rope that lashed his wrists together behind his back.

Bukayev pointed his weapons at Misha. "You move, he dies."

Next to Misha, Davit stirred, but Maggie knew that Bukayev could get off two good shots before either of them would be able to fire one.

Maggie withdrew before Bukayev caught sight of her. She couldn't shoot. Roger was in her direct line of fire. But if she didn't do something, Bukayev would kill Misha, Davit, and Roger.

She let out a long breath and inched forward.

"Give me your guns," Bukayev barked at Misha and Davit.

They complied, shoving their weapons toward him out of their reach.

A smile spread across Bukayev's face. When Roger tried to wrench himself free, Bukayev grunted, pushed him to the floor, and pointed his gun at the center of his forehead.

"Imran!" Maggie shouted.

The Chechen startled, confused.

Maggie took one step forward and aimed.

"You're alive." Bukayev leveled his weapon at her.

"And not in critical condition." Maggie could feel Roger's eyes on her.

"You killed Zara." His voice pulsed with rage.

"I did. And I'd do it all over again."

"You bitch," he roared. His shaking hands gripped the weapon as he inched toward her.

"Maggie, run!" Roger shouted, distracting Bukayev for a split second.

Maggie squeezed the trigger.

Bukayev's left shoulder jerked backward. He yowled in pain but raised the gun in his right hand.

Their eyes met. She fired again but missed, the bullet sailing over the Chechen's head. He stumbled momentarily before righting himself and firing wildly at Maggie as he ran for the front door.

Maggie flew through the living room, giving chase after the terrorist.

"No!" Roger shouted.

"Imran!" she called.

He stopped and whirled around, shooting in a frantic, haphazard frenzy. Maggie dropped to one knee, steadied her breath, and fired. Bukayev's hands flew to the left side of his stomach. Wide-eyed, he looked from Maggie to the dark stain blooming under his fingers. Without a word, he lurched forward, landing face first on the ground, where he remained motionless.

The next thing she knew, Misha was at her side, then Davit.

"Maggie!" Roger stood in the front doorway, hands and feet still bound. Sprinting toward him, she knew that nothing else mattered. Only Roger. She threw her arms around him. "I thought you were dead."

"Then I guess we're even," he said, his voice heavy with emotion.

She pressed her lips against his.

"Ouch, yeah, that hurts."

She pulled back, touched his mouth with her finger, and examined the dried blood on his jawline. "You need stitches." She took in the rest of him. "You're a mess, Roger."

"You always know how to make a guy feel special. Now, do you mind untying me?"

She made quick work of the ropes.

Roger groaned as he moved his arms in wide circles.

Across the lawn, Davit secured Bukayev's gun and patted him down to make sure there weren't others.

Misha checked his pulse. "He's not dead yet."

"It's a gut shot. Could take a while to bleed out," Davit said. "Should we finish him off?"

Maggie looked at Roger. "No. Leave him." He was as good as dead. *Let my bullet be the last thing he feels.*

Roger glanced at Bukayev's body, then back at the house. "We've got to get out of here."

Just then, Karina came running across the yard, tears streaming down her face. "What am I supposed to do now?"

"Karina," Roger said, his tone soothing. "It's okay. We're going to call your father as soon as we can. But right now, you should gather a few essentials. You won't be back here for a long time."

"I'll help." Maggie took the younger woman's arm. "We're going to walk straight into the house. Don't look around. Let's just go to your room."

Five minutes later, a shaken Karina emerged from the house with Maggie and a suitcase full of her most precious belongings.

Misha brought the car around. In the backseat, Maggie sat between Karina and Roger. "Davit, I'm so sorry about your friends."

"They were mercenaries, not friends."

As they pulled away, Maggie looked out the rear window. She could've sworn she saw Bukayev move his leg. *There's no way,* she told herself. "Is it terrible that I want him to suffer?" she whispered to Roger.

"No. He would've killed all of us if he'd had the chance."

As they pulled out of the road, a black sedan came roaring past them.

Karina gasped. "It's Samir!"

"He wasn't in the house?" Roger asked.

"No. He went to get Imran a phone charger," Karina explained.

"Who's Samir?" Maggie twisted around in the seat to watch the speeding car.

"One of Bukayev's thugs," Roger replied. "I figured one of you shot him outside or something."

"Should we go back?" Maggie said, a thread of panic lacing her voice. "Take him out?"

Roger clasped her hand. "Trust me, he's not going to call the police, but we've got to get the hell out of Dagestan before someone does."

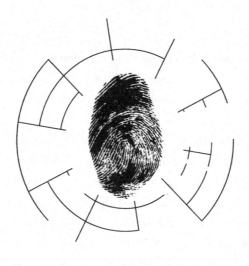

CHAPTER FIFTY-ONE

Hatteras Island, North Carolina
Saturday, August 6, 2005

Maggie leaned into Roger as they walked along the sand at Hatteras Inlet, the southernmost tip of the island. "This has been a wonderful vacation, Roger." She hated to see it come to an end, but work and reality beckoned. Warner had been gracious enough to refuse her resignation. And after all the drama and chaos of the summer, she owed him her full professional attention, especially since he'd kept her rescue mission to Dagestan a secret.

Without a doubt, there'd be congressional hearings this fall about Imran Bukayev's demise. Warner would tell the relevant congressional committees what he'd told the president—that an Agency officer had gone to Dagestan to help an asset in danger and had witnessed the

Russian assault on Bukayev's safe house. Unfortunately, he would add, Moscow had refused to share details about the operation, including how its intelligence agencies located one of the world's most wanted terrorists.

It was a detail that weighed on Maggie too. She couldn't help but wonder if Roger had provided the safe house address to Anna Orlova. Or if he'd given the information to Warner to pass on as he saw fit. Perhaps, she thought, she was better off not knowing. As for Anna, she hadn't shown her face at the gym since the day of the bombing. And with any luck, their paths would never cross again.

Roger turned her toward him and leaned in for a kiss. "Thank you for the best week of my life."

She smiled and tugged him farther down the beach toward the inlet, to the place where the Atlantic and Pamlico Sound meet. "The sun's starting to set. Let's pick somewhere to watch it."

"Here?" Roger pointed to a pile of washed-up seagrass.

She leaned over, grabbed a slimy strand, and threw it at him.

He ducked.

"How about here?" She stopped at a spot with smooth, undisturbed sand.

Roger took the backpack from his shoulders and unzipped it. "An amazing time topped off with an even more amazing invention: a backpack cooler." He pulled out a beach towel and spread it before them. Then came the bottle of chilled pinot grigio, a corkscrew, and two glasses.

They sat and Roger poured the wine. Maggie ran her fingers over the sand.

"Remember when we communicated using your whiteboard?"

She laughed. "Yeah, what initials did we use for him?" Since their time in Dagestan, she'd never said Bukayev's name aloud.

"EB. The evil bastard."

"That's right." She wrote *EB* in the sand then drew a giant X through it.

"Rot in hell, EB," Roger said.

A wave of unease passed through her. It always did when she thought of Bukayev. It shouldn't. He was dead. The Russians said so. Of course, they'd claimed that Rasul Makasharipov had been killed multiple times before he actually was. What if Bukayev's man, the one who'd shown up when they were leaving Karina's house, had managed to stop the bleeding? She sipped her wine. *No.* The odds of him surviving his wounds were minute. As far as she was concerned, unless and until there was proof otherwise, Imran Bukayev was dead.

"Maggie?" Roger studied her. "You in there?"

"I was just thinking about everyone we've lost. But also about how great life is now." Their relationship would never fit the conventional definition of normal. It couldn't, not with the demands of the intelligence world. She'd always known this was true, at least in the abstract. But now, she fully understood that if she and Roger were going to make a go of it, she would have to learn to operate in the gray zones. He'd never be able to give her everything she wanted, but she'd take what she could get. Like this perfect week on the island. Because he was worth it.

He raised his glass. "To Steve."

"And Jane," she said. "And Daud."

"And Rich," he added. "And to us."

They clinked glasses and sat in silence, Maggie's head on his shoulder.

THE END

ACKNOWLEDGMENTS

To the team at CamCat Books, thank you for your endless support for me and for the Wayward series of spy thrillers. Special thanks to CamCat's founder and CEO, Sue Arroyo, for believing that readers will want to "live in" these books. And to Helga Schier, editorial director extraordinaire, whose insight and direction continue to elevate my storytelling. And to the entire production and marketing team who have worked tirelessly to get *The Wayward Target* ready for its readers—thank you.

Many thanks to my wonderful agent, Steve Hutson, at Word-Wise Media Services and to Ruth Hutson for her keen eye and guidance along the way.

For my husband, Dan, and my children—thank you for continuing to support my writing career.

Finally, thank you to everyone who read *The Wayward Spy* and *The Wayward Assassin*. Your enthusiasm for these stories motivates me to continue writing and dreaming up thrillers that will keep you up reading way past your bedtime.

ABOUT THE AUTHOR

Susan Ouellette is the author of the award-winning and critically acclaimed Wayward Spy thriller series. The series includes *The Wayward Spy*, named Best Thriller of 2021 by the Independent Publisher Book Awards and called a "gripping debut and series launch . . . Ouellette, a former CIA analyst, brings plenty of authenticity to this fast-paced spy thriller" by *Publishers Weekly*. The second book in the series, *The Wayward Assassin*, has been hailed "a must read that should be on every thriller fan's bookshelf" (*The Strand Magazine*).

Susan was born and raised in the suburbs of Boston, where she studied Russian language and culture and international relations at both Harvard University and Boston University. As the Soviet Union teetered on the edge of collapse, she worked as an intelligence analyst at the CIA, where she earned a commendation for her work done during the failed 1991 Soviet coup.

Subsequently, Susan worked on Capitol Hill as a professional staff member for the House Permanent Select Committee on Intelligence (HPSCI). There, she participated in several overseas staff and congressional delegations focused on intelligence cooperation with allies and classified operations against adversaries. She also played an integral role in a study about the future of the post-Cold War intelligence community. It was there, during quiet moments, that Susan conceived of Maggie Jenkins, an intrepid female character thrust into a dangerous situation borne of tragedy. Next came the threads of a plot, and from that blossomed her first espionage thriller, *The Wayward Spy*.

Susan lives on a farm outside of Washington, DC, with her family, cat, chickens, turkeys, and too many honeybees to count. In her spare time, she loves to read, root for Boston sports teams, and spend time staring out at the ocean on the North Carolina coast.

If you've enjoyed

Susan Ouellette's *The Wayward Target*,

you'll enjoy

Jonathan Payne's *Citizen Orlov*.

CHAPTER ONE

In which our hero meets a new and unexpected challenge

On a frigid winter's morning in a mountainous region of central Europe, Citizen Orlov, a simple fishmonger, is taking a shortcut along the dank alley behind the Ministries of Security and Intelligence when a telephone begins to ring. He thinks nothing of it and continues on his daily constitutional, his heavy boots crunching the snow between the cobbles.

The ringing continues, becoming louder with each step. A window at the back of the ministry buildings is open, just a little. The ringing telephone sits on a table next to the open window. Orlov stops, troubled by this unusual scene: there is no reason for a window to be open on such a cold day. Since this is the Ministry of either Security or Intelligence, could an open window be a security breach of some kind?

Orlov is tempted to walk away. After all, this telephone call is none of his business. On the other hand, he is an upright and patriotic citizen who would not want to see national security compromised simply because no one was available to answer a telephone call. He is on the verge of stepping toward the open window when he hears footsteps ahead. A tight group of four soldiers is marching into the alley, rifles on shoulders. He freezes for a second, leans against the wall, and quickly lights a cigarette. By the time the soldiers reach him, Orlov is dragging on the cigarette and working hard to appear nonchalant. The soldiers are palace guardsmen, but the red insignia on their uniforms indicates they are part of the elite unit that protects the Crown Prince, the king's ambitious eldest son. Orlov nods politely, but the soldiers ignore him and march on at speed.

The telephone is still ringing. Someone very much wants an answer. Orlov stubs his cigarette on the wall and approaches the open window. The telephone is loud in his right ear. Peering through the gap, he sees a small, gloomy storeroom with neatly appointed shelves full of stationery.

Finally, he can stand it no longer. He reaches through the window, picks up the receiver, and pulls it on its long and winding cable out through the window to his ear.

"Hello?" says Orlov, looking up and down the alley to check he is still alone.

"Thank God. Where have you been?" says an agitated voice, distant and crackly. Orlov is unsure what to say. The voice continues. "Kosek. Right now."

"I'm sorry?" says Orlov.

"Kosek. Agent Kosek."

Orlov peers into the storeroom again. "There's no one here," he says.

"Well, fetch him then. And hurry, for God's sake. It's important." Orlov is sorely tempted to end the call and walk away, but the voice is so angry that he dare not.

"One minute," he says, and lays the receiver on the table. He opens the window wider and, with some considerable effort, pulls himself headfirst into the storeroom, where he tumbles onto the floor. Picking himself up, he slaps the dust from his overcoat, opens the storeroom door, and peers along the hallway; all is dark and quiet.

With some trepidation, Orlov returns to the telephone. "Hello?" he says.

"Kosek?"

"No, sorry. I'll have to take a message."

The caller is still agitated. "Well, focus on what I'm about to say. It's life and death."

Orlov's hands are shaking. "Hold on," he says, "I'll fetch some paper."

Before he can put the receiver down, the caller explodes with anger. "Are you a simpleton? Do not write this down. Remember it."

"Yes, sir. Sorry," says Orlov. "I'll remember it."

"Are you ready?"

"Yes, sir."

"Here it is. We could not—repeat not—install it in room six. Don't ask why, it's a long story."

The man is about to continue, but Orlov interrupts him. "Should I include that in the message: 'it's a long story'?"

"Mother of God," shouts the man. "Why do they always give me the village idiot? No. Forget that part. I'll start again."

"Ready," says Orlov.

This time the man speaks slower and more deliberately, as if to a child. "We could not—repeat not—install it in room six. You need to get room seven. It's hidden above the wardrobe. Push the lever up, not down. Repeat that back to me."

Orlov is now shaking all over, and he grimaces as he forces himself to focus. He repeats the message slowly but correctly.

"Whatever else you do, get that message to Kosek, in person. No one else. Lives depend on it. Understood?"

"Understood," says Orlov, and the line goes dead.

Orlov returns the receiver to the telephone and searches for something to write on. He remembers the message now, but for how long? He has no idea who Agent Kosek is, or where. Now that the caller has gone, the only sensible course of action is to make a note. He will destroy the note, once he has found Kosek. On the table he finds a pile of index cards. He writes the message verbatim on a card, folds it once, and tucks it inside his pocketbook.

Standing in the dark storeroom, Orlov wonders how to set about finding Agent Kosek. He considers climbing back into the alley, going around to the front entrance, and presenting himself as a visitor, if he could work out which ministry he is inside. But it's still early and it might take hours to be seen. Worse than that, there is a possibility he would be turned away. He imagines a surly security guard pretending to check the personnel directory, only to turn to him and say, "There's no one of that name here." Perhaps agents never use their real names. Is Kosek a real name or a pseudonym? Orlov decides the better approach is to use the one advantage currently available to him: he is inside the building.

He lowers the sash window to its original position and steps into the hallway, closing the storeroom door behind him. All remains dark and quiet. The hallway runs long and straight in both directions, punctuated only by anonymous doors. He sees nothing to suggest one direction is more promising than the other. Orlov turns right and tiptoes sheepishly along the hallway, now conscious of his boots as they squeak on the polished wooden floors. He walks on and on, eventually meeting a door that opens onto an identical dark corridor.

As he continues, Orlov becomes increasingly conscious that he is not supposed to be here. He imagines an angry bureaucrat bursting out from one of the many office doors to castigate him and march him off to be interrogated. However, he has walked the length of a train and still he has seen no one.

Finally, Orlov sees the warm glow of lamplight seeping around the edge of another dividing door up ahead. He is both relieved and apprehensive. He approaches the door cautiously and puts his ear to it. It sounds like a veritable hive of industry. He takes a deep breath and opens the door onto a scene of frenetic activity. Banks of desks are staffed by serious men, mostly young, in formal suits, both pin-stripe and plain; the few women are also young and dressed formal-ly. Some are engaged in animated conversations; some are leaning back in chairs, smoking; others are deep into reading piles of papers. A white-haired woman is distributing china cups full of tea from a wheeled trolley. At the far end of this long room, someone is setting out chairs in front of a blackboard. Above this activity, the warm fug of cigarette smoke is illuminated by high wall lamps. Orlov hesitates, but is soon approached at high speed by a short, rotund man in a three-piece suit. He has a clipboard and a flamboyant manner.

"You're late," says the man, gesticulating. "Quickly. Overcoats over there."

"No, no. You see," Orlov says, "I'm not really here."

The man slaps him on the back, taking his coat as they walk. "You seem real to me," he laughs.

Orlov protests. "I have a message for Agent Kosek."

The man rolls his eyes. "Do not trouble yourself regarding Agent Kosek. He is late for everything. He will be here in due course."

He directs Orlov to take a seat at the back of the impromptu classroom, which is by now filling up with eager, young employees. Orlov is suddenly conscious of his age and appearance; his balding head and rough clothes stand out in this group of young, formal-ly dressed professionals. He also feels anxious about being in this room on false pretenses. However, he need only wait until Agent

Kosek appears; he will then deliver the message, make his excuses, and leave. He could still make it to the Grand Plaza in time for the market to open.

The flamboyant man, now standing in front of the blackboard, bangs his clipboard down onto a desk to bring the room to order. "Citizens," he says, "I would appreciate your attention." The room falls silent, and he continues. "I am Citizen Molnar, and I will be your instructor today."

Orlov turns to his neighbor, an earnest young man who is writing the instructor's name in a pristine leather notebook. "I'm not supposed to be here," says Orlov. The young man places a finger on his lips. Orlov smiles at him and returns his attention to Molnar, who is writing on the blackboard. Molnar proceeds to talk to the group for some time, but Orlov struggles to follow his meaning.

The instructor repeatedly refers to the group as *recruits*, which adds to Orlov's sense of being in the wrong place. He becomes hot under the collar when Molnar invites every recruit to introduce themselves. One by one the impressive young recruits stand and detail their university degrees and their training with the military or the police. When Orlov's turn comes, he stands and says, "Citizen Orlov. Fishmonger." He is surprised when a ripple of laughter runs through the group.

Orlov is about to sit down again when Molnar intervenes. "Is there anything else you'd like to tell us, citizen?"

Orlov says, "I have a message for Agent Kosek."

"Yes," says Molnar, gesturing for Orlov to sit down, "the agent will be here soon, I'm quite sure."

Orlov's hopes pick up some time later when Molnar says he wants to introduce a guest speaker. Orlov reaches inside his pocketbook to check that the message is still there. But Molnar is interrupted by a colleague whispering in his ear.

"My apologies," says Molnar. "It seems Agent Kosek has been called away on urgent business. However, I'm delighted to say that his colleague, Agent Zelle, is joining us to give you some insight into the day-to-day life of an agent. Agent Zelle."

Orlov is disappointed at the change of plan, but perhaps this colleague will be able to introduce him to Kosek. Taking her place in front of the blackboard is the most beautiful woman Orlov has ever seen. She is young and curvaceous but with a stern, serious expression. Her dark curls tumble over pearls and a flowing gown. Several of the male recruits shift uneasily in their chairs; someone coughs. Agent Zelle seems far too exotic for this stuffy, bureaucratic setting. She speaks with a soft foreign accent that Orlov does not recognize.

"Good morning, citizens," says Zelle, scanning the group slowly. "I have been asked to share with you something of what you can expect, if you are chosen to work as an agent for the ministry. I can tell you that it is a great honor, but there will also be hardship and danger."

She paces up and down in front of the blackboard, telling them stories of her life in the field. Orlov is entranced; these real-life tales sound like the adventure books he used to read as a boy. There are secret packages, safe houses, and midnight rendezvous in dangerous locations. There are car chases and shootouts, poisonings and defused bombs. It is so engrossing that, for a while, Orlov forgets that he has no business here aside from finding Kosek.

As he focuses on Zelle's lilting voice, Orlov is struck by a thought that has never before occurred to him in more than twenty years of fishmongering. Perhaps he is cut out for something more challenging, even thrilling. Perhaps, even at his age, he is capable of taking a position in a ministry such as this one where, instead of standing all day in the cold selling fish, his days would be full of adventure, danger, and even romance. Zelle's stories fill his head with possibilities.

But perhaps this is foolish. After all, he and Citizen Vanev have a good business and a monopoly situation, since theirs is the only fish stall in the Grand Plaza. What's more, Vanev has always been loyal to him, and he has always tried to be loyal in return. Orlov tries to banish these silly ideas from his mind.

When Agent Zelle finishes, spontaneous applause fills the room. The agent seems surprised, almost embarrassed, and gives a slight curtsy in acknowledgement. She turns to talk to Molnar as the class breaks up and the recruits begin to mingle. Orlov sets off in the direction of Zelle, but several recruits are in his way, now forming into small groups, discussing what they have just heard. Orlov attempts to get past, saying "Excuse me. Sorry. May I . . ." but by the time he reaches the blackboard, Agent Zelle has gone.

"Is everything all right, citizen?" asks Molnar, seeing Orlov's distress.

"I really need to see Kosek," says Orlov. "It's very important. I have a message for him."

"I'm sure he'll be here, before induction is completed," says Molnar. "He always likes to meet the new recruits."

"That is what I was trying to explain," says Orlov. He gestures in the direction of the window through which he climbed. He is about to explain his entry to the building, but thinks better of it. "I'm not supposed to be here."

Molnar eyes him with a puzzled expression. "I assure you, citizen," he says, "that we rarely make mistakes." He brandishes his clipboard, showing Orlov a sheet of heavy, watermarked paper with a list of neatly typewritten names. Molnar runs his finger down the list ostentatiously, stopping in the middle of the page. "Here we are," he says. "Orlov."

CHAPTER TWO

In which our hero sets out on a journey

The next morning, Citizen Orlov forgoes his daily constitutional and sets out early for the Grand Plaza. In consideration of his new situation, he wears the dark suit he last wore at his father's funeral. It appears that the waistband has shrunk since those days, but Orlov finds that he can tuck it under his belly by wearing the trousers a little lower. This unattractive arrangement is hidden by his heavy overcoat, since it is another frigid day.

As he walks to the market, Orlov's head is full of possibilities. He understands that very few recruits are chosen to be agents. Most of the positions in the ministry are mundane and menial—clerks, copyists, mailroom operatives, and the like. And he should remember that no one has offered him anything so far. He needs to focus on delivering the telephone message. Already a day has gone by, and he has failed to find Agent Kosek. If he can find Kosek today and successfully deliver the message, perhaps that will stand him in good stead when the ministry comes to decide on the allocation of positions. Not wanting to incur the considerable wrath of his employer,

Orlov determines to tell Vanev only about his short-term task, for now. He will keep the possibility of a position at the ministry to himself, until it is confirmed.

Orlov is disappointed, but not surprised, to see that Citizen Vanev has arrived at the market stall before him. Vanev—an obese, unshaven man who perpetually wears the same fish-stained overalls—is busy setting out the wooden display boxes. In a vain attempt to lessen the inevitable anger of his employer, Orlov rushes up to the stall, grabs a bag of ice, and begins to fill a display box.

"So, he's not dead after all," says Vanev.

"My apologies, citizen," says Orlov.

"What happened yesterday?" asks Vanev. "I was slaving away over cold fish all day without so much as a cigarette break."

"I have a job," says Orlov.

"Exactly," says Vanev, slamming a box full of ice into position. "And it's traditional to do your job, if you expect to get paid for it."

"No," says Orlov, "for the government."

Vanev stops in his tracks. "Doing what?"

"I'm not sure, exactly," says Orlov, "but it's very important."

"Which ministry?" asks Vanev.

Orlov hesitates. "Security. Or perhaps Intelligence."

Vanev continues. "So, you don't know what the job is or who you're working for, but you're going abandon me anyway. Sounds like an excellent plan."

"I won't be gone forever," says Orlov. "There's just one task I need to complete. It's life and death. As soon as that's done, I'll be back."

"And how long will this take?" asks Vanev.

"I just have to find someone and deliver a message. That's all."

"I need you to be here on Saturday," says Vanev, reaching over to spread a dozen haddock across the ice. "I have some political business to attend to."

"The People's Front," says Orlov.

"The People's Front," repeats Vanev. "One day, you will join us."

"I don't care for politics," says Orlov.

"I don't care for tyranny," says Vanev.

"How can you be sure a republic would be an improvement?" asks Orlov.

"How can *you* be sure you or your mother will not end up disappeared, or worse?" asks Vanev.

"Let us leave my mother out of this," says Orlov, a little more sharply than he had intended.

"I mean no offense," says Vanev. "I am merely concerned for your wellbeing, as well as my own."

"I understand," says Orlov. "But I do not share your conviction that a revolution is in the best interests of our great nation."

Vanev sighs. "It is the least terrible option available to us."

Since versions of this exchange have played out between them many times, Orlov knows it is futile. He is anxious not to be late for his appointment at the ministry.

"Do not fear, citizen," says Orlov, turning to go. "I shall return." He trudges away across the snow-covered square, pausing while a tram trundles past slowly before he continues down the hill and across the bridge into the government sector.

Orlov arrives at the foot of the stone steps that lead up to the grand front doors of the Ministries of Security, on his left, and Intelligence, on his right. He felt sure, while walking here, that he would know which door to approach, but now he is singularly lacking in enlightenment. He thinks back to the remarks made yesterday by Citizen Molnar and Agent Zelle; they had plenty to say about security, but then again, they also talked about intelligence. It could be either. He imagines being interrogated by skeptical security guards in the lobby of either or both buildings. Finding this a distinctly unattractive proposition, Orlov walks around to the back of the buildings, where the dark, narrow alley is familiar and comforting compared with the formal front entrances. He finds the rear entrance through which he and the young recruits exited the previous afternoon, but the door is closed and a surly security guard leans against it, smoking a cigarette. Orlov nods politely and keeps walking, feeling the guard's eyes following him all the way up the alley and around the corner.

Once he is out of sight, Orlov leans against the wall at the end of the Ministry of Security and enjoys a cigarette of his own. He takes a couple of peeks around the corner, but the security guard is still there. He is just about to build up the courage to try one of the front entrances when he hears voices. A gaggle of besuited men is approaching at high speed, led by Citizen Molnar. Orlov stubs his cigarette on the wall and steps forward to attract their attention. Perhaps he can follow them into the building. But Molnar speaks first.

"Ah, the very man," says Molnar, holding out a hand so that one of his aides can pass an envelope to him. He hands the envelope to Orlov. "We need you on the next train to Kufzig," he says. "Your ticket is in here. Check into Pension Residenz. Kosek will meet you there."

Orlov is stunned and for a while is unable to speak. Eventually he says, "I'm not going to be working in the mailroom?"

Molnar looks surprised, and his aides laugh. "We know talent when we see it," says Molnar. "We need you in the field."

"And Kosek will be there?" asks Orlov.

"Yes, he's expecting you," says Molnar.

"What will I be doing?" asks Orlov.

"Kosek will explain your task," says Molnar and begins to walk away.

Orlov calls after him. "How will I recognize him?"

"He will find you," Molnar replies over his shoulder.

Orlov cannot believe his good fortune. He grins involuntarily while watching Molnar and his aides disappear around the corner. Agent Zelle's stories of espionage and danger flash through his head. He is both elated and nervous. Could he really be about to leave fishmongering behind for the life of an agent?

He opens the envelope and finds a first-class ticket to Kufzig, leaving in less than an hour. It is a small town in the mountains about two hours south of the capital. Orlov has visited it only once before, as a child. He has never before travelled in the first-class carriage of a train.

He considers returning to the market to explain this change of plan to Vanev, but it is a shorter walk to the railway station. He will find Kosek, deliver the message and, all being well, return in time to cover the stall on Saturday.

⋯⋯⋯

ORLOV STEPS OUT onto the platform at Kufzig and pauses to admire the view while fastening his overcoat against the thin, freezing air. The picturesque little town is surrounded by rugged, snow-capped mountains. Well-dressed travelers rush past him, lifting suitcases down from the train. Others run to board before the train continues its journey south. When the train pulls away, Orlov is still in the middle of the platform, admiring the view, and finds himself engulfed by a cloud of steam. By the time the steam has dispersed, all the other passengers have gone on their way, and Orlov is left alone on the platform with a guard, a haggard old man who limps toward his hut as though in a hurry to get out of the cold.

Orlov waves at the guard and walks toward him. "Excuse me," he says. "I'm looking for Pension Residenz."

The guard stops at the door to the hut. "Residenz, you say?"

"Yes," says Orlov. "It was recommended." He is about to say who gave the recommendation, but thinks better of it. "Is it a good place to stay? Reasonable?"

"Oh, yes," says the guard. "Quite good. And quite reasonable. Only . . ." He pauses.

"Only?" asks Orlov.

"Some people mistake it for Penzion Rezidence," says the guard. "It's an easy mistake to make." He heads inside the hut.

Orlov leans into the doorway. "I'm sorry," he says. "There's another pension called Rezidence? Here in Kufzig?"

"Oh yes, sir," says the guard. "It causes all sorts of confusion."

"I imagine it would," says Orlov.

"That's why I always like to check," says the guard.

"I'm quite sure it's Pension Residenz that was recommended," says Orlov, confidently.

"Straight down the hill, sir," says the guard, "a short walk along Feldgasse—that's our beautiful main street—and you can't miss it."

Orlov thanks the guard and sets out down the hill, admiring the view of the town beneath him. He was confident that Molnar had said *Residenz*, but the farther he walks, the more he wonders if he had misheard *Rezidence*. He would like to call Molnar on the telephone to confirm this but, even if he could find a telephone, he has no idea how to reach the ministry. Only now he realizes that he missed an opportunity this morning to ask Molnar which ministry he works for. Perhaps it would have been embarrassing to admit that he didn't know, but the embarrassment would have been over in a second, and then he would have been quite sure. As it stands, he will have to live with the uncertainty a little longer. He determines to ask Agent Kosek this evening, as soon as they meet. He hopes Kosek is a kind person, the sort of person who will not be cruel about this simple misunderstanding.

In any case, Orlov is bringing with him an important message, and he is therefore confident of striking up a good rapport with the agent. He will deliver the message, complete whatever task Kosek has in store for him, and return home without delay. Given Citizen Vanev's mood this morning, he does not want to be away from the market any longer than absolutely necessary.

At the foot of the hill, Orlov sees the sign for Feldgasse and follows it into the heart of the town. The scene in front of him stirs memories of his childhood visit to Kufzig: a quaint main street with a steepled church at one end and, at the other, a square with an ornate fountain. Between these two landmarks, the busy thoroughfare is full of restaurants, bakeries, and street cafés. Half way along Feldgasse, equidistant between the church and the square, sits Pension Residenz.

Like many of the pensions in this part of the world, it is a tall, elegant townhouse that was once the home of a wealthy family but has long since been converted into a boarding house, with guest rooms spanning four floors. A faded picture of Beethoven at his piano decorates the sign that hangs above the door.

Now that he has seen the sign clearly showing Pension Residenz, Orlov is feeling more confident that this is the right place. He steps into the cramped reception area and, since no one is at the desk, he rings the bell, which elicits no immediate response. While waiting, Orlov peruses the newspaper rack and sees an interesting headline: "Kufzig Prepares for Royal Visit." He considers removing the newspaper from the rack in order to read the article but, before he does so, a curious little woman in thick spectacles appears from the back office and stares at him sideways, as though her peripheral vision is better than her ability to see straight ahead.

"How may I help you?" she says.

"I'd like a room, please," says Orlov.

"You know the king is visiting?" says the woman.

"I just saw it in the newspaper," says Orlov.

"Full up," she says. "Quite full. A lot of people want to see His Majesty. Those people booked in advance. On account of our excellent views along Feldgasse. Those with a balcony can see all the way down to the fountain."

Orlov is nonplussed. "I was supposed to stay here. I have to meet someone." She shrugs and Orlov continues. "Could you tell me if," he is about to say *agent* but corrects himself just in time, "Citizen Kosek checked in yet?"

"Can't say," she says. "Against the rules."

"But he is booked to stay here?"

"Against the rules."

"May I leave a message?"

She shakes her head. Then, to Orlov's surprise, she says, "Go to the Bierkeller later." She points along the road in the direction of the square. "Every man in town will be there tonight."

"Why?" asks Orlov.

"Trust me," she says.

"Is there anywhere else to stay nearby?" says Orlov.

The woman looks at him and for a while seems to be weighing something up. "She might have a room. Across the street." She pulls a face, as though making this recommendation is distasteful. "She's always slow to fill up. On account of the inferior views."

Orlov turns to look out through the front door and across the street. "There's another boarding house opposite?"

"Directly across the street," says the woman.

"That wouldn't be Penzion Rezidence, would it?" asks Orlov.

The woman raises her eyebrows, as though he has used inappropriate language at the dinner table. "If you say so," she says and disappears into the back office.

Orlov heads outside and crosses the street, where he finds an almost identical townhouse. Hanging above the door, under the words Penzion Rezidence, is a sign with a faded picture of Gustav Mahler waving his conductor's baton. Orlov steps inside to a similar reception area.

This time, he does not need to ring the bell because someone is at the desk. She looks much like the proprietor opposite, except that her spectacles are not so thick.

"Good day, sir. May I help you?" she says.

Orlov sounds a little more desperate than intended. "Do you have a room?"

The woman looks down at the ledger on the desk. "How many nights?"

"Just tonight, please," says Orlov. "I'm meeting a colleague this evening. Returning home tomorrow, I hope."

"You're not planning to stay for the royal visit, sir?" she asks.

"No, this is strictly business," says Orlov, and he enjoys how that sounds—much more impressive than fishmongering.

"Room three is the only one available," says the woman. "It doesn't have much of a view, but if you're not staying for the king, I dare say you won't mind that."

She fetches the key while Orlov signs the ledger. Room three is a drab affair on the second floor with a restricted view of the street and a shared bathroom in the hall. Since Orlov has no luggage to unpack, he decides to go out again. He takes a stroll around the town, but it is too cold for a prolonged walk. He eats an early dinner of sausages and cabbage at the least expensive restaurant on Feldgasse and then makes his way to the Bierkeller. It is mostly empty when he arrives, and he drinks two beers alone at the bar before the place begins to fill up. It is a literal cellar and a typical pub in most respects, with the addition of a small stage, complete with lights and curtains.

Orlov watches all the newcomers closely, wondering which one is Kosek. By the time he is on to his third beer, Orlov is becoming agitated that Kosek has not made himself known. He does not like the sense of being powerless.

He wants to take control of the situation.

At the other end of the bar, a serious, middle-aged man has been drinking alone for some time. He is well dressed and appears to be surveying the busy cellar with eagle eyes. Orlov might be just a simple fishmonger, but he has good intuition. He picks up his beer, walks slowly toward the man, and leans against the bar next to him. He takes a sip of beer and smiles at the man, to ensure he has been noticed. The man looks uneasy; he half-smiles back.

"Good evening," says Orlov.

"Evening," says the man.

"Are you, by any chance, Citizen Kosek?"

"Leave me alone," says the man. "I'm just here for the show." He nods toward the stage, where the lights are going up and a weaselly little man with a shaggy moustache calls the room to order.

"Ladies and gentlemen, your attention please," he says in the shrill tones of a carnival barker as oriental music begins to emanate from a tinny loudspeaker. "We are very proud to announce, by popular demand, for one night only, the return of the one, the only, Mata Hari."

To Orlov's surprise, the whole cellar erupts in applause. Some men bang their beer glasses on the tables as others stamp their feet. The cacophony dies down as the music swells. From behind the curtain emerges an exotic, barefoot dancer, dressed in nothing aside from carefully placed jewels and flowing veils. She gyrates into the center of the stage to begin her act. Only when she arrives in the full glow of the spotlights does Orlov sense that this dancer is familiar. In fact, he saw her only yesterday. It is Agent Zelle.